THE GHOST OF HOLLOW HOUSE

A Mina Scarletti Mystery Book Four

Linda Stratmann

Also in the Mina Scarletti Mystery Series
Mr Scarletti's Ghost
The Royal Ghost
An Unquiet Ghost

THE GHOST OF HOLLOW HOUSE

Published by Sapere Books.
11 Bank Chambers, Hornsey, London, N8 7NN,
United Kingdom

saperebooks.com

Copyright © Linda Stratmann, 2019
Linda Stratmann has asserted her right to be identified as the author of this work.

All rights reserved.
No part of this publication may be reproduced, stored in any retrieval system, or transmitted, in any form, or by any means, electronic, mechanical, photocopying, recording, or otherwise, without the prior written permission of the publishers.
This book is a work of fiction. Names, characters, businesses, organisations, places and events, other than those clearly in the public domain, are either the product of the author's imagination, or are used fictitiously.
Any resemblances to actual persons, living or dead, events or locales are purely coincidental.

ISBN: 978-1-913028-41-1

Prologue

When Mr Honeyacre brought his young bride to Hollow House in December 1871, he could never have imagined that his peaceful country retreat would soon become a scene of relentless terror.

Mr Honeyacre was a gentleman of sixty, a hale and active sixty, kind and charitable, serious and scholarly. Mrs Honeyacre, the second of that name, was the former Miss Kitty Betts, aged thirty but admitting to twenty-five. She had once enjoyed a glittering career on the popular stage as Princess Kirabampu the oriental contortionist, but had been looking for something a little more permanent. Although Kitty lacked great beauty, she more than compensated for this with her cheerful and engaging personality, coquettish charm and a remarkably supple spine.

As the newlyweds' carriage approached the manor house, Mr Honeyacre had to admit to a growing unease, but that, he told himself, was merely anxiety as to whether his dear Kitty would love her new home as much as he did. He had purchased the estate in the summer of 1866. The building had then been lying empty and neglected for some time, but although much had decayed within, its external structure, apart from that eternal curse of old houses, the roof, was strong and sound. Mr Honeyacre, recognising the potential of Hollow House on his very first viewing, had been irredeemably charmed. Nestling in a dip between Sussex hills, with land bordering the village of Ditchling Hollow, it was the home he had long been seeking, a place of calm repose, of pleasurable study, where he might entertain friends and display his collection of art, books and antiquities. There were grasslands suitable for pasture, a winding brook bubbling under an old stone bridge, gardens that had once been laid out with bowers and shrubberies, and provided generous fare for the kitchen. There was even a quaint little church. All could be made fresh and useful again. On that day, with the old windows of the aged manor smiling in the summer sun, everything had seemed possible. He had then been married to his beloved first wife, and she too had admired the house, and was eager to acquire it.

Tragically, before the much needed repairs and renovations could commence, the first Mrs Honeyacre had been taken gravely ill, and the anxious husband had devoted much of his time to caring for her during a long and painful decline. They had never lived in Hollow House, preferring Brighton so as to be within easy reach of the best medical advice and refreshing sea air. Following his inevitable bereavement, Mr Honeyacre had gone abroad to salve his grief, leaving Hollow House in the care of servants, who had attended to the most immediate repairs and brought the garden back to life. The planned improvements and extensive redecoration had never been carried out.

On his return to Brighton, he had found the town society all abuzz on the question of spiritualism, something that attracted his curiosity, and soon became a consuming interest and a new subject for his studies. As a result, he had been plunged into a series of extraordinary events, which for reasons he had never quite understood, centred around an unusual little lady, Miss Mina Scarletti. He had also made the acquaintance of Miss Kitty Betts, who quickly consented to becoming his second wife.

As soon as the engagement was announced, Mr Honeyacre ordered a small army of persons to create, in Hollow House, the delightful home he had always desired, somewhere that would be suitable for his studies, and provide every comfort and delight for his dear Kitty. Once the roof was declared sound, the house was cleansed from top to bottom. There was dusting and polishing and painting, restoring of old panelling, hanging of paper, laying of carpets, replacing threadbare draperies with the most luxurious velvets to guard against any possibility of draughts. New lamps cast a brilliant glow, the kitchen was fully equipped, the fireplaces and chimneys scoured and restored, and the antiquated plumbing and hygiene facilities brought up to the most modern standards.

With all this activity, the one thing that busy Mr Honeyacre had not yet done was study the history of his new home. That was a delight lying in store. How eagerly he anticipated poring over the registers in the little church of St Mond, copying the inscriptions on gravestones, collecting documents and portraits, and finally gathering together all his work into a little volume on the history of Hollow House. It would be a slight but useful publication, which would give pleasure for generations to come. Mr Honeyacre had looked forward to the quiet enjoyment of his senior years, the care of his collections, the rewards of scholarship and the sparkling company of his amusing wife.

It was only as they approached the entrance to the estate that he began to have doubts. It was a chill December day, and the hills were shrouded in rain. The manor house, peering through a damp haze, looked dark, dull and forbidding. His dear Kitty, he reminded himself had been used to a world where everything was painted in bright colours and covered in spangles. There had been music, acrobats, illusion and the noisy acclaim of the multitude. Unwillingly, he began to see his new home through the eyes of his wife, and it did not look inviting. Glancing at her as she gazed out of the carriage window for her first glimpse of Hollow House, he began to feel afraid. Gently, he took her hand, and it felt cold even through her glove. 'I hope we will be happy here, my dear,' he said, pressing her fingers affectionately.

He hoped he did not see a touch of uncertainty in her expression, which quickly vanished as she rallied herself into a smile. She returned the pressure of his fingers. 'It is — quite breathtaking,' she said.

It was only a few weeks later that Mr Honeyacre was obliged to ask himself why it had all gone so horribly wrong…

Chapter One

January in Brighton was cool and wet, the lower lying centre of town rendered mysterious with a grey mist that flowed from the chilly sea and veiled everything into unfamiliarity. Mina Scarletti, her lungs and chest cramped by the distortion of her twisted spine, was obliged more than most to avoid winter coughs and chills, and ventured out only if strictly necessary. When journeys were required, she faced the dangers with her slight form guarded by so many shawls and cloaks that she was amplified to more than twice her actual width. Thus clad, she thought she must resemble a misshapen sea monster that had swum in from the northern wastes, and half expected that one day she would be harpooned by an overeager hunter and put on display in a curiosity museum.

Anxious friends were always on hand to ensure that she took no chances with her fragile health. Dr Hamid, her wise and cautious advisor, proprietor of an Indian herbal steam bath emporium and natural successor to the renowned 'Dr Brighton', Sake Dean Mohamed, watched over her with especial care. Once a week, Mina visited the baths and luxuriated in the aroma of exotically scented vapour, after which Dr Hamid's sister Anna applied her special oil massage to soothe away the pain in her strained back muscles, and gave instruction in callisthenic exercises.

Her days were unusually quiet for the season, since Mina's mother, Louisa, was currently in London, tending to the voluble misery of her married daughter, Enid Inskip. The previous autumn, Enid had been indiscreet to the point of folly and her current delicate state of health was therefore incompatible with the prolonged absence of Mr Inskip abroad. His return was not anticipated with any pleasure.

In Brighton, Mina's home, lacking Louisa's perpetual complaints and Enid's outbursts of self-pity, was hers alone to enjoy. Her mornings always began with exercises, using a set of dumbbells, which she kept carefully hidden so as not to invite the ridicule of her family. She then proceeded to a light breakfast. After that she sat at her desk, perching on the wedge-shaped cushion that improved her posture, where, after dealing with correspondence and household matters, she could undertake her real work, writing chilling stories of hauntings and horror, which were published under the *nom de plume* Robert Neil.

Unfortunately, Mina found herself unable to enjoy the contemplative peace generally believed to be so vital to the writer's mind, and found herself, instead, idle, dull and lacking imagination. The still quiet, the daily round of repeated events, the very pattern on the pale lemon wallpaper, seemed to be mocking her. The only subject she could think of addressing was a story about a woman driven to madness with boredom, and she couldn't think that anyone would be interested in reading that. It was with some relief, therefore, that she received a note from her good friend Nellie Jordan, begging to be allowed an urgent visit as there was a matter of some importance she wished to discuss.

Nellie had once ornamented the stage as the bewitchingly costumed assistant to the noted French conjuror, M Baptiste. He had been generous enough to marry her, an arrangement that, in his eyes, did not exempt him from enjoying the affections of other women. Nevertheless, Nellie had understandably believed herself to be that gentleman's legal wife until another lady unexpectedly arrived from France with a brood of small children and a marriage certificate that pre-dated her own. Time had healed all hurts, and a contrite M Baptiste had reconciled with his loving if tempestuous family, who, in Nellie's estimation, were more than welcome to him.

Nellie's new husband, Mr Jordan, was a partner in an establishment providing the best Parisian fashions. He was not likeable, but he was rich, and Nellie's fine features and voluptuous figure displayed the latest ensembles at leading society gatherings to both her and his great advantage. The early months of the marriage had been a dazzling whirlwind of purchases to enable Nellie to live in the manner she felt she deserved; a new home, servants, a smart carriage, and of course, costumes and jewels. She had often declared herself to be as happy as it was possible for any woman to be when married to Mr Jordan. In the last few months, however, Mina had sensed that her friend's happiness had become tarnished.

Mina asked the maidservant to deliver a reply to Mrs Jordan, and purchase some of the sweet treats Nellie enjoyed with her tea. Within an hour, Nellie was at the door in her pretty little carriage, a perfumed vision in wine-coloured fur and velvet.

Rose, the general maid, who had been instructed by Dr Hamid as to how best to fuss over Mina, had tended the parlour fire well and secured the room against draughts. That ultimate horror of any good household — dust — had been eradicated and replaced instead with the sharp nostril-twitching tang of whatever cleansing mixture the chemist had devised that week.

A table had been set before the fire. There was a tray of delicate little wafers with crisp pink icing and an inviting thread of hot vapour was twisting from the teapot lid. Nellie embraced Mina warmly and settled herself before the table with a sigh. 'You look very well, my dear,' she said.

'As do you,' said Mina, pouring the tea. In truth, Nellie did not look as well as she once had; she was like a bright ornament that had lost its glow and it was a question as to how, or indeed whether, she might be restored. Mina knew exactly how much milk and sugar Nellie liked, so there was no need to ask. Once, she might have enquired whether Mr Jordan was well and if Nellie was happy, but in the last few weeks, she had deemed that both questions were better avoided. 'But I am interested to know what brings you here so urgently.'

Nellie thrust a white hand into her reticule and produced a letter. 'This,' she said. 'It is a cry for help and impossible to ignore! My dear friend Kitty, Mrs Honeyacre as she is now, is in dire need, and I feel sure that you are just the person who can assist her!'

Mina had been a guest at the nuptials of Mr Benjamin Honeyacre and Miss Kitty Betts the previous December. The reception had been unusual in that Kitty's family had provided all the entertainment. Her mother Hilda — or Little Owl Feather, as she was known on stage — had been sawn in half by her father Arthur Betts, otherwise known as Chung Ching the Chinese illusionist and sword-swallower, after which her brothers put in an energetic performance as a troupe of Greek acrobats. The newly married couple had appeared to be as happy as anyone could reasonably have expected, and Mina hoped that nothing had happened to spoil what should have been their honeymoon.

'I am sorry to hear that Mrs Honeyacre is in need of help,' said Mina, 'and mystified as to why I might be her saviour.' She proffered the tray of wafers and Nellie made a great show of trying to resist temptation before she gave in and took two.

'Let me reassure you on one point,' said Nellie. 'Dear Kitty says that Mr Honeyacre is the best of husbands. He is dedicated to providing her with every comfort and pays attention to her slightest whim. She has all the clothes and jewels she could desire and a carriage in which she can drive out every day if she wishes.' She bit into a wafer and crunched the icing with pleasure.

'I had wondered if she would find life in the country dull after Brighton,' said Mina, cautiously. 'I assume she has given up the stage. Is she missing her old life and friends?'

'Not at all,' said Nellie with a dismissive wave of her confectionary. 'It was always her intention to retire from the stage when she married. Also, Mr Honeyacre has promised that she will be able to visit her friends as often as she likes and attend all the events of the Brighton season. Oh, and her greatest friend Miss Pet is with her; they are utterly devoted.'

Mina sipped her tea thoughtfully. 'Is Miss Pet on the stage? I don't recall her at the wedding.'

'She is a quiet, shy creature and does not perform, but her great art and skill lies in tending costumes and dressing hair, at which, I can promise you, she is second to none. She could not bear to be parted from Kitty and is now her personal maid and companion, almost like one of the family.'

Mina nodded. Now she thought about it, there had been a very shy young lady at the wedding, who had ensured that the bride's gown and accessories were perfectly arranged and then faded quietly into the background.

'There is, of course,' said Nellie, with a meaningful expression, 'a certain proud gentry of Sussex who might take a little time to accept Kitty as one of their own, ladies who, because of her history, might consider her to be beneath their notice, but Mr Honeyacre is determined to change all that by throwing extravagant entertainments where she will be bound to win them over. You know how amusing Kitty can be, even when she does not do her famous backbend with her head between her ankles.'

'Then there appear to be no clouds on the horizon,' observed Mina. 'Except, of course, those you have not yet described.'

'You may laugh when I tell you,' said Nellie. 'Kitty tells me that the house is haunted. As you may know, many theatrical people are superstitious, and Kitty is no exception. Oh, she is a sensible girl, not inclined to strange fancies, but she declares that she cannot deny the evidence of her eyes and ears.'

'Eyes and ears may easily be deceived,' said Mina. 'She must know this more than most.'

'She does. But apart from that, the servants are becoming distracted and upset, and Mr Honeyacre, whose interest in spiritualism you are aware of, feels that he cannot open the house to the county quality until the ghost has been laid to rest.'

'But you do not believe in ghosts?' asked Mina.

'I have never met a conjuror who did.' Nellie ate another wafer.

Mina reflected on what little she had been told of the history of Hollow House. 'Has Mr Honeyacre not owned the house for some years? He must have visited it before he came to live there. How has he not been aware of this before?'

'He has never lived there, or even spent the night. When he purchased the house its condition was such that he was obliged to stay at the Railway Inn in Hassocks while it was being surveyed. Then, of course, he went abroad. The only occupants during his absence were Mr and Mrs Malling, the housekeeper and groundsman. They live in their own separate apartment above the stables and have never made any complaint.'

Mina refreshed the teacups. 'What has Mrs Honeyacre seen and heard?'

'Her letters are a little vague on that subject, almost as if she is unwilling to commit the words to paper. But she says that there have been noises and the appearance of a figure. She goes no further than that.'

Mina spent a few moments in contemplation. 'You have known Mrs Honeyacre far longer than I. What do you think is the explanation?'

Nellie restrained herself from taking another wafer. 'It is a very old house. Floorboards may creak, draughts may move curtains, there will be shadows everywhere. I feel sure it is all a work of the imagination and as Kitty becomes more familiar with her new home, she will come to realise that. But it seems that the maids are terrified and one of them even fainted dead away and now refuses to tell anyone what it was she saw. Neither of them will spend a night in the house. They live in the village and will only go there during the hours of daylight.'

'It is hard for me to give an opinion without visiting the house and speaking to the inhabitants,' said Mina.

Nellie smiled. 'My thought precisely. And that is what Kitty would like you to do. She has invited me to stay for a few days and absolutely begged me to bring you with me. She has heard your reputation for solving such mysteries, and although Mr Honeyacre is a believer in phantoms, he respects your opinion. You are like one of the wise women of old to whom all men listen. I am convinced that you will be able to set everyone's mind at rest.'

Mina hesitated. The winter wind moaned softly down the chimney making the firelight flicker, the slivers of flame waving like warning fingers.

'It is an easy journey,' said Nellie soothingly. 'We will go to the railway station by carriage and take the train to Hassocks Gate. It isn't far at all. Mr Honeyacre will send his carriage to take us from there to Ditchling Hollow. And I have an excellent maid who will attend to you.'

'I fear that Dr Hamid will rule against it,' said Mina. 'Not that I always obey him.'

'Oh, I have thought of that,' said Nellie with a laugh. 'I will ask Dr Hamid to accompany us. If the Honeyacres' maids are in a state of terror his services will be needed and he will be able to reassure himself that you are well cared for.'

'When will you go?' asked Mina.

'I thought we could depart next Friday and return on Monday. We can't stay too long as there is so much to be done to prepare for next month's costume ball. I am to be Madame de Pompadour and Kitty is considering a gypsy girl, although I have thought of a better idea. You must come, Mina.'

'I am not so sure that would be wise,' said Mina. 'Large assemblies of people in winter always bring the danger of catching cold. The winter costume ball is a boon for sellers of medicine and if I take a chill on my lungs I am more likely to trouble the undertaker.'

Nellie smiled away the objection. 'Oh, I have thought of how to prevent any risk and have the very thing for you. You will be a Spanish lady with a beautiful fan. You may use it to cover your face and so protect yourself against bad air and coughs and chills. We will ask Dr Hamid to add a little sachet of his wonderful herbs.'

'I have never attended a costume ball,' Mina reflected, realising that since her mother and Enid would still be in London there was nothing to prevent her. 'Are there any tickets remaining?'

'Leave it all to me!' said Nellie. 'And the costume, too, I know exactly what is needed. Only come to Hollow House with me and we will have a very amusing visit.'

'I imagine that preparations for the ball are keeping Mr Jordan extremely busy in Brighton,' said Mina.

'Yes, the provision of costumes is a new venture for the business and occupies his every thought and all his energy,' said Nellie cheerfully.

'Well,' said Mina, who had decided to agree to the scheme at its very first mention, 'if you can persuade Dr Hamid to accompany us, I will go, and with great pleasure. I hope Mrs Honeyacre is not too distressed by the situation.'

Nellie allowed a trace of concern to cloud her face. 'From what she has written — and in some part what she has chosen not to write — she is principally disturbed by her husband's attitude. Since he wishes to study supernatural phenomena he is plunging ever deeper into the world of the psychic. It is not the marriage nor the home she had hoped for. But we will mend that, my dear, we will.'

Chapter Two

Mina's greatest dilemma as she instructed Rose on packing for the excursion was whether or not to inform her mother that she would be absent from home for the better part of four days. If she did, she knew that she would receive an urgent telegram ordering her not to leave the house and refusing her permission to undertake such a perilous winter journey. The fact that Mina was a twenty-five-year-old woman of independent means did not make any difference to her mother's perception of her as a difficult child who required constant instruction. Mina knew that if she disobeyed that order, or hurried away before the inevitable telegram arrived, a torrent of maternal outrage and recrimination would fall upon her head. She had survived many such storms before, but preferred not to invite them unnecessarily. It was tempting, therefore, to say nothing and hope that her mother would remain ignorant of the visit, in which case, all would be well. There was, however, the possibility that a family matter would arise during her absence, which her mother, as she so often did, would insist required Mina's immediate attention. If she was found inexplicably not to be at home the consequences were something she did not wish to contemplate.

At length, Mina decided to write to her older brother Edward, sensible, serious, diligent Edward who managed the Scarletti family publishing business in London; and inform him of her intentions, reassuring him that she would be accompanied by a respectable lady friend, a maid and a medical attendant. Edward was in a constant state of annoyance with their mother and therefore well aware of what it was advisable to conceal from her for a quiet existence.

Early on the Friday morning, Nellie, in an exuberant mood, dashed up to Mina's front door in a hired cab. The smart little equipage that was her usual mode of transport around Brighton was, of course, quite insufficient to carry the volume of luggage necessary for such a long stay.

The cab driver descended and assisted Mina into the vehicle, then loaded her modest luggage, one carpetbag handed to him by Rose. Nellie's maid, Zillah, was sitting composedly in a corner of the cab. Quickly, deftly and unfussily, she provided Mina with a foot-warmer and a fur wrap. She had, thought Mina, been very carefully chosen; youthful and good-looking enough to be an ornament to her mistress, but not sufficiently so as to outshine her. Zillah's manner gave Mina some confidence that at least one of the servants would be unflappable in the face of spectral visitations.

Dr Hamid, carrying a gentleman's overnight bag and a medical bag, was waiting for them at the station. He assisted the ladies down from the cab, although in Mina's case he took care to give her only as much help as she needed, allowing her the independence of doing as much as she could for herself without risk. In Mina's experience, this was a subtlety that few gentlemen were able to appreciate.

Dr Hamid was the only doctor Mina had ever fully trusted and, along with his sister Anna, he had made a special study of scoliosis, since his older sister, Eliza, whom Mina had befriended, had been dreadfully afflicted with that condition. The losses of both his wife and Eliza in the last year were blows that had crushed all joy from Dr Hamid's life and he had turned to his work for solace, devoting himself to the good of others. Mina's scoliosis was less advanced than that of Eliza's and she often thought he saw in her a special focus for his care, a hope that she could be saved from worsening, even

19

perhaps achieve some improvement. His dedication to his profession meant that he was oblivious to the fact that a well set up widower in his forties with a profitable business was an object of keen interest to the single ladies of Brighton. Many had cast an eye in his direction, but to no avail. Mina had often wondered if she ought to draw his attention to the situation, but realising that the knowledge would cause him the most painful embarrassment had decided to remain silent. Having been warned many years ago that her deformity precluded any possibility of marriage and children, Mina was content to regard the doctor as a valued friend.

As the little party approached the station, Dr Hamid cast a watchful eye over Mina's ungainly limping gait. No one better than he could see the incipient signs of a dangerous deterioration. Thus far, he appeared satisfied. 'So I am obliged once again to protect you from yet another madcap scheme,' he said, but he was smiling as he spoke.

'Four days in the country,' said Mina, dryly. 'Is there no end to my folly? Who knows what I will attempt next?'

'Mrs Honeyacre has assured us that every possible comfort will be provided,' said Nellie.

'Fresh air, warm fires, ghosts,' said Dr Hamid.

'I have a feeling that the ghosts will vanish as soon as we arrive,' said Nellie with a laugh. 'From what Kitty says, the maids have been frightening each other with fantastic tales, so they see spectres in every shadow. You will need to dose them well with something to quell their imagination. And Mina's sound advice will soon show them that there is nothing to fear. Then we can amuse ourselves by seeing the countryside, which is very pretty thereabouts, and Mr Honeyacre does keep an extremely good table.'

Dr Hamid, who was an enthusiastic trencherman, brightened up at that last prospect.

'You must admit that the weather is very mild,' said Mina. 'No snow or frosty air.'

They glanced up at the sky, which was darkening ominously.

'Yes, the rain is uncommonly warm for the time of year,' agreed Dr Hamid, as the first drops began to fall.

Nellie had secured tickets for the best class of carriage and they soon made themselves comfortable. It had been more than two years since Mina had travelled by railway. She and her family had then been removing to Brighton from London for the sake of her ailing father's health. The consumption that eventually claimed his life had not yet taken away his voice during that previous trip and once her mother had fallen into a doze he had regaled Mina, whom he knew had a taste for dramatic tales, with a vivid account of the terrible railway accident that had taken place on that very same line in 1861. The tragedy, caused by the collision of two trains in Clayton Tunnel, had inspired Mr Charles Dickens to write his story, *The Signal-Man*, in which a ghost gives warnings of disasters. Mina thought that the actual incident was quite horrible enough without the addition of a ghost, but she supposed that that was what the public liked to read.

'A gloomy place,' said Dr Hamid as their train entered the tunnel where so many lives had been lost. Mina wondered if the line had a reputation, an atmosphere even, that encouraged further tragedy. Only three months previously, a young Brighton man, despondent through ill-health, had chosen to end his life there by throwing himself from a second-class carriage. Dr Hamid's expression made her think that the youth might have been one of his patients. She decided not to enquire, but once they had emerged into the light she took out a pencil and the little notebook she carried with her to record ideas for stories and quickly jotted some thoughts.

Before long they were at Hassocks Gate railway station, where they alighted. The rain was coming down harder now, in large misty grey drops, and they hurried into the ticket hall where a middle-aged man in a coachman's uniform holding a large black umbrella was waiting for them. 'Mrs Jordan and party?' he asked.

'Ah, you must be Malling,' said Nellie. 'Yes, please assist my maid with the luggage.'

Dr Hamid took the umbrella and conducted Nellie and Mina to the carriage that awaited them outside the station. He then returned to ensure that Zillah was not soaked as her mistress's boxes were brought to the carriage. It was a small kindness, but Mina wondered how many gentlemen would even have thought to protect a maidservant from a wetting.

'Malling is a man of many parts,' said Nellie as they took their seats. 'He is coachman, gardener and general handyman. Mrs Malling is the housekeeper. They have lived on the estate and cared for it ever since Mr Honeyacre purchased it, so I think they will have some interesting stories to tell.'

Mina glanced at Mr Malling as he finished stowing the luggage and climbed back onto his perch. He had a face like granite, immovable, expressionless. If he did have any stories to tell, Mina doubted that he would be telling them.

Hassocks was a small farmstead only a mile north of Clayton Hill. The carriage soon left the few cottages behind and travelled down a narrow road flanked by hedgerows and trees. Thin bare branches straggled to the sky, but others had been savagely cut back, their blunt ends making them look like the clawed fingers of skeletal hands driving up out of the earth.

Mina found the appearance interesting and made some more notes in her little book.

The road passed the railway line and they were briefly able to see the extravagantly ornate north entrance to the fatal tunnel, which looked like a crenellated gothic castle in miniature, before turning onto an even narrower road, the surface of which was already dissolving into mud. Rain was cascading from clouds the colour of iron and there were distant rumbles of thunder.

'Why did Mr Honeyacre choose to purchase a home in Ditchling Hollow?' asked Mina, as she felt her hopes of comfortable accommodation fading into the distance.

'He encountered it while touring Sussex looking for antiquities,' said Nellie. 'It was perfect for his needs and even allowing for the fact that it required substantial renovation, it came at a very good price. It had lain empty for so long that the owners accepted his first offer at once.'

Mina said nothing but she thought that such eagerness to sell was not a good sign. She hoped that Mr Honeyacre would not discover an unsuspected fault in the building that would cost him dear in the long run. She jotted another story idea in her notebook. This one was about a man who bought a beautiful house very cheaply, which he found was plagued with strange noises and then, one day, the foundations collapsed and the whole edifice crumbled away, crushing the owner and all his property. She wondered if she ought to put a ghost in it.

The carriage turned right again. At the junction between the roads was a small signpost, its legend so worn by time and neglect that it was impossible to read it. This time the way was narrower still. Two vehicles would have been unable to pass each other without one of them veering off the road into one of the small entranceways that led to a farm gate.

The carriage lurched over deep ruts and splashed through rain-filled pools. The road was dipping down a slope and for a while Mina was afraid that they would slip into a watercourse or lake at the bottom, but then to her relief, it levelled out. She peered out of the window and saw ahead a small stone bridge over a brook, its waters plunging and rushing with great energy. There were hills encircling them and far away through the curtain of glittering rain she caught a glimpse of what looked like two windmills.

'I think we are almost there,' said Nellie. 'From Kitty's description this is Ditchling Hollow.'

The carriage juddered over the bridge and passed along a single street flanked on one side by a row of labourers' cottages and on the other by larger properties that Mina assumed were farmhouses. As they continued a curtain was pulled back from the window of a farmhouse and a face peered out, the head turning to follow the progress of the carriage down the road. The expression, as far as Mina could see, was not welcoming. An upper window then opened slightly. Mina was unable to see who was within, but one fitful ray of light from the clouded sun was briefly reflected from something like a mirror or a glass. Even allowing for the weather there was something dreary and dejected about the place, a sense of joyless existence in its grim façade. There was a single provision store, a smithy and the inevitable beer shop, which had some pretensions to being a public house since there was a faded signboard on which she could just read the words 'Goat and Hammers'.

Mina said nothing but glanced anxiously at Dr Hamid, who seemed similarly perturbed.

They neared a low wall built from large blocks of dressed stone enclosing a graveyard, behind which stood a small and very ancient church. There were no more cottages; in fact, they seemed to have seen all that Ditchling Hollow had to offer. The wall continued to their left and to their right there was an expanse of wet pasture with a few animal sheds. As the church retreated into the distance they finally saw their destination. Within the same perimeter wall that enclosed the church and the graveyard was a fine large house of unusual design.

'Is that Hollow House?' asked Mina.

'I believe it is. Kitty told me it was like three houses put together,' said Nellie.

'I am no expert,' said Dr Hamid, 'but it does look like the central part was constructed first and the two wings added later.'

As the carriage brought them closer, they saw that the main part of the house, almost certainly the oldest portion, was a three storey edifice, built of large, irregular slabs of stone with vertical windows on the two lower floors and small square casements above. The projecting two storey porch was undoubtedly a later decoration, built of smaller, flatter stones, its high doorway gaping like a large toothless mouth and a bay window above with supporting stonework carved into sharp pointed traceries. The decorative bosses in the form of carved heads did not, thought Mina, add to its charm.

To the right, as they faced the house, there was a newer wing of the same height and of the same material as the porch. The opposite wing was quite different: a wall of dull brick with an arch leading into a stable yard and plain windows of the rooms above.

'I expect Mr Honeyacre originally saw it in better weather,' said Mina.

'I understand it was much neglected when he purchased it and did not look as well as it does now,' said Nellie. 'The grounds were a veritable wilderness and what we see today is the result of the Mallings' hard work.'

The carriage paused before an ornamental gateway, which Mr Malling briefly descended to open, then it continued along a curve of driveway, a sinuous path with a double turn like Mina's spine. The grass on either side had been clipped. There was a border of rounded stones and behind those were broad beds planted with evergreen shrubs. The drive ended in a semi-circular area in front of the porch, which was flanked with urns containing small ornamental trees and some comfortable looking benches. A round stonework construction, not yet completed, looked as though it would eventually become a piece of statuary or even a fountain.

As they alighted from the carriage, Mr Malling wielded his umbrella with a dexterity that spoke of long practice. Two maidservants came from the house to meet them and attend to the luggage, together with Mr Honeyacre's manservant, Gillespie, who indicated without the necessity of saying a word that he would wait upon Dr Hamid. A robust lady in housekeeper's gown with a chain of keys, presumably Mrs Malling, was there to direct the maids in an authoritative yet not unkind manner.

Mr and Mrs Honeyacre soon appeared in the porch-way to greet the visitors. The last time Mina had seen Mr Honeyacre was at the wedding, when he had been blandly yet cheerfully mystified by everything that was going on around him. Kitty had been her usual vivacious self, laughing and twirling about to show off her gown with apparently unlimited energy. That morning, Mr Honeyacre was doing his best to put on a cheerful welcoming face, but he kept casting concerned glances at his wife and Kitty, despite her smiles, was quiet, still and strained. She was hugging what appeared at first glance to be a bundled shawl, but then the fabric appeared to move of its own accord and a small brown face peeped out with large dark eyes and pointed furry ears. It was the smallest dog Mina had ever seen and Kitty held it as a child would hold a doll.

A tall, very plainly dressed young woman stood in Kitty's shadow and Mina recalled that she had been at the wedding, giving delicate attention to the bride's gown and coiffure. Miss Pet, for that must be she, had a modest eye and a curious posture, as if ashamed of her height and wanting to conceal it.

Mina could not help glancing up at the façade of the house as she approached the shelter of the porch and it was then that she saw the figure at an upper window of the stone built wing. A woman, she thought, clad all in flowing white, the face indistinct through the rain and the misted glass. She looked up at Dr Hamid, on whose arm she was leaning, to see if he had noticed the figure, but his attention was on herself. 'I hope the journey was not too tiring for you,' he said. 'The sooner we are inside the better.'

'A warm fire and a hot drink will soon restore me,' she reassured him and looked back at the window, but the figure had gone. Mina had the presence of mind to note which window it was; one at the furthest end of the property. Could the lady in white be another visitor, she wondered, or a maid preparing the guest rooms? It would be foolishness to think she might be anything else.

'Oh, come in, come in, do!' exclaimed Mr Honeyacre, 'I am sorry the weather has been so unfavourable. We must hope it will improve later on. Did you have a comfortable journey here?'

'Thank you, the way was a little muddy, but no harm done,' said Nellie. Kitty gave the little dog into Miss Pet's care and Nellie came forward to embrace her friend warmly. 'My dear, you look well, the country air must suit you.'

Kitty smiled bravely.

'And what a charming little puppy dog!'

'Oh yes,' said Kitty, 'he is such a tiny scrap, but so very clever and affectionate!'

With wet umbrellas and cloaks placed in the porch to dry, the new arrivals were conducted into an entrance hall, which alone was twice the size of many a family home. Freshly painted walls, velvet hangings and gilded lamps were a welcome sight, and despite the age of the house there remained still the scent of the new. As tiled floors gave way to wood and carpet, so the sense of comfort seemed to reach out and envelop the slightly chilled and dampened visitors.

'If you come into the dining hall, you will find a tray of hot toddies to warm you through,' said Mr Honeyacre. 'Then Mrs Malling will show you to your rooms and luncheon will be served in one hour. I promise our cook is second to none! We have a perfect blaze of fires everywhere and no one will be in danger of catching cold. After luncheon, if the weather permits, we can make a tour of the grounds and our little church. In any case, I know you will want to view the house. The renovations are not yet complete but we have come a long way in the last weeks.'

Mrs Malling departed together with the housemaids and Zillah and their host conducted the visitors to a set of double doors that opened onto a room of almost baronial importance. The space was dominated by a long table, which was fully able to seat twenty guests to dinner in comfort. For more intimate gatherings, a smaller round tea table nestled in one corner. The fireplace, which was loaded with blazing logs in a brass grate, was a masterpiece of the carver's art, with pillars entwined glossily in ivy and topped by lions' heads. Above it was a mantelpiece and an importantly tall mirror. The walls were decorated with a rich red paper dotted with gilt ornaments, the pattern thick and raised. Above the table there was a magnificent central chandelier, a thick brass stem from which there curved more delicate branches, each ending in a gilded glass lamp. The effect was of a burnished efflorescence of light. Six matching pairs of lamps were placed around the walls.

Around the perimeter of the room were carved oak settles of obvious antiquity and plinths displaying Chinese vases, while on a long sideboard, well-furnished with decorated tableware, was a tray of glasses in silver holders. When the maids re-entered, each was carrying a jug which exuded inviting clouds of hot vapour.

Mina observed that both maids were clad in dark grey uniforms with starched and frilled white aprons, caps and collars. The figure she had seen in the upper window had been clad entirely in white. Or had she been mistaken and some distortion of the glass, enhanced by the rain, had magnified the white and concealed the dark? Had there been time for one of the maids, both of whom had been occupied with the luggage, to appear briefly at the window? She would need to discover in which room the figure had appeared. Perhaps, she thought, this was the origin of the supposed haunting, a simple error, the distortion of an image seen through glass. She determined to make a written note of the experience and her theories at the first opportunity.

Cradling the comforting drink in her hands Mina felt the heat rise up to her face, like one of Dr Hamid's fragrant vapour baths. She inhaled the aroma and then sipped the hot buttery liquid. As she did so, she considered the demeanour of the occupants of Hollow House. The senior servants, older and experienced, Mr Gillespie and the Mallings, were able to conceal their inner thoughts behind the calm exterior that it was their duty to present to their employers. The much younger and greener maids, however, hurried about their business in a more obviously nervous manner, eyes staring straight ahead as if afraid of what they might see if they were to look about them. The Honeyacres were clearly troubled and Miss Pet was a model of silent anxiety. Whatever the reason for the reported haunting, even if it was all down to a simple error, Mina could see that she must treat it in all seriousness. No idle dismissal or reassurance would do here. No one was going to be humoured out of their discomfiture.

Until this moment, Mina's only experience of hauntings were the ghostly productions of spirit mediums; manifestations of faces and hands, and even complete figures whose glowing robes, appearing gorgeous to the untrained eyes of those who sat in darkness, owed more to the properties of phosphorus than heavenly radiance. Many of these self-professed 'psychics', as they had come to be known, offered entertainment to the curious and comfort to the bereaved for a modest sum, and Mina had no concerns about that. There were others, however, who, while proclaiming themselves to be the selfless servants of suffering humanity, attached themselves to their hapless victims, demanding ever-increasing fees for private séances, sometimes to the point of ruin. When no more fees could be paid, they moved on to another target. They were like the spider who traps a fly in its web, wraps it in silk, sucks it dry and then abandons the husk to look for another meal. In Mina's opinion, these people were heartless extortionists and it was to her great satisfaction that, due to her efforts, several of them were now in prison where they belonged.

She wondered if anyone in the house professed to be a medium. If this was not the case and the family and servants were in the middle of a disturbance that they had not invited and could not control, it was a situation with which she was wholly unfamiliar.

Although Mina had never experienced a genuine haunting, she accepted that such a thing might be possible and it might transpire that this was the case in Hollow House. If so, it would have to be dealt with, most probably by the clergy. If, on the other hand, it was all a mistake, this would need to be demonstrated beyond a doubt in order to set everyone's mind at rest. It was a hard thing to achieve in a few days and Mina was unsure of how to begin. She could treat the visit as a social call and simply observe, listen to what was discussed and form her own conclusions. Or, with Mr Honeyacre's permission, she could start asking questions and gathering information. The next hour or so would tell her what to do.

Kitty and Nellie, as old friends, were on one of the settles talking quietly together and Mina saw Nellie pat Kitty's hand reassuringly. Kitty took the little dog back into her arms and Miss Pet went to sit nearby, her long fingers curled modestly together on her lap. It was hard to read how she felt about the uncomfortable atmosphere in the house, but from time to time she glanced at Kitty with concern and Mina deduced that she was more worried for her mistress than for herself.

Mr Honeyacre, making jerky little motions with his arms, spoke enthusiastically to Mina and Dr Hamid of the dining hall, which he said had been almost uninhabitable when he had first purchased the house. Most of his collection of paintings, sculptures, porcelain and curios were still stored away in readiness to ornament the rooms and he anticipated that in time the whole house would represent a gallery of exquisite art. Despite his confidence, his manner was brittle and he appeared to be talking about his home and his collection in order to ease his discomfort and avoid discussing the subject which had brought them there.

'What an interesting house!' Mina exclaimed. 'I could not help but notice there has been more than one architect at work. What do you know of its history?'

'I confess that I have been so occupied with the task of making it comfortable that I have made little progress with that study, a neglect I fully intend to remedy in future,' said Mr Honeyacre. 'But the old title deeds of the estate reveal that there was a house on this site in the days of the Tudors. A courtier, Sir Christopher Redwoode, was granted the land by Henry VIII and built a fine manor here, but as far as I know, hardly any part of that building remains. I assume it was essentially timber framed and was eventually pulled down. If there was a brick hearth I haven't discovered it yet, but there are some very interesting cobbles outside.'

Mina appreciated the sight of a handsome building but was unable to match Mr Honeyacre's enthusiasm for cobbles.

'The largest central portion of the present house,' he continued, 'judging by the style, dates from the early Hanoverians. The addition of the east wing and porch, which, as I am sure you have already observed, match each other, was perhaps some fifty years ago. The western wing is much more recent and of no architectural interest. There is a stable yard and servant accommodation above. But you will see it all after luncheon.'

Mina made no comment, but thought that a house composed of so many fragments, all constructed at different times and of different materials, offered a world of opportunity for draughts and unstable crevices, and the creaking of old wood, not to mention vermin and other creatures making their homes in its darker spaces. Perhaps, she thought hopefully, the ghost of Hollow House would prove to be flesh and blood after all.

Chapter Three

Once the luggage was dealt with and the cups cleared, Mrs Malling reappeared to show the visitors to their rooms. Unlike the maids, she appeared to Mina to be perfectly comfortable in her surroundings, but how she actually felt under the façade of quiet service could be another matter.

'You must know the house very well,' said Mina as Mrs Malling conducted them up a set of stairs that led from the entrance hall. The carpet was soft underfoot and still smelt new. The lamp glow that lit their way brushed the gilded frames of oil paintings depicting views of Sussex.

'Oh, that I do,' said Mrs Malling, readily. 'We have lived here quite a number of years, Mr Malling and me, while Mr Honeyacre was away on his travels.'

'I expect there was a great deal for you to do,' said Mina in her most sympathetic voice. 'I believe it was very dilapidated at first. Having seen it now, I would be most interested to know what work was required.'

Mrs Malling smiled as she reminisced. 'When we came here, most of it was not fit for anyone to live in, except for the newest part, the west wing, where we have some nice rooms. The rest was sorely in need of repair, the roof letting in water and the damp getting everywhere, and the garden was a wilderness. There were no drains at all. I think a barbarian gentleman might have found the sanitary arrangements to his liking, but not an English lady. We have done a great deal, but there is still much to be done.'

'I look forward to Mr Honeyacre's tour of the property,' said Mina. 'I have been very impressed by what I have seen so far.'

'Most of the decoration — the paint and the papers and the lights — that was all done in the last few weeks, ever since Mr Honeyacre was married and said he was coming here to live. There were workmen here, there and everywhere, and no end of noise and dust and smell. Mr Malling had to be everywhere too, to oversee them. Then there were the floors and the carpets and the furniture.' Mrs Malling paused. 'Of course, it looks very splendid now, but if you ask me, Miss, the old house didn't like it, being disturbed like that. Sometimes houses don't, you know. They just want to be left alone.'

They reached a landing where a wide, well-lit corridor drew the eye pleasingly towards the east. A plain door suggested access to the newer western part of the house and the servants' quarters. The staircase continued upwards, but it was changed in character, being narrow, uncarpeted and less inviting than the lower part. A red rope strung across on brass hooks suggested that its use was not recommended. Mina paused to look up, but the walls were bare and unadorned and nothing could be seen beyond an upper landing that disappeared into a grey gloom and led only to an unlit second floor.

'We don't advise that visitors go up there,' explained Mrs Malling. 'The roof in the old part of the house was in a dreadful state. It has been made sound and all is now dry, but the floorboards are rotten and not safe to walk on. We are expecting men to come in next week and replace them.'

They proceeded down the corridor, which was flanked on either side by doors, most of which bore ornamental enamelled plaques with gilded lettering.

The first door they came to announced itself discreetly to be the water closet and the second was a bathroom. 'If anyone should require a bath we would need some notice to make sure there is enough hot water,' said Mrs Malling. 'It comes up in pipes now, which is very convenient. But all the rooms are supplied with washstands and a jug of hot water will be brought to you every morning.' Opposite the bathroom there was a door bearing a plaque marked 'Cicero' and they walked past it. Since that room would enjoy a view over the estate, Mina assumed it was the master bedroom.

The next door was entitled 'Socrates' and here Mrs Malling paused. 'This is your room, Dr Hamid. Mr Gillespie, who is Mr Honeyacre's gentleman, will be up directly to assist with your things and bring you anything you might need.'

Dr Hamid opened the door and a waft of fragrant herbs drifted into the corridor. He smiled and entered.

Opposite Socrates was a door marked 'Minerva'. 'Miss Scarletti, this is your room. The one opposite, "Atalanta", that is Mrs Jordan's.'

Mina, who had seen another door further on from her own, did not enter her room at once, but walked on, gazing about her. 'How very charming it is here!' she said admiringly. 'I do so like the little plaques. They show what a scholar Mr Honeyacre is. But this other room does not have one. Is it waiting for one to be made? I am quite fascinated to know what it will be.'

'I'm not sure,' said Mrs Malling. 'That room is not a bedroom; it is presently used to store the antiquities and paintings that are yet to be displayed.'

'Are we the only guests?' asked Mina, 'or is anyone else expected?'

'It is just your party,' said Mrs Malling.

Mina walked to the end of the corridor where a tall window admitted pale light reflected from the cloudy sky and found a narrow winding staircase leading both up and down. The upper part was roped off.

'Those are the servants' stairs,' said Mrs Malling. 'They go down to the kitchen and laundry room. The upper part is not yet used.'

'Where will Zillah sleep?' asked Nellie. 'I shall require her to unpack my luggage, and my coiffure is a perfect fright.'

'Zillah has been given a room in the west wing,' said Mrs Malling. 'She will be here directly to attend to you.'

Having established that her guests required nothing more, Mrs Malling, saying that she should be called at once if she was needed, departed.

Mina entered a room in which a small, freshly-tended fire took the chill from the air and a vase held bunches of dried lavender. There was a comfortable-looking bed, against which a small footstool had been placed, the better to enable a person of her small size to climb between the sheets. There was a washstand with a basin and jug of patterned porcelain, scented soap, fresh towels and a small dressing table. The mantelpiece was provided with figurines of shepherdesses and, rather more usefully, a pair of stout brass candlesticks, which Mina thought she might make use of for her exercises, as she had not been able to pack her dumbbells. On the night table was a pierced work candleholder of oriental design that reminded her of the Royal Pavilion and a box of candles and matches.

Thick window curtains had been pulled aside to afford a view over the grounds and Mina went to look out. The room was at the front of the house and directly below her window she saw the terrace and one of the ornamental urns. It occurred to her that the urns would be a perfect guide as to the location of the rooms as seen from the outside. The window at which the white-clad figure had appeared, the one at the furthest end of the house was, she felt sure, the window of the room next to hers, the one that had been designated a storeroom. Perhaps, she thought, what she had observed was a maid who had gone into the room to fetch something required for a guest.

Mina opened the door of her room and glanced out. Zillah arrived and was admitted to Nellie's room. Knowing Nellie, Mina judged that the task of unpacking the boxes and tending her mistress's hair would occupy Zillah for some little while. The corridor was deserted. Mina slipped out of her room and moved as quickly and quietly as she was able to the storeroom door, where she tried to turn the handle. After a number of unsuccessful attempts, she realised that her inability to do so was not due to lack of strength but the fact that the door was locked. She spent a few moments listening with her ear pressed against the door, but there was no sound inside the room. Fortunately, no one appeared to discover her in that undignified position. Of course, thought Mina, if Mr Honeyacre was using the room to store valuable antiquities and works of art then it was not at all unreasonable that the door should be kept locked.

Returning to her room she drew from her bag the little wedge-shaped cushion that made it possible for her to sit on an ordinary chair in an upright posture. Tucking it under her hip she sat at the dressing table, took out her notebook and made a record of what she had learned so far. She also tried to recall which individuals had been in her company when she had seen the figure at the window. They included all the party of visitors, Mr and Mrs Honeyacre, Mrs Malling and Miss Pet.

The maids, Mr Gillespie and Mr Malling, however, had been busy with their duties and she could not with any certainty place any of them at the time of the unusual appearance.

Mina's previous experiences of séances meant that she was, more than most people, aware of the fallibility of memory. Nellie had assured her that much of the success of a magician's tricks depended on this, as well as the ease with which audiences could be distracted and the quirks of the human eye, an organ very prone to lead its possessor astray.

Had the figure she had seen not disappeared so quickly, Mina might have concluded that what she had seen was only a garment stand or a painting. A shape which was there one moment and gone the next was far more concerning. The glowing apparitions commonly produced by spirit mediums could only be convincing in a dark séance. This daylight figure was different. Had she really, for the first time, seen an actual ghost?

Mina was impatient to know more and decided not to wait until she was called for luncheon, but went downstairs, where she found Kitty and Miss Pet playing with the dog in the hall. The little creature was bounding about as if it wore tiny springs on its paws, uttering sharp yaps of excitement, its pointed pink tongue glistening. Kitty gathered it up and buried her face in its silky fur. 'Isn't he a pretty angel?' she exclaimed.

'Most endearing,' said Mina. 'What is his name?'

'I call him Little Scrap, because he is one,' said Kitty. 'But are you not chilled here, Miss Scarletti? Come into the parlour where we can be warm.'

Miss Pet opened the door of a small but comfortable parlour and Mina noticed that she was careful to close it securely when they were inside. It was a room designed for ladies with beautifully upholstered armchairs, a small pianoforte and a tea table with silver dishes for sweetmeats. A fire crackled busily in the grate and when Miss Pet took some twigs from a Japanese vase and tossed them onto the glowing logs there arose a fresh perfumed aroma.

Kitty fondled the little dog on her lap and uttered a deep sigh. 'We do not know each other very well, Miss Scarletti,' she began, 'but I hope that that will be corrected very soon. I am told that you are brave and clever and know all about how to lay ghosts. I would be so grateful if you agreed to help me.'

'I am at your service,' said Mina, relieved that the unspoken subject was to be broached at last. 'I promise that I will do whatever I can. Please tell me everything.'

Kitty's gaze wandered about the room, as if searching for the right words. 'I did not visit Hollow House before I was married,' she said at last. 'Benjamin said that it was being decorated and wished to spare me the discomfort and inconvenience and, in any case, he wanted it to be a surprise. He is so considerate — I wish all ladies had a husband as kind and thoughtful.' She sighed again. 'My first impression when he brought me here was what a curious house it is. I was quite prepared to like it as much as Benjamin does and make it my home. But —' she fondled Little Scrap's ears, which twitched in response — 'something here is wrong. Oh, I don't just mean the haunting, though that is disturbing enough. It is not a happy house. I feel it has bad memories — secrets — things in the past it cannot forget that linger even now and affect everything that happens within.'

'Forgive me,' said Mina, 'but you are only telling me your impressions. What I need to know is what have you seen? What have you heard? And what have you been told?'

'How practical and sensible you are!' exclaimed Kitty with a smile. 'I knew I did the right thing to ask your advice. Yes, of course. We have two maidservants, Mary Ann and Susan. They live in the village and their families are hardworking and devout. Both girls are respectful, industrious and as sensible as anyone can be under the age of twenty. Not long after I came to live here, Mary Ann came to me and asked if anything was needed for the lady visitor. I told her there was no lady visitor expected. She said that a lady was here as she had seen her. I knew nothing of this, but I supposed that Benjamin could have invited a lady and forgotten to mention it. He can get very absorbed in his studies, you see. I went to ask him and he was as surprised as I was. He sent for Mary Ann and questioned her and she said that she had seen a lady, dressed all in white, in the first floor corridor just outside the room where he keeps his paintings and curios.'

'The one next to Minerva,' said Mina.

'Yes. When we asked her for a better description she said that she had only seen her in a moment's glance and then when she next looked the lady had gone away. Benjamin and I both went up to look, but no one was there and there was no sign of any lady visitor. We discussed it and I said that I thought it must have been a mistake, perhaps Mary Ann had only seen the moonlight shining through the window. Benjamin agreed with me, but I could tell from the way he said it that he thought it might be something more. You know about his studies, of course.'

'I do,' said Mina. 'He is very eager to have his beliefs justified. That is not to say he is mistaken, but in cases of doubt he will be too willing to accept the explanation that most closely matches his opinion. We are all guilty of that in one way or another. I do not exclude myself. What did you say to Mary Ann?'

'I told her it must have been a trick of the light and she should not worry about it. But even as I did so I began to think of other things that had happened, things I had dismissed, strange noises that I had assumed were natural in a house of this antiquity, scraping and creaking and tapping.' She gave a little shiver. 'I have not slept well since. Every small noise wakes me and when I do sleep I have strange dreams — at least, I think they are dreams — but how can one tell?' She looked appealingly at Mina.

Mina was not sure she had an answer. 'You may well have been correct about the light. Its quality will change with the seasons, the weather and the waxing and waning of the moon. Have you yourself witnessed anything that disturbed you?'

Kitty allowed a little frown to mar her forehead, but quickly dismissed it. 'Yes, but not clearly. Sometimes it seems to me that I see something out of the corner of my eye, something moving, gliding, just slightly apart as if it does not want to be fully seen, but when I turn my head, hoping to catch it, nothing is there. I am fearful that my mind is playing tricks on me.'

Kitty said nothing further on the subject, but Mina realised that her hostess was beginning to have doubts about her sanity and understood the reluctance to express herself in any greater detail. If a man had such experiences he would write a book about them and travel the length and breadth of England to give lectures. A woman might find herself drugged with sedatives and confined to her bedroom.

'Mrs Honeyacre,' said Mina encouragingly, 'I think that on that point, at least, I can reassure you. I recently had a most interesting interview with an oculist, a Mr Marriott of Brighton, who was able to demonstrate to me that the eye, even when in perfect health, is the most easily deceived of all the organs of sense. A shadow, a ray of light, a patch of mist, all quite natural things, can seem in some circumstances to be more than they are.' Mina considered mentioning the white figure she had seen as an example, but decided against it until she had made an examination of the room. At this juncture she might only spread further alarm.

'Thank you,' said Kitty, 'I will remember that. But Mary Ann was most insistent that she had seen a lady, seen her so clearly that she thought she was a living person. And then —'

'Yes?'

'Not long after that, Susan came to me in a great fright and said that she had seen the lady, too, and was so certain that she was a real person she had actually gone to ask her if there was anything she required, but the lady ignored her and walked into the storeroom.'

'The storeroom?' Mina almost protested that the room was kept locked and just stopped herself in time. It was not something she would be expected to know. 'Perhaps she merely lost her way? A new visitor to the house might do that. Or — since I assume the room was once a bedroom — the lady could have been a former guest or servant who made a mistake?'

'No, Miss Scarletti, that is not possible,' said Kitty with great firmness. 'The only persons who have a key to that room are Benjamin and Mrs Malling and it is always kept locked. Benjamin tells me that the things he keeps there are extremely valuable and that seems like a wise precaution, especially as there are so many workmen coming here. Only when the collection can be put on display will the room be opened up and redecorated for use. Also —' she paused and stroked the little dog, gazing down at it affectionately — 'the room was not formerly a guest bedroom. It was once a nursery and also we think it was where the nursemaid slept.'

Mina nodded. 'And you are sure that it was not Mrs Malling that Susan saw?'

'No, the figure was far younger — and a great deal more slender. Besides —' Kitty hesitated — 'Susan said that the lady did not open the door to enter the room. She — she walked right through it.'

Chapter Four

The room was silent and even in front of the warm fire, Mina felt a chill. 'Miss Pet?' she asked. 'Have you anything to add? Have you seen anything of a similar nature?'

'No, Miss Scarletti,' said Miss Pet. Her voice was soft, like a carefully modulated exhalation. She was not unhandsome, although her face was over-long with sharp prominent bones. Mina could not help wondering if Miss Pet was being untruthful and trying to conceal any exhibition of feeling. If she had witnessed something alarming she might well wish to keep it to herself so as not to disturb Kitty.

'What of Mr Honeyacre? Has he seen this figure? Or anything else? If so, he has not mentioned it to me.'

'No, he has seen nothing,' said Kitty with a humourless laugh, 'and believe me, I would know of it if he had. He would not be able to keep it a secret from me, or indeed anyone else. He has heard the noises, of course, we all have, and I have known him to leave his bed in the middle of the night, take a candle and go searching about, hoping to find their origin, but without result.'

Mina understood. 'Then he is unafraid of spirits and eager to encounter one?'

Kitty nodded. 'Oh yes! He would welcome it, run to question it, embrace it as his dearest friend. In fact, I have been wondering if it is this very eagerness to make contact with the spirit world that has encouraged these appearances. Perhaps the spirits were always here in the house, but quiet and unseen, just waiting for the right person to come and live here. Perhaps Benjamin, through his studies, his thoughts, has unwittingly created an atmosphere that has brought them out. You know that half his library is now composed of books about the spirit world? Can that be a good thing? I don't think it is. I know we all enjoy a good ghost tale, something with which to amuse ourselves as we sit around the fire at Christmas, but as to pursuing them — that is a sport I would rather leave to others.'

Mina could see that, despite Kitty's affection for her husband, his devotion to his spiritualism was causing her unease. While Mr Honeyacre was aware of his wife's concerns about the haunting, how fully had she expressed herself to him about his pursuits? That was a subject which Mina would not broach. But, she wondered, to what extent did Kitty's fears affect her perception of events in the house?

'Tell me about your own beliefs,' she said. 'Before you came here did you believe it possible for us to contact the spirit world, or for spirits to contact us? Did you attend any séances? Did you see or hear ghosts?'

Kitty and her companion exchanged glances.

'In the world of the theatre,' Kitty replied, 'there are ghosts everywhere: stories, legends, tales of tragedy. Not only in plays, but in the buildings themselves. When the audience has departed, when all is quiet, then the ghosts come. They appear on darkened stages and act out their mysteries; they sit in the auditoriums and lurk in dressing rooms and in the wings. People see and hear them; they are shadows constantly watching, voices in conversation, echoes. We smell them even; hints of perfume, of tobacco smoke. It's the emotions, you see. Theatrical persons, whatever part of that profession they occupy, are creatures of great passion. Rivalry, jealousy, love stolen, love disappointed. These feelings are so much greater and more concentrated than in other walks of life. But we don't fear our ghosts, we treasure them, we never seek to expel them. They are old companions; they can bring us good fortune. In some theatres, a dark figure watching from the gallery predicts full houses and a long and successful run. Myself — I have heard things; whispering voices, distant music and I have seen moving shadows, but mostly I just feel when someone is there.'

Mina felt the surge of excitement she always experienced when confronted with a new and valuable mine of story ideas, but took care to restrain herself. There would be time enough to learn more about haunted theatres when she had laid to rest the ghost of Hollow House. 'Mrs Jordan might think differently,' she observed.

'Dear Nellie,' said Kitty affectionately. 'But, of course, her business is conjuring and illusion. Conjurors can create ghosts to order out of nothing. So they cannot find it in themselves to believe in the real thing.'

'What about Mr and Mrs Malling? What do they say? In all the years they have lived here, have they not been troubled?'

'Their apartments are in the newest part of the house, the stables wing. There has never been a haunting there. But I often feel that they might know more about the white lady than they say. Mrs Malling has been trying to calm and soothe the maids, so she would not want to pass on any tales of her own in case it upset them further. I think she might be willing to talk to you. Shall I ask her?'

'Yes, please do. And if you don't mind I should very much like to look inside the storeroom.'

'Of course. I will let her know. And if anything should occur — if I or Miss Pet should see or hear anything, we will tell you at once.'

'Thank you, but I beg of you, don't go looking for strange things. Even if there is nothing there your eye and your mind can make shapes out of shadows and all you will do is frighten yourself. And, after all, consider this — even if there is a spirit here, is it something to fear? It might be a troubled soul. Perhaps we should pity it and give it comfort and peace.'

Kitty nodded, but she looked dubious. 'But there are bad spirits, too. If we let in the good the bad might come with it.'

'I see no sign of that,' said Mina, firmly.

'Then what do you advise? What must I do?'

'Try to be your usual self. Find some pleasurable occupation for your mind. I will do what I can to solve this mystery, as will Nellie and Dr Hamid. They have helped me before and we have had some good results.'

Kitty smiled. 'I think I feel better just for having spoken to you.'

A soft melodious rumble sounded from the hallway. 'We are being summoned to luncheon,' said Kitty, rising to her feet and cuddling Little Scrap who, judging by his alertness, knew exactly what the gong heralded.

Miss Pet rose and peered out of the window. 'The rain has stopped at last.'

'Then I anticipate a tour of our little church this afternoon,' said Kitty. 'It is very old indeed, dedicated to St Mond.'

'I have never heard of a St Mond,' said Mina.

'His story has been lost,' said Kitty. 'Another mystery. But then Ditchling Hollow is a place full of mysteries.'

In the long dining hall the curtains had been thrown back to reveal a sky washed by pearly clouds with a milk-white sun glowing through.

Mr Honeyacre took his place at the head of the long table and looked about him at the assembled company. 'How delightful to see you all here! I declare that this is the first such gathering since we took up residence. The first of many, I hope.'

'I expect the house has seen many a grand dinner or ball in its history,' said Mina, in an effort to prise useful conversation from her host.

'Oh, I do so hope it has!' exclaimed Mr Honeyacre with some feeling. 'This should be a place of sweet content, of the higher pleasures of the mind, of music and art and learning and laughter, and good food.' He gave a sharp little exhalation of regret.

'How long had the house been empty when you purchased it?' asked Dr Hamid, as the maids, under the eagle eye of Mr Gillespie, brought the luncheon dishes in.

There was a pause as a steaming platter of hot cutlets in gravy was brought in, together with a dish of cold roast chicken garnished with salad and devilled eggs. Cheese, biscuits and fruit compote were put on the sideboard.

'I believe it had then lain empty for some fifteen years,' said Mr Honeyacre, looking more cheery to see the eyes of his guests brighten with anticipation. 'I purchased it from a nephew of the former owner, a Mr Lassiter. The family were racing people and intended to run a stables here, which is why the west wing was constructed, but the plan never came about.'

'Why was that?' asked Mina, as the maids passed around the table, offering the dishes and pouring wine and water.

'I am not sure. They did not live here long; less than a year, I think. I asked Mr Lassiter why his uncle had departed and he said he didn't know. Perhaps he found it unsuitable. Or the cost of repairs, even then, was too great for his purse. That must be why the estate failed to attract a buyer until I saw it. In the intervening years, the west wing has been used for stabling but the house has lain unoccupied.'

'You mentioned the east wing and porch,' asked Dr Hamid, helping himself to a cutlet and digging into it with relish. 'They are particularly striking.'

'Ah, those slender traceries and arched windows point to a passion for the Gothic, do they not? Quite a different style. Hard to date, as is anything when the creator harks back to times past. The original owners, the Redwoode family, appear to have left Sussex, at least I have been unable to discover when and why they did so, or when the Tudor mansion was demolished. The deeds only show that, in the last century, the estate was purchased from the Redwoodes by a gentleman called Wigmore and he was who built the main part of the house. The east wing and porch were undoubtedly added later. On his death, the estate was sold to the Lassiters.'

'Is there anything to be learned from the church records about the families who lived here previously?' asked Mina.

'I'm afraid not. When I bought the estate I consulted Reverend Tolley who took Sunday service at our little church, but it appears that, since the earliest of records, no occupant of Hollow House has ever been baptised, married or buried here.'

There were murmurs around the table, but no member of the company saw fit to express any special concerns. There was an interlude of appreciative hush as the luncheon absorbed all thoughts. Despite the generous fare and Mr Honeyacre's strenuous efforts to appear cheerful, Mina sensed that the diners were unusually restrained and uncontroversial in their comments. The real reason for the visit was like a ghost in the room that no one wanted to admit they had seen.

Mina put down her knife and fork. 'Mr Honeyacre, I happen to recall that some months ago, when you first told me about Hollow House, you were adamant that despite its age and history it was not the haunt of spirits, yet I am given to understand that you have since found you were mistaken. This is a very interesting subject and I would like to know more.'

There was a concentrated silence in the room as the guests prodded their cutlets with more than the usual attention.

'Ah yes,' said Mr Honeyacre softly. 'We have all been avoiding that subject, have we not? Yet, I suppose we all know that there is a special reason for this gathering.' He glanced around the table and met with no dissent. 'Miss Scarletti is well aware of my great interest in the supernatural, which I have been studying for some little while. Yet, as I have discovered, there is a difference between an academic pursuit which may engage and stimulate the mind and actually existing in the centre of a haunting. That, I can assure you, is another matter altogether. I had planned to pay visits to houses that are known to be haunted, but I can't say that I have ever had any ambitions to live in one. In every account I have read they seem to cause their owners such a mountain of trouble.'

'Has there been any record kept of the experiences of those living here?' asked Mina. 'I ask because memories can sometimes be faulty and it would be best if any unusual sights and sounds were recorded almost immediately after they occurred. The date, the time, the location and a full description of what was observed are all of vital importance.'

Mr Honeyacre contemplated the devilled egg on his plate as if he had suddenly lost his appetite. 'I regret, no. Although, now you suggest it, I agree, that would seem very sensible. Why did I not think of it? I promise you, it will be done from now on. For myself, I have heard curious noises in the night, footsteps along the first floor corridor, and sounds like sighing or weeping, but very distant. Yet, when I go to look, there is nothing to be seen. I can assure you I have no fear of ghosts. They are, I think, only unhappy earthbound spirits and were I to see one I would be more likely to try and engage it in conversation to try and discover the reason for its distress than run away in fright. Who knows — there might be something the living can do to give those troubled souls the rest they clearly crave?'

'Have you made any attempt to contact the spirits?' asked Dr Hamid.

'Through a medium, you mean? No, not as yet. My acquaintance with Miss Scarletti has taught me how hard it is to find one who can be trusted. So many of them are charlatans. I did write a letter to Mr Arthur Wallace Hope, or Lord Hope as he should properly be called, who gave such an inspiring lecture on spiritualism in Brighton last year that I thought he might have some good advice. However, he has not responded. He may have gone to Africa again, of course. I know he was planning to mount an expedition to try and discover the whereabouts of Dr Livingstone.'

Mina was unable to repress an angry frown at the name of the noted explorer and author who had made an impression in more ways than one during his visit to Brighton the previous autumn. She picked up her knife and fork and attacked her portion of chicken with grim determination. Mr Honeyacre appeared not to have noticed her discomfiture, but Nellie gave her an enquiring glance. Mina said nothing.

Mr Honeyacre coughed gently. 'In fact, I was rather hoping that Miss Scarletti would be willing to try the experiment.'

Mina stared at him and took great care before she replied. 'I am not a medium, Mr Honeyacre, and have never professed to be. I appreciate that the newspapers may say differently. In fact, most of the practising mediums in Brighton will not allow me over their doorsteps, claiming that I radiate negative energy that will dissuade the spirits from appearing. Their real reason is that they know there is a danger that I will try to expose them as frauds.'

'They cannot all be frauds, surely?' pleaded Mr Honeyacre. 'What of those who will permit you to visit?'

'It is a question of what they choose to demonstrate,' said Mina. 'The ones most easily found out are those that use the skills of the conjuror to create illusions. But there are others who claim to pluck prophecies from the air, or relate messages that are mere platitudes, so it is impossible to prove them false or true, and they know it.'

'Then you do not hold with the idea that some individuals possess an unusual sensitivity which allows them to communicate with the spirits?' asked Mr Honeyacre. 'Surely you cannot deny it! There are a thousand examples.'

'I neither deny nor agree. I simply await with interest the proof that will satisfy me.'

Mr Honeyacre could only shake his head and Kitty leaned forward and said, 'Then what would you advise?'

Mina felt suddenly quite sorry for the Honeyacres and reminded herself that she was there to help. 'Before I can advise you, I need to learn as much as I can about what has been happening here,' she said gently. 'With your permission, I will begin with interviews.'

'With the spirits?' asked her host, hopefully. 'How do you propose to do that?'

'No, Mr Honeyacre. For the present, my enquiries will be with the living.'

'Oh, yes; yes of course,' he said. There was no mistaking his profound disappointment.

After luncheon, Mr Honeyacre requested a brief conversation with Dr Hamid on a private matter, which Mina assumed must be of a medical nature, and she took the opportunity to converse with Nellie.

'You will have observed that all the people living here are in a state of agitation, which will induce them to see and hear anything,' she said.

'And yet so far there is nothing to be seen or heard,' replied Nellie.

Mina decided not to mention the white figure at the window, which she felt sure must be a trick of the light and the rain. 'You, better than anyone here, know how illusions may be produced by the simplest of circumstances.'

'That is true, although I feel that this may not be the occasion to amuse everyone with a display of *legerdemain* after dinner. The maids especially would be convinced that I am a witch.'

'Or worse than that, Mr Honeyacre would decide that you are a medium.'

Mina felt sure that she had thus far witnessed only a small part of her friend's conjuring skills. Nellie could make cards and coins appear and disappear with a flick of the fingers, only inches from the eyes of astonished onlookers. When assisting M Baptiste, she had performed a mind reading act, as the Ethiopian Wonder, wearing little more than a coat of paint and some beads. Nellie had even appeared as Miss Foxton, the spirit medium on the popular stage, performing sensational miracles of levitation. She had then been under the patronage of a Signor Ricardo, a dashing fellow with a black mask, false moustache and an execrable Italian accent. The Signor was none other than Mina's younger brother Richard, a good-hearted scallywag who spent more time devising schemes to avoid work than he did actually working. Richard and Nellie had undoubtedly been fond of each other, but they had parted in friendship when she married Mr Jordan for money, of which Richard had none. Difficult as Richard could be, his absence created a gap in Mina's life that often begged to be filled with trouble, excitement and unpredictability.

'We dare not risk a séance,' said Mina. 'If something really is happening here I might not be able to deal with it without a clergyman present and if nothing is happening then imagination and panic might provide the rest.' She paused, thoughtfully. 'Mr Honeyacre mentioned Reverend Tolley. I shall take the opportunity on Sunday to speak to him and see if he has any suggestions as to how to proceed. He may also know some history of the house and its owners, which would assist me.'

'And I promise to weave no magic while I am here lest I be taken out and burnt,' said Nellie. 'I will, however, be on the watch for conjurors.'

Once everyone had rested and refreshed themselves after luncheon, Mr Honeyacre was eager to conduct his visitors about the house. He was especially proud of his collection of oil paintings, each of which, he advised them, required an investment of time to fully appreciate and learn their history. In the drawing room, where deep divans and cabinets of sherry, brandy and cigars invited luxurious leisure, a substantial portrait of his late wife occupied a prominent place over the mantelpiece, itself a monument in marble. The much-lamented first Mrs Honeyacre had been a lady of unexceptional beauty with a round face, clusters of grey curls and a gentle expression. Mr Honeyacre gazed on her features with misty-eyed affection, describing her kindness and good temper, her charity and piety.

Kitty, cuddling her little dog, viewed the picture of this avowed paragon with an uneasy smile, fixed as if in amber. There were a number of smaller portraits of Mr Honeyacre's ancestors, looking serious and stiff in velvet and brocade. For the rest, his taste ran to landscapes and the sea.

'What you see here is only a part of my collection,' he added proudly. 'Some is being stored, some is still in my Brighton apartments and I have, in addition, two paintings of considerable antiquity purchased from the Lassiters, which they themselves acquired from the previous owners. The paint is dark with age. In fact, it is almost impossible to see the subject matter and considerable cleaning and restoration will be needed, therefore they are not yet on display, but might prove interesting. I can promise that once everything has been placed to the best advantage there will be twice as many works to give pleasure to the eye.'

Dr Hamid said nothing but looked politely approving, Mina made kind and thoughtful comments and Nellie did her best to admire everything without revealing her profound relief that there was only so much to admire.

They were allowed a brief examination of Mr Honeyacre's study, a quaintly masculine room, all leather and dark wood and parchment with comfortable armchairs and a handsome writing desk, and adjoining it, the library, where his collection of both venerable and recent books was ranged. Chairs and a reading table with a good lamp provided all that was necessary.

'You are a great reader, I understand, Miss Scarletti?' observed Mr Honeyacre, seeing that she was taking an interest in the contents of his shelves.

'Very much so,' said Mina. 'I was wondering if I might be permitted to look at some of your books?'

'Oh, please do. You may peruse any of them you like.'

Mina cast her eye over the volumes, many of which were scholarly works on antiquities, art, furniture and coins. There were also histories of Sussex and Brighton. A substantial section, however, was devoted to his recent studies and there were such titles as *The Logic of Table Turning*, *Modern Spiritualism* and *The Soul and its Survival of Bodily Death*. She also saw to her annoyance a copy of *The Brighton Hauntings* by Mr Arthur Wallace Hope. Mina also owned a copy of this book and deemed it to be the most egregious waste of five shillings she had ever spent. The volume, which had naturally enjoyed considerable sales, and which she suspected had been dashed off in careless haste, was comprised of a jumble of sensational folk tales described with easy assurance as wholly true and an account of séances that had taken place during Mr Hope's time in Brighton, which she knew to be mostly invention. He had even had the effrontery to refer to that patent fraud, Mystic Stefan, as one of the finest exponents of mediumship he had ever seen and the wicked Miss Eustace as a much injured innocent. Both these rascals were, as a result of Mina's tireless efforts, currently and deservedly in prison. Worse still in Mina's eyes the book contained a veiled reference to herself with the strong implication that she was a gifted medium who had not yet acknowledged her powers. She hoped fervently that Mr Honeyacre had not noticed this, or at least not understood the allusion.

A volume entitled *Glimpses of the Supernatural*, describing itself as a 'compendium of witches, hauntings, dreams, ecstasy and magnetism', looked more entertaining and she selected it for further study.

A moderate improvement in the weather was enough to allow the promised delight of a visit to the church of St Mond. Mina put on her warm cloak and gloves and braced herself for the outdoors before joining the party. On the terrace she turned and faced the house, judging the positions of the decorative urns in relation to the windows. She had been careful to position her curtains in a way that enabled her to readily identify her bedroom when seen from the outside. She could now confirm that the urn on the furthest right was directly below her own window. Mina felt certain that this was not the window where the white figure had appeared; it was the next one — that of the locked storeroom. The curtains of that room were now closed and she could not see within.

The rain had stopped but its memory hung in the air. As Mina emerged from the house she could feel a prickle of damp on her cheeks. Mr Honeyacre was keeping up an appearance of hospitality and good cheer, offering his arm to Nellie with a gentlemanly flourish, leaving Mina to the quiet ministrations of Dr Hamid. Kitty had elected not to accompany them and drifted away, pressing her little puppy's silky ears to her cheeks, with Miss Pet close by her side.

There was a set of steps leading down from the front terrace, broad, smooth and new, but devolving soon into something older and more hazardous. Mina gazed down onto a winding arrangement of rough undressed slabs with chipped edges, giving only the most perilous purchase underfoot, slick with rain and muddy residue. Dr Hamid looked at her anxiously, but she placed a firm grip on his forearm and moved down the stairs in a slow and deliberate fashion.

Nellie, resplendent in a voluminous cloak with a fur-trimmed hood, picked her way nimbly as a dancer in her neat little boots to the voluble admiration of Mr Honeyacre.

The steps led to the entrance of the tiny church wallowing in a broken, grassy landscape dotted with tufted hillocks and waterlogged pits. A row of stone pillars linked by chains marked the boundary of the graveyard, whose few remaining headstones tilted in the soft earth, swept clean of any readable markings by the prevailing breeze. Beyond the posts the graveyard showed signs of care, the grass between the stones had been recently clipped and a few green posies, fresh but sodden, lay beside some of the graves.

On the far side of the graveyard was the low boundary wall of the estate that Mina had passed in the carriage that morning. An elderly man emerged from behind the building, trudging a narrow stony path around the perimeter. He was dressed in loose trousers and a coat of some sturdy brown material, much worn and grimed. There were tangled wisps of grey hair about his ears and almost-white stubble on his cheeks and chin.

'That's Ned Copper from the village,' said Mr Honeyacre. 'He likes to walk about the graveyard and keep an eye on things. Most of his family are buried here.' He made a polite nod in the man's direction. Ned responded with a low growl and a surly salute, and walked on.

'He seems to be of indifferent temper,' said Nellie. 'I hope he is more cheerful in clement weather.'

'You must excuse Ned's strange moods,' said Mr Honeyacre. 'He is quite harmless, but he dwells too much on the less fortunate events in village history. You know, of course, about the terrible accident in the Clayton Tunnel — it seems that Ned was close by when it occurred and gave assistance to the injured. He has seen sights that no man should ever see. It has preyed upon his mind ever since and given him an unhappy outlook on life. He will tell endless stories of that day if he is not stopped and they are quite unfit for a lady's ears. I have absolutely forbidden him ever to mention the subject to my dear Kitty.'

Mina said nothing, but determined to engage Ned Copper in conversation at the earliest opportunity. She hoped there were enough blank pages in her notebook.

A simple gate led to a path fortunately provided with robust stone flagging that led to the church door, framed by a simple arch. There was an insufficiency of high narrow windows giving little relief to the rough stone blocks of the church walls and promising a dark interior.

'The date of the church's construction is lost, of course, but it has clearly been here for centuries,' said Mr Honeyacre. 'The roof is more recent and therefore of little interest. Church roofs are always a trial — I have been told that this one is especially vulnerable to storms and has collapsed into the nave more than once. The small size suggests that it might originally have been a chapel, for the sole use of the estate owners, the villagers having to walk to Clayton to worship. But in recent years, it has been in general use.'

'Do you know when the village was first established?' asked Mina.

Mr Honeyacre smiled. 'Ditchling Hollow has a brief mention in the Domesday Book, the attraction of fertile fields and the mill brook, meaning that settlement was made very early. But it has never flourished,' he added sadly. 'It is not as sheltered from wind and weather as it might be. For much of the year the prospect is delightful, but at times it can be harsh.'

As if in response, the wind cut a severe course across the visitors and Mina flinched and pulled her cloak more closely about her. Dr Hamid did his best to shield her from the gusts.

Ned Copper, untroubled by the elements, had paused in the graveyard and leaned forward, his fingertips sweeping fallen twigs from a headstone, then he straightened and looked about him with an expression of contemplative melancholy. The rain began to patter again, but he didn't move.

Mr Honeyacre pushed open the church door and they walked in, brushing beads of moisture from their garments. 'Please don't concern yourselves about the rain,' he said. 'I have asked Mr Malling to come for us with the umbrellas if need be.'

They were standing in a small entrance porch. On one side there was a recess with a place to put muddy overshoes. A board hung there with a sign announcing that Sunday services were conducted by a Reverend Ashbrook. Another sign listed the clergymen who had preached there in the past, the last of whom had been the man Mr Honeyacre had mentioned, Reverend Tolley. A third notice devoted to special services showed that there had been one christening in the last month but nothing was determined for the immediate future.

'Reverend Ashbrook cannot be kept busy here,' said Nellie.

'Oh, he is not a Ditchling man,' explained Mr Honeyacre. 'He resides in Clayton and only comes in for the services. You will see him on Sunday. He is new to the parish and —' there was a meaningful pause — 'in my opinion, has yet to wholly understand it. But I am sure he will in time.'

Mina was disappointed. A new man was unlikely to be such a generous source of history as his predecessor.

Opposite the recess was a small door. 'The vestry,' said Mr Honeyacre. 'It contains a parish chest of great antiquity and I am sure that if you were to ask Reverend Ashbrook he would be delighted to show it to you.'

'I shall be sure to do so,' said Nellie, smiling brightly as if she had been promised a great treat.

As they passed into the nave, Mina became aware of the kind of chill peculiar to churches, a deep ingrained pervasive cold that was part of the stones and the air, an eternal sunless winter. The ancient church smelled of dust and things too old and dry and decayed to recall what it had once meant to be alive. There were no pews. Instead, there were double rows of straight-backed chairs without cushions and a grey stone pulpit that appeared to have grown out of the wall a thousand years ago, remaining there despite all adversity, clinging on like a limpet. The altar, low plain and humble, was covered by a simple linen cloth.

Mina wondered what a service there might be like and imagined herself seated, shivering on one of those unwelcoming chairs, her back muscles crying out at the discomfort, hands clenched against the cold, trying to draw warmth from Reverend Ashbrook's words. Did the clergyman's fervent devotion warm his blood, or did he thrill instead to the asceticism of suffering?

She glanced up anxiously at the roof timbers above her head, but thankfully there was no sign of their imminent descent.

They moved down the stone flagged aisle with Mr Honeyacre exclaiming excitedly about the carved plaques on the walls. A few were dated and the names could be read, memories of the village dead, and the same surnames appeared often, like an echo: Copper, Jesson, Tuckfield, Gateley, Parker.

Beneath her host's animated chatter Mina heard another sound, a faint shuffling noise. She looked about her, half expecting to see a mouse scuttle across the floor, but there was nothing. 'Did you hear that?' she asked Dr Hamid.

'Yes,' he said, with a frown.

Mina glanced at Nellie, but she had not put back her hood. Mr Honeyacre appeared not to have heard, but he was deeply engaged in his enthusiasm. He paused to indicate a bronze plaque ornamented with scrolls. 'And this is of especial interest

— the commemorative plaque for the Redwoode family who once occupied Hollow House. I mean to discover more about them if I can, but all I have at present is their names.'

Mina peered closely at the inscription. 'In memory of Sir Christopher and Lady Matilda Redwoode of Hollow House, whose generosity gifted the altar ornaments to the Church of St Mond, Ditchling Hollow, for the greater glory of God.' The altar was bare of ornaments, which Mina presumed were safely in the custody of Reverend Ashbrook. 'But you said that the Redwoodes are not buried here,' said Mina.

'Sadly not,' said Mr Honeyacre. 'There is no mention of them or any owner of the house in the parish records.' He shook his head and in that moment of near silence, Mina heard the strange sound again, but only briefly, like the rustling of rodents in a nest. It reflected from the walls, rising and mingling with the wooden rafters until it was impossible to tell its origin.

Dr Hamid glanced at Mina and nodded to indicate that he too had heard the noise. 'The proverbial church mouse?' he queried.

'Is there some difficulty?' enquired Mr Honeyacre, seeing their worried expressions.

'I heard something just now, which leads me to fear there may be an infestation of vermin in the church,' said Dr Hamid. They stood quite still and listened, but all was perfectly silent, as if the intruders had also suddenly become still and were holding their collective breath.

'I don't hear anything,' said Mr Honeyacre, 'although I confess my ears are not as they once were. Poor creatures, perhaps they have been driven indoors by the wet. I am loath to deny them shelter, but, of course, we must not alarm the ladies. I will speak to Malling about it.' He paused suddenly.

'Unless …' He looked about him, his eyes darting hopefully to and fro in case there was another explanation. Mina suspected that her host was wondering if, in the darkness of the old church, a spectre would rise up from between the stone slabs in a formless mist, shape itself into a man and shake its gory locks at him. His expression of disappointment told the rest of the tale.

The tour of the little church was soon done. The rain had eased and they were able to walk around the pathway to view the rest of the graveyard and the narrow track that led to the main street. A man was walking briskly past in the direction of the village. He wore a stout tweed coat and a peaked travelling cap. A leather strap was hung about his neck, supporting a small case of the same material. Mina had seen such cases before, carried by visitors to Brighton who liked to gaze out to sea and knew that it must contain a set of binocular glasses.

As he passed by he gave a swift glance at the party emerging from the church and there was a small but significant hesitation in his step before he walked on. Mina judged him to be between thirty and forty. He was of medium height with sallow features and a thin mouth.

'Do you know that man?' asked Mina, since Mr Honeyacre was frowning.

'I have not spoken to him but I believe he may be a land surveyor. He has been lodging at Hollow Farm with the Gateleys for the last few days and spends his time walking about and staring at everything. We get such men here from time to time, as the land is good and city folk, the men of property who employ these persons as their spies, think nothing of the countryside and want to build their horrid factories here.' Mr Honeyacre gave a sorrowful shake of the head. 'I hope I never live to see such a thing.'

When they returned to the front path Ned Copper was still trudging his way between the gravestones, his bristled chin thrust forward pugnaciously. He made little grunting noises as he walked, as if having an angry conversation with himself.

They had reached the boundary markers and were approaching the steps to the house when something made Mina glance back over her shoulder. She felt sure that Mr Honeyacre had closed the church door behind them as they left, but now saw that it had opened an inch or two, though what, if anything, lay behind it was concealed in the darkened interior. The door was surely too heavy to be moved by the breeze. As she thought this the door was pressed shut again.

It was a relief to be back indoors and pass their damp cloaks to the maids. Mina and Nellie retired to the ladies' parlour and warmed themselves before the fire.

'Poor Mr Honeyacre,' said Nellie, 'the very man who most wants to see a ghost and never can.'

'*If* they exist,' said Mina, 'and I cannot say yea or nay since I have never seen one. Do you think some people are more likely to see them than others? I do not speak of séances, of course, where anyone may see a ghost if they pay the medium handsomely enough.'

'Oh, every theatre has at least one ghost and many people claim to have seen or heard them, though I have often thought that spirits of another nature are involved.'

'Did you chance to see or hear anything in the church? Both Dr Hamid and I thought there was a strange noise. I had assumed it was mice, but after we left I looked back and the door was open then it closed again.'

'Well, then it cannot have been a ghost, as they are notorious for walking through walls and it would not have troubled itself to open a door. Perhaps we surprised a traveller come to shelter from the elements.' Nellie paused. 'If anyone saw a ghost today it was I.'

'Truly?' said Mina.

'Not precisely a ghost, but a familiar face and one that I was not expecting. The man we saw walking along the street.'

'The surveyor?'

'Yes, but he is no surveyor. I don't know his name, but his features are not such as I would forget. I have seen him before and I do not wish to see him again.' Nellie uttered a sigh and bit her lip before she went on. 'He is a private detective. I believe he has been engaged by my husband to watch me.'

Chapter Five

Mina did not ask Nellie if her husband had reason to distrust her, since she was aware that there was some substance to Mr Jordan's suspicions. Prior to the marriage, Mina's brother Richard and Nellie had been far closer in their affection than either would openly admit and it was obvious that the warmth of their regard had not abated afterwards.

Mr Jordan's husbandly discomfiture was increased by the fact that the business of his emporium necessitated frequent excursions to the continent to buy fashionable fabrics and view the latest styles. It could not be chance that Richard's visits to Brighton for the proclaimed purpose of seeing his family had often coincided with Mr Jordan's absence. On those occasions Richard was usually missing for most of the day, only returning to the Scarletti house in the small hours of the morning, hungry, the worse for drink and in a dishevelled state. Mina had quite deliberately never asked him where he had been. Some things, she thought, it was better not to know. Mr Jordan, however, was clearly determined to find out.

Another person might have tried to comfort Nellie by persuading her that she was mistaken, but Mina was sure that she was not. She thought of their arrival that morning — the carriage passing through the village, the reflection from the open window which might well have been the detective staring at them through his binocular glasses.

Fortunately, there would be no scandal for the detective to see, since Richard was in London, lodging with their sensible older brother, Edward. Richard had found employment in the family business, the Scarletti publishing house, making sketches for a ladies' magazine, *The Society Journal*. The few shillings he earned hardly paid for his entertainment, however, his mother, who doted on him and declared him to be the handsomest and most agreeable and talented of her children could always be relied upon to lend him money. The fact that their mother was currently staying in London, thought Mina, ought to be sufficient to keep him there and hopefully out of trouble.

Nellie was clearly concerned — not at the prospect of being discovered in any malfeasance — but by the knowledge that her husband was spying on her. Mina reassured Nellie that even if the spy was to spend all of his days observing her visit to Hollow House he would be obliged to make a report that Mrs Jordan had occupied herself in the most decorous of diversions in the company of respectable people.

There would be no more excursions out of doors that day as the rain was coming down again, cutting through the air like bright blades, and the sonorous roar of thunder was an ever present though distant threat. Kitty and Miss Pet joined them in the parlour and the little dog amused itself by biting the toes of the visitors and jumping on and off its mistress's lap in an endlessly fascinating game until it was time to refresh themselves for dinner.

Mina returned to her room and was composing some notes of the events she had witnessed so far when there was a polite knock at the door and she bid the visitor enter. It was Mrs Malling, showing just the right combination of dignity and respect.

'Miss Scarletti? I just wanted to make sure that you have everything you need. Zillah will be along directly to attend to you.'

'Thank you, Mrs Malling, everything is more than satisfactory. I am very comfortable here and luncheon was excellent.'

'I am very pleased to hear it,' said Mrs Malling. She paused. 'Mrs Honeyacre said that you would like to speak to me.'

'I would — if you can spare the time from your duties.'

'Of course, Miss.' Mrs Malling remained where she stood.

Mina smiled engagingly. 'Please, do sit down.' She waved at the easy chair beside the fire and Mrs Malling, surprised at being asked to take a seat in front of a guest, hesitated for a few moments before she complied. Mina, hoping to have placed the housekeeper at her ease with the friendliness of her request, took advantage of the other chair, taking her little wedge-shaped cushion and putting it carefully in place before sitting down. 'I was hoping that since you and Mr Malling have lived in Hollow House longer than any of its current residents you could tell me something of the history of the house and the various unusual incidents that have been reported as occurring here.'

Mrs Malling looked concerned. 'Well, I don't know about incidents, Miss. We've had none in the servants' wing.'

'There have been no incidents of any kind in that part of the house? No hauntings, apparitions, noises that you can't explain?'

'No, nothing of the sort at all. As to the rest of the house, well …' Mrs Malling pursed her lips thoughtfully and her fingers moved as if each hand was stroking the other for reassurance. 'It's so hard to say. We don't come to this part of the house at night time when it is full dark. Then, of course, in a half light, one can always see things that —' she shrugged. 'My eyes aren't as sharp as they once were and it's easy enough to imagine something or make a mistake. One can get quite fanciful in an old house like this one. I wouldn't trouble yourself about it, Miss.'

'I understand, of course,' said Mina. She could not help suspecting that the housekeeper was not telling all the story so as to avoid worrying her. 'I promise that I will not be frightened by anything you tell me, but I am very curious about these things and eager to learn more. Please can you describe what you have seen?'

Mrs Malling took a deep breath. 'It was only out of the corner of my eye, but I was up in the corridor, this one, where the bedrooms are, and I thought I saw something. It looked like a lady dressed all in white. I wasn't afraid — I wondered if it was someone from the village who had wandered in to look about the house. I called out to her, but she took no notice. And then she —'

'Yes?'

'That was when I knew it was my mistake, my old eyes playing tricks. She walked right through the closed door of the storeroom. Or at least, the light just seemed to vanish.' Mrs Malling glanced down at her hands, as if seeing for the first time how work had imprinted its memories on her skin.

'How many times have you seen this?' asked Mina, her voice firmer, more demanding of a reply.

'Several, now, always in the same place. That's how I know it was just something about the light. I looked everywhere to see how it came about, but I couldn't find it.'

'And the thing you saw — it always looked and moved in the same way?'

'It did.'

'And that is all that you have found disquieting?'

From Mrs Malling's hesitation, this was obviously not the case. 'Well — it's the only thing I have seen. There have been noises — but then all old houses have them, don't they? Creaks and bumps, and things that sound like footsteps, and sighing noises like the wind, or someone crying.'

'When was the first time you saw the white lady?'

'Oh, it wasn't long after Mr Honeyacre first took the house. But it only happened once or twice afterwards, until …' She paused and Mina waited. 'Just lately, I think the house has been — well — stirred up if you like. It was mostly quiet when it was just me and Malling here. But then last year, when Mr Honeyacre determined to come and live here, it all became very busy. There was charladies who came in to clean and then the maids arrived and then the workmen came to finish off the repairs to the roof and there were the decorators, and the plumbers and then the men came to bring all of Mr Honeyacre's effects. There was that many folk coming and going I hardly knew where I was. All the hammering and sawing made more noise than any ghost. But once that was all done, and I don't think it was my imagination, I started to hear the other things more. And I saw the white lady twice in one week.'

'Has Mr Malling seen her too?'

'I think so, but he won't speak of it. He doesn't hold truck with things like that and if you ask him he won't admit to it.'

'Tell me about the maidservants. I was told they won't come here during the hours of darkness.'

'That's true. When they were first engaged they used to come in early to dust and light the fires, but then they said there were strange things going on and they were too afraid. Malling lights the fires now.'

'The maids don't sleep here?'

'No, they live in the village.'

'I shall have to speak to them.'

She gave a sharp nod. 'They're good girls and they work hard, but they have their fancies, like so many young girls do. Susan is the younger and she is very timid and easily frightened. A shadow, or a bird, is enough to startle her. Mary Ann is more composed but she is full of stories. I don't know where she gets them from, but I think they are very common about here.'

'Do any of these stories relate to this house?'

Mrs Malling kneaded her hands together. 'One of them does, yes. I don't know how much truth there is in it, mind, but it's about the Lassiters, the folk Mr Honeyacre bought the house from.'

'True or not, a good story always interests me,' said Mina, encouragingly. She left a meaningful silence.

Mrs Malling gave a nervous cough. 'It's a very tragic tale, Miss.'

Mina smiled. 'Oh, those are the best sort.'

Mrs Malling gazed at Mina carefully, as if trying to assess how disturbing she might find the tale. Mina remained firm and gazed back.

'Well,' Mrs Malling began, with noticeable reluctance, 'it seems that the Lassiters came from somewhere out of the county and settled here to start a stables. They thought they would use the land to exercise the horses. And the Brighton railway had not long been built, which was a good thing for these parts, or so they thought. There was Mr and Mrs Lassiter, quite a young couple they were, and very devoted. They had a child, a boy, their first born, and they had great hopes for him, as people do. The nursery was all beautifully decorated and crowded with so many playthings and they engaged a nursemaid to look after him. But —' here Mrs Malling gave a little gasp and winced as if in pain, although it was only the hurt from the story — 'there was something wrong with the child. The parents knew it from the start, but they couldn't admit it to themselves. They thought that with the right diet and good doctoring and his mother's love he would get well and be just like other boys. I don't know what was wrong because they always kept him hidden away. No one in the village ever saw him. It was just stories. Some said that the child would never grow up and others said it would be best if it didn't if you see what I mean. There were those —' her voice took on a hushed tone, as if there was some danger of her being overheard — 'who said it was a child sent by Old Nick, if you'll pardon the expression. That maybe he wasn't even a real boy at all, but a demon or some such thing.' Mrs Malling took a moment to compose herself before she went on. 'And then, one day, the child was nowhere to be found, and the nursemaid had disappeared, too. The rumour in the village was that she had taken him out to play in the fresh air and he had fallen in the brook and drowned.'

'Was the body ever discovered?' asked Mina.

'No, never, Miss. In fact, neither of them was ever seen again. It might have been an accident, of course, and the nurse was afraid she would be blamed for it and ran away. But some said it was deliberate and that she killed the demon to save the souls of the parents. Of course, Mrs Lassiter went quite distracted with grief. She took to wandering about the house sighing and crying out for her boy. It got so that her poor husband had to have her locked away for her own safety, but she wouldn't eat and so she wasted away and died.'

'But she wasn't buried here?' said Mina. 'I was told there are no church records relating to anyone who once lived in this house.'

'No, it's thought that Mr Lassiter left Hollow House and took her to be buried in a family plot; somewhere in Kent, I believe.'

'What is his history after that?'

'No one knows. Some say he went mad and had to be put away, others say he blew his brains out. Either way, it wasn't him but a nephew who sold the house to Mr Honeyacre.'

Mina was obliged to compare Mrs Malling's lurid tale with her host's brief and less dramatic account of the Lassiters. 'Mr Honeyacre has not told me this story. Either he does not know it or he is keeping it from me. Which is it?'

Mrs Malling looked uncomfortable. 'I didn't like to tell it to him, especially with him being newly married and such. It's not a nice thing to think about. But he has just now asked me to write down all I know about the house, so I suppose I shall have to do it. Only he might not tell Mrs Honeyacre because he won't have her upset, not for anything, and I would never say a word to her.'

'I promise to respect that wish and say nothing of this to Mrs Honeyacre,' said Mina, provoking a faint look of surprise from Mrs Malling. 'Would Mr Malling have anything to add to this story?'

'Oh no, he never listens to village gossip.'

'What about your excellent cook — was she in service with Mr Honeyacre during the lifetime of his first wife?'

'Yes, Mrs Blunt. But she was with him when he was in Brighton. She never lived here till now. She has a room in the new wing. She hasn't made any complaints.'

'If there is time before dinner, I would very much like to take a look inside the storeroom,' said Mina. 'The room next to this one. I have been told that it was once a nursery.'

'It was. And —'

'Yes?'

'It is supposed to be the room where Mrs Lassiter died.'

'How interesting. Then I must view it at once.'

'Yes, of course,' said Mrs Malling. She rose to her feet. 'Was there anything you especially wished to see?'

Mina was unwilling to tell anyone that she had seen an apparition in that room and it was for this reason that she would like a closer look. 'No, I intend to learn all I can about the house and Mr Honeyacre said I could explore any room I liked. I see you carry the keys about you.'

'Yes, at all times.'

'I understand that Mr Honeyacre has the other.'

'Yes, he has all the household keys, but he doesn't carry them about, he keeps them in a safe in his study. I don't think he has had occasion to use them since he moved here.'

Mina eased carefully from her chair and followed the housekeeper into the corridor. Mrs Malling turned the key in the lock of the unmarked door and pushed it open, stepping aside to allow Mina to enter first. 'We like to keep this room as clean and well-dusted as any in the house,' said Mrs Malling. 'Mr Honeyacre is very particular about his art and antiquities. Everything in here has its final place already determined once all the rooms are ready.'

Mina looked about her and had to admit it was a very well-ordered room. The floor was uncarpeted but thoroughly mopped. There were two tall wooden cabinets, each with many shallow drawers, and three more with double doors inlaid with marquetry. Two weighty chests of obvious antiquity had layers of thick rugs rolled on top. Objects that were presumably framed artworks were carefully wrapped in dust cloths and leaned against one wall. The item that particularly attracted

Mina's attention was a cheval mirror on wheels. It was far taller than she and draped with a white cloth. Could this be what she had seen through the window?

The curtains were closed. 'I can tell that this room is aired regularly,' she said, approvingly.

'Oh yes, we take great care over that. We open the curtains and air the room every morning just for a little while.'

Mina walked over to the window, pulled aside one curtain and peered out. If she turned her head she could just see the decorative urn, the one on the extreme right as she had faced the house, which was directly below her bedroom window. The mirror, however, was not currently in a position where someone standing outside the house could see it and she knew that it had moved in the few moments between her first seeing it and looking again. Had that been an illusion? If the floor was being mopped it might have been moved, but, on her arrival, both maids had been occupied with the luggage. Mina touched the carved frame as if to admire it. 'What exquisite work,' she said.

'Oh, Mr Honeyacre has the most wonderful taste, I'm sure.'

'How convenient as well, as it can easily be moved to wherever one wishes it,' Mina added, demonstrating with a gentle push that the mirror moved smoothly and without sound. 'And these fine cabinets are where Mr Honeyacre keeps his collection of antiquities?'

'That part of the collection which has not already been placed in its final location. He has the key to those.'

Mrs Malling stood by patiently as Mina studied the room. The walls had not been papered but painted, a pale wash on which were images of horses and ponies in watercolour. In one corner was something covered in draperies. Despite its concealment, Mina could guess from its shape and location what it was. 'So this was where the Lassiter's son slept — and where he played?'

'It was,' said Mrs Malling. 'I was told that it was Mrs Lassiter herself who painted the pictures on the walls to amuse her son. And after she lost her mind this is where she was locked away.'

Mina knew it would have been impertinent to ask to search inside the cupboards and drawers without Mr Honeyacre's permission, but she allowed herself a little inquisitiveness. Limping over to the shape in the corner she drew back the dust sheet and found as she had suspected, a rocking horse, painted in bright colours and well-varnished. 'I have two brothers,' she said, 'they played with a toy such as this. Was this the Lassiters' property?'

'It was. We found it behind some old bedsteads in one corner with some blankets over it, looking all forgotten. Except sometimes...'

'Yes?' Mrs Malling seemed unwilling to reveal more. Mina gave the toy a little push and it moved smoothly, making a soft rhythmic creaking noise before it came to rest.

Mrs Malling drew away as if afraid of the sound. 'I think we should go now,' she said.

Soon after Mina had returned to her room, Zillah arrived to help her prepare for dinner, bringing with her a box of hair ornaments loaned by Nellie. This was a comparatively simple task as Mina had only one suitable gown to wear. The maid said nothing as she observed the unusual cut of Mina's clothes, the better to accommodate her slight, twisted frame. When Mina was at home the general maidservant Rose often helped with her hair. It was simply styled, so that Mina could dress it herself for every day, although doing so sometimes made her shoulders and back ache. For family meals and occasions when her mother was present and especially demanding and unsparing of her criticism, Rose's help was always required and she had done well enough, but Zillah showed why she had become so invaluable to Nellie in so short a time. Mina, who only looked in a mirror when strictly necessary, now did so to admire Zillah's work, the fingers skilled, the brush never tugging, just smoothing and coaxing the long waves into a shiny cascade.

'I would be interested to know your opinion of the maids here,' said Mina, 'since it seems to me that so much of what troubles the Honeyacres comes from them. Do you think they are sensible girls?'

'No, Miss, not at all,' said Zillah, briskly, 'they are both very foolish and have tried to draw me into their way of thinking. Mary Ann tells ghost tales, some of which are very silly, and Susan even told me that she sees things that I don't, as if the very idea will cause me to have visions. They have claimed that books and plates and ornaments, even furniture, have started to move about on their own. There have been broken plates, but I was not there to see them fall. When I said that dropped dishes are always the result of carelessness, not ghosts, they gave me the most pitying looks.'

'Are they playing tricks on you, do you think?'

Zillah began to twist Mina's hair into long slender plaits that could be arranged to frame the contours of her face. 'That is hard to tell. They both profess to be afraid, Susan especially. Even though the servants' quarters are free from spirit visitations they refuse to stay in the house at night, as they think, should they be called upon to attend their employers or guests, they will encounter a ghost or some such horror walking about. I think it is a good thing they go home at night or we would all be troubled with their hysterics. Mr Honeyacre has asked Dr Hamid to interview them this afternoon, as he seeks a doctor's opinion.'

'What of Miss Pet?'

Zillah's expression softened. 'Oh, she is so devoted to Mrs Honeyacre; they are almost like sisters. She is quiet and sensible and affectionate. I think — in fact, I hope — we may become friends.'

Mina, as she gazed into the mirror, thought she saw a slight blush form on Zillah's cheeks. 'Do you know if she has seen or heard anything strange?'

'I don't think so, but if she has she does not like to talk about it, as she knows that Mrs Honeyacre believes in spirit visitations what with being a theatrical person and she would do anything rather than upset her. Also —' she paused.

'Also?' Mina queried.

Zillah completed the styling by holding it in place with a silk ribbon bow and then selected some jewelled combs. 'It's a delicate matter, Miss, but Miss Pet believes that Mrs Honeyacre thinks she might be on her way to providing her husband with an addition to the family.'

'Ah,' said Mina. 'I noticed that he has been very protective of her and I had wondered if he was concerned for her health. Now I understand. Of course, he would be taking especial care for her not to be alarmed by anything, so that is all the more reason for me to try and resolve this matter quickly, if I can.'

Zillah stood back to admire her handiwork.

'Thank you, Zillah; my hair has never looked better. I shall make sure to engage you if I am to go to the costume ball.' Mina had not mentioned it to Nellie but she was still undecided about attending.

'The Spanish lady? Oh yes, Mrs Jordan has ordered the gown and the combs and mantilla are all ready for you. You're to see the dressmaker next week.'

Conversation was kept artificially light over dinner, where the table was resplendent with a handsome roast joint, savouries, sauces, jellies and custards. That morning's visit to St Mond's was the main subject and Mr Honeyacre made some amusing comments about church mice before discussing the antiquity of the pulpit and the improvements he meant to make to the steps leading down to the churchyard so that the ladies would not be in danger of tripping up. Kitty was very quiet and ate sparingly and her husband occasionally urged her to eat more beef, soliciting approval from Dr Hamid for this advice, which he was glad to give.

The conversation moved on to the impending costume ball and the gentlemen remained silent and nodded appreciatively as the ladies talked of the silken elegance they planned. Nellie was eager for Kitty to visit Brighton to take tea with her at the Grand Hotel and view the latest fashionable arrivals from France. By the end of the meal it was determined that Kitty would ornament the ball by recreating her costume as Princess Kirabampu, only in fabrics more gorgeous than were sufficient for the popular stage.

Once dinner was done Mr Honeyacre drew Dr Hamid aside for a private consultation, though from overheard whispers it appeared that what he most required was advice on the merits of a special bottle of brandy he kept in his study. The ladies retired to the drawing room where Miss Pet brought Kitty her little dog and amused it with a piece of coloured ribbon. Mr Malling came to tend to the fire from which Mina guessed that the maids had already departed.

The quietness of the country enveloped them. They were far from any woodlands or livestock and could not expect to hear the cry of birds or nocturnal creatures through the thick draperies. There was the comfortable popping of wood and hiss of coal, the thrum of flames caught by wind from the chimney. Little Scrap entertained them with squeals and growls, but did not seem inclined to bark.

'I hope you have found some reading in Benjamin's library to amuse you,' said Kitty.

'I have indeed,' said Mina, deciding not to mention her choice.

'And you also write?'

'I do.'

'Perhaps you could tell us one of your stories?'

Mina paused. Few people were aware that the majority of her works, which were published under the name of Robert Neil, were tales of demons, ghosts, sprites and monsters. Her family believed that she wrote uplifting moral stories for children, something none of them would think of reading. Mina had first begun to write several years ago, in order to compose comforting stories to recount at the sickbed of her sister Marianne who was dying of consumption. It was not long, however, before she found her true calling in creating bloodcurdling mysteries. The only person party to her secret was Dr Hamid, as Mina had entertained his late sister Eliza with terrifying tales of which she had been particularly fond.

Mina delved deep into her memory and extracted a tale written long ago, one that Marianne had liked, of a pet dog, which had saved the family fortunes by discovering a treasure.

Kitty listened with careful attention, stroking Little Scrap as she did so. 'There you are, my darling,' she murmured, when the story was done, 'what a clever little dog that was. And you are clever, too.' She smiled at Mina. 'I should like to hear more stories about dogs.'

Mina decided not to recount the only other one she had written, in which a dog released vengeful ghosts after digging up the corpses of executed murderers. 'I will be sure to compose some more,' she said.

The gentlemen joined them and Mr Honeyacre assured the ladies that although Mr and Mrs Malling had retired for the night they could always be summoned if necessary.

Mina decided to return to her room early as she wished to complete her notes on the day's events. As she prepared for bed it occurred to her that she was, for the first time, about to spend the night in a reputedly haunted house. Was there anything she ought to be doing to brace herself for this dreadful ordeal? Should she be more alert than usual, or was that a mistake, since it would be a stimulus to her imagination and therefore open her to errors of observation. She couldn't be sure.

Sitting up in bed by candlelight with her warmest wrap about her shoulders, Mina rested her notebook on her lap and wrote. The old house was cooling and now and then there were little creaks and squeaks, or the sighing of the wind. Absorbed in her work she was not yet ready to sleep.

Her eyes became accustomed to the grey dark. She looked about the room at the simple but refined furnishings. Nothing moved, nothing appeared or disappeared. If there were monsters in the wardrobe they were monsters only from her own stories and therefore imaginary. Even if she were to hear footsteps in the corridor, they would be the steps of someone seeking the water closet in preference to the simpler amenities.

The sound that did alert her was none of those things, and nothing to which she could attribute a cause. A shushing, sweeping sound, like some heavy object being dragged along the corridor and then a noticeable thump on her bedroom door as if something had collided with it. Was someone moving furniture about in the middle of the night?

It took Mina a while to slip safely from the bed, wrap herself closely against the cold air, find her slippers and ease them onto her feet. She crept to the door and opened it. Outside the corridor was dark, the moon that might have lit it occluded by heavy cloud, and she saw nothing. Returning to her night table she took the candle and stepped out into the corridor. There was nothing to see and the noise had ceased.

She decided to inspect the storeroom next door but it was locked as usual. She pressed her ear to the door, but all was quiet within. After a few more moments she returned to her bedroom and write down all that she had just experienced.

In her warm bed once more she finally completed her notes, hoping that this would bring an end to the events of the day, then extinguished her candle and settled down to sleep, but sleep did not come easily. Even after committing her thoughts to paper they still troubled her. Moreover, the wind had risen once again and its squally protests threatened to keep her awake. She slipped out of bed once more, descending carefully in the darkness, and went to the window to ensure that the curtains were drawn as securely as possible when she saw, from between the velvet folds, a light moving up the terrace steps towards the house.

Mina watched the light for a time and, judging by the way it moved, it was clear that it was not some bright object borne by the wind, but was being carried by someone or something, though whether its bearer was human or animal, living or deceased, it was not possible for anyone to determine. Mina's natural inclination tended towards the living but she felt sure that there were others who would think differently.

Her candle had been snuffed out, so the unknown presence could not see its glow in her window, but it had been lit only a short while before and she wondered if it was that which had drawn the visitor to the house. She remained still and watched carefully. The sky was like a flood of dark ink, almost impenetrable apart from the occasional brief suspicion of a full moon that seemed to glide into being and then quickly disappear. There were no lights from the church or the village. All was deadly quiet. If the presence had footsteps they were muffled by window glass, curtaining and distance.

As far as Mina was aware no visitors were expected and certainly none that would creep up to the door in the middle of the night. She felt curiosity rather than fear. The simplest explanation was that the arrival was simply a lost traveller, or someone in need of assistance, in which case she might expect to hear a knock at the door. She waited, but the light moved back and forth a number of times, as if searching for entry and there was no knock.

It then came to Mina that the shadowy figure could well be Mr Jordan's detective, come to spy out the house in the hopes of surprising Nellie in some act of infidelity; a secret assignation on the terrace, a passionate embrace viewed through a window. It was all very distasteful and if Nellie chanced to leave her room there was the danger of an innocent chance encounter being subject to misinterpretation. The other and far more worrying theory was that a robber had come to examine the house to discover how easy it might be to enter and steal the valuables known to lie within.

Mina debated with herself as to her best course of action. She could not return to her bed, leaving the dangers unaddressed and her curiosity unsatisfied. The sensible thing to do was, of course, to fetch Dr Hamid or summon Mr Malling and ask for their assistance. No doubt the gentlemen would order her back to her room, telling her to lock her door and draw the curtains tightly. Only then would they go and assess the danger for themselves. If there was any excitement she would miss it all.

It was not an action of which great stories were made, she reflected. Would Sister Ireyna of the Convent of the Immaculate Heart have gone running for the assistance of an Archbishop in *The Haunted Nun*? Would *Bessie the Pirate Queen* have hidden in her cabin shaking with terror every time the monster of the deep left its evil smelling glutinous trail on deck as it searched for hidden gold? No, they would not.

What if the light proved, after all, to be no more than an artifice of nature, or some roaming animal, a large hound, perhaps, with a studded collar that gathered and reflected faint slivers of moonlight? How foolish she would look then! How like the heroine of *Northanger Abbey*, whose excitable imagination caused her to see Gothic terrors in the commonplace.

Mina made her decision. She put on her warmest wrap and slippers, lit her candle, placed it in the lantern and then slipped out into the corridor. The pierced metal of the holder, like an oriental dome, threw flowery shapes on the wall that spun around prettily as she walked. All was quiet. Mina crept along the corridor, even more slowly than was usual for her, hoping not to disturb anyone. The head of the stairs soon loomed in front of her and she began to descend, holding tightly onto the bannisters and reaching out carefully with each foot to judge the position of the steps.

The hall was peopled with unfamiliar shapes. Had she been susceptible she might have seen a ghost in every corner. She wondered if the presence outside had noticed her. She had no intention of opening the front door to look. Instead, she entered the parlour where the banked embers of the fire still warmed the air, put down the candle holder and approached the window. As she gently shifted the curtain aside so that she could peer out she was taken aback by seeing a large silhouette very close to the glass in the unmistakable shape of a man. Mina retreated, but knew that she had been seen. Now was the time to do the sensible thing, probably the thing she ought to have done before, and summon the servants. She was going to pull the bell cord when she heard a soft tapping on the window and a whisper.

'Nellie? Is that you? Let me in, oh, please do!'

To Mina's alarm she recognised the voice as that of her wayward younger brother Richard and realised that she would ten times rather he had been a burglar. Abandoning any intention of summoning another person she returned to the window.

The figure outside raised a candle to his face. He was wide-eyed and damp, his blond curls plastered to his forehead beneath the brim of his tweed travelling cap. Rather than have him make more noise she managed with a struggle to unfasten the window catches and open the lower pane the merest crack, just sufficient to enable them to converse.

'Richard?' she whispered.

He gave a little gasp. 'Mina! Oh, do let me in, there's a dear girl, it's cold outside and it's starting to rain again.'

'Richard, I can't.'

He shivered and gazed at her pleadingly in the way that always earned him a donation from his mother's purse. 'But I want to see Nellie! I miss her!'

'How did you know she would be here? Have you been corresponding?'

'Just little notes. I got a message saying that she would be coming here with you and I thought it would be such fun to see her without that awful husband of hers always snooping about. So I suggested to the *Journal* that they send me here to do some sketches. Not that there is anything here worth the paper, apart from this house and the windmills and the old church.'

Realisation dawned on Mina. 'Was that you in the church earlier today?'

'Yes, I heard Nellie's voice and didn't know who was with her, so I thought it best to climb up and hide in the pulpit. Did you get a fright?'

'Not as much as the one I am having now. Richard — I am not letting you anywhere near Nellie. Have you seen the man who is staying at the farm? The one with the binocular glasses?'

'Oh yes, the surveyor — Stevenson, I think his name is. Why? Is he after Nellie, too? I wouldn't blame him, of course, but he might make himself a nuisance. Should I challenge him?'

'You will do nothing of the sort. He's not a surveyor, he's a detective, almost certainly engaged by Mr Jordan to follow Nellie and keep watch for any suspicion of infidelity.'

'Oh! I thought his face looked familiar — I have seen him about in Brighton. He's a detective?'

'Yes. If you enter this house at night and he gets to hear of it he will report to Mr Jordan that you had a secret tryst with his wife. And then she will be divorced, abandoned, penniless. I'm sure you don't want that to happen.'

There was a brief silence outside then something that sounded like a sniffle. 'But I miss her! I never met any girl I liked half as much.'

'In that case you won't do anything to destroy her reputation and her marriage. Just go. I can't let you into any part of this premises.'

'And I think I have a toothache coming!' he wailed.

Mina hardened her heart. 'I can't help that. And it is all the more reason for you to go home. Do you have somewhere to stay tonight?'

'Yes, a room at the Goat and Hammers. It's not very nice.'

'Then this is what you are going to do. You will return to your room for the rest of the night. Tomorrow, early, you will hire a cart to take you to Hassocks Gate and you will then take the first train back to London. If you don't — Richard listen carefully to me — if you don't, I will tell mother everything.'

He gasped. 'Oh, Mina, darlingest, you wouldn't do that!'

'I would,' said Mina. There was a short pause and Mina felt spots of rain on her fingertips as they rested on the window ledge.

'Can I give you a note for Nellie?'

'Sometimes, Richard, I think you are quite mad,' hissed Mina. 'At this moment I am sure of it. No! You must put nothing in writing. You will not come near this house again. You will not try to see Nellie. You will not write any notes. You will go.'

Richard gave a little groan of acceptance. 'Then tell her from me — tell her I think of her every day. Tell her I wish — oh, I hardly know what I wish. If I was rich, it would all be so simple. Has Nellie told you that Mr Jordan is unkind to her? And she doesn't deserve it, not a bit!'

Mina said nothing. The fears that had lurked in her mind for some while had just become all too real.

'Very well,' said Richard, miserably, 'I have decided. I shall go back to London and write Mr Jordan an insulting letter. Then he will call me out and I will dispatch him.'

'He might dispatch you, which would be a great grief to all of us, including Nellie. And supposing you did prevail? You would go to prison, or be hanged, and if the law thought Nellie encouraged you it would be the worse for her, too. Nellie has a past and that will weigh against her in people's estimation. Even if she has not been indiscreet people will believe it of her.'

'But I can't agree never to see her again!'

'You may have to, or else only see her when you are both in a large assembly of people. But please, Richard, for now, just go. And promise me you'll do nothing to interfere with Mr Jordan.'

He uttered a ragged sigh. 'Oh, very well. But I have one more sketch to complete for my mission or I may not be paid. I shall go up to the windmills at first light tomorrow morning and finish my work and then I will return to London. I don't suppose you could write a little history of the windmills for me? The readers seem to expect it and you're better with words than I am.'

'Of course I will. Now, no more standing about in the cold and wet.'

'You're the best sister in the world!' Richard blew her a fond kiss and then, to Mina's great relief, he turned back and the little light moved away.

Mina refastened the window and crept back to her room, thankful that no one else in the house had been disturbed and that Little Scrap had yet to acquire any skills as a guard dog.

The restfulness of sleep still eluded her. There were times when it was hard to know if she was dreaming or awake. Her mind drifted through stories; those she had been told and new ones that insisted on composing themselves in her head and would not let her rest. There was a grieving white lady in the corridor, a strange child in the nursery, a mysterious maid who might be a murderess, a beautiful witch and a hound that glowed in the dark. She heard a child's footsteps moving quickly, a squeal of laughter and the creak creak creak of a rocking horse...

Chapter Six

Kitty arrived late to the breakfast table, looking strained and pale. Despite the tempting array of hot dishes she was able only to sip milkless tea and take small bites of dry toast, which she chewed without any appearance of enjoyment. Mr Honeyacre tried to tempt her to an egg but she merely shook her head listlessly.

'I am sorry to say that Kitty did not sleep at all well last night,' said the anxious husband. 'Myself, I always sleep very soundly, but Kitty was disturbed by some noises.' He patted her hand. 'Perhaps the wind and the rain are to blame.'

'I am sure that is the answer,' said Mina, thankful that hers was the only other bedroom that faced the terrace and therefore no one else had witnessed Richard's unwise attempt to see Nellie.

'I also thought I heard someone walking about,' said Nellie, 'but I was asleep again almost as soon as I heard it. I assume there were no late visitors?'

'No, or the Mallings would have come to the door,' said Mr Honeyacre. 'The house, I wish to reassure everyone, is most securely locked at night. All the doors and windows are fastened. No one can enter from the outside.' He frowned suddenly. 'Maybe it was that surveyor creeping about outside like a spy. We must all look for footprints this morning and if we find them I will go down to the village myself and give him a piece of my mind.'

'I do hope we have better weather today,' said Dr Hamid. 'I have been looking forward to a pleasant walk to view the country. And I prescribe one to Mrs Honeyacre, who needs to breathe good fresh air as much as possible!'

Kitty gave a little gulp and dropped her toast. 'Please excuse me,' she said, pressing a napkin to her lips and hurriedly rose and left the table.

Mr Honeyacre turned to Mary Ann, who had just brought in a pot of coffee. 'Mary Ann, do go and let Miss Pet know that Mrs Honeyacre is indisposed.' He sighed. 'She must have her rest, of course. My plan for today, if the weather holds, is for us to go up and inspect the windmills. There is a very fine view from the top of Clayton Hill and you can also see the north entrance to the railway tunnel, which is a particularly fine example of the modern Gothic style, although in a rather curious spot.'

'I was wondering if you have any books in your library about the windmills?' asked Mina, remembering her promise to Richard.

'Not specifically, but there are histories and a guide book, and also a gazetteer of Sussex which will help you.'

'Then I would very much like to read them.' Mina declined the coffee. 'In fact, I will go now and choose a book so I will be well read before our walk, the better to appreciate my surroundings. Mrs Jordan, would you care to accompany me and help me select a book?'

Both Nellie and Dr Hamid appeared surprised at this request, as Nellie was not famed for her reading of historical texts, but Nellie quickly understood that this was a subterfuge for a private conversation.

Once in the library Mina quickly told Nellie about her encounter with Richard the previous night. 'At least he now knows that the man with the binocular glasses, who is going under the name of Stevenson, is not who he pretends to be.

But since Richard intends to complete his sketch of the windmills this morning before he goes I think it would be most unwise for you to join the party in case you encounter him and Mr Stevenson is following us and observes your meeting.'

'I agree,' said Nellie, 'and I am sorry for it, but I must make every effort not to meet Richard again unless in a large company. If we should chance to meet on Clayton Hill Mr Stevenson will think it was by arrangement and Mr Jordan will be unforgiving on a mere unconfirmed suspicion.' She looked profoundly regretful and Mina felt sure that, to Nellie, a meeting with Richard would have been far preferable to one with her own husband.

Nellie glanced out of the window. 'Although, from the look of the sky, the expedition to see the windmills may not take place.'

Nellie was right. The weather was taking a turn from bad to worse. The cloud cover had darkened and a suspicion of rain was rapidly becoming a certainty.

Mina found a visitors' guide to the county of Sussex that included a paragraph on the Clayton Hill windmills and borrowed it for further reading. 'I doubt that Mrs Honeyacre would have been able to accompany us in any case. She did not appear at all well this morning.'

'Yes, and I believe it may be more than lack of sleep that ails her,' said Nellie, meaningfully.

'What is it, do you think?' asked Mina, pretending innocence of the subject.

'I have my suspicions, as I am sure you do, that she may not be actually unwell, but expecting a happy event. However, even allowing for that, I have never in all the years I have known her seen her as out of sorts as she is at present. She is fearful, which she never was before, and a mere semblance of her former self. Her husband, having known her for only a short while, is not as aware of the great change, which he will put down to other causes. Myself, I am not so sure.'

They both returned to the dining room where the coffee was being replenished. Just as the new downpour appeared to be easing it mocked them by descending afresh like a thick grey curtain, billowing in the wind. Mina fervently hoped that Richard would be able to make his escape back to London.

'I am sorry to say that, in view of the weather, the windmills will have to wait for another day,' said Mr Honeyacre. 'But I do have good news. Kitty is feeling a little better. Mrs Blunt is making her some ginger root infusion to Dr Hamid's special recipe. She is in the parlour now, keeping warm.'

Mina and Nellie found Kitty reclining in an armchair that had been piled with cushions and drawn up before the fire. She was having her temples bathed with a cologned handkerchief by Miss Pet, who knelt by her side. Little Scrap was curled up on his mistress's lap, nibbling a biscuit. The room was warmed with the fragrance of burning wood and flowery perfume.

'Miss Scarletti!' exclaimed Kitty, reaching out to clasp Mina's hands. 'Please tell me — is it wrong for me to feel so afraid? We can never know what the future will hold and sometimes it can seem that everything is against us and wishes us ill!'

'There are those who claim to know the future,' said Miss Pet, 'but I do not trust them.'

'Nor should you,' said Nellie. 'They are conjurors all, but they juggle with our feelings and play upon our weaknesses. Kitty, my dear, you need to keep your strength up. You should take care of yourself and not give in to idle fancies.'

Kitty pushed away the handkerchief and sat up straight, gathering her puppy dog into her arms. Her eyes were bright, her cheeks pale, each with a single patch of red. Had she been on stage, she would have looked fragile and enchanting, but close up she seemed far from well. Miss Pet rose to her feet and placed her fingertips very gently on Kitty's forehead.

'Are you feverish, my dear?' asked Nellie anxiously.

Kitty shook her head and Miss Pet said, 'We were afraid of that, but Dr Hamid has examined her and can detect no fever. Her forehead has a natural warmth but she feels a little weak and faint and her stomach is disordered.'

'There is something in the house that does not like me,' exclaimed Kitty. 'It wants me to go away. I can't sleep because I hear strange noises. I lie in my bed and I try to sleep and I dare not open my eyes because I am afraid of what I might see.'

'There are always strange noises in an old house,' said Mina soothingly. 'I hear them too.'

'You do?' gasped Kitty.

'Yes, but they are nothing, they mean nothing. They are the sounds made by old wood responding to changes in the weather. I take no note of them and neither should you.'

'The other day,' said Kitty, 'I was walking along the corridor and I heard a noise from the room where the antiquities are stored. The door was locked and there was no one inside, but still there was the noise. On and on it went, as if it would never stop. It was the old rocking horse, I know it. Moving, all by itself. I heard that there was a child that once lived here, who rode that horse. Long ago. Do you think the child died and its ghost comes back here to ride the horse?'

'Kitty, are you sure that was not a dream?' said Nellie.

'I don't know,' said Kitty. 'Sometimes I can't be sure. I am thinking I ought to ask Benjamin to take it away, but would that make things worse? And then there is the painting.' Kitty shivered and her lips trembled. 'How I hate that painting! I can hardly ask him to remove that. He does so dote on it.'

'The portrait of the first Mrs Honeyacre, you mean?' asked Mina.

'I am never happy when I look at it. She stares at me so. She doesn't care for me being here, I know it!' Kitty burst into tears and Miss Pet comforted her as best she could.

Mina and Nellie glanced at each other and, by mutual unspoken agreement, withdrew to the hall for a conversation.

'This is worse than I thought,' said Nellie.

'I agree. Perhaps Dr Hamid will have a draught that can soothe her,' Mina suggested. 'I would not make light of her anxiety, as I know that in a half-dream it is easy to imagine things. If, as we both suspect, she is in a delicate condition that could make her fears appear to be more than they are.'

'Her health must be the first concern,' said Nellie, thoughtfully, 'and I have a plan which would solve everything. Kitty's upset is partly due to her unease in Hollow House and the rumours that it is haunted. I will propose that Kitty visits Brighton earlier than intended. In fact, I shall insist that she travel with us when we return on Monday. That is only two days from now. She can stay with me. If Mr Honeyacre wants a reason I will tell him that I urgently need her advice on the preparations for the costume ball. And I can arrange entertainments and distractions during her visit. I am sure that, before long, she will quite forget her fears.'

'I think that is a very good scheme,' said Mina.

They were on their way to speak to the gentlemen on the subject when they were met by Mr Malling, who appeared very troubled.

'Oh, Mrs Jordan, Miss Scarletti, I have just come from informing Mr Honeyacre. A boy has come up from the village just now to say that the mill brook has burst its banks and the bridge is underwater and in danger of coming down.'

'What about the road to Hassocks Gate?' asked Mina.

'I'm very sorry, Miss, but for now, it's impassable. All the roads out of the village are. You might have to stay at Hollow House longer than you had planned.'

Mina and Nellie exchanged shocked glances. Their plan to remove Kitty to the haven of Brighton at the earliest opportunity had just vanished and Mina could already hear her mother's fury at her prolonged secret absence from home echoing in her head.

'Please do not worry,' said Mr Malling, not appreciating the reasons for their dismay, 'we have everything we need here for your comfort.'

'What did the boy say about the road?' demanded Nellie.

'Only that it was under water and what wasn't under water was mud. He's wet to the skin himself.'

'The poor boy,' said Mina. 'I hope he was rewarded for daring to come here with the news.'

'Oh, he's a farmer's lad, weather is nothing to him. Wet and dry is all alike, they don't mean anything,' said Mr Malling with a careless shrug. 'Besides which, he has a cape to cover him. Mrs Blunt has given him some hot soup and he is properly grateful for it.'

'Where is he now?' said Mina. 'I would like to speak to him.'

Mr Malling blinked. 'Well, he is in the scullery, Miss, but I wouldn't bring him up here and I wouldn't advise you to go down there.'

'Mina never does what she is advised to do,' said Nellie with a smile. She linked arms with Mina. 'Come, Mr Malling, show us the way.'

Mr Malling had no option but to comply and on the way they learned that the youth was aged fifteen and called William Jesson. There was a set of stairs descending from the hallway, leading to a short passage that opened out into a large warm kitchen.

Having been recently refurbished by a man who prided himself on an excellent table the kitchen of Hollow House had every resource possible. The walls hung with banks of shining pans, moulds and implements, while long deep shelves held serving dishes, trays and crocks. The range, which boasted an impressive roasting jack, was easily of a size to prepare a feast for twenty. The floor was well cleansed and there was a long table which had been scrubbed spotless.

Mrs Blunt, the cook, stood at a butcher's bench. She was a large woman in every possible dimension. Before her was a carcass of beef on a bloodstained board which she was attacking with a large chopper and an expression of grim determination. She looked up, mildly astonished at the arrival of two fashionable ladies where fashionable ladies never went. 'Is everything satisfactory?' she asked.

'Oh, everything is quite splendid,' said Mina. 'Please don't let us interrupt your work. We are only here because we would like to speak to young William.'

'He's in the scullery, Miss.' Mrs Blunt had laid down the chopper and taken up a large knife with which she gestured towards a door. 'He's none too clean. Take care you don't dirty your clothes.'

Mr Malling followed Mina and Nellie into the scullery, which was furnished with two large sinks and a boiling copper and smelled of washing soap and vinegar. Mary Ann, her sleeves rolled to her elbows, was busy scouring the serving dishes and chinaware that were the residue of breakfast. William was crouching on a stool, under which some brown paper had been laid, and gulping at a bowl of hot soup. Most of his clothes were wringing wet, including the heavy woollen cape he wore, and his boots were coated in mud, although there had been some attempt at scraping off the worst of it. His hair was glistening.

His jaw dropped open with amazement at the sight of Mina and Nellie and he nearly tumbled off his stool in his eagerness to stand up respectfully, narrowly avoiding spilling his soup.

'I am glad to see you have been given some refreshment for your trouble,' said Mina, kindly. 'No, please don't stand, and do go on with your soup. I insist. It will do you good.'

He sat down with some relief, but his eyes remained on Mina. She wondered if her appearance would result in yet another village legend — that of the twisted lady.

'I just wanted to ask you some questions. Tell me — have you lived in Ditchling Hollow all your life?'

'I have that, Miss.'

'And have you ever known the weather to be as bad as it is now?'

'Yes, every three or four years it comes down like this. Then the brook rises up and the road is under water and there's no going back and forth, not for days.'

Behind him, Mary Ann nodded vigorously in agreement. Mr Malling saw the gesture and dismissed her from the room with a jerk of his head. She did not look pleased to go, but she obeyed.

'Do you think a carriage, a good carriage like Mr Honeyacre's, would be able to travel from here to Hassocks Gate railway station?' asked Mina.

William shook his head vigorously. 'Oh no, Miss, it could never get through. Water's too high.'

'What about the footpath from the house down to the church. Is that clear?'

'Yes, but it's awful slippy, especially the old stones. I came up that way from the lane.'

'Only we are due to return to Brighton on Monday morning,' said Nellie. 'Will that be possible?'

'Naw,' said William, with another shake of the head. 'There'll be no carriages going that way on Monday. Nothing to Clayton nor Hurstpierpoint neither. A horse might do if it's a strong one, but it's not fit for ladies.'

Nellie and Mina looked at each other. He saw their expressions, his eyes flickering from one to the other. He gulped his soup and licked his lips. 'If you ask me, ladies, you shouldn't have come to Ditchling Hollow. It's not for outsiders.'

'Now then!' exclaimed Mr Malling, quickly. 'No one asked you and that is no way to speak to your betters!'

'Oh, let him speak, please do,' said Mina, 'I want to learn more.' She drew closer to the youth, her crooked body rocking from side to side as she walked, and he stared at her in alarm.

As she neared, the savoury scent of hot soup mingled with the smell of damp clothing and earth and all the decaying things that lay within it brought back to life by the rain. Seated as he was the boy's face was level with hers and it made him uneasy. His thin features were smeared with wet grime and the hands clasping the soup bowl were dotted with scabs and scratches, the nails black with mud. 'Tell me William, what is the matter here?'

'The matter?'

'Yes, in Hollow House. Is it an unlucky place? Some people seem to think so.'

He licked the bowl clean, thoughtfully. 'My grandmother came from outside to work in this house and it never brought her anything but trouble.'

'What kind of trouble?'

'Worst kind,' said William. 'You want to talk to Ned Copper, he knows. And it's not just the house. He says the whole village is under a curse and coming here never brings any good to those who weren't born here.'

'What is the nature of this curse, and what is its cause?' asked Mina. 'Can it be avoided, or lifted?'

William wiped a grubby fist across his mouth. 'I don't know. It's only what I've been told. Ask Ned Copper. Ask him to tell you about the devil child. He saw it with his own eyes, he did.'

'That's enough!' said Mr Malling. 'I'll not allow language like that in front of ladies.' He seized the boy by the arm and quickly hustled him away. Mina decided not to pursue the matter since she felt that William had said all he was going to.

Mina returned to the kitchen. 'Mrs Blunt?'

The cook turned to her. She was wielding the meat chopper again and looked larger than ever. Fortunately, largeness never troubled Mina since all adults were larger than she. 'I just wanted to ask you — have you seen anything strange in the house? Anything you couldn't explain?'

Mrs Blunt gave a laugh like the sound of a pepper grinder and cracked her knuckles. 'A ghost, you mean? I'd like to see the ghost that would try and haunt me! I'd soon send it packing! I'd chop it into little pieces, I would! No, they stay away from me. They know what'll happen!'

Much to the relief of Mr Malling, who had been quite unsettled by the sight of the quality descending to the kitchen, Mina and Nellie retraced their steps to the hallway, where they encountered Mrs Malling on her way to the kitchen stairs.

'Miss Scarletti, Mrs Jordan,' she said, 'I'm to advise you that, in view of the weather situation, Mr Honeyacre asks that everyone should come to the drawing room where he will have something to say. I have made sure that the room is well-warmed and will ask Mrs Blunt to arrange for a jug of hot cocoa and her best spice biscuits to be brought to you all.'

They thanked her and she hurried on her errand.

Despite the comforting fire that blazed in the grate and the promise of warming refreshments it was a sombre party that gathered in the drawing room under the watchful painted eye of the first Mrs Honeyacre. Only Kitty was not present, as she and Miss Pet had taken Little Scrap to play.

Mr Honeyacre tried to put a brave face on the situation. 'As you have all no doubt learned by now, the flooding has rendered the road from Ditchling Hollow to Hassocks Gate impassable to carriages and I believe that the other roads are little better. I fear that Reverend Ashbrook will not be able to come in from Clayton tomorrow morning to take Sunday service at St Mond's, something I know we were all very much looking forward to. If it is still possible to travel to church safely on foot we will have to be content with assembling there for prayers. Otherwise, we can always gather here to pray.

'I am, however, hopeful that in four or five days' time, if the weather clears, the waters will recede and the roads will once again be clear for carriages. I would like to reassure the ladies that they are not in any danger of missing the grand ball and there will still be ample time to make all the arrangements for costume and coiffure and — whatever else may be required. But, in the meantime, we can make the best of things here.'

Everyone stared out of the window where the prevailing deluge seemed to be implying that the best course of action would be to start building an ark.

'I especially wish to set your minds at rest regarding the remainder of your stay here. There are ample supplies to keep everyone well fed and warm. I am only sorry that you will not be able to explore the surrounding countryside and villages as I had hoped, but that is a pleasure to be reserved for another occasion.

'I am also happy to say that we are well able to keep ourselves amused. I know that Miss Pet would be delighted to entertain us on the piano and anyone able to sing will be encouraged to do so. I have a few volumes of poetry and I am sure that some readings would be appreciated. Also, I could give a lecture about art and antiquities, so there will be a great deal to entertain us and the time will just fly by.'

'We are very grateful to you,' said Dr Hamid. 'You have been more than kind and generous, and the weather is hardly your fault.'

Mr Honeyacre acknowledged the compliment with his customary modesty.

'I am assuming,' said Mina, wondering if she should send an explanatory letter to her brother Edward, 'that there is no possibility of any post being received or sent?'

'None, I am sorry to say. All the mail for Ditchling Hollow goes to the main post office at Hurstpierpoint and it is one of Mr Malling's duties to go up there to collect it, as well as ordering supplies. He also likes to visit his son who lives there. That is of some concern to me, too, since Mr Albert Malling is a clerk employed in the estate office and I have expressly requested that he write to warn me the instant he learns of any of those dreadful developers making enquiries about the estate or sending their agents here as scouts. I had hoped to learn more about that man who has been staying in the village and spying on everything, but I shall just have to be patient, I suppose.'

'Have there been any such enquiries?' asked Dr Hamid.

'Not in recent months, no. Last year, before I commenced the improvements, a Mr White wrote to me and offered an insultingly small sum to buy the estate. He actually admitted that he intended to convert it to industrial use. Shocking! I can only hope that Mr White and others of his ilk who wish to despoil the English countryside might find themselves with an enemy in the Sussex weather.' It was an unusually uncharitable burst of feeling for the normally gentle Mr Honeyacre. Although he did not say so, Mina thought he envisaged all such intruders sinking into a muddy grave never to be seen again.

'There is, of course, the reason for our visit here, which I will continue to pursue,' said Mina. 'With your permission, of course, I would like to speak privately to the maidservants concerning the unusual events that they have witnessed here. My feeling is that the frights they have had might have their origins in simply mistaking quite natural occurrences for something more sinister. I hope to be able to put their minds at rest, although I doubt that I will be able to fully undo the effects of any fanciful tales that have been passed around the village. People are too willing to believe the unusual over the commonplace and the result is that they go about in fear of a great deal of nothing.'

'I would be grateful for that,' said Mr Honeyacre. 'When would be convenient?'

'The sooner the better,' said Mina.

Chapter Seven

Mina decided to interview the maids in her room, where their conversation was less likely to be interrupted. She made it especially clear that she did not want a senior servant present. Mr Honeyacre agreed to this and Mrs Malling was asked to send the maids to her individually. Mina held her notebook and pencil ready and waited.

The first to arrive was Mary Ann. She was a sturdy girl with a round face and sand-coloured curls. There was a steady look in her large grey eyes and while her expression showed that she was a little curious as to what was to occur it revealed no trace of timidity or fear. Mina made sure that she was comfortable, offering her a seat by the fire, facing her own. Mary Ann took it with alacrity, the friendly gesture not appearing to cause her any unease.

'Mary Ann, do you know why I wish to speak to you?'

'Yes, Miss. Mrs Malling said you know all about ghosts and hauntings and wanted me to tell you about what I have seen here,' she said, her voice confident and even.

'But first of all, I would like you to tell me about yourself,' said Mina.

Mary Ann, it transpired, was the granddaughter of Ned Copper. She was eighteen and had been born in Ditchling Hollow, where she had lived most of her life. She had been sent out to service in Clayton at the age of fourteen, but had not been happy in that place as she thought her mistress was unkind and she had therefore been eager to return to her family and home village when she heard that the big house was to be occupied and needed maidservants.

Mary Ann lived in a cottage with her grandfather, widowed mother and two brothers. Her brothers worked on the land and her mother kept house and did washing and mending. All were regular attendees at the church of St Mond.

'I saw your grandfather when I visited the church,' said Mina. 'He was walking in the graveyard. I was told that he has many interesting stories to tell about the history of the village.'

'My grandfather has second sight,' said Mary Ann, with a note of defiant pride in her tone. It was clearly not something that occasioned her any discomfort. 'He sees things other people don't see and sometimes it turns his mind to strange thoughts. He thinks things that no one else can even imagine. Some people say he has lost his mind, but I don't believe it. There are those in the village who are afraid of him and some of them send him little gifts to keep on his good side. He knows more about strange things than anyone else round here and more than he will ever let on.'

'Do you have second sight?'

Mary Ann smiled. 'I think I might have a bit of it. Mother don't. My brothers don't. At least they say they don't, but sometimes I think they do and don't want to admit it, or people might think they are like grandfather. They just want to do their work and get their wages and not be bothered. I've been used to strange things all my life and I know that some are not to be feared.'

'What about in Hollow House? Do you know what is happening here?'

The maid looked thoughtful and her gaze moved about the room, as if looking for spectres. 'The goings on here are different. It's not like when I dream of Father or see Grandmother standing at the foot of my bed. I feel safe then. Here — I can feel it sometimes; it's something that lives here but doesn't always want to be seen. It doesn't like other people in the house and it will do what it can to make them go away.' She leaned forward a little, as if imparting a confidence, her voice hushed. 'I think that there will come a time when the old part of the house will fall down. It might catch fire, or sink into the mud, or just crumble away. The new part might remain, because no one cares about that, but no one will want to live there. And that will be the end of Hollow House.' She sat back, triumphantly.

'So,' said Mina, her pencil poised, 'tell me what things you have seen and heard here that you think are not natural. When did it start?'

Mary Ann settled comfortably into her story, her manner suggesting to Mina that she had told it often. 'The very first week I was here, at the end of December, it was, I saw the white lady in the corridor. I didn't know who she was and I said "excuse me", but she didn't reply. I thought maybe she was a deaf lady, so I went and asked Mrs Malling what was wanted, only she said there was no lady staying here. We both went and looked but there was no one. Mrs Malling said it was a trick of the light but I knew better.'

'What time of day did you see her?'

'It was evening. I carried a candle and saw this great thing that was all pale like a bride.'

'Did you see her face?'

'No, she had her back to me and after I spoke she went away.'

'Did you see where she went?'

'No. When she didn't answer I went back down the corridor to see Mrs Malling and when I looked back the lady had gone.'

'Was it a moonlit night?'

'Oh yes. Full moon. That's when the ghosts come out. It's like day to them. When Mrs Malling said no lady was here that was when I knew what it was I saw. After that I never went down there after moonrise.'

'Whereabouts in the corridor was this lady?'

'Outside the room we use for storing things. The one painted with horses.'

'Do you ever go into that room?'

'I do; just to air it and dust and mop the floor. Mrs Malling has the key and lets me in. I don't like that room.'

'Why not?'

'It's just a feeling I have. It's cold. And I think there's something in there, watching me. I don't like that big mirror. I won't look in it. I think if I was to look in it I might see something I don't want to see.'

'But what have you seen apart from the white lady?'

Mary Ann gave a little smile, the smile of someone who knew something that others did not. 'Things move. All sorts of things. I put them down and then when I next look they are somewhere else. I thought at first it was Susan playing tricks on me, but she said not and I believe her. She sees it too. Cups and plates — they sometimes slide along the shelf on their own. I've seen that happen with my own eyes. And when I go to look at them there isn't anything there, no reason why they should have moved. It's almost like — a child playing. A bit of mischief. I heard it laugh once. At least that was what it sounded like. Not a nice laugh, either. Grandfather said —' she paused.

'Yes?'

'It's not nice to think about, but he said that there was a bad child lived in this house once. And a bad nursemaid. And they both disappeared and no one knew what became of them. But sometimes he hints that he knows something more. And it isn't anything good.'

Susan Parker was aged sixteen. She was a small, slight, pale girl and unlike Mary Ann she looked frightened. Her father John was an agricultural labourer and her older sisters were in service in Clayton and Burgess Hill. Before coming to Hollow House she used to help her mother at home and she and her younger brothers tended a small plot of vegetables and looked after some chickens. When the owner of the big house was looking for maidservants it had seemed like a good opportunity to work indoors where it was warm and clean and she was very happy to be given a place. She had no complaints about the work. Mr and Mrs Malling had treated her very fairly and Mr Honeyacre was a kind gentleman. Mrs Honeyacre used to smile and be cheerful when she first came, but then that all changed. Things happened that were very upsetting, things she couldn't explain and she knew that they were not natural.

'Tell me about these things,' said Mina.

Susan's mouth trembled as she spoke. 'Soon after I came here I saw the white lady upstairs and I knew what it was because Mary Ann had seen her too. Only, when I saw her, she walked right through the closed door. I saw her face, too. She had a horrible expression — eyes sunk right into her head, mouth open as if she was crying and couldn't stop. I thought that she was suffering a great sadness that nothing could make better. And then things started to move — little things at first, like plates and bowls, they would slide along the shelf without anyone touching them. I have seen things jump right off a shelf when I was on the other side of the room and no one else was there. Or I would hear them falling to the floor and breaking when I was outside the room and when I went in there would be broken pieces on the floor and no one about. Once I went into the dining room and all the chairs had been turned over.' She took a deep gulp of breath. 'But that wasn't the worst thing.'

Mina said nothing but waited for the girl to go on.

'I feel things, too. I hear things. Sometimes there is a hand laid on my arm when no one is beside me. I can feel it is a hand; I can feel the fingers and the nails. And it's not warm like a living hand, but cold like a corpse. Often I hear a woman crying. I remarked on it but no one else could hear it. They said it was my fancy, or the wind in the chimneys, but it wasn't.' Susan's eyes were wide and bright. She pressed the hem of her apron to her forehead and shuddered. Still, Mina said nothing; she sensed that there was more to come.

Susan wiped her face and tried to compose herself. 'One day, Mrs Malling asked me to go into the storeroom to dust. I didn't like to as I thought there might be bad things in there. But I had to do what I was told. She has the key and let me in. I started to work and then I saw it. There is a child's toy there, a rocking horse. It comes from a time past, before Mr and Mrs Honeyacre lived here. I never touched it, I never went near it, but it started up all on its own, back and forth, back and forth, and the wood creaked like it was hurting and then I heard the child laughing, only it wasn't a nice laugh, it was a wicked laugh and I think I screamed. Then Mrs Malling came running and found me on the floor. I think I must have fainted. And the horse was still rocking away. It was still moving. Mrs Malling saw it. She said it was just the floorboards settling because of me walking about, but I don't think it was. So I won't go in there anymore. And Mary Ann and me, we don't come in when it's full dark. And even now, even in the light, I still feel afraid.'

When Susan had gone Mina studied her notes and was quite absorbed in them until there came a knock at the door. It was Mrs Malling.

'I am sorry to say, Miss, that the rain has ruined all our plans,' she said, 'but we are to have luncheon at the usual time and tea at five o'clock. Mrs Blunt has made her special sponge cake and a fruit loaf, which you really must try. And there will be steak pie for dinner. That is Mr Honeyacre's favourite.' She paused. 'I do hope Mary Ann and Susan were properly respectful and told you what you wanted to know.'

'They have been very helpful, thank you,' said Mina. 'I have a great deal to think about now. I only wish I could see one half of the things that they have seen.'

'Oh, you don't want that, do you, Miss?' asked Mrs Malling with some surprise. 'Why, most ladies would go a long way not to see such things, if such things exist. I know you have been to séances and all, but this is something very unsettling.'

'It is. I was considering consulting Reverend Ashbrook, but now it looks as though I shall not be able to meet him before I go home.'

'Do you think he should come here and say some prayers?' asked Mrs Malling. 'I'm not saying there is anything in what Mary Ann and Susan say, but it might make them feel better.'

'Susan told me you saw the rocking horse move on its own after she had fainted.'

'I did. I was outside the room and heard her fall to the floor in a faint and when I went in it was moving, but I told her that was just the floorboards. They are old boards, Miss, and will bend a little in some places as you step on them. I don't think there was anything more in it than that.'

'You are almost certainly right,' said Mina. 'Have you ever seen plates and cups fall off the shelves as Susan has?' She glanced about the room, but the ornaments on the mantelpiece resolutely refused to fling themselves to the floor.

'There have been some things broken, but I put that down to carelessness. Things not put away properly.'

Mina nodded and closed her notebook. 'Is Dr Hamid about? I would like to speak to him.'

'Yes, I believe he is in the library. He was with Mr Honeyacre this last hour looking at antiquities and now says he needs to consult a book.'

Mina thanked Mrs Malling and sought out Dr Hamid in the library. He was seated at the reading desk, poring over a volume entitled *The Antiquities and Customs of Sussex*. Whatever it was he was looking for he had clearly not found it and was content to put his book aside. It was an opportunity for Mina to advise him fully of all she had learned thus far. He listened carefully and with some concern about the tragedy of the Lassiters, the supposed curse on the village, the infernal child, the missing nursemaid, the sightings of the white lady, the mischievous rocking horse and disobedient chinaware. She also felt obliged to mention Richard's visit and the fact that her brother had been responsible for the noises in the church, upon which he pressed a hand to his forehead and groaned. Mina reassured him that since Richard had not tried to repeat his visit she was hopeful that he had been able to return to London before the roads were flooded and Dr Hamid expressed his sincere wishes that this was the case.

They studied Mina's notes together and agreed that thus far there was no real evidence of anything attributable to spirit visitations other than old legends and sights and sounds that could all be explained by natural events.

'My main concern at present is not the laying of ghosts or placating wandering spirits, but the health of the living,' said Dr Hamid.

'Yes, I was hoping that Reverend Ashbrook could come here after church and offer some comfort and good advice, but that will not happen this Sunday. I am less worried about Mary Ann. She has had fewer troublesome experiences than Susan and since she is Ned Copper's granddaughter she has a more robust attitude to such things. Susan, on the other hand, is easily frightened and sees and feels and hears ghosts everywhere. I can only assume it is Mr Honeyacre's kindness to his servants that keeps her here. I am also very worried indeed about Mrs Honeyacre. Mrs Jordan had planned to bring her back to Brighton with us on Monday, but that is now impossible.'

Dr Hamid tapped the volume on the desk with his fingertips, deep in thought.

'Have you learned anything of interest?' asked Mina.

'Possibly. This story you have just told me of the Lassiters' missing son. There may or may not be a connection, but Mr Honeyacre asked me to look at some items amongst his collection of curios. There are some unusual fragments and he wondered if I could comment on them from a medical point of view.'

'Fragments?' queried Mina.

'Yes. He showed me some splinters of wood. They were dressed and varnished wood — he thought perhaps the remains of a casket, but so old that it was hard to tell. And there was a piece of fabric that had been found with them, which appeared to be velvet. It was dark with age and decay, but I think it might once have been red. There was another object found together with these things that Mr Honeyacre wanted me to identify. Of that one I had no doubt. It was a tooth. Almost certainly a mammalian tooth. If human it was far too small to be that of an adult. Beyond that, I could not offer an opinion.'

'It sounds like the remains of a burial,' said Mina. 'Where were these things discovered? In the graveyard at St Mond's? Given the heavy rains we have experienced I would not be at all surprised if old burials were sometimes exposed to the elements by the weather. Surely such things should not be made part of a curiosity collection, but given a proper Christian reburial?'

Dr Hamid looked very serious and took a deep breath before he replied. 'It appears that the items were discovered by one of the villagers, who drew a little map to show the location and brought it and the remains to Mr Honeyacre. They were not found in the graveyard, but just outside it. They were buried in unconsecrated ground.'

Luncheon was a gloomy affair. Kitty ate almost nothing and Nellie's efforts at brightening the atmosphere by discussing the costume ball fell on stony ground, even after Mr Honeyacre tried to join in the conversation with desperation flickering in his eyes.

The dishes were not yet ready to be cleared when there was a patter of rapid footsteps outside. 'Is that the ghost?' whispered Mina to Nellie. 'I rather wish it was, as I would have something to say to it.'

When the door opened they saw not a ghost but the flushed face of Mary Ann. 'Oh, Mr Gillespie,' she gasped. 'I am so sorry to interrupt, but there is a gentleman and his companion come to the back door as it would not be right to do anything else in their condition as they are dreadfully travel-stained. Their carriage broke down in the mud on the way from Clayton and they have walked all the way here. They say they have come to stay.'

'To stay?' remarked Mr Gillespie, with the slightly raised eyebrow that, on his features, served as astonishment. 'Well that cannot be right as no other guests are expected.' He glanced quizzically at his master.

'That is true,' said Mr Honeyacre, who seemed equally mystified. 'I have invited no one else. But perhaps they are bound elsewhere and in view of the weather could go no further. A gentleman, you say?'

'Yes, sir. The older man was very well-dressed and both are respectable looking.'

'Well, if he is a gentleman and he and his companion are in need of accommodation in such dreadful weather we can hardly turn them away,' said Mr Honeyacre mildly. 'Did he give a name?'

'Yes, sir, he said he was called Hope. Mr Arthur Wallace Hope.'

Chapter Eight

On hearing this momentous news, Mr Honeyacre, with profound apologies to the company, left the table at once and hurried to speak to his unexpected guests.

Mina was silent. Out of the corner of her eye she could see Nellie and Dr Hamid glancing at her with concern, but she did nothing to acknowledge this. Viscount Hope, who preferred the humbler appellation of Mr Arthur Wallace Hope, was the last man in the world Mina might wish to encounter. Her friends were well aware of this, but even they did not know all the reasons.

While Mina waited for further news she clung desperately to the idea that Mr Honeyacre would soon rejoin the company to reveal to his great regret that the new arrival had proved to be a flagrant impostor who had been peremptorily sent away.

That pleasant anticipation was swept away like a fool's dream when, a few minutes later, Mr Honeyacre returned in a froth of excitement.

'Well,' he gasped, 'it is true and what a remarkable thing! Our visitor is indeed the renowned Lord Hope and there is a young gentleman called Mr Beckler who has come with him on purpose to see the house. It appears that his Lordship's letter replying to mine did not arrive, but no matter! It is such an honour to entertain a man of his erudition and courage.'

Mina clasped her fork hard enough to leave imprints on her fingers.

Mr Arthur Wallace Hope was a man of immense presence and influence, a tall deep-chested vigorous individual with expressive eyes, winning voice and flowing hair, who had created a sensation in Brighton the previous autumn. Fate had decreed a gilded life for Mr Hope, awarding him both a title and a landed estate. Most men with his advantages would have been content to idle away their days with empty and frivolous pursuits. Mr Hope, however, thrived on travel and danger. A hero of the Crimean War he had later earned renown as an explorer, having accompanied Dr David Livingstone on his expedition to Zanzibar in 1866. He had published a memoir of his African adventures, which was already in its third printing. Mr Hope, priding himself on possessing the common touch which enabled him to converse with men of all stations in life, had toured Britain to deliver stirring lectures on his adventures to enthralled audiences of susceptible youths and even more susceptible ladies.

He had recently taken to the study of spiritualism in a substantial way and his compelling words had brought numerous others into the fold of believers. Mr Hope's enthusiasm had, however, led him to dismiss out of hand any accusations of fraud perpetrated by those mediums he championed, even where there was convincing evidence of their guilt. He was neither a foolish nor a gullible man, but having once formed an idea nothing could sway him from the conviction that he was entirely right. This flaw led him either to ignore any evidence that suggested that he was mistaken or recast it in his own mind to the contrary purpose.

As far as Mina was concerned Mr Hope was as entitled to hold his opinions as she was to disagree with them, but on his visit to Brighton he had taken up a cause that she had been unable to ignore. Mr Hope had appointed himself the champion of self-proclaimed spirit medium Miss Hilarie Eustace, who had recently been confined to prison after being found guilty of extortion. Undeterred by the clearest evidence of criminality, Hope had started a vigorous campaign to exonerate Miss Eustace with the intention of obtaining her freedom, restoring her reputation and then using his fame, position and fortune to promote her as a psychic. Mina had been one of the most prominent prosecution witnesses at the trial of Miss Eustace and her confederates. It had therefore been an essential part of Mr Hope's campaign that Mina should make a public statement that she had changed her mind and he had made considerable efforts to convince her to do so.

To his astonishment Mina had been immovable; immune both to his masculine charm and his powers of persuasion, in both of which he had formerly enjoyed complete confidence. His next ploy was to win her over by securing the admiration of her family, a plot that had included financing her brother Richard's hare-brained scheme to produce a play in the Royal Pavilion. When this plan, too, failed, Mr Hope had finally shown his true colours by stooping to threats and blackmail. Mina had resolutely refused to succumb to either and he had then determined to engage a London medical consultant in an attempt to have her declared insane. Fortunately, this had never been carried out.

It would have been easy to denounce Mr Hope as wicked, but Mina was sure that he was not. He was convinced that his espousal of the world of the spirit and dissemination of his message was for the ultimate good of all mankind and was therefore prepared to take whatever action he thought necessary, however cruel, however destructive it might be of the individuals who stood in his way, to achieve his desired result. This was nothing less than that every human being in the world should come to agree with him.

Mina's last encounter with Mr Hope had ended stormily when she had made him a public laughing-stock by exposing one of his delusions in front of the Lord Mayor and Aldermen of Brighton. Finding himself about to be implicated in a scandal involving the wife of a prominent gentleman he had been obliged to quit the town in a hurry. Mina had therefore been most relieved to learn that he was planning to return to Africa where she hoped he would remain as long as possible and it was her most fervent hope that their paths would never again cross.

Dr Hamid had been present at Mr Hope's shaming and Nellie had been regaled with an account of the affair. However, there was another and far more painful reason why Mina never wanted to see Mr Hope again, one which she was obliged to keep to herself. Her sister, Enid, who was married to Mr Inskip, a solicitor she frequently declared to be the dullest man in the world, had developed an uncontrollable passion for Mr Hope, feelings he had done nothing to discourage. With her husband abroad on business, Enid had conducted a dangerous intrigue with the handsome explorer and had been devastated at his sudden departure. Unless her sister had committed another indiscretion that Mina knew nothing about it was Mr Hope who was responsible for Enid's current delicate state of health. She was residing in London, her emotions running the full gamut between crushing misery and hysterics, being attended to by her mother, anticipating a family event which was due to take place in the summer and dreading her husband's return.

Mr Hope and his travelling companion Mr Beckler had had a hard time reaching their destination. Mr Hope, although a seasoned veteran of battlefield and jungle, a man of determination and courage in the face of all adversity, the word 'failure' having not yet appeared in his vocabulary, had just discovered that he had still to overcome the tribulations of a wet morning in Sussex.

His story, with which he regaled the company later, was that he had informed Mr Honeyacre of his arrival by letter, but had not been aware when he set out for Hollow House that the ill weather might have prevented its delivery.

All had gone moderately well until the approach to Clayton when his carriage had become solidly mired in the road and broken an axle. One of the horses stumbled and sprained a fetlock; the other lost a shoe in the mud. Mr Hope had given the animals into the care of the local farrier, but discovered to his dismay that no suitable replacement carriage or horses could be procured. The residents of Clayton had decided for themselves that to proceed any further would be the act of a madman and declined to risk their property at any price.

Mr Hope would not be denied. His elderly manservant, whom he deemed insufficiently robust to continue such a strenuous journey on foot, was ordered to remain in Clayton where he would assume charge of carriage, horses and the bulk of the luggage and continue on to Hollow House as soon as suitable transport became available. He and his young companion Mr Beckler had unloaded such bags as two men could easily carry and pressed ahead, fighting their way through fresh assaults of howling rain.

It soon became apparent that the road, churned into a semi-liquid sea of slippery brown slime and pebbled with invisible traps for the feet, was too fraught with dangers even for the seasoned traveller. After a brief struggle Hope had decided that the only possible means of progress was to cut across the fields. Here, the rain-pummelled sodden grass, matted into the mud, gave them a little more purchase, but it was an exhausting business, especially as their boots were not designed for such terrain. Some parts of the fields were little more than shallow lakes, reflections of the dull grey sky, and they were obliged to skirt around them as best they could, so as not to sink into the clinging mire; this exercise doubling the distance they needed to travel.

A small wooden bridge across the mill brook had been swept away, but by now both men were so thoroughly wetted that traversing the stream made little difference to the state of their clothing. Mr Hope had waded worse rivers, ones clouded with stinging insects in which dangerous reptiles and savage parasites lurked. Here, he had only to keep his feet, weighed down by the ballast of his luggage, while he and Mr Beckler, who fortunately was young and active, linked arms against the power of the surging waters.

As they finally approached Hollow House they were obliged to acknowledge the impossibility of making themselves presentable to company and sought admission at the servants' entrance to give the least inconvenience to their host. Mr Hope's commanding and assured manner, and the quality of his sodden clothing, had enabled him to gain the proper attention and once Mr Malling had heard his tale the visitors were admitted and Mary Ann dispatched to carry the intelligence.

When Mina received the news she bit her lip but elected to make no comment. She glanced at Nellie and Dr Hamid with the merest shake of the head. Both of them understood by this that they were to remain silent.

In any other circumstances Mr Hope's arrival would have been the signal for Mina's immediate departure. However, the rain was still roaring outside and any possibility of returning home soon had long since vanished into the watery mist. All parties, thought Mina, would simply have to make the best of it. If they were fortunate the remainder of the visit, which she hoped would last no more than a few days, would pass in an icy politeness, nothing of any moment would occur and better weather would eventually provide a thankful escape.

'I have arranged for hot baths, fresh attire and a late luncheon for both the gentlemen and, of course, there will have be some changes to the accommodation,' enthused Mr Honeyacre, blissfully unaware that anyone else in the room was not as enamoured of the situation as he. 'I am sorry to inconvenience guests but needs must. Have no fears, Mr and Mrs Malling will see to everything. I was wondering —' he turned his most appealing expression to Mina and Nellie — 'Miss Scarletti and Mrs Jordan, would you be kind enough to agree to share a room? I will make sure to have a second bed provided and I promise that there will be no diminution of your comfort. Lord Hope must, of course, have a room to himself. His companion, Mr Beckler has kindly agreed to take a room in the west wing and Miss Pet will share her accommodation with Mrs Jordan's maid Zillah. No arrangement is without difficulty but that does seem to be for the best.'

'I am sure we will be perfectly comfortable,' said Nellie.

'I think that will be the best arrangement,' Mina added. Privately she thought that since Mr Hope was a known seducer with a taste for young, married women it would be a good thing if Nellie were to share her room. There would be no opportunity for him to satisfy his predatory instincts. No roaming ghost instilled as much terror in Mina as the prospect of Mr Hope prowling the corridors of Hollow House at night in search of his favourite game. Despite this precaution there was still a danger. Both Nellie and Mr Hope would be living under the same roof for some little time and if Mr Stevenson, the detective, came to know of it the suspicion alone might prove damaging.

Having addressed his guests, Mr Honeyacre, clearly in a state of breathless excitement about the arrival of Mr Hope, began darting back and forth as new ideas for the comfort of the honoured arrival occurred to him with every passing minute. On one occasion, Mina saw him clutching his copy of *The Brighton Hauntings* and trembling with the anticipation of receiving the author's signature on the revered volume.

While the maids made the necessary changes to the rooms, Mina took the opportunity of discussing Mr Hope's unsavoury reputation with Nellie. 'We must be sure that you are never left alone with him,' said Mina. 'There must be no opportunity for any misinterpretation.'

'And what of Kitty?'

'I don't want to alarm her,' said Mina. 'She is agitated enough already without adding to her concerns.'

'True,' Nellie admitted. 'I will warn Zillah about Mr Hope's proclivities and ask her to speak to Miss Pet. They are both endowed with more than the usual common sense and between them, they will make a plan to keep Kitty safe. I am thankful that they are sharing a room and the younger girls do not sleep here.'

'That only leaves Mrs Blunt who sleeps alone,' observed Mina. There was a brief pause as they both imagined the consequences of Mr Hope making an attempt on the cook.

'Perhaps we should advise her to sleep with an axe under her pillow,' said Nellie with a smile.

'Perhaps she already does,' said Mina.

The two visitors, having been refreshed and provided with dry clothing as near as could be found to fit them, joined the others in the drawing room a little later and Mr Honeyacre, still in a state of high excitement, made the introductions.

On their first entering the room it was almost instantly apparent to Mina that Mr Honeyacre, who had been busily occupied in ensuring that his noble visitor had every possible comfort, had been so distracted that, while he might have mentioned that there was a good company present, he had not actually named them.

As a result of this oversight, Mr Hope was clearly thunderstruck to be confronted with Mina. His friendly smile vanished and there was a moment when his cheeks lost their accustomed ruddy outdoor complexion and turned the colour of parchment. He hesitated and misstepped so abruptly that Mr Beckler, who was a few paces behind, very nearly collided with him and was obliged to make a sudden stop. Mr Hope recovered himself quickly. During the introductions performed by Mr Honeyacre he greeted Mina with the briefest acceptable inclination of the head. Nevertheless, his mouth twitched with anxiety while his eyes settled into a cold stare and he was obliged to look away.

Mr Hope was, if anything, even more displeased to see Dr Hamid and adopted towards him an attitude of rigid courtesy. An observer not acquainted with Mr Hope might have imagined that his initial slight recoil on seeing the doctor was due to a prejudice against persons of colour, but Mr Hope, to his credit, judged all men on their individual worth and often said that he had met African guides whom he trusted above any English gentleman. Dr Hamid he knew to be both a good friend to Mina and a man of intelligence, whose opinions were much valued. Both these attributes inevitably gave him cause for concern.

In the atmosphere of restrained politeness it was clear that no-one thought it wise to reveal to their host that the three of them were already acquainted. That could have led to a difficult conversation regarding the circumstances of their last confrontation, something that none of them felt impelled to describe. It was a weapon that Mina knew she could hold in reserve, but she had the uncomfortable feeling that were she to use it Mr Hope could talk his way out of any blame and give a contrary account of the matter that would be believable to anyone who had not been present. The result of the unexpected encounter in the drawing room was therefore an unspoken chilly truce.

Mr Hope, perhaps in an effort to create a distraction, ushered forward his companion for the approbation of the company. 'Allow me to recommend to you my friend Mr Beckler,' said Mr Hope. 'He is a great expert in the art of photography and very much in demand by ladies and gentlemen of position in the county of Middlesex for portraiture.'

Mina thought herself to be the very last person to judge a stranger by appearances. To be born beautiful or ugly or plain was a mere accident and said nothing about character, which was the only thing that mattered. Plainness in a person with a fine character could look pleasing and, conversely, when character was wanting outward beauty seemed flawed and artificial. Nevertheless, she could not help disliking Mr Beckler at the very first view. He was aged about thirty and taller even than the towering figure of Mr Hope, but unlike Hope's broad and muscular physique his form was slender. Mr Hope had a still and unbending stance. Mr Beckler appeared restless, constantly turning his shoulders or his head, as if searching about him for some opportunity, the nature of which he kept to himself. His face was long and pale, with a patchy tuft of beard, short bristly moustache and small, probing dark eyes that peered from behind unruly wisps of hair like a snake through grass.

'How interesting,' said Mr Honeyacre, blandly. He gave Mr Beckler that meaningful look which indicated that he had identified him in the scheme of things as being not quite a gentleman. 'But tell me, Mr Beckler, do you believe that the photograph can replace painting or drawing? I am not at all sure that it can. I say that as a collector of art.'

Mr Beckler, who obviously cared nothing for Mr Honeyacre's artistic pretensions and may well have heard this argument many times before, afforded him an intense stare. 'I think that they both have their place.'

'Oh, well, there is the *carte de visite*, of course, when a picture must be made many times over. I understand that,' said Mr Honeyacre dismissively. 'My first wife had a collection of them and they can be very informative and useful. And I suppose, too, that a photograph may be achieved more quickly and cheaply than a painting, for those that require such a service.'

'But there is far more to it than that,' said Mr Hope. 'A photograph by its precise chemical nature can produce a picture of something which the human eye is unable to see. I do not refer to something purely from the imagination of an artist, or even something artificially presented to the camera and intended to cheat the lens. No, I refer to what is true and real, and undeniably a fact of nature. And,' he added with a complacent smile, 'it is a truth that can no longer be derided or denied by materialists since it is their acclaimed science that reveals it.'

'Photography is a valid scientific process,' said Dr Hamid. 'One cannot deny that. And there are many things that exist but are beyond the capacity of the human eye to see. The microscope and the telescope have taught us that. There are animals whose perception in some areas is far beyond the power of man, such as the sensitive nose of the dog.'

'And yet, materialists say that they will believe in nothing but what they see with their own eyes,' said Mr Hope, scornfully. 'That is their great fallacy, one which I intend to cure them of.'

Mina wasn't sure that this was exactly what materialists said and wished she had a convincing answer that would not be trampled upon by Mr Hope. 'But perhaps Mr Beckler would like to tell us about his pictures?' she said.

Mr Beckler smiled. He had teeth like a wolf. 'One of my very special services to clients is the memorial photograph. The *memento mori*, as it is sometimes known. I create a portrait of a loved one who has recently passed away, something for a bereaved family to treasure.' His eyes roved about the company and settled on Mr Honeyacre, as if assessing him as the most likely potential subject for the near future.

'You take portraits of people lying on their deathbeds?' asked Nellie.

'I do. If the deceased has never been photographed in life it will be the only picture of that individual the family will ever have. It must, of course, be done with sensitivity and good taste. Sometimes the client wishes the loved one to be seated in a more natural pose, such as in a favourite armchair, surrounded by family members and they will then seem to be sleeping. Or, a grieving mother will hold her dead child in her arms. I can, if the family so requests, paint open eyes on the photographic print so that the subject appears to be alive. But, recently, I took a picture that showed more than just the body of the deceased. There was something in that portrait which I could not see through my camera lens, which no one present saw and yet it was recorded on the plate.' He paused and his gaze slithered about the room, passing over the rapt faces of his listeners. 'I had taken a portrait of a spirit.'

There was a moment of astonished silence before Mina could not help but venture a query. At least, she thought, Mr Beckler did serve a useful purpose, since she could address questions to him without having to engage with Mr Hope. 'Excuse me, but could you describe the form this took and how you knew it was a spirit?'

'But, of course. Its appearance on the plate was like a dark smudge and I was fully prepared to find that the picture had been ruined by the intrusion of dust. Once I had developed it, however, I could clearly see a transparent white cloud in the shape of a head. It hovered above the body of the deceased, whose features it closely resembled. I should add that when the family saw the portrait they were astonished and all said that the face of the spirit was, without a doubt, that of their loved one. It was a very great comfort to them.'

'Did you know before the photograph was taken that such a form might appear?' asked Mina.

'Not at all. It was a very great surprise. But, following that incident, I have resolved to make a study of the matter and conduct experiments to better understand the conditions required to produce portraits of spirits.'

'Have you had much success?' asked Mr Honeyacre, his interest in photography newly kindled.

Mr Beckler gave a smile of regret. 'Not as yet. The spirits are fickle; they do not come at my command.'

'Mr Beckler knew of my interest in spiritualism since I had given a lecture on the subject in Twickenham, where he resides,' said Mr Hope. 'And he was astute enough to realise the importance of what he had achieved. Another man might have dismissed the spirit portrait as a mere artefact of the photographic process and even striven to make changes to his methods to eliminate what might have seemed to him to be an imperfection. Indeed, it is very possible that other, less perceptive men have done precisely that and so destroyed valuable evidence of the persistence of life after bodily death. Fortunately, Mr Beckler brought the picture to me. It was a significant moment. Pictorial proof of the existence of the spirit.'

Mr Beckler looked quietly triumphant.

'Are you a medium?' asked Mr Honeyacre, breathlessly.

'It is hard to be sure,' said Mr Beckler, doing his best to appear modest.

'Myself, I am certain of it,' said Mr Hope. 'But, as I have learned, mediums vary in their skills. Some produce visible manifestations, others demonstrate spirit messages written on slates, still others do no more than hear voices. Mr Beckler's psychic talent lies in the production of photographic impressions. At present, therefore, I am loath to attempt to develop him in other areas as I fear that might diminish his already proven powers. For the future — who can tell?'

Dr Hamid addressed the humble psychic. 'So your visit to Hollow House is for the purpose of photographing the spirit or spirits reputed to be haunting here?'

'That was the case,' admitted Mr Beckler, 'but unfortunately my camera, its stand and plates, all had to be left behind in Clayton in the charge of Mr Hope's servant. They are too heavy to transport across muddy fields on foot and too fragile to risk. As far as capturing spirit images goes I shall therefore be obliged to rely on my powers of observation and memory, and with Mr Honeyacre's permission I hope to return another day.'

Mina glanced at Mr Honeyacre, but it was obvious to her that some portion of the reverence he held for the famous Lord Hope had now, by the process of proximity, attached itself to his protégé. This did not promise well.

The conversation was interrupted by the sound of the dinner bell. As Mina entered the dining room she reflected on what she knew about photography and discovered that it was almost nothing. She had never sat for an individual portrait and her only experience was the photographs taken at her sister Enid's wedding, when, as part of the family group, she had been placed carefully so as to conceal her unusual shape. In the finished portrait only her face had appeared, a small round disc like the moon with dark eyes like craters, hovering without a body between the shoulders of her brothers. She recalled that there had been a great deal of fussing with glass plates and chemicals, but the result had been forthcoming before too long and fortunately did not include any family ghosts.

There were, of course, photographers aplenty in Brighton and she was familiar with the appearance of cameras. But how they actually acted to produce the final picture she had no idea. Was the camera a kind of eye? And if it was, was it more or less accurate, more or less easily confused than the organ it mimicked? She felt she would like to know more.

As they took their places at the dining table it became clear that Mr Hope was fully recovered both from the ordeal of his journey and the shock of seeing Mina and Dr Hamid. Despite the fact that he was dressed in a suit belonging to Mr Gillespie that did not fit him, as it was too tight, he carried off that inconvenience with aplomb and good humour. Mr Beckler was in what must have been Mr Malling's Sunday best, loose around the shoulders and several inches too short in the leg, the deficiency being overcome by a long pair of shooting socks.

Once, in the days before they had acknowledged themselves as enemies, Mr Hope had dined with Mina's family and his object on that occasion had been to charm the ladies and ingratiate himself with Richard, the better to influence Mina. Now that she saw him in different company she made a careful observation of his manner towards the other diners, to try and judge his intentions, while making an effort not to appear to be doing so.

Kitty sat quietly at the table with downcast eyes and said almost nothing throughout the meal. She ate sparingly and occasionally slipped a small item into her pocket, a wafer or a morsel of pastry, undoubtedly a treat for Little Scrap. Mr Hope regarded her with politeness and courtesy, as befitted her status as lady of the house, but did not address her. Perhaps, thought Mina, Kitty's wan features did not appeal to him, or did he draw the line at attempting to seduce his host's wife under their roof?

Nellie was quite another matter, an undoubted beauty with a fine figure and a married lady not in the company of her husband. The glances Mr Hope threw at her were more than just appreciative, they were predatory. To such a man, fully aware of his attractions for the opposite sex, she was a prospect ripe for adventure without the danger of incurring the wrath of the host. Nellie very sensibly paid him no attention, even when he smiled at her and raised a glass of wine in tribute.

Mr Hope took care to address neither Mina nor Dr Hamid and since Mr Beckler was already his acolyte it was scarcely necessary to pay any attention to him. His conversation was almost entirely directed at Mr Honeyacre. Just as Mr Hope had once been the 'mark' of fraudsters who had rightly assessed him to be the type most easily taken in by their schemes, so he had weighed Mr Honeyacre and found him ideal for his purposes, a man who owned and lived in a haunted house, a dedicated believer in spiritualism and overwhelmed with delight at entertaining a member of the aristocracy. Mr Hope was fully at his ease.

Dinner began with savouries and soup and Mr Hope especially fell to with gusto. 'I cannot fully express to you, Mr Honeyacre, the excitement I experienced when I received your letter. I must apologise profoundly for the delay in my response — my letter to you that sadly did not arrive — but I was away from home making arrangements for my proposed return to Africa to find Dr Livingstone. I saw your letter only a few days ago and it filled me with tremendous eagerness to visit Hollow House. I have attended many séances, of course, with the most excellent mediums and received results that were highly evidential. But your invitation to experience an actual haunted house was something I could not ignore.'

'Your expertise in this area will be most appreciated,' said Mr Honeyacre. 'I should also tell you that Miss Scarletti is knowledgeable on these matters and I am sure she will be delighted to assist you.'

'What I need to do first of all,' said Mr Hope, as if Mina's name had never been mentioned, 'is to locate the focus of the psychic energy.'

Mr Beckler nodded in agreement. For some reason he chose to turn his eyes towards Mina with a grin then stuffed savouries into his mouth and chewed energetically. It was not a pleasant sight and she turned away.

'The location you seek is almost certainly the first floor corridor and the room where the antiquities are stored,' said Mr Honeyacre. 'It is where the activity has occurred and the ghost of the white lady has been seen, as well as some curious movements of a rocking horse.'

'Ah yes, the unhappy Mrs Lassiter, as you have told me, searching for her lost child. The account of that matter, supplied by your housekeeper, has been of very great importance. That is a highly significant location without a doubt, but we must always consider that it might not be the primary one.'

Mr Honeyacre opened his eyes very wide and leaned forward to catch his guest's words of wisdom.

'Sometimes,' said Mr Hope, 'where there are hauntings they are merely the symptoms of a larger incursion, one that has spread from somewhere quite different, a place we might not suspect and it is that place that we need to find. The secret might lie far back in time, beyond living memory, existing only in folklore, the spoken word never recorded but passed down through the generations.'

'I am afraid I learned nothing from the gentleman from whom I purchased the property. In fact, he had never lived here,' said Mr Honeyacre, regretfully.

'And you tell me that Mr and Mrs Malling reside in the new wing, where nothing psychic has occurred,' said Mr Hope. 'Of course, we cannot rule out the possibility that that wing is a hotbed of psychic activity which is only apparent to a sensitive.'

'There were some curious noises in the church while we were there,' said Dr Hamid, eliciting raised eyebrows from Mr Hope and a smile from Mina, 'but I rather thought they were due to mice.'

'So many incidents of psychic activity have been explained away by accusing innocent vermin,' said Mr Hope with a laugh, as if psychic phenomena were a far more probable explanation, which to his mind they probably were. 'But yes, the little church which we saw on our way here, that could well be another focus.'

'You should speak to Ned Copper,' said Mina mischievously. 'He is an elderly resident of the village and has many tales to tell of its history.'

Mr Hope said nothing to Mina, but glanced at Mr Honeyacre for confirmation.

'That is true,' said Mr Honeyacre. 'I can't say how reliable he is, but I think it would be a good thing to interview him and write down what he says.'

The maids arrived to remove the soup plates and bring in the fish course.

'I ought to mention,' said Mr Honeyacre, 'that Mary Ann is Ned Copper's granddaughter.' He nodded towards the maid. 'The maids both live in the village as neither of them feel comfortable about sleeping here after dark. Both have witnessed disturbances in several locations and seen the ghost of the white lady.'

Mr Hope's eyes brightened. 'I shall certainly interview them both, as well as Mr Copper. Despite the lack of Mr Beckler's photographic apparatus our time here will not be wasted. In fact, I can already see that we will be extremely busy.' He glanced up as his plate was laid before him and the fish was served. 'I should like to know from Mary Ann if she has any stories of the village which she might like to describe, something that might explain what has been happening here.'

Mary Ann hesitated. 'Don't be afraid, Mary Ann,' said Mr Honeyacre, encouragingly. 'You may speak.'

'Well, sir, I only know what my grandfather has said, but he has always told me that there is a curse on the village.'

'A curse?' exclaimed Mr Hope, with some anticipation. 'Well, that is extremely interesting. Does he know its origins?'

'He says it goes a long way back, before the last people who lived here.'

'As far back as the family who built the house?' asked Mr Honeyacre. 'The Wigmores?'

'More than that. Long before Queen Bess even, when there was a cruel King who cut off the heads of his wives.'

Mr Hope was now all attention and turned around in his chair, his eyes on Mary Ann. 'Do go on.'

Mary Ann, having been given permission to speak, allowed a sly smile to play around her lips. 'Grandfather says that, in those old days, on the top of Clayton Hill there was a gallows. And there were cruel laws so many folks were hanged there who didn't deserve to die and then they were left hanging till their flesh was all rotted away. Soon there were just the bones left behind. Afterwards the bones were gone, too, and so they never got a Christian burial. And now all those folks have been forgotten and there is no one to pray for them and they are lost souls forever a-wandering and a-crying out.'

There was a profound silence in the room.

'Mary Ann, continue to serve the fish,' said Mr Honeyacre.

'Yes, sir,' she said and moved on.

Mr Hope turned to his host. 'Did you know about this?'

Mr Honeyacre shook his head. 'Executions in the sixteenth century? No.'

'Hmmm.' Mr Hope's broad brow furrowed in thought. 'I will need to consult a map. I want to see where that place is with reference to Hollow House and the village and the church. If I could draw a line between them it might reveal a flow of psychic energy. The gallows is long gone, I suppose.'

'Oh yes, there are just the two windmills there now.'

'The windmills!' exclaimed Mr Hope, excitedly. 'I saw them as we came across the fields. So they are on the site of the old gallows? How extraordinary! How long have they been there?'

Mr Honeyacre searched his memory. 'The post mill used to be elsewhere and it was dismantled and brought here maybe ten or twenty years ago. The tower mill is more recent. At the time I purchased Hollow House it had only just been built.'

'And prior to the windmills? What was on the hill?'

'I'm afraid I don't know.'

'It shouldn't be hard to discover. Oh, this is wonderful news! It would not surprise me if a windmill could act as a psychic focus. It is so much in touch with the elements, with the forces of nature. If it was on the site of a former gallows that would be a powerful influence. And two windmills together! How unusual! I have never known of such a thing.' He turned to his companion and pointed an authoritative finger. 'Beckler, if the weather permits we must go up there tomorrow. And we must make sure to speak to Ned Copper and see what tales he has to tell.'

'Yes, sir,' said Mr Beckler, automatically.

'Mr Honeyacre,' said Mr Hope cheerfully, 'I now have every expectation that I will discover the reason behind the haunting and then the unhappy souls that have been troubling you may finally be laid to rest!'

'Oh, I do hope so!' said Mr Honeyacre. 'And I know Miss Scarletti will be eager to play whatever part she can. I have found her good sense and sound advice most valuable.'

Mina glanced up from her plate at the mention of her name and saw Mr Beckler's eyes slide an amused gaze in her direction. She suspected that, following the awkward encounter in the drawing room, Mr Hope had taken the opportunity to tell Mr Beckler about her, suggesting either that she was an unacknowledged medium, or a determined opponent whom he intended to tame, or a woman who lived on the brink of insanity. There was no reason he could not have represented her as all three.

'And now I must ask you all an important question,' said Mr Hope, looking about him. He waited until he was certain that he had the full attention of everyone at the table. 'Does anyone present have mediumistic powers? Please speak up if you think you do. This could be the key to the resolution of the mystery. I myself have only the smallest of gifts, if my poor efforts are anything to judge by,' he added, with a little exhalation of regret.

'I quite am sure that I do not,' said Mr Honeyacre, 'and neither does my dear wife. If we did then I might have been able to resolve this unhappy situation without appealing for assistance.'

'Most emphatically no,' said Nellie, in a tone that discouraged any contradiction.

'I also answer no,' said Dr Hamid, mildly.

'And Mr Beckler's abilities lie in the photographic portrait,' said Mr Hope. 'There is however, I believe, a sensitive at the table.'

All eyes turned to Mina.

'Miss Scarletti!' exclaimed Mr Honeyacre, in astonishment. 'Why have you hidden this from us?'

'I have nothing to hide,' said Mina. 'If Mr Hope is referring to me then he is dreadfully mistaken.'

'Ah, but time will tell,' said Mr Hope, with a superior smile. 'One day your powers will burst forth and that will be a great and glorious day for spiritualism!'

Mina finished her fish as the table fell into silence, waiting for her powers to burst forth. 'But not today, I fear,' she said.

'I can be patient,' said Mr Hope. 'Mr Honeyacre, I assume that Mr and Mrs Malling and your excellent cook have not claimed any mediumistic powers?'

'They have not. And I can speak for my manservant, Mr Gillespie, and Kitty's maid, Miss Pet, as well.'

'I can say the same for my maid,' said Nellie.

'Well, we shall see what emerges,' said Mr Hope, undeterred. 'In my experience, those who believe they have no powers often experience an unexpected awakening when in a location of concentrated spiritual energy. Just such a location as this, in fact.' Not everyone at the table viewed this prospect with such obvious enthusiasm as did Mr Hope.

The fish plates were removed and were succeeded by a large and fragrant steak pie with vegetables.

'Do you expect anything further to transpire today?' asked Mr Honeyacre, anxiously.

'I do indeed,' said Mr Hope, who was becoming more confident by the minute. 'It is very clear to me that the best course of action would be to hold a séance. And we must do so without further delay. This room would be ideal.' He turned a searching eye to his host. 'Have you held a séance here before?'

'Er — well, no, I mean, I thought one had to engage a medium to do so and we have none.'

'Oh, we have more than enough psychic power in the house and I am confident that we shall achieve good results. Once dinner is done I will see to the best arrangement of the room.'

'But Mary Ann and Susan will be frightened out of their wits!' protested Mr Honeyacre. 'And my dear wife — I will not have her disturbed for anything!'

'If the maids are nervous they may be sent home before we begin. It will be for the best, as malevolent spirits have been known to be attracted to young girls of the servant class and play their tricks and frighten them, and we do not want anything of that sort preventing innocent unhappy entities contacting us. Mrs Honeyacre,' and here Mr Hope turned his most appealing expression towards Kitty and his tone dropped and softened like the touch of silken velvet, 'I would like most earnestly to reassure you that you will be in no danger at all. In any case —' he pressed his hand to his chest — 'I am here to protect you.'

Kitty, as so many ladies had done before her, melted under his earnest gaze and smiled. 'Oh, Mr Hope, you are too kind!'

Mr Honeyacre sighed. 'If it was only possible to send Kitty away, I would. My dear, what would you like to do?'

'I think,' said Kitty, bravely, 'that if there is an unhappy spirit here it should be given comfort. And I am content to be a part of the company.'

The pie was consumed without relish, although the meat was tender, the gravy delicious and the pastry crisp. The hot pudding that followed brought little consolation. Mr Hope, who had placed himself in charge of the arrangements, expounded on his plans for the séance as if he had now become the master of the house, in which Mr Honeyacre had been demoted to chief steward. As he did so, Mina saw her host's expression harden and grow less comfortable. A viscount Mr Hope might be and an honoured guest, but he had hardly been in the house a few hours before his welcome was wearing thin.

Chapter Nine

'Well,' said Nellie, as she and Mina headed for the parlour, 'we should have expected that, I suppose.'

Immediately on completing his dinner, Mr Hope had risen from the table and begun striding busily back and forth the length of the dining room, issuing orders to the other gentlemen as to how everything was to be made ready for the séance. The ladies had all decided to make their escape. Mina dared not look at Mr Honeyacre, but had no doubt that he was already reconsidering the wisdom of inviting Mr Hope to his home.

As they crossed the hall, which was filled with the authoritative boom of Mr Hope's commands, they encountered Mr Malling, umbrella in hand, conducting Mary Ann and Susan, heavily cloaked against the rain, to their homes in the village. Miss Pet was bringing Little Scrap to her mistress and the two decided to avoid contemplating what was to come by playing with the pampered puppy.

'My fervent wish is for an uneventful evening,' said Mina, as she and Nellie made themselves comfortable before the parlour fire.

'Really?' said Nellie, arching a mischievous eyebrow. 'I could arrange something different if you wish.' Mina was sure that her friend could easily delude Mr Hope. Nellie had always maintained that the best conjuring tricks, assuming a skilled performer, were the simplest ones that required little in the way of special equipment or preparation and therefore appeared all the more mysterious. Her brief career as Miss Foxton the medium had necessitated only several yards of black fabric, which, due to Richard's impecuniosity, Mina had been obliged to purchase, and a loan of the Scarlettis' best oriental vase.

'Please promise me you will not,' begged Mina. 'In fact, I am relying on you to look out for trickery and put a stop to it if you can. If there should be any manifestation during the séance it will only strengthen Mr Hope's delusion that I am a medium and I will never hear the end of it.'

'Perhaps you ought not to attend,' suggested Nellie.

'I will still be in the house, so I doubt that that will make any difference.'

'Do you think Mr Hope is a cheat?' asked Nellie.

Mina considered this. 'He is a true believer and I suppose he would imagine cheating to be unnecessary, but I also know that he will stoop to anything in pursuit of his goal, which is to draw others to his cause. So I would not dismiss the idea. If he does cheat, however, I think he will not be adept at it. You would easily find him out.'

'And what about his faithful follower, Mr Beckler?'

'I don't know. It is worrying enough that he is Mr Hope's disciple. I would not be at all surprised if Mr Hope is funding his experiments in photographing spirits. He has some knowledge of chemicals and optics, so may have a host of tricks that he can play to deceive us. However, both gentlemen arrived here with little more than a few necessities and that may limit what they can achieve.'

Mina cast her mind back to the séances of Miss Eustace, which she had attended with her mother. Crucially, while all the attention of the sitters was on the medium, events had occurred which were only possible if there was an accomplice present. Sometimes the accomplice posed as one of the sitters, sometimes the accomplice lurked outside, waited for darkness and then crept in and walked about invisibly to wreak fear in the hearts of the faithful. Accomplices could also be placed outside the séance room throughout the performance, rapping on walls.

She rose to her feet. 'There are at least some precautions I can take,' she said. 'Come with me. It would be extremely valuable if you could take a look at the room and see if there are any opportunities for cheating.'

When they returned to the dining room, Mr Hope was still giving orders, which were being carried out by Mr Beckler, Mr Gillespie and Dr Hamid. Mr Honeyacre was on one of the settles looking helplessly miserable. The large dining table had been moved against one wall. The linen runner folded, silver candlesticks, cruet set and other dishes had been placed on the sideboard. The round tea table had been granted pre-eminence and was placed centrally under the efflorescence of ceiling lamps. Seven dining chairs circled the table and the rest were being placed in a line next to the sideboard.

'Mr Hope,' said Mina. 'Might I suggest something?'

He looked around. There was a pause during which he appeared to be considering asking her to leave, but thought better of it. 'By all means,' he said coldly.

'With Mr Honeyacre's permission, of course,' Mina added.

Mr Honeyacre looked up as if surprised that he had been addressed. 'Oh, yes; yes, please do.'

Dr Hamid and Mr Beckler had both stopped what they were doing and were staring at Mina. On both their faces was the expression of anticipation that often appears in a theatrical audience which has just seen a curtain go up.

'I am sure,' said Mina, 'that everyone would like to avoid any possibility of an accusation of cheating.'

'There will be no cheating,' said Mr Hope, curtly. 'I forbid it and will do everything I can to prevent it.'

'Of course, but when we relate the circumstances to others who are not present will not some people criticise the arrangements and say that this or that thing could have been done? And would it not be an idea to dismiss those doubts before we begin?'

Mr Hope appeared to be biting back a firm retort. Instead, he chewed at his lower lip and gave her a hard stare. 'What do you suggest?'

'You have just seven chairs about the table.'

'Yes, they are for myself, Mr Beckler, Mr and Mrs Honeyacre, Dr Hamid, yourself and Mrs Jordan.' He glanced around to see Nellie, who was walking around the room, looking for all the world like a fashionable lady with no thought in her head other than taking a refreshing turn to banish *ennui*. His eyes lingered on her form a little longer than they ought to have done.

'You consider the smaller table to be preferable to the large one?'

He turned back to Mina. 'I do, for the better transmission of energy between the sitters.'

'What of the other persons in the house? Will they not be here?' asked Mina.

'The servants you mean?'

'Yes.'

He considered this. 'That would make us —' he began to make a calculation.

'Thirteen,' said Mina. 'The remaining six are Mr and Mrs Malling, Miss Pet, Zillah, Mr Gillespie and Mrs Blunt.'

He grunted agreement. 'Thirteen at the table. Not the most propitious number for such a proceeding. And, in any case, the table is not large enough. Besides, none of the servants has shown willingness to be a part of this. Mrs Malling will come in to sweep once the furniture has been rearranged, but after that she will retire from the room.'

'My suggestion is that they should all be in the room when the séance is conducted. They do not need to participate; they may observe from a distance, no more. This is to avoid an accusation of complicity from someone outside. It does happen; do not deny it. I have attended séances of that nature.'

His expression darkened. 'You know my opinion on these matters. It is only when the spirits are unwilling or unable to appear, or the medium has temporarily exhausted his or her powers that certain practices are resorted to in order to ensure a result. It happens no more than one occasion out of a hundred, perhaps a great deal less. The intention of the medium is not trickery, but to avoid disappointing the clients, many of whom are in a grieving state. That is the reason for these ridiculous accusations of cheating.'

'Do you agree,' Mina persisted, 'that it would do no harm to have all persons present in the room?'

After some consideration, he said with some reluctance, 'I agree, it would do no harm.'

'Then let it be so. And there should be light in the room.'

This was a demand too far and Mr Hope's ability to control his annoyance with Mina finally expired. 'Oh, this is quite unreasonable! You know very well that the spirits deplore light. We shall never have any results that way.'

'But,' said Mina patiently, 'we both know that it is the constant theme of the doubters that darkness only serves to give opportunities for fakery. Results from a dark séance will never convince them. This, however, I will concede. It will not be necessary to provide a bright light. Just sufficient to satisfy everyone that no one has left their place.'

Mr Hope was not appeased. 'But this is not an experiment to convince the materialists; it is a sincere effort to contact and comfort the spirits that are causing a disturbance in this house. Nothing more.'

'If you don't mind my saying so,' offered Mr Honeyacre nervously, 'Miss Scarletti's proposals seem very sensible to me. I would like to be as sure as I can of the evidential nature of anything that transpires. The gas can be lit but turned low.'

Mr Hope folded his arms and stared at Mina in what he hoped was an intimidating manner. Mina refused to be cowed. 'I suppose you would like everyone to swear on the Holy Bible that they will not resort to trickery?' he said angrily.

'That is an excellent idea,' said Mina. 'I had not thought of that. I agree with your suggestion.'

He gave an irritated grunt. 'It should not be necessary to point out to you that no one here claims to be a séance medium. No one is taking money to be here. All of us around the table are genuine seekers after the truth.'

'Then I await the results with interest,' said Mina. She turned and left the room. Behind her, she could hear the plaintive tones of Mr Honeyacre's voice asking Mr Hope to comply with her requests.

'I believe we both had the same thought,' said Nellie when they were back in the parlour. 'The large dining table would be hard to tilt; it must have taken several men to move it, but the round one could easily be manipulated. While you were engaging Mr Hope's attention I looked underneath it. With a company seated around, especially if there are gentlemen with long limbs, there would be no room for anyone, even a small child, to hide under it undetected and tap out messages. However, anyone seated there might knock it with a foot. I saw nothing in the way of apparatus to assist with movement, but artifice is still possible without.'

'An eminent professor once said that table tipping was the result of the energies of the sitters combining and producing the movement without their being aware of it,' said Mina. 'Of course, even if correct, that theory cannot explain the levitation of a table.'

'Oh, that is simple,' said Nellie, airily, 'any conjuror knows how to do it. Provided the table is not too heavy it requires only the connivance of two people on opposite sides, materials that can be procured anywhere and a little planning.' She gave an enigmatic smile. As a conjuror's assistant she knew many secrets and while she often hinted at them in a tantalising manner she knew that she ought never to fully reveal them.

It did not take long before the dining room was arranged to Mr Hope's liking. Once Mrs Malling had seen it swept and tidied she called on Mina and Nellie to announce that all was prepared and their presence requested.

When Mina and Nellie followed her to the dining room they found Zillah, Miss Pet, Mr Malling, Mrs Blunt and Mr Gillespie seated on the dining chairs that were ranged against one wall. The gas lamps were still fully lit and Nellie cast her eye about the room without appearing to be too obviously looking for cheating.

Mr Hope, chin resting in his hand, was regarding the small table where the other participants were already seated. 'We have four gentlemen and three ladies,' he said. 'It might lead to a better result if there was an even number at the table, alternating male and female.' He glanced at the row of servants. Mrs Blunt looked like something that had been carved out of a block of stone and left on the banks of the Nile and therefore not likely to move in the near future, and Mrs

Malling, who had taken a place beside her husband, shrank back in her chair as if trying to make herself invisible. After a brief whispered conversation between Zillah and Miss Pet and much encouraging patting of hands Miss Pet rose and stepped forward shyly. 'I might be the fourth lady,' she said.

'And a very charming one, too,' said Mr Hope, gallantly, bringing an eighth chair to the table and offering it to Miss Pet, the others moving to make room for her. Having taken charge of the order of seating he had managed to position himself between the two most desirable females: Nellie and Miss Pet. Next around the table was Mr Beckler then Mina, Dr Hamid, Kitty and Mr Honeyacre.

As Mina took her place she made note of the location of the sitters. The only two persons she might have considered cheats, Mr Hope and Mr Beckler, were not opposite each other where they might have been able to connive at lifting the table, but placed with only Miss Pet between them. The unlikely sets of conspirators were therefore Mr Hope facing Dr Hamid and Mr Beckler facing Mr Honeyacre. The other opposites were herself and Nellie, and Kitty and Miss Pet.

'And now,' said Mr Hope, with a little sneer, 'at the insistence of Miss Scarletti we are all obliged to swear on the Holy Bible that we are not liars and cheats. I personally did not think this to be necessary in a company of this quality, but the lady will have her way.' Mr Hope went to fetch an elderly Bible from the sideboard and while his back was turned Mina took a rapid glance under the table. She saw nothing unusual, but as an added precaution slid her hands, palms up, beneath the table top, feeling for hidden hooks or shelves. All was smooth and free of places where objects might be hidden. As she did so she became aware that Mr Beckler had turned his head to look at her. She glanced at him. He was smiling. She glanced away.

Mr Hope brought the Bible and circled the table offering it to each of the participants in turn, each of whom placed a hand upon it and made a solemn oath to be honest and truthful.

The volume was then placed in the centre of the round table and Mr Hope placed his hand upon it and made the same oath, his voice thundering especially loudly. The volume remained where it was, perhaps as a reminder to the company that their enterprise was a holy one and did not infringe any precepts of the Christian religion.

'Mr Malling,' said Mr Honeyacre. 'You can confirm that Mary Ann and Susan are at their homes?'

'Yes, my Lord, I conducted them there myself,' said Mr Malling.

'Then we may safely assume that we in this room are the only living persons in this house,' said Mr Hope. 'I have agreed, again upon the insistence of Miss Scarletti, that the gas will remain lit, but it will be turned down, although not so low that we cannot see each other.' He turned to Mina. 'Does that meet with your requirements?'

Mina ignored the challenge in his tone. 'If it does not I will be sure to let you know.'

Mr Hope nodded to Mr Malling, who rose and attended to the gas. Even in the deepening gloom his figure could be seen as he moved about the room. Finally, he returned to his seat.

'I would like to ask one thing,' said Mina.

'You have asked several already,' said Mr Hope, heavily, as he took his place at the table. 'Well, say it and be done.'

'I ask only that if any person here makes a noise such as a cough or a movement of the foot, perhaps striking the table by chance, that they own to it at once. Then we need not be distracted or unnecessarily alarmed.'

'That seems very sensible,' ventured Mr Honeyacre.

Mr Hope made a sound like a snarl. 'Very well. We will begin by placing our hands upon the table where they can be seen by us all, grasping the hands of the persons on either side. Then we will say the Lord's Prayer and after that I command everyone to be silent and still.'

Mina placed her tiny hands on the table in front of her. To her left Dr Hamid clasped her fingers in a manner that offered reassurance, to her right Mr Beckler's large hand enclosed hers completely.

Mina closed her eyes to accustom her vision more quickly to the dimness. All present, led by Mr Hope, recited the prayer aloud in unison. As the last whispers died away Mina allowed her breathing to settle into as even a rhythm as possible. There was always a point when her lungs, cramped by the distortion of her ribcage, could not expand as far as she might want and she could feel it like an obstruction in her chest. All exercise had to be taken with care and emotional exertion was no less difficult. Now she needed to remain calm and observant, open-minded, so that her senses would not be deluded by expectation.

Mina opened her eyes and looked about her at the persons seated at the table and the servants sitting in a row against the far wall. In the soft light all could be readily identified. No one moved. The only sound in the room was that of breathing and the soft hiss of gas. Every so often there was a distant creak of old wood settling, which provoked a sharp intake of breath from Kitty, then all fell quiet again. Outside the rain throbbed like a beating pulse, the wind gathering it up and hurling it against the windows.

Mina tried to estimate how much time had passed; she thought some fifteen to twenty minutes. Despite the assistance of her little cushion the lengthy immobility began to irk her back and shoulder and she had no idea how long the sitters were expected to remain there before Mr Hope declared the attempt a failure. A failure, she reminded herself, for which she would undoubtedly be blamed.

Time passed. The hallway clock struck the hour. There was another creak and this one appeared to come from directly above. Mina, her back muscles protesting, hoped that she would not have to wait until the clock struck again. Another creak followed, then another, and it became plain to everyone that it was moving, slowly and rhythmically as if someone was walking along the upstairs corridor. Now they were all controlling their breathing, not daring to make a sound. There was a sudden loud echoing bang like a fist pounding on a door and a startled little gasp from Kitty. Once again it struck and was followed by a moaning that might have been the wind, or something else.

The sound slowly died away into nothingness. Everyone was breathing a little faster and the rain was tapping on the window like fingernails.

They became aware of a new noise, a squeaking like metal grinding against metal, and the light above them began to move, flowing back and forth, brushing its glow up and down the walls, revealing frightened faces. Mina glanced up and saw that the central inflorescence of lamps was swaying back and forth.

Then the linen runner on the sideboard unfolded itself and flew across the room.

Those who had witnessed it gasped and squealed in unison.

'Stay quiet!' exclaimed Mr Hope. 'No one move! There is a spirit present and I will try to question it.'

One of the candlesticks began to slide across the sideboard, not smoothly, but in little jerking steps. They watched it reach the edge and tumble to the floor. Even though they had expected to hear a clatter as it struck it was still a shock in the stillness.

'Spirit — can you answer me?' called Hope.

The other candlestick tilted a little but it didn't fall, instead it regained its upright position with a slight thud.

Kitty uttered a slight squeal and her husband tried to hush her.

'Do you have a message for the living?' asked Mr Hope.

Another tilt and a thud.

'Are you the spirit of someone who once lived in the house?'

Another thud.

'Were you once a man?'

The candlestick remained still.

'Were you once a woman?'

A thud.

'Did you die a natural death?'

No sound.

'Were you killed?'

And then it came — a scream of the most piercing intensity and thunderous noises from above like the hammering of angry feet, and the candlestick rose up and flew across the room, striking the far wall. One of the plinths tilted and Mina expected a valuable Chinese vase to crash to the floor, but miraculously it stayed in place. Then a row of plates began to cascade from the upper shelves of the sideboard, one after the other, tumbling like leaves, shattering into pieces as they struck the floor, and a shower of tiny stones cascaded from the ceiling, striking the glass lamps like a carillon of tiny bells, then falling onto the table, bouncing and rattling across the polished surface, overflowing into people's laps. Kitty stood up and shrieked. Mr Honeyacre also stood. 'Enough, I beg of you, enough!'

Mr Honeyacre, whimpering as he went, hurried to comfort his distressed wife, his arms flapping distractedly like the wings of a bird trapped in a snare. All efforts at stillness and quiet were over. Even Mr Hope was aware that the proceedings could not be rescued and remained seated, making no attempt to resume the séance or bring the company to order.

Mr Malling, looking confused, left his seat but could only stand and stare at the displaced and broken property, contemplating the fortunate survival of the Chinese vase in wonderment. Mr Gillespie remained calm and turned up the gas lamps while Dr Hamid stepped forward with quietly spoken advice. Kitty's terror finally dissolved into convulsive sobs and before long she had been sent off to bed with Miss Pet and Dr Hamid to attend her. Mr Honeyacre wanted to accompany them but was gently persuaded to wait until his wife was comfortably settled and assured that he would then be sent for. He sat miserably on a dining chair and Mina went to sit beside him.

'She is so delicate,' he whispered, 'so very delicate.' There were tears glistening in his eyes.

Nellie took the opportunity of the distraction to examine the sideboard, the plinth, the candlesticks and the linen runner. Mina glanced at her but received only a shake of the head.

Once Kitty was safely away Mrs Malling took on the task of clearing up the mess in the dining room and Mr Malling, assisted by Mr Gillespie, Mr Hope and Mr Beckler, busied themselves with replacing the furniture and silverware to its usual position. Mina expressed the wish that everything should be left as it was until the room could be examined in daylight, but her suggestion was overruled, Mrs Malling looking especially horrified at the idea that all should not be restored to order well before breakfast.

The work was still not complete when Dr Hamid returned to reassure everyone that Kitty was very much better and no harm had been done. 'Mrs Honeyacre requires only a good night's rest in a quiet room and she will be perfectly well by morning.'

'We are so very grateful to you, Dr Hamid,' exclaimed the anxious husband and hurried away to see his wife.

Due to the lateness of the hour and the excitement it was naturally assumed that they would all shortly be retiring to their rooms and Mina and Nellie were already making their way to the door when Mr Hope rose to his feet and spoke.

'And now,' he announced, 'it is essential, while the events of tonight are fresh in our minds, that we gather together to discuss them. The drawing room will be ideal for my purpose. Come with me!' He strode purposefully to the door with complete confidence that everyone would meekly follow. At the door he paused and glanced back. 'Mr Gillespie, I think a restorative glass of sherry would be appropriate for the ladies and brandy for the gentlemen.'

Mr Gillespie's expression did not change. 'I will see to it at once, my Lord,' he said.

'And once Mr Honeyacre has satisfied himself that his good lady is well, please fetch him. I am sure he will want to join us.'

'Yes, my Lord.'

Eventually, Mina, Nellie, Dr Hamid and Mr Beckler were all assembled in the drawing room and, after a short wait, Mr Honeyacre arrived and the restoratives were served.

Mr Hope was in a state of the most inordinate excitement. He was unable to sit for long, but after a brief period of deep contemplation he rose and paced up and down the room with long energetic strides, while Mr Honeyacre clutched at his head as if the movement alone was causing him pain.

'It must be apparent to the meanest intelligence that what we have experienced this evening is of the very highest order!' exclaimed Mr Hope. 'The materialists and doubters who refuse to accept that raps are a method of communication used by the spirits cannot deny it now! In the past the difficulty has always been that raps at séances are only heard and we never see what produces them. This results in the most uncalled for and nonsensical attacks on mediums, who are actually accused of making the sounds themselves by tapping their feet on the table legs and other such nonsense. Tonight, however, we have ushered in a new era of belief. We are fortunate to have had the observation of several respectable and reliable persons, one of whom is a photographer and therefore with a discerning eye second to none and one, dare I say it, a former opponent of spiritualist matters who has now seen the evidence for herself and cannot fail to admit her former error.'

He gazed meaningfully at Mina and it was not a pleasant expression.

'It is my belief that the testimony of persons of education and quality should be admitted as wholly and unquestionably true. Indeed, it should be regarded as actual scientific proof. We saw with our own eyes, all of us, the raps giving answers to my questions being made by the movement of an object, which no human hand or foot could have reached. Really,' he went on, 'I cannot understand how so many people refused to believe in it before. Raps are one of the oldest and most widespread means of communication by the dead. They were known in Ancient Egypt and by the Greeks and the Romans. Independent witnesses, from all corners of the world and across the centuries, have experienced the same phenomena. It is impossible for it to be either chance or invention.'

'That is true,' said Mr Honeyacre, wearily, although he looked relieved to have a distraction from his woes. 'I have made a study of this and while the old myths of the barbarous races have been explained by natural events and are no longer current in modern civilisation, there are, today, scientifically trained witnesses, sane and credible, who can attest to spirit rappings, apparitions, clairvoyance and even levitation.'

'And let us not forget,' said Mr Hope, nodding approvingly, 'that modern science now accepts as true many phenomena which past centuries rejected and ridiculed.'

'But what can we do?' wailed Mr Honeyacre. 'How can we comfort the unhappy spirits that exist in this house? We really cannot hold another séance as my poor wife is so distressed.'

Mr Hope looked shocked. It really seemed that, until that moment, it had never crossed his mind that he would not be permitted to hold another séance. He narrowed his eyes and bit his lip, as if hardly knowing how to respond. Clearly, he cared nothing for Kitty, whose distress he considered a small price to pay in his pursuit of the truth, but he declined to mention this. He paced again, thoughtfully stroking his chin. 'It has been revealed tonight that the spirit who is haunting Hollow House is that of a woman who once lived in the house and was murdered. Do you know of any such individual?'

'No, I don't,' said Mr Honeyacre.

'But someone must surely know of this. A murder — and almost certainly one where the culprit has not been found to pay the price of his villainy. How is this not the common talk of the village?'

'It might be,' said Mr Honeyacre, 'that the body of the victim has never been found and the individual is simply assumed to have gone elsewhere. The Lassiters' nursemaid for example; we do not know for certain what became of her. There may be others we know nothing about.'

Mr Hope nodded meaningfully. 'That could be it, yes — a murder that is not yet suspected to be a murder. I suggest that we make it our business to bring Ned Copper here and question him closely. His memory may well hold the secret.'

'Very well,' said Mr Honeyacre, 'I will ask Mr Malling to bring him here after church tomorrow.'

'And if the weather improves,' Mr Hope continued, 'then Mr Beckler and I will go up to view the windmills. It may be necessary in time to bring a powerful medium to the site and then we may learn more.'

It was by now obvious, even to Mr Hope, that the company was weary and he graciously but reluctantly permitted them to retire to their beds.

Zillah came to help Mina and Nellie prepare for bed, moving about them with quiet attentiveness.

'Do you have any observations about the séance?' Mina asked Nellie.

'Only that some of the activity took place inside the room and some on the floor above. I saw no one leave their places, but such things can be done on stage. I was once in a tableau representing a haunted mansion. There were ornaments on a mantelpiece and a man poked a stick through a hole in the scenery and pushed them off. Then a vase of flowers slid across a table and fell on the floor. One of the actors had a black thread attached to it, which the audience was unable to see. Distance renders many things invisible. So does darkness.'

'But you saw no threads.'

'No, none. And, of course, on stage we all know what is about to happen and everything is carefully planned and arranged. The setting of the stage for such tricks takes far longer than the performance of them. As far as we know no one here has the experience to carry out such a convincing deception with so very little notice.'

'And the noises above, the swaying of the chandelier and the cascade of stones? What was the cause?'

'None of it was chance, which means either some human agency or a ghost. Again, it was like a piece of theatre — everything was timed to coincide with events.'

'I agree with Mr Honeyacre that we should not attempt another séance,' said Mina, 'but in one way it is a pity. If we did some trusted person could conceal himself or herself on the upper floor and keep watch. I would be glad to do it. If a ghost should appear I would not allow it to leave until I had interviewed it and written its story.'

'Zillah, did you notice anything that particularly struck you?' asked Nellie.

Zillah, brushing out her mistress's cascade of auburn hair, looked thoughtful. 'There was something, but it was before.'

'Oh?'

'It was when the gentlemen were moving the furniture about. Before the servants were sent for. Miss Pet came upstairs to fetch one of Little Scrap's toys for Mrs Honeyacre and she was halfway down again when she thought she heard a strange noise and went back up to listen.'

'What sort of a noise?'

'She said it like a little bird in a cage, chirping. But before she could find out where it was coming from it stopped.'

'There are no caged birds in the house, are there?' asked Mina.

'No, Miss. I asked Miss Pet and she said not.'

When they were ready to sleep Nellie insisted that Mina take the more comfortable bed. She did not need to insist very hard.

A clock began to chime and Mina, against her better judgment, found herself counting the strikes. One, two, three, four. Four in the morning, an ungodly hour to be awake. She usually slept soundly, but something had awoken her and she was confused as to what it might be. An ache in her back, the unfamiliar bed, or a draught? None of those applied. She eased into a more comfortable position and pulled the covers warmly to her throat. Nellie was asleep, her breaths soft and even.

If she closed her eyes, Mina thought, and lay very still and measured her breathing to resemble that of one asleep then she might be able to drift into slumber again. Mina drowsed contentedly, consciousness sliding away, and that was when she heard it, the creaking of wood on wood, rhythmic, insistent. A voice was whispering softly, a woman's voice, gentle, as a mother would speak to her child. She found herself listening, concentrating, trying to make out the words, but it was too far away. The voice was just the rise and fall of a tone. A child laughed, a happy sound, and still the creaking, creaking, and suddenly, abruptly, it stopped. Then a scream ripped through the air, once, twice, a cry of terror and pain.

Mina sat up in bed. Nellie too was awake. The screaming didn't stop, although it gradually reduced to sobbing and gurgling. There were footsteps running along the corridor. Mina struggled to separate dream from reality and, as one faded and the other remained, realised that the creaking and the voice and laughter had been a dream into which some very real screams had intruded. Nellie got out of bed and put on her wrap then helped Mina out of bed and made sure she was warmly enfolded. They both went to the door and peered out. Mrs Malling, blinking away sleep, stood in the corridor holding a candle.

'What has happened?' asked Mina.

'Mrs Honeyacre,' said the housekeeper grimly, 'woke up to see the figure of a woman standing by her bed. Dr Hamid is with her now.'

Chapter Ten

Kitty did not appear for breakfast that morning. Mr Honeyacre, his eyes red-rimmed from lack of sleep, came to the table without an appetite, it being apparent that he was only there from a sense of duty to his guests. He apologised profusely for the disturbance, but said that Kitty had awoken in a fright and had required careful soothing. She was calm now and Miss Pet was sitting with her. Dr Hamid, he said, had prescribed a nourishing broth and rest. He bewailed the fact that he was unable to remove his wife from the house but expressed his profound relief that there was a doctor present to attend to her.

Dr Hamid arrived to say that after speaking to Kitty he had been able to reassure her that what had happened was simply a dream occasioned by recent events. 'Her health is a little delicate but she is in no danger. She has now been able to sleep. Once she is awake and has managed a little nourishment she should make the effort to take gentle exercise and engage in conversation. It would not do for her to be alone, or dwell too much on the events of last night.'

He seemed distracted as he ate breakfast and Mina saw him glance up at the ceiling more than once. She realised that he was examining the light above the table. Whatever he saw, it did not assist his thoughts.

As they prepared to go to church, Mr Malling, who had braved the muddy footpath to make enquiries in the village, came to advise them that Reverend Ashbrook had not arrived from Clayton to conduct the service and it was to be assumed that he had been unable to make the journey due to the inclement weather and bad roads. Mr Honeyacre, looking as if the miseries of the world had fallen upon his shoulders, debated with himself whether they should attend church or hold a prayer meeting at the house.

Mr Hope, who appeared to have as much energy as all the rest of the company put together, was all for attending church, indeed his eyes lit up at the prospect, and Mr Beckler, whom no one expected would disagree, was equally enthusiastic.

'Very well, we will walk down to the church,' said Mr Honeyacre. 'I am sure we will find our prayers comforting and beneficial.'

'One word of caution,' said Mr Malling. 'The steps leading down to the church have become more difficult due to the weather. The ladies will require some assistance if they are to use them. There is the pathway to the rear of the graveyard, the one the villagers use, but that is very muddy indeed and I wouldn't advise anyone here to attempt it.'

'Is the path up to Clayton Hill clear?' asked Mr Hope. 'We intend to view the windmills this afternoon.'

'It might be better to visit them on Monday, my Lord, if the rain holds off. Also, the miller will be there to show you the site and answer your questions.'

Mr Hope grunted with impatience, but seemed to accept Mr Malling's advice.

Sunday morning worship usually started at 10 a.m. and the band of participants began to assemble in their most waterproof boots in the hallway shortly before. Kitty was not amongst them and since Mr Honeyacre had not yet appeared Mina took the opportunity to speak to Dr Hamid about his patient. Nellie arrived, although, like Mina, she was not dressed to brave the outdoors, but rather to contemplate it from within and decline further acquaintance.

'Mrs Honeyacre has decided to take prayers in her room with Miss Pet,' said Dr Hamid.

'I hope she is recovering from her fright,' said Mina. 'It so happens that I had a disturbing dream last night and it was only on awakening that I became truly certain that it was indeed a dream, as it felt very real at the time.'

'She is better, yes, but I think her imagination does not permit her to understand the difference between dream and wake as well as you do. There is one difficult subject I will have to broach with Mr Honeyacre. Mrs Honeyacre is extremely nervous about the portrait of her predecessor. She thinks the eyes follow her as she walks past. I fear I might have to suggest he move it elsewhere.'

'Have you come to any conclusion as to the origin of the stones that fell on the table at the séance?' asked Mina.

'I put some of them in my pocket,' he said. 'I mean to look about and see if I can identify something similar.'

'Mrs Malling was so quick to tidy up I did not have the opportunity of examining them,' said Mina.

He delved into his pocket and brought out a few stones. They were quite small and rounded and regular. 'Now where would these be found?' he asked.

Nellie examined them thoughtfully. 'Are you a gardener, Dr Hamid?'

'Er — no, why do you ask?'

'When you walk down to the church I suggest you look in the ornamental urns on the terrace. I have something of a similar nature in my garden and the soil is protected from weeds with small pebbles like these.'

'If that is the case then anyone might have picked them up,' said Mina. 'What I would like to know is how they came to fall from the ceiling onto the tea table. If it had been a dark séance the answer would have been obvious. Someone would have come to the séance with a pocket full of stones and simply thrown them on the table at the right moment. But we all saw that they cascaded down from above. We even heard them striking the brass fittings and glass shades of the chandelier.'

'I was looking this morning at breakfast,' said Dr Hamid, 'and the only place they could have come from was the chandelier which was directly above the centre of the tea table. But there was nowhere in the chandelier to store the stones unseen and, even if there was, how could their descent be achieved and so well timed with the séance?'

'Then we must take a close look at the chandelier and consider the possibilities.'

Mr Honeyacre arrived, well cloaked and booted, and Mina went to speak to him.

'I think it would be advisable for me to remain here and join Mrs Honeyacre for prayers,' she said.

'Oh, yes, of course, I quite understand. She will appreciate the company.'

'And I was wondering if you have such a thing as a plan of the house. It would be of great assistance to me.'

He was surprised at the request, but delved into his study and soon provided her with the plans of the house in three sheets, drawn up floor by floor.

'And now,' said Mina to Nellie when the little party had gone, 'let us take a close look at the chandelier and determine how the stones descended from the ceiling.'

Nellie laughed.

'I'm not sure I could persuade Dr Hamid to climb up on the table,' said Mina, 'and he would have a perfect fit if I was to attempt it, but I am sure you would enjoy the adventure.'

'I have danced on tables before now,' said Nellie, 'but not in such a confining costume.'

In the dining room they laid a cloth on the table and Nellie stepped up on a chair and then to the table top, where she could reach up and touch the glass lampshades.

'How easy is it to see?' asked Mina.

'There is no obvious place to store any stones. I can see one or two small ones that must have fallen into the bottom of the shades when they all came down. If stones had been held up here, attached to the ceiling perhaps, it might have been in a cloth bag, or some paper. I don't believe either of us examined the ceiling before the séance began.'

'But how were they released and how was the descent so well-timed?' asked Mina.

'That is a good question. The only other possibility is if there was a gap in the place where the chandelier is attached to the ceiling and the stones somehow came down from the floor above, but it is tightly fitted and there is not a space large enough, even for such small pebbles.'

'But the chandelier did sway,' said Mina. 'We all saw it. Can you make it sway now?'

Nellie carefully pushed the fitting but it was firmly fixed and hardly moved at all. 'Curious,' she said. 'If it was possible for it to move last night, perhaps motivated by the hand of a spirit, then it ought to be possible for me to move it now. There is no damage to the ceiling.'

'Ah, but spirits know nothing of ceilings and walls,' said Mina. 'And there are mediums who claim to fly through the air and make their entrance into houses through brick and plaster without leaving any sign. How strange it is, therefore, that Mr Hope's wonderful Miss Eustace is still in prison.'

'Would you not consider that the stones might have been carried into the house by a spirit passing through solid walls before being dropped the table,' asked Nellie.

'I will consider that, of course, as I might consider every explanation,' said Mina. 'But, unlike Mr Hope, I see it as the last possibility and not the first.'

Nellie descended from the table and the cloth was put away.

'Now then,' said Mina, 'I have here the floor plans of the house and we will use these for our next expedition.' She laid out the plans on the table top. 'This sheet shows the ground floor. Here is the dining room and that —' she pointed — 'is approximately the location of the chandelier.' She took the next sheet. 'This is the first floor of the main house and east wing, showing the bedrooms and other amenities. If I lay it over the first one we will find our match.' She adjusted the two sheets to reveal as far as possible the position of the first floor rooms in relation to those below. She then examined the arrangement, carefully turning the top paper aside until she saw the location of the chandelier. 'There it is,' she said. 'The room directly above the position of the chandelier is the one marked Socrates. The one occupied by Dr Hamid.' She paused. 'Eager as I am to continue this enquiry I feel I ought to ask his permission to examine the room.'

Mina and Nellie made a further tour of the house, but were unable to discover anything that might explain the unusual phenomena. They called on Kitty, who had awoken from her slumber somewhat refreshed and a little ashamed of herself for having disturbed the sleep of her guests. There was a breakfast tray by her bedside, which looked as if she had eaten well and some of the usual fresh colour of her complexion had been restored. Mina, Nellie, Kitty and Miss Pet said prayers for the restless spirits in the house, asking God to grant them peace and content so they could leave the troublesome earthly world and reside in Heaven.

The Hollow House party that had gone to pray at St Mond's was back within an hour of leaving, cold, damp and much muddied. In the absence of Reverend Ashbrook the church service had passed rather more quickly than was usual and, according to Dr Hamid, mainly consisted of the private prayers of a congregation anxious to return to their homes.

Dr Hamid paid a visit to Kitty and, on finding her much improved, left her to the kindness of Miss Pet and the anxious soothings of Mr Honeyacre. Mr Hope and Mr Beckler were making plans for the afternoon, so it was not hard for Mina and Nellie to engage Dr Hamid in a private conversation.

'I wonder,' he said, 'what the two of you have been doing this morning?' He glanced at the rolled-up plans in Mina's hand. 'It was not all prayers, I think.'

'We have been exercising our minds on the conundrum of the stones that fell at the séance,' said Mina. 'One way they could have been introduced by a living hand is through the ceiling in the place where the chandelier is fitted, but it is impossible to see how it could have been done. However, I obtained the plans of the house, which have been very helpful. I am fairly sure that the precise place where the chandelier is attached to the ceiling is directly below the room you are occupying.'

Dr Hamid gave her a very firm stare.

'Naturally, we would not intrude without your permission.'

'Naturally,' said Dr Hamid, looking a little surprised that they had not already done so.

'So, the next thing to do, with your permission, is to examine the floor of the Socrates room and see how, if at all, the stones might have been introduced from above.'

'But by whom?' he argued. 'Everyone was in the séance room, as I seem to recall you insisted.'

'That is a difficulty,' Mina admitted. 'I will have to address that question once I have solved the first.'

'I see. Are you planning to take up carpentry?'

'Well, that would be amusing. Whyever not?'

He threw up his hands. 'There are many things I would venture to solve the puzzle, but I am not about to tear up Mr Honeyacre's floorboards. I fear we would not be invited again if I did.'

'If it comes to that,' said Nellie, 'I think Mr Honeyacre would go much further to ensure Kitty's comfort and safety.'

Dr Hamid could only agree. 'Very well,' he said, with the resigned air of a man who knew that his fate was already determined. 'Let us take a look and then I suspect we will find that the theory is impossible.'

The first thing Mina noticed in the Socrates chamber was that the floor was not carpeted but covered by a large rug. She consulted the floor plan and calculated where the location of the chandelier fitting could be found. It was necessary only to move one item of furniture, an armchair, before the rug could be rolled back and the floorboards of that area exposed. Even Dr Hamid was obliged to admit that it was not so difficult a task as he had anticipated.

'Well, there is the floor,' he said, 'and the boards should all be nailed down.'

Mina and Nellie said nothing but looked at him.

He sighed and got down on his hands and knees to inspect the floorboards.

After a few moments he glanced up at them with a rueful smile and pointed at one of the boards. 'I think we have something.'

'You mean that one is not nailed down?'

'No, and deliberately I think, as, if your map reading is correct, it should give access to the fastenings of the chandelier. Of course, it makes sense as, if the chandelier needed to be repaired or replaced, one would not want to be tearing up the floor.' He used a pocketknife to prise at the edge of the board, which was a short one, and was easily able to lift it out. Mina and Nellie crept closer to look.

The fittings of the chandelier protruded though the ceiling joists and were held in place by substantial bolts. A quick inspection by Dr Hamid showed that all was firmly in place, so it should have been impossible for the chandelier to sway as they had seen it do and neither was there any gap through which even small stones could be thrown down into the room below.

'But this is not logical or sensible,' said Mina after a long pause.

'Séances rarely are,' said Dr Hamid, getting to his feet with a wince and rubbing his knees.

'Supposing,' said Mina, 'I was to concede that the arrival of the stones is an example of psychic activity and they simply passed through the ceiling by some means no one can understand, I still don't see why a spirit should choose to act in this way.'

'As to how it is possible, I cannot explain,' said Dr Hamid. 'The very nature of these incidents do suggest a principle which is yet to be discovered.'

'I will consider that, of course,' said Mina, 'but the purpose of the activity remains mysterious. It conveys no message, other than to reveal a presence. It is mischievous rather than informative. A prank more appropriate to the schoolroom than some higher location.'

'The action of a child,' said Nellie.

Dr Hamid replaced the floorboard and the rug. Mina felt dejected as they made their way back down the corridor. She had hoped to solve the mystery, but was as puzzled as ever. As they reached the stairs leading to the upper floor she paused and gazed up into the shadowy space above. Then, impulsively, she unhooked one end of the obstructing rope, fastened it to the opposite fitting, took a firm hold of the rail, and began to climb.

There were horrified gasps behind her. 'Miss Scarletti, whatever are you thinking!' exclaimed Dr Hamid. 'I beg you, go no further! We have been warned of the dangers and to you it is doubly unwise!'

Mina knew she was being foolish and, just two steps on her way, she stopped. 'I just feel that somewhere in this house lies the answer. And we have not yet seen the upper floor. The plans show me that there are two attic rooms, both connected. It is the only part of the house that has been forbidden us.'

'For a very good reason!' said Dr Hamid, crossly. 'Come down and I will go.' He climbed up to Mina and took her hand. She made no protest as he helped her descend. 'Stay there,' he said. 'Mrs Jordan, see to it that she does not move from that spot.' He began to climb the stairs, cautiously. There were no alarming noises, just the occasional protest of aged wood, and at the top of the staircase he turned the corner and vanished from their sight. Mina and Nellie waited. Mina thought that, had this been one of her stories, the intrepid adventurer would have encountered a monster chained up in the attic. Perhaps it would be a scion of the Redwoodes, the rightful heir to the estate, but locked away because of a morbid taste for human flesh? It had been obliged to subsist only on the bodies of vermin, but at the sight of the valiant doctor, crazed by the prospect of the first proper meal in many years, it would rend its chains and attack. Would her story conclude with a loud scream following which the bold explorer would fail to return? She rather preferred an ending where he stood his ground and ended the creature with a perfectly placed bullet.

Mina listened intently but heard neither screams nor gunshots. Instead, there were only a few shuffling sounds and creaks after which Dr Hamid reappeared. 'The upper rooms are unfurnished, but there is considerable evidence of water damage and the floorboards are rotted in places. There are no ghosts.'

'How disappointing,' said Nellie. 'I had expected the decaying corpse of a hanged man at the very least.'

Mina realised that she was being jested with, but the comment reminded her of some information she still required. While Nellie and Dr Hamid went to see Kitty with the object of persuading her to come downstairs and make herself comfortable in the parlour, Mina headed in the direction of the library, hoping to discover a reference to the gallows on Clayton Hill. The visitors' guide she had borrowed had described only the present windmills, while *Glimpses of the Supernatural* had not proved illuminating and she had decided to return them both.

'Miss Scarletti,' said a voice from the shadows of the hallway. She stopped to see the tall figure of Mr Beckler leaning against the wall. 'Sorry if I startled you,' he added, although he didn't look at all sorry.

'You were lurking in a corner like a long case clock,' she observed. 'I wasn't expecting it to speak.'

'Where are you going?' he asked, as she moved on.

'The library. Mr Honeyacre has kindly agreed that I might read any book he has there.'

'Then I'll keep you company.' He eased away from the wall and offered her his arm.

Reluctantly, she took it and they walked on. It was some moments before he could adjust his long strides to her slow limping progress. She could not help thinking that they must make a curious couple, as he was rather more than six feet in height to her four foot eight. 'What books interest you, Miss Scarletti?' he asked.

'Books in which the author is discussing a subject of which they have profound knowledge. Books from which I can learn something new. Books that entertain.'

'Chemistry, now there's a subject,' said Mr Beckler. 'And optics, there's another one.'

Mina had never read a book on chemistry, although, following her interview with Mr Marriott, the Brighton optician, she had read a book on optics, since she wanted to know more about how the eye sent pictures of the world to the brain. She was not about to reveal that to Mr Beckler. In Mina's experience people were far more likely to show their true selves when they underestimated others and new acquaintances always underestimated her.

'Mr Honeyacre's library is chiefly composed of history, art and spiritualism,' she said. 'I do not believe there is any science, which is a lack I shall suggest he corrects. I have just read a book about hauntings and other curious events, but it was hard to say how much was fact and how much imagination. By the time a story has been passed from one person to another over a hundred years or more it has been embroidered so much that none of the original fabric remains.'

Mr Beckler laughed, a noise somewhere between a honk and a growl. 'Mr Hope said that you were a difficult one to draw into the way of spiritualism.'

'I am not impervious to the truth,' said Mina. 'I deplore nonsense and lies and deceit.' She glanced up at him. He was still chuckling. 'Has he sent you to talk me into believing him? I had better warn you, it will take more than that.'

'Ohhhh, I can see it will.' He glanced at her again with an odd little smile. 'If only I had my camera you might see the proof for yourself. The dead do not lie.'

That point was debatable, Mina thought, but she was not prepared to debate it. 'What were you intending to do had you been able to bring the camera here?'

'I wanted to identify the exact site where the hauntings chiefly take place and then take photographs. Even if there is nothing for the eye to see there might still be something the camera can capture. Now that we know it is possible, a world of discovery lies ahead.'

They had reached the library and Mina replaced her books and selected two more, a gazetteer of Sussex and a county history. Taking them to the reading table she sat down and opened her notebook. She had no intention of continuing her conversation with Mr Beckler but applied herself to her studies.

Mr Beckler did not take a book, instead he sat opposite Mina and hunched forward, leaning his elbows on the table, holding his long forearms parallel, the palms of his large hands several inches apart. When she glanced up he was staring at her intently, tilting his head first one way then the other.

'What are you doing?' she demanded.

He laced his fingers and placed his chin on them. 'I take photographs, so I am always looking for interesting subjects. You, Miss Scarletti, are extremely interesting.'

Mina bridled in a way that she did not normally do. There was something about him she found highly irritating. 'Why, because of my twisted body? Don't try to be polite, Mr Beckler, say what you think. I am a curiosity of nature. Is that it? That's no surprise to me. I have a mirror; I have eyes. Do you want to take a picture of my back and publish it in a book of medical marvels?'

He smiled, but in the deceptive manner of a predator about to pounce on a helpless prey. 'No, Miss Scarletti,' he said softly. 'I want to photograph your face. You have fine features, pretty eyes. I spend too long with the dead. If I could capture that spark of life that lies within you, now that would be an achievement.'

Mina, unused as she was to any kind words about her appearance, was obliged, in the face of this blatant flattery, to remind herself that Mr Beckler must address all potential lady clients in that way to secure their custom. To the plain, he promised beauty, to the aged he offered youth, and to Mina he suggested that she had both inner and outward attractions that rendered her frail and crooked body of no account.

Mina closed her books, snapping them as if she hoped to squash unwelcome insects between their pages, and rose to her feet. Mr Beckler also rose and offered her his hand. She ignored it. 'I suggest, sir, that you find another subject.'

He gazed at her steadily. 'I have seen none I like better,' he said.

'I find that hard to believe.' She made for the door and he turned with the clear intention of accompanying her. 'Please don't follow me.'

Mina left the library and did not look back. She escaped to her bedroom, where she felt sure that Mr Beckler, if he had any small shred of decency, would not pursue her. The annoyance had made her heart race and she sat alone, unable to concentrate on her books until she felt calmer.

Finally, she was able to resume her studies. The gazetteer described the building of the first post mill on Clayton Hill in 1765. This had been demolished and replaced by the present tower mill. There was unfortunately no account of what, if anything, might have been on Clayton Hill prior to 1765, and no mention of any gallows.

The history book told her that between 1307 and 1830 the Sussex County Assizes had been held at the town of Horsham some twenty miles away and it was there that executions, mainly of highway robbers, burglars and horse thieves, had been carried out; but there were exceptions. Several criminals, usually murderers, had been hanged at other locations such as hills or common land, often near the site where the crime had been committed, where there was presumably a good chance of attracting a large and appreciative crowd of onlookers. There was no specific mention of a gallows on Clayton Hill, but that did not mean that there had not been one.

Mina decided to retire to the relative comfort and warmth of the ladies parlour. Taking the history book, she peered out of her door and, on seeing that the corridor was clear, went as quickly as she could down the stairs. It was with some relief that she reached her destination unmolested.

There she found Nellie together with Kitty, Zillah and Miss Pet. Kitty was very quiet and wrapped in soft shawls, nuzzling her face into Little Scrap's soft fur, while Miss Pet was watching her carefully and embroidering a handkerchief, occasionally demonstrating the niceties of stitching to Zillah.

Mina sat down and began quietly reading her book.

'Are you quite well?' asked Nellie with a frown, 'I can see that something is troubling you.'

Mina put down the book and sighed. 'Oh, only Mr Beckler, who suggested that I should be a subject for a photograph. He was quite insistent, but I refused. He is idle now as he does not have his camera and is trying to flatter people into becoming new customers. I expect he has already asked you.'

'He has not,' said Nellie and glanced at Kitty.

Kitty pouted and shook her head. 'Not even Little Scrap here, who would make such a pretty picture.' Little Scrap's ears twitched as if he knew he was the subject of a compliment.

'Well, I am sure he will ask you both in due course,' said Mina. 'Be warned, he is very persistent.'

Mina found her history book entirely lacking in any reference to Clayton Hill or Ditchling Hollow and set it aside. 'I am sorry that Reverend Ashbrook could not be here today, as I had hoped to be shown the parish chest,' she said.

'You have a taste for church antiquities?' asked Nellie. 'That is a new thing.'

'I wanted to examine the parish records,' said Mina. 'Mr Honeyacre said that they did not have any reference to the past owners of Hollow House, but there may be some information about others who have lived here. I expect Reverend Ashbrook has the key, so I am to be disappointed.'

Unexpectedly, Kitty gave a little laugh and Nellie smiled.

'I think Kitty was remembering the tricks performed by M Baptiste. He was a great admirer of the late M Robert-Houdin and studied his methods, to which he added his own original ideas. He taught himself how to escape almost instantly from ropes and chains, even when sealed in a sack and locked in a trunk. Sometimes, it was I who was thus confined and we changed places, much to the astonishment of the audience.' Nellie looked wistful, as if the years of toil and hand-to-mouth living with a bigamous spouse had been a paradise by comparison to her present circumstances.

'I see,' said Mina. 'But —'

Nellie glanced at Miss Pet and Zillah, who were absorbed in their sewing and each other's company, then leaned towards Mina, patted her beaded reticule and whispered, 'A lady should never travel without her lock picks.'

Mina spent a moment or two contemplating what Nellie was suggesting. It was reckless, foolish, dangerous and bordering on the criminal; exactly the kind of thing her brother Richard would have done without thinking about it. Mina made a decision and it did not take her long. Perhaps she and her brother were not so different after all.

'If the rain has stopped for a little while then a visit to the church might be possible,' said Mina. 'I would like to go, if only to escape the company of Mr Beckler and Mr Hope. What are they doing now, I wonder?'

'I have seen them prowling about the house with very serious expressions and talking in low voices,' said Nellie. 'From what I managed to overhear, they are looking for concentrations of psychic energy.'

'Really? How will they know if they find them?'

'I believe Mr Hope has some idea that those places will be very cold, or possibly very warm.'

Mina rose and went to peer out of the window. It was not actually raining, although the land was still wet and muddy. She felt sure it was possible for active men to walk down to the village if they kept to the carriage drive and main road, and the path and steps down to the church were still passable with care. 'It has not yet begun to rain frogs and scorpions,' she observed. 'Shall we take the air while air remains?'

'I thought the way was too difficult for ladies,' said Nellie, teasingly.

'I am sure it is not too difficult for you. I will lean on you as we go. And Dr Hamid is not here to order me not to attempt it.'

'Then we have a plan,' said Nellie. She turned to Kitty, who looked disinclined to take a walk in the cold and wet. 'Kitty, will you come with us? A walk in the fresh air might do you good.'

'No,' cooed Kitty, fussing over her little dog, 'I shall stay here with my darling Little Scrap or he might take a cough. And Miss Pet has promised to show Zillah a new way to trim a bonnet with lace.'

'Then we shall go,' said Nellie. 'Come, my dear, and remember, as long as we say our prayers, whatever our sins, we shall be forgiven!'

Securely wrapped against all the intrusions of cruel nature, Mina and Nellie emerged onto the rain slicked terrace and ventured down the damp steps once again, only more cautiously than before. Nellie made sure to place her feet very carefully to prevent slipping and Mina clung to her friend's arm as if her life depended on it, which it probably did.

It was almost twilight and the clouds were thick and hung overhead in great deep dark clumps, like mountain ranges turned upside down. They reminded Mina of the time when, as a child, she had thought that thunder was the sound made by clouds bumping into each other. They looked so menacing and solid that her uninformed childish impression now seemed not unlikely.

As they neared the church they saw a number of villagers wandering pensively in the graveyard, their slow bent shapes pausing to peer at illegible words on the headstones. Curious eyes turned to the approaching ladies, then, after dipping in respect, turned away. Mina and Nellie passed along the path and entered the church.

All was quiet. A solitary parishioner seated before the altar with bowed head, rose up and moved away. The outer doors closed and they were alone. Mina consulted the list of clergymen and established that Reverend Tolley had preached at St Mond's between 1840 and 1871, which meant that he must have known the Lassiters. Presumably he was deceased or at any rate retired, but either way he was not immediately available for questioning.

She glanced at Nellie who was examining the lock on the vestry door. 'This shouldn't take long,' Nellie said and, removing what resembled a bunch of small keys from her reticule, carefully selected one.

Mina was already beginning to regret agreeing to the adventure and glanced nervously at the door. 'I hope no one comes in and sees us,' she said. 'How would it look if we were caught?'

'Oh, I am sure that with your talent for composing stories you will be able to make up a dozen excuses if we are,' said Nellie cheerfully. 'But the church doors make a noise as they open and I should have ample warning.'

Mina remained near the doorway, listening carefully. She wondered if the reading public was ready for the adventurous tales of a lady burglar.

A few moments passed and there was a gentle click. 'There!' said Nellie.

'Will anyone be able to guess what has happened the next time the vestry door is opened?' asked Mina.

'No. I pride myself on a delicate touch. There will be no sign.'

'The lock picks are very small. I had imagined them to be larger.'

'I used to hide them between my toes,' said Nellie, wistfully. She turned the handle and the vestry door opened.

Mina hesitated and followed Nellie into the room. 'If we are discovered here we can always say that we came to church to say our prayers and found the door to be accidentally left open.'

'The perfect explanation,' said Nellie, closing the door behind them. 'No one would dare contradict us. It is well known that ladies are too delicate and timid to pick locks.'

The vestry office was furnished with a chair and a writing desk, which was nothing more than a small square table supplied with a blotter, paper, pens and ink. A shelf, hanging precariously from the wall, was piled with worn prayer books. The parish chest, which lay against the opposite wall, was constructed from thick slabs of age-darkened oak and looped about with broad bands of iron. The lid was secured with a heavy padlock that passed through iron loops.

'This may take a little time,' said Nellie. She took the chair over to the door and tilted it so the back rested underneath the handle.

'I had not realised you were so adept at burglary,' said Mina, thankful that the law was less strict on such crimes than it had been in the days of the Horsham gallows.

'A magician needs many skills,' said Nellie, selecting her largest lock pick. 'And his assistant should study them, too. They will reward her on stage and also in her daily life.'

Mina said nothing. As her friend worked a hundred questions hovered on Mina's lips but she did not feel it would be right to ask them.

'There,' said Nellie as the lock emitted a noticeable click. They both waited, breathing carefully, but a minute passed and no one came to investigate. Carefully, Nellie eased the padlock from the loops and placed it on the desk. 'Now, as quietly as possible, in case the hinges squeak.'

Together, they raised the lid, which was a struggle because of its weight and Mina's lack of it and the necessity to do so without attracting attention, but at last it was securely leaning against the wall, held in place by the substantial mass of the body of the chest.

The first things Mina noticed inside the chest were some items carefully wrapped in soft cloths, which she guessed must be the church silver. She felt a sudden sick lurch of fear in her stomach. In wanting to look at the books, which had no special negotiable value, she had entirely failed to consider that she and Nellie were conniving at what might look to another person as an attempted felony, which could potentially result in a conviction and a term of several years in prison.

The chest also contained a number of venerable leather-bound books and Nellie began to lift them out, bringing with them the harsh scent of decayed leather and a sickly odour of vellum. Some were stamped on the back with dates, others simply had dates inked on the spine in thick black strokes.

Mina located the book that covered the time when the Lassiters had occupied Hollow House and opened it. Since the parish was so small it did not require separate books for births, marriages and deaths, but entered them all in the same book in different sections.

From what Mr Honeyacre had said the Lassiters had lived in Hollow House for a period between 1850 and 1852. The small number of records made Mina's work simple. No one of the surname Lassiter had been christened, married or buried during those years and also for the few years on either side. There was also no mention of anyone resident in Hollow House, or pursuing an occupation that suggested that they had lived there. The Lassiters, Mina recalled, had purchased the estate from a family called Wigmore, who had in turn purchased it from the Redwoodes. She explored further back in time, the pages growing older and browner and stiffer as she went, but found nothing apart from records of the villagers.

Nellie, in the meantime, had delved further into the chest and found some old prayer books, their bindings in need of repair, and a package wrapped up in strong paper and tied with string. It took some doing for her to untie the knots, but at last she teased them apart and opened up the paper.

'What do you have there?' asked Mina, looking up from the book she was studying.

'A lot of dust and parchment,' said Nellie, coughing. 'Church records, the cost of repairs, here's a mention of the Redwoodes and the installation of their plaque. A map of the village, hand drawn, no date that I can see, very faded, I'm afraid. Oh, and some pamphlets. Religious tracts — the sort of thing one might expect.' She stopped. 'Ah.'

'Yes?' said Mina.

'This one should interest you.' Nellie handed it to Mina, who read the title, her excitement growing with every word.

The Authentic Narrative of the Astonishing and Unaccountable Events at Hollow House, Ditchling Hollow, in the County of Sussex, in the month of March 1851, as observed by a Reverend Gentleman.

Mina examined the end pages without learning more. 'The author is not named and it has been privately printed, but given the year, I suspect Reverend Tolley to be the author.' She could not resist starting to read the pamphlet. 'Oh, this is more than just interesting. It is an account of a previous haunting of Hollow House. And there is an explanation of why the Lassiters left so abruptly.'

It was too much of a risk for Mina to spend time copying the contents of the pamphlet, but an unfamiliar name that appeared in its pages sent her on a second fruitless foray into the parish records, after which she wrapped and tied the little package of documents and tucked it into her reticule. It looked as though the package had not been disturbed in a long time and, since Reverend Ashbrook was a recent incumbent, it was doubtful that he had ever opened it. With care, she ought to be able to study the papers at her leisure, wrap them so they did not look as if they had been disturbed, and return them before his next visit.

With the exception of the papers the contents of the chest were replaced as they had been found, the lid carefully lowered, the padlock restored and locked. The chair was once again placed before the desk. After listening at the door, Nellie opened it a tiny way, peering out to ensure that they would not be seen emerging from the vestry. To their relief, the church was empty. The two malefactors, one of them far more nervous than the other, were thus able to make their escape undetected.

'If anyone should ask,' said Mina, 'we simply said our prayers.'

Their return to the house was observed only by Mrs Malling, to whom Mina explained that she and Nellie had taken a turn about the terrace. Mrs Malling seemed surprised, but after observing that they were both looking chilled, insisted on providing hot coffee as a warming restorative.

Thus refreshed, Mina took the purloined papers to her room for detailed study. The village map was, as Nellie had commented, badly faded, and there was some writing on it, including what appeared to be a date, all of which was illegible. From her slight knowledge of the village and the estate, Mina was able to make out the shape of fields with some markings which she guessed were the names of the tenants, the main street, a farmhouse, the church and a manor house, which, from its shape, was almost certainly the one that had existed before the Wigmores had built Hollow House. Apart from the pamphlet the remaining documents were surveys of the condition of the church roof made during the time of Reverend Tolley, the cost of the Redwoodes' plaque which dated from 1794, and some accounts of collections for the parish poor.

She saved the most interesting part for last and, tucking her little wedge-shaped cushion more firmly under her hip, settled comfortably to read the Reverend Gentleman's account of the remarkable transactions at Hollow House.

In this, my faithful account of the haunting of Hollow House and the unfortunate Lassiter family I hope I will not be accused of being too fanciful or too trusting. My enquiries have been most thorough and I have made good use of both my senses and my experience of human nature. A lifetime spent in the service of the church has, I believe, well fitted me to understand both the strengths and weaknesses of the human condition. All the circumstances I place before the reader are therefore those that I have either seen with my own eyes or have been divulged to me by reliable persons, whose veracity I have no reason to doubt. My fervent faith in the Almighty and the promised hereafter have, as always, shored me up at times of great anxiety.

There came to Ditchling Hollow, towards the end of the year 1849, a most excellent family who had previously dwelled in the county of Kent. The family consisted of Mr Edward Lassiter, who was in the business of breeding and training racehorses and had many successes to his name. He was then thirty-two years of age and of the most agreeable disposition. His wife, to whom he had been married above four years, was the former Sophia Peele, whose late father, an honest and industrious corn chandler, had left her with a not inconsiderable marriage portion. Mrs Lassiter was a gentle, kind, devout lady and much skilled in the art of watercolour painting. I have never seen, either before or since, a married couple so devoted as the Lassiters.

The Lassiters had one child, a son called George, although he was affectionately known as Georgie by the family, and he was then just three years of age. He was a lively, active and cheerful child, and his parents doted on him. The other residents of the house were a cook/housekeeper, Mr Lassiter's servant, a general maid and a ladies' maid, all of whom had come with the Lassiters from Kent. On their arrival in Ditchling Hollow, the Lassiters engaged a nursemaid to take charge of the child, their previous one having decided to remain in Kent where she was to marry. This nursemaid was Abigail Falcon, of Burgess Hill, who was then eighteen years of age. All persons resident in the house were sober and respectable, and despite the strangeness of the stories they had to tell, I have every confidence in the truth of their observations for reasons that will become clear.

The family and servants were regular attendees at the church and the Lassiters gave generously to charity. Mr Lassiter also employed a great *number of men in the construction of a new wing to Hollow House, the object being to provide stabling for horses and accommodation for the riders and grooms.*

The Lassiters had not been here four months when Mr Lassiter came to me in a very troubled state. He said that there had been disturbances in the house, which he was unable to explain and his wife, who was in that happy but delicate state of health particular to young married ladies, was becoming very frightened by it and as a result he was extremely anxious for her safety. It had occurred to him that a man of the cloth might be the best person to advise him.

Naturally, I was intrigued by this information and humbly gratified by the confidence reposed in me. I stated at once that I would do everything in my power to assist him.

He told me that, one afternoon when Abigail was with little Georgie in the parlour, several ornaments were sent crashing to the floor, some of which were broken beyond repair. When Mrs Lassiter heard the commotion, she went to enquire what had happened. Georgie at once said that he was not responsible for the breakages and Mrs Lassiter had no reason to disbelieve him. Suspicion naturally fell on the only other individual present, Abigail, who it was thought had carelessly knocked them to the floor. Abigail, however, protested that she had not touched any of the ornaments and claimed that they must have fallen down by themselves.

Mrs Lassiter decided not to press matters further, hoping that such an incident would not happen again. The very next day, however, Abigail came running to Mrs Lassiter saying that some dishes in the kitchen had fallen from the shelf while her back was turned. Mrs Lassiter went to look and saw broken plates lying on the kitchen floor. Before she could say a word, a whole row of dishes tumbled from the shelf and broke. Neither Mrs Lassiter nor Abigail were near to the shelf at the time. No other person was in the room. As they contemplated this alarming event there was a loud noise from the scullery. They ran in and discovered that some china basins had fallen to the floor. From that moment on it appeared that nothing in the house was safe. Jars of preserves, ornaments, lamps, candlesticks and even a clock would jump to the floor or throw themselves against the wall while no person was within reach of them.

As one might imagine, I received this account, told to me in great sincerity, with a certain degree of scepticism. I was careful not to dismiss it out of hand, however, as my parishioner was undoubtedly very concerned. Mr Lassiter, to some extent, saw through my doubts and begged me to go to his house and see for myself, which naturally I did. He confided his suspicions that there was a disturbed spirit haunting Hollow House, which would not let his family alone and asked me if I knew of any unhappy person who had expired there.

I have conducted services in the church of St Mond Ditchling Hollow for many years and so I cast my mind back in the hope of providing Mr Lassiter with an answer. The Lassiters had purchased the house from a family by the name of Wigmore, who had originally built it about 1795 on the site of an old and much decayed Tudor mansion. At the time I knew old Mr Wigmore, he was a very unhappy gentleman. His wife was an invalid who had been sent to Switzerland for her health but unfortunately this measure had not been effective and she had died there. His three daughters had all married and no longer resided in Sussex. He had begun to wander in his mind and repeatedly expressed the idea that a maidservant who had lived in his house many years ago had suffered ill-treatment at the hands of his butler, a circumstance which he had not done enough to prevent, but what had become of her no one could recall, least of all Mr Wigmore. At length, one of his daughters, concerned for the old gentleman, had him removed and placed in the care of a nurse.

I examined the church records very carefully and they show no burials in the churchyard of St Mond of anyone who had once lived in Hollow House.

I duly paid a visit to the house and carefully interviewed all those who had witnessed unusual incidents. It transpired that all the inhabitants *had, on occasion, heard items tumbling to the floor, either in an adjoining room where no one was present, or in the same room when no one was near enough to move them. Sometimes they had not actually seen the things fall, but there had been incidents when they had actually seen plates or jars fly across the room while not being touched by any human hand. Everyone seemed very sincere and all were willing to attest on the Bible to the truth of their accounts.*

I am not a believer in spirit visitations, which I have always suspected are a result of overheated imagination, and decided to seek a simpler explanation. I considered the important fact that Mr Lassiter was having the new wing constructed and wondered if this could be causing the disturbances. I therefore suggested that Mr Lassiter call upon the services of a reliable builder of Burgess Hill, who paid him a visit and examined the property and expressed his belief that the construction of the new wing had unsettled the foundations and it was for this reason that objects slid off shelves onto the floor.

Mr Lassiter was most relieved at this explanation and was quick to inform his wife that the solution to the mystery had been found, and it only wanted some improvements to the foundations to be made for the incidents to cease. This work was duly carried out by the aforementioned builder, at some considerable expense, and Mr Lassiter invited me to view the completed new wing of the house.

As we sat down before partaking of dinner it was suggested that we take a glass of sherry, but as the butler went to fetch the bottle the tray on which it and the glasses sat flew off the side table and all the glassware was dashed to pieces. He proceeded to sweep up the fragments, but as he did so the whole room was thrown into a state of consternation by a shower of stones, which appeared to have descended from the ceiling. These incidents I saw with my own eyes. Mrs Lassiter at once began to weep and ran from the room in a state of great distress.

Mr Lassiter went to comfort her and it will not be hard to imagine that the evening did not end happily. It was decided that Mrs Lassiter, together with little Georgie and the nursemaid, should leave Hollow House at once and pay a visit to her sister, where she would be more comfortable. This was done and the disturbances in the house ceased. However, only a week later, Mrs Lassiter, little Georgie and the nursemaid all returned.

Mr Lassiter came to me again. He looked like a desperate man, so much so that I was afraid for his health and possibly even his sanity. He informed me that the distressing incidents had continued at the house of Mrs Lassiter's sister, who had been greatly upset, this being the reason for the party's early return. It had been observed, however, that the events only occurred when Abigail Falcon was nearby, either in the same room or the next one. He further told me that she of all the people in the house was unafraid of the events and had even been heard to comment quite unconcernedly that it was a commonplace thing to happen. He suspected that the girl was the focus of a discontented spirit and he and his wife had begun to feel afraid of her. He asked me to perform a ceremony of exorcism on her, which I naturally refused to do, it being a custom of the dark ages of superstition. My advice was to dismiss the girl, but he went away shaking his head in a most peculiar fashion, saying that he felt unable to do so. That was the last time I saw him.

Only two weeks later, I learned that the Lassiters had decided to vacate the house. I was told that the servants who had come with them from Kent went with them, but Abigail Falcon did not and I never heard what had become of her afterwards.

Thus ends my narrative, in which I have endeavoured to describe only the simple facts, neither exaggerated nor diminished, in the hope that one day the truth of the matter will be made apparent.

A Reverend Gentleman. Ditchling Hollow, 1852.

Mina would have liked to show the pamphlet to Dr Hamid, but that might have led to awkward questions as to where she had obtained it. If, as was very probable, he should mention it to Mr Honeyacre on the natural assumption that it came from his host's library the situation could become highly embarrassing. A life of crime, she reflected, was not without its complications. She rather hoped that her current possession of the pamphlet would remain a secret forever and it would soon be safely back in its proper home.

The only person she could share it with was Nellie, who was eager to read it. 'How similar to the events reported here,' she observed, 'including the stones. But from the appearance of the packet I doubt it has been opened since the pamphlet was printed.'

'I agree,' said Mina, 'but the coincidence is very strange.'

'I wonder what became of Abigail Falcon?'

'I did go back to the parish records to look, but I didn't see anyone there with that surname.'

'So, does that mean that since the house was built no resident has died here?' asked Nellie.

'Not necessarily,' said Mina. 'The church books record burials, not deaths. No one who was resident in the house has been buried in the graveyard of St Mond. If someone died here or in the village and was buried elsewhere there would be no entry in the books.'

She wrapped the papers and secreted them in a drawer of the night table. Abigail Falcon, if still alive, would be about forty. Mina wished she could interview her, but for the time being she would have to remain a mystery.

Chapter Eleven

The occupants of Hollow House gathered for a substantial luncheon of ham, chicken rissoles and potato croquettes, followed by fig tart. Mr Hope ate heartily, attacking his food like a lion that had just made a kill and was excited by the aroma and taste of fresh blood. If he at all repented the disturbance he had caused the previous night it was not apparent from his manner. Mr Beckler, the only other person at table with any relish for food, tore at his meat with large sharp teeth as a hyaena might. Mina hoped that Mr Beckler was a single man, otherwise she would have to sympathise with a wife who was obliged daily to face him across the cruets. Even Dr Hamid's usually robust appetite was subdued, while Kitty ate sparingly and avoided looking at anyone.

'Mr Honeyacre,' said Mr Hope in a burst of enthusiasm, 'I really must congratulate you on your table. I can assure you that there are lords and ladies who do not dine as well.'

Mr Honeyacre murmured his appreciation of the compliment, but his manner towards Mr Hope was more coolly polite and less admiring than before.

If Mr Hope noticed any change in his host he did not reveal it. 'You have been more than generous with your time and hospitality and, of course, your agreement to hold a séance here. The results have been quite extraordinary and will undoubtedly advance the knowledge of mankind. I predict that in years to come the events of last night will be spoken of with reverence. Our séance will be talked about all over the world, as the one that ushered in a new understanding of psychic matters. And now I can inform you that Mr Beckler and I, after an exhaustive examination of the house, have found several powerful concentrations of psychic energy. There is an especially strong one in this very room! With that in mind I do not think we should lose the opportunity of repeating the experiment as soon as possible.'

Mr Beckler nodded. 'If the carriage should arrive with my camera that would be all the better,' he said. 'The house has many things in it which are deserving of a photograph.' He smiled at Mina. She did not smile back.

Mr Honeyacre, moving slowly and deliberately, put down his knife and fork, which were barely used, dabbed his lips with a napkin and coughed gently. 'Lord Hope,' he said in a carefully even tone, 'am I to understand that, despite the distress caused to my wife by the séance we held last night, you actually intend to hold another?'

Mr Hope paused, surprised by this unexpected hint of dissent. 'It is essential that we do. Of course,' he added reluctantly, 'we could wait until Mrs Honeyacre has recovered from her upset. But I do not think that will take long. A few hours perhaps? But we must proceed sooner rather than later or the energy might dissipate.'

Under his calm exterior, Mr Honeyacre was simmering with emotion. He chewed his lips while deciding how to reply. Mina, too, was appalled by Mr Hope's manners, since it was hardly his place to discuss the health of his host's wife in front of them both.

Kitty rose from the table in some agitation and Nellie at once went to her side and linked arms with her. 'Let us go and sit together in the parlour,' she said. 'If the weather improves we might take a walk on the terrace with Little Scrap.'

Kitty agreed with a tired smile, much to the relief of her husband, and they departed.

'I feel quite sure that a walk in the fresh air will soon restore Mrs Honeyacre,' Mr Hope went on, breezily. 'And, who can tell, it might be that she is a medium and unaware of it, with powers she has yet to understand. If I am correct she could be developed into a new shining beacon of spiritualism!'

'That is not an issue here,' said Mr Honeyacre, sharply. 'The issue here is the wellbeing of my wife, which I will not endanger for any consideration of fortune or fame.' Mina could see that, under the table top, his hands were clenched and trembling. Meek and mild he might be, but Mr Honeyacre in defence of his wife was a giant amongst men.

'If I might make a suggestion,' said Dr Hamid, interrupting the awkward confrontation, 'I will continue to attend to Mrs Honeyacre's health and all here present must agree to abide by my decision as to when she is fully restored.'

'I approve your suggestion,' said Mr Honeyacre warmly.

Mr Hope attempted to conceal his displeasure, but his eyes were hard and his smile unfriendly. 'How soon might that be, Dr Hamid?'

'I make no predictions.'

The meal continued without further conversation.

As the dishes were being cleared, Mr Malling appeared. 'I have persuaded Ned Copper to come to the house and be questioned,' he said, his tone implying that it had been no easy task. 'He is currently at the kitchen table enjoying a hearty meal. In view of the state of his clothing I regret that he is not fit to be brought into the family part of the house.'

'I understand, of course,' said Mr Hope, rising to his feet, 'and I will go to him. I have served in the army and walked the jungle with men of all classes and races, and do not judge them by birth or appearance, but by what they do. I do not believe that I am lowering myself to sit with a wise and aged man in a kitchen, and learn from him.'

It was, therefore, Mr Hope, Mr Beckler, Dr Hamid, Mr Honeyacre and Mina who went to hear Ned Copper.

'Are you sure about this?' asked Mr Honeyacre of Mina. 'I know I would not have Kitty listen to him, although I am sure you have better nerves.'

'Miss Scarletti has nerves that strong men would envy,' said Dr Hamid.

'Oh, I'm sure, I'm sure,' said Mr Honeyacre and, while it was not clear if he agreed with Dr Hamid, he looked on Mina with renewed respect.

As they approached the short flight of stairs leading down to the kitchen and scullery, Dr Hamid, as was his habit, offered to assist Mina and she extended her hand to take his arm, but found herself instead being grasped firmly by Mr Beckler, who flashed her a conspiratorial smile. She looked away quickly but not before she had seen Dr Hamid's expression of astonishment.

Ned Copper sat at the kitchen table with a large plate of bread and meat and something foaming in a tankard. Mrs Blunt, unchallenged queen of her domain, eyed him with suspicion. The room smelt of old clothing and lemons and from the connecting door came the fragrance of a laundry with a hint of hot soapy vapour.

When the little party arrived, Mrs Blunt departed as far as the scullery, where there was some metallic clattering indicating violent activity, but not loud enough to conceal voices.

Ned Copper wiped his grey muzzle with the back of his hand, but had the decency to rise to his feet as his visitors arrived.

'Oh, please do be seated and enjoy your meal,' said Mr Hope amiably. 'I am very pleased to see you and glad too that you have been given some refreshment.' He sat down at the table in what was intended to be a friendly manner inspiring confidence and Mr Beckler drew out a chair for Mina. Everyone else remained standing. 'I am eager to hear what you know about the history of Ditching Hollow and this house in particular.'

Ned Copper eyed the unexpected gathering with a certain degree of suspicion. 'I know too much and that's a fact,' he said. 'I know what I wish I didn't know. I know what ought never to be spoken of.'

'But for the safety and comfort of others it is best that you tell all,' said Mr Hope, who knew how to wheedle when wheedling was required.

'I don't know about that,' said Ned. 'Some things are better not said. People hereabouts, we understand that, we just try to get on day by day and hope for nothing worse.' He took a deep draught from the tankard. 'Some say that it all began when the trains ran into each other in the Clayton Tunnel. But it was before that.' He took a bite of bread and meat and chewed it thoughtfully. Everyone waited for him to speak but when he swallowed that mouthful he simply took another bite.

'What can you tell us about that day?' asked Mina, hoping, as this was apparently his favourite subject, to at least get him talking again.

He took another pull from the tankard. 'More than ten years ago it was, but for those who saw it, it will always be like it happened yesterday. I was working in the field then and I heard the noise so loud it was worse than any thunder. It was like the ground opening up all the way down to the fiery pit. A grinding of metal and the steam and the shrieks of the poor souls being roasted alive. I went running to see what I could do, but inside the tunnel it was too dark to see. Then out of the smoke and the mist there came people, staggering, limping, half burnt, their faces black, clothes in rags. And deep inside there was the screaming of men and women and children in their last agonies, the ones that couldn't be saved.' He took another gulp. 'Even now, as I sit here, I can still hear the dying as they cry out for help, but they were past all help.'

'But you say that was not the start?' prompted Dr Hamid.

Ned gave him a grim look. 'No, it was long before that, so long that no one alive today remembers it. There are those who say that Ditchling Hollow is forever cursed. Cursed by the spirits of those who swung on the gallows and whose bodies were left to rot away unburied. It's said that all who were not born here or wed to one who is are cursed and especially — yes, most especially — all those who live in this house, the masters, the magistrates, the ones who sent innocents to be hanged. No one who lives in Hollow House can ever find contentment.'

'I can assure you that no one who lives here now has ever sent anyone to the gallows, guilty or innocent!' exclaimed Mr Honeyacre.

'Well, that's the thing about curses,' said Ned Copper. 'They got long memories.'

'I spoke to William Jesson recently,' said Mina. 'He came here to tell us about the road being flooded. He said his grandmother came from outside the village to work here. Here in this house. But she was unhappy. What do you know about her?'

He gave a strange laugh. 'Unhappy? Is that what you call it? Just a young thing she was, no more than a child, and next thing she had a child of her own and no father to be seen.

There were some who said it was old Mr Wigmore because he left her a few pounds in his will.'

'I think, perhaps, we will not discuss that subject,' said Mr Honeyacre, uncomfortably.

'What do you know of the ghost that haunts this place?' asked Mr Hope.

Ned put down the tankard and stared into it, as if willing it to fill itself.

Mr Hope quickly signalled Mr Beckler to fetch more beer. He found a jug on the sideboard and brought it to refill the tankard.

Ned Copper sniffed at the tankard with its dark bitter foam and took another gulp. 'I don't know nothing about that. But I don't set foot in here more often than I need to, and not at night.'

'You must remember the Lassiter family,' said Mina. 'The last people who lived here. I was told they went away quite suddenly. Why was that?'

'Oh, there was all sorts happened that made them go. Things flying about all over the place when there was no one near them. I heard say that Mr Lassiter murdered his wife and went mad. And there was a child, a peculiar child, and the story is that the nursemaid made away with it, but I don't rightly know what happened to her as she was never seen again.' He took another bite of bread and meat. 'It was my father who found the thing,' he said, his voice muffled.

'What did he find?' asked Mr Hope eagerly.

Ned hesitated and looked up with a watery gleam in his eye. Mr Hope nodded to Mr Beckler, who obediently took a coin from his pocket and put it on the table. There was a pause and the coin was joined by a second one. Ned picked up the coins, rubbed them between his fingers and put them in his pocket.

'It was a coffin. A small one, all broken up. Not a proper coffin, more like a wooden box, like they use for tea. And it had a body in it, a child's body dressed in red. Only, he said it wasn't the right shape. Like it was an imp or a hobgoblin. It was a bad thing, it was a wicked thing.'

Mr Honeyacre gave a little gasp. 'Why that —'

'Where did he find it?' demanded Mina. She glanced at Mr Honeyacre and shook her head. He looked surprised but fell silent.

'I don't rightly know, but it wasn't in the churchyard. Just outside it maybe. Not on holy ground, I can tell you that.'

'Do you still have it?' asked Dr Hamid, who had seen Mina's look.

Ned gave a laugh and shook his head. 'Who would keep something like that? No, he burnt it. To this day, I don't know if he did right.'

It was all that Ned Copper had to say and, on receiving another coin from Mr Honeyacre, he departed without protest.

Mr Hope gestured Mr Beckler aside and they had a brief but urgent conversation, a conversation that largely consisted of Mr Hope talking rapidly and Mr Beckler nodding his agreement. Mr Hope then turned to the others in the little group, inflated his chest as if he was about to address a large company and made an announcement. 'Our course of action is now obvious. The slight break in the weather affords us better light and clearer air and will enable Mr Beckler and I to go and look for the burial site of that small coffin. While it was not in the consecrated earth of the graveyard, in my experience such questionable items are often buried nearby as Mr Copper suggested. Perhaps it is felt that the proximity to holy ground will redeem the evil that lies within. That location will be an important focus of psychic energy.'

'But —' began Mr Honeyacre.

'Have no fear, we will not disturb church land,' Mr Hope, interrupted. 'We will also make enquiries in the village to see if anyone other than Mr Copper can provide more information. But there is no time to lose. Mr Beckler!' he called, as if summoning a hunting dog. 'Come with me!'

They departed and no one was sorry to see them go.

'I could not help noticing,' said Dr Hamid, 'that we all failed to mention to them that the location of the strange burial is already known. Do we plan to do so?'

'I rather thought we ought to have done,' said Mr Honeyacre.

'We may do so in time,' said Mina mischievously. 'But their expedition, if they but knew it, is by nature of a test. If Mr Hope and his lackey are able to find the burial place without a map then I will be more impressed with their skills.'

'Ah, I understand,' said Mr Honeyacre, nodding approval. 'That is a clever device.'

'I suspect,' added Mina, 'that he is also in search of more ghost stories as material for his next book, since he seems incapable of writing his own. If the villagers have any sense they will be composing them as fast as they can and demanding gratuities.'

After an interlude with her book and her notes, Mina decided to join Nellie and Kitty who had decided to take a stroll around the terrace. She found them looking out over the rear gardens, the tidy arrangement and tilled earth awaiting a spring planting, a testimony to the hard work of the Mallings. Miss Pet and Zillah were keeping them company, walking together arm in arm in friendly fashion. All too soon the breeze stiffened into a cruel wind and they were forced to retire indoors.

In the warmth of the parlour the ladies begged Mina to relate another story and she was obliged to make up one on the spot. In this tale, Mr Hope and Mr Beckler decided to walk up the steep path to Clayton Hill to visit the windmills, even when they had been warned not to as it was too muddy. The two men climbed as hard as they could, but just as they neared the top they encountered a large dog which barked at them and this frightened them so much that they both slipped and fell. They could not stop themselves rolling down the muddy path and so they rolled all the way down, over and over, arriving at the bottom of the hill so covered in mud that they couldn't be recognised. When the villagers found them they were thought to be vagabonds and thrown into the mill brook. Everyone laughed heartily at the story — even Miss Pet, who was usually so solemn, dabbed her eyes with amusement.

'Perhaps that will happen when they go up there tomorrow,' said Kitty. 'Then I will order Malling to turn them away.'

Mina was reminded that Nellie's party of visitors was supposed to be returning to Brighton that day, although it continued to look unlikely. She would have liked to be home before she was missed, but at the same time did not want to leave when there was still a mystery to be solved and Mr Hope and Mr Beckler were creating agitation for Mr Honeyacre and Kitty. She went to look out of the window to see if the weather might be clearing and saw four men walking up the path towards the house. As they drew closer she realised, with a surge of dismay, who they were.

For a moment or two she could hardly believe what she was seeing and then, when it was impossible to deny, beckoned Nellie over.

'Nellie!' she whispered. 'Go somewhere — anywhere — just don't be found here!'

'Why, what is it?'

'What is the matter?' asked Kitty. Little Scrap was nestled on her lap, being fed morsels of biscuit from her pocket.

'Mr Hope and Mr Beckler have not after all got lost in the mud but are coming back in time for tea,' said Mina. 'And they have brought two visitors with them.'

Nellie, also looking out of the window, managed to swallow a horrified gasp. The two men accompanying Mr Hope and Mr Beckler were Mina's brother Richard and Mr Stevenson, the detective.

'You had better go back to your room at once, before they see you,' Mina whispered. 'Let us hope their visit is a brief one. I will tell everyone that you have a headache.'

'I never have headaches.'

'You must have one now. Quickly! Before they arrive!'

Nellie sighed. 'Very well, I will do my best.' She clutched her hand to her forehead in dramatic fashion, groaned loudly and hurried from the room.

'Whatever is the matter?' asked Kitty, staring after her. 'Is Nellie ill?'

'Nellie is taking care to avoid Mr Hope, since she dislikes him so,' said Mina.

Kitty accepted the explanation and seemed disinclined to leave the cushioned comfort of the parlour, while Miss Pet and Zillah went to stare out of the window.

'Why it is young Mr Scarletti!' exclaimed Zillah. 'I don't know the other gentleman.'

'Oh, Mr Scarletti is much more amusing than Mr Hope!' said Kitty. 'Now we shall have some fun!'

'Amusing' was not perhaps the word Mina would have used to describe her brother. She decided it would not be a sensible question to ask Nellie's maid how she recognised him. She peered out into the hallway and was relieved to see that Nellie had climbed the stairs and was out of sight before the new visitors reached the front door and were admitted by the servants.

Mr Stevenson, whose air of confidence suggested that he was unaware that his true identity was known, looked about the hall approvingly, while Richard entirely failed to appear repentant at the unexpected intrusion. 'And we have arrived not a moment too soon,' said Mr Hope, as the rain began to descend once more. A distant crackle of lightning and dull boom of thunder rolling across the hills and into the valley seemed to Mina like the harbingers of all that she had most dreaded.

She braced herself, doing her best to appear friendly and calm, and left the parlour to greet the arrivals. As she did so, Mr Honeyacre and Dr Hamid arrived. Neither man was able to conceal his astonishment and when Mr Honeyacre perceived Mr Stevenson he rocked a little on his heels so that Dr Hamid was obliged to grasp him firmly by the elbow to prevent an accident.

'You are surprised I can see that we have brought new friends!' said Mr Hope. 'But you will soon understand the reason for my invitation.'

Mr Honeyacre recovered his balance and made an effort far beyond the normal requirements of civility to remain, if not exactly welcoming, polite. While he was not displeased to see Richard he fixed Mr Stevenson with a look of mingled distress and revulsion and for a few moments was unable to speak.

'Miss Scarletti,' said Mr Hope, raising a cynical eyebrow, 'were you aware that your brother was in Ditchling Hollow or are you as surprised to see him as I was? I rather think you must have known it all along and have deliberately kept it a secret from us. Now why should that be?'

'I believed him to be in London,' said Mina, truthfully. 'Richard, what can you be doing here?'

'Oh, it's my work, you know,' said Richard, blithely, 'doing sketches for the *Society Journal*. I ought to be back home now, only the infernal weather prevented me from returning and I have been obliged to keep warm and dry at the Goat and Hammers.'

'And I,' uttered Mr Honeyacre in a voice that sounded like the last gasp of a half-strangled man, 'have not had the honour of meeting this gentleman.'

'Stevenson,' said that person with a polite little bow. 'I am a naturalist and travel the country looking for rare species.' He tapped the leather case of binocular glasses on his chest, as if to add verisimilitude to this account. 'I am compiling a volume to be entitled *The Pleasures of Sussex*.'

Mr Honeyacre appeared unconvinced. 'Indeed. And who is it to be published by? A Mr White, perhaps?'

Mina searched her memory and recalled Mr Honeyacre's angry denouncement of a Mr White, the developer who had wanted to purchase the estate and convert it to industrial use.

Mr Stevenson, however, looked genuinely puzzled. 'No, it is a private publication. I am not acquainted with a Mr White.'

'Well,' said Mr Honeyacre, his suspicions far from allayed, 'I suggest we all go to the drawing room and I will have tea sent.' He bowed stiffly and departed, while Mr Malling arranged for the new arrivals to hand over their damply misted coats and have their muddy boots cleaned.

Mr Beckler approached Mina with one of his odd little smiles. If it was meant to look friendly and inviting it failed. 'I do hope the ladies will join us for tea?' he asked and it was apparent from his tone that by 'ladies' he meant Mina. 'I should like that very much.'

'I expect so, but I wish to have a private conversation with my brother first,' said Mina, coldly.

'Very well, I anticipate your company with pleasure.' He raised his hand and for one dreadful moment, Mina thought he would kiss his fingers to her, but he simply gave a little wave, inclined his head and drifted away.

Dr Hamid stared after the departing figure and gave a little cough. 'Miss Scarletti, I hope that fellow has not been annoying you,' he said awkwardly. 'I could not help but notice his behaviour, which smacks of more familiarity than one might expect on so short an acquaintance. Of course,' he added, stiffly, 'if it should chance that his attentions do not annoy you then you must let me know.'

'He annoys me very much,' said Mina, 'but that is only his manner. He has been making flattering remarks about my appearance which are quite uncalled for.'

'The scoundrel!' exclaimed Dr Hamid. 'That is — I mean — not that you do not warrant — I mean, it is not his place to make such remarks if you do not wish him to. That was what I meant.' Dr Hamid clenched his teeth as if to force himself to be silent.

'Oh, I don't think he means anything by it. Remember, he is a photographer and I suppose he flatters all people to gain their custom. He tells ladies that they have pretty faces and no doubt he tells gentlemen of their noble countenances which, it is essential, must be preserved for posterity. I expect he has said as much to you.'

'No, he has not.'

'Well, it is only a matter of time before he does.' She glanced across to where Mr Stevenson was strolling about the hallway, as if estimating the value of its contents. Richard was pretending to be interested in his surroundings but she could tell that this was only an excuse to lurk nearby. She might have expected her brother to go where there were both refreshments and the chance to hide in full company to avoid Mina's recriminations. Instead, he appeared to be waiting to speak to her and, for once, his expression was unreadable.

'I will not come to tea just yet,' said Mina to Dr Hamid. 'I have family business to attend to. You should join the others.'

Dr Hamid inclined his head and followed Mr Hope and Mr Beckler to the drawing room, but it was obvious that he was not happy with that company. Richard favoured Mina with the ghost of one of his most disarming smiles, the kind that melted all hearts except hers.

'Richard —' she began.

'Ah, my dear sister!' he exclaimed. 'How extraordinary and unexpected that we should meet here! And what a delight! How well you do look! I saw mother and Enid the other day and I am pleased to say that they are both flourishing. Mother in particular has an important message for you.' He turned to Mr Stevenson. 'I hope you don't mind, old chap, but we have a few private matters to discuss. We'll be along for our tea shortly.'

'Of course,' said Mr Stevenson, reluctantly, and left the hallway to follow the others.

Richard linked his arm in Mina's and as he did so looked down at her and the smile dropped from his face. 'Where can we talk?' he said urgently.

'The library. I'll show you the way,' said Mina.

Once the door was closed behind them, Mina faced her brother. She had been about to reprimand him for his failure to leave the area and his folly in coming to the very place she had warned him to stay away from, but his changed manner had stopped her and she decided instead to listen to what he had to say.

Richard spent a moment or two listening at the door then carefully eased it open and peered out and finally closed it softly before beckoning Mina to the far side of the room. 'No one must hear us!' he hissed.

'Richard, what is the meaning of this?'

He took a deep breath. 'You're not angry with me?'

'Of course I am; I am always angry with you. Now explain yourself.'

'I was going to do as you said, really I was, but I had to finish my work first. The day after we spoke I went up to Clayton Hill to finish my sketch of the windmills and, as it happened, Stevenson was up there too. Then the rain came down and we had to shelter inside. Mr Hammond, the miller, was very happy when he saw my sketch and gave us tea and told me all about the history of the mills, which I thought very dull, but a good thing for the *Journal* and I wrote it all down, so you don't have to do it now, except for the wretched spelling. So, Stevenson and I, we were there for hours and we talked and I said I was employed by the *Journal*. As it happened I had some old letters from the editor in my pocket, so I think he believed me. He asked if I was related to the famous Miss Scarletti who has been in all the newspapers and I couldn't really deny that I was your brother, as I expect he already knew that, and he said that he had seen you visiting the church here with a party from Hollow House. He said he found it hard to believe that I didn't know you were here. So I had to admit that I did. But here is where I was clever —'

Mina groaned inwardly, since Richard's idea of cleverness often led to dreadful consequences that she usually had to put right.

'I told him I did know because you had told me that you were looking into some hauntings and I was worried about you in case you got into any danger and coming here had been my idea as I wanted to be nearby in case you needed my help. So, Stevenson and I became very friendly and then, when the rain stopped, we went to refresh ourselves at the Goat and Hammers.' Mina's face must have shown what she was thinking because he added quickly, 'No, really, Mina, I could never get inebriated on what they serve there.'

'Did your new friend reveal his true purpose in being here?'

'No, and I didn't expect him to. He did ask me if I knew Nellie. Of course, I couldn't lie about that because he already knows I do, so I told him that I know her because Mrs Jordan is your friend and I entertain the greatest respect for her.'

'I hope he believed you. But why, Richard, why, after all the warnings, did you come here?'

'It wasn't my fault. Stevenson and I were in the Goat and Hammers when Mr Hope and Mr Beckler came in. They started buying beer for everyone and asking if there were any stories of ghosts and demons and strange burials in Ditchling Hollow, especially relating to Hollow House. Of course, he recognised me and after that I couldn't avoid him. But here's the thing.' Richard stopped speaking suddenly and Mina saw he was in the grip of strong emotion. His face became flushed and he dragged his hand through his dishevelled blond hair, raking it into tufts as if it was standing up with fright. 'Here's the thing,' he repeated, trying to calm himself. 'Mr Hope told me that you were at the house and then he mentioned Nellie. I must tell you he referred to her in very coarse language. I won't repeat a word of it. So I said "Mrs Jordan is not what you are thinking; she is a respectable married woman".'

'I trust he accepted your words.'

'He did — in a manner of speaking. He said that that was the best kind for his purposes.'

'His purposes?' exclaimed Mina. 'What an unpleasant man he is. I have seen that he admires her, as so many men do, but — purposes?'

'I don't think I need to say anything further, do I?'

'No, you don't.'

'So I decided then and there not to express any more opinions on the matter, as I thought it best for him not to know what I thought of him. And I tried to think of a good plan to get a message to Nellie to warn her of the danger.'

'Did you think of one? Because this is not it.'

'No, there wasn't time. Because the next thing was that Mr Hope invited us here, whether or not he was entitled to, and that gave me a proper reason to come here and be on hand to protect Nellie. Mr Hope is a vile man when it comes to women.'

'Why did he invite you both here, do you think?'

'He told us that there had been some wonderful things happening in a séance and he was going to hold another one, but he needed more witnesses. Since Mr Stevenson claims he is a naturalist and I am making my way as an artist Mr Hope said that we are men who use our eyes and we see the truth.'

'He doesn't want the truth,' said Mina, 'he just wants people to agree with him that what he believes in is the truth.' Mina thought quickly and took hold of her brother's hands. 'But, Richard,' she continued in a gentler tone, 'now that you have warned me you have accomplished what you came here to do. I will make sure to warn Nellie and I will also ensure that Dr Hamid knows of the danger to her. We can all protect her. But we need Mr Stevenson to go. Once you have had your tea, I suggest that you find some reason to leave Hollow House and persuade him to go with you.'

'How can I do that?'

'I don't know. I'll think of something. Is all your drawing complete now?'

'Yes, it's been a frightful bore and it doesn't pay as well as I thought it would. I don't know if I shall go on with it. Being a detective sounds like much more fun. Maybe, once this is all over, I could tell Mr Stevenson that I had seen through him and ask if he needs an assistant.' He gave a sudden laugh. 'You know that is a bit of joke that — about him being a naturalist. When we were in the Goat and Hammers, which is none too clean, there were cobwebs in every corner and even a nest of dead spiders, all dried and shrivelled up. When he saw them I thought he would faint and he confessed to me that he hates them. Don't naturalists like that sort of thing?'

'Well, he won't find any cobwebs or spiders here,' said Mina. 'Let us have our tea and I promise to speak with Nellie later. Then you must go.'

'I do need to get back to London,' Richard admitted gloomily, rubbing his cheek. 'That tooth is no better. The blacksmith said he would help me out with it, but I'm not sure of his methods. Does Dr Hamid have his medical bag with him?'

'He does, and I am sure that he can give you something to ease it.'

'I couldn't see Nellie, just for a minute before I leave?'

'No, Richard, better not.'

'Where is she?'

'She is avoiding seeing you by claiming a headache.'

'She never has headaches.'

'And she and I are sharing a room, which seems doubly wise now. Don't worry, we'll keep her safe from Mr Hope and you keep her safe from Mr Stevenson.'

'I wish someone would keep her safe from Mr Jordan,' said Richard to which Mina could think of no suitable reply.

Mina linked her arm in his and was turning to the library door when Richard said, 'Oh, and there was one more thing.'

'Oh dear.'

'I think you should know that Mr Beckler rather admires you. He told me that he would like to take your photograph.'

'He does not admire me,' said Mina. 'He is a photographer. It is a part of his trade to flatter people about their appearance, whether it is warranted or not, in order to obtain custom. I expect he has flattered you, too.'

'Er, no, he has not.'

'Well, I am sure he will do before long,' said Mina with the uncomfortable feeling that this was a conversation she had had too many times.

Mina and Richard joined the group in the drawing room, who were awaiting their tea with expressions of deep solemnity. Even the portrait of the first Mrs Honeyacre looked less happy with her surroundings than earlier. The grumbling thunder was moving closer, as if mocking their discomfiture.

Mr Hope was on his feet, in mid-declamation. 'And there,' he said, excitedly, 'only a few feet from the gate, we saw, or to be more accurate, both of us sensed, a disturbance that could only have been the location of the strange burial. Beckler knew it before I did,' he added with a rare generosity and Mr Beckler dipped his gaze and allowed himself a modest smile. 'There was an aura about the very soil, the appearance of the vegetation, that spoke to him, and when he pointed it out, I saw it too. Mr Stevenson!' Mr Hope turned expectantly towards the detective with a suddenness that made him start. 'As a naturalist, we must engage you for your expert advice on that matter.'

Mr Stevenson did his best to appear flattered by that prospect, but his eyes darted about as if looking for inspiration. 'I — er — it would be best for me to avoid commenting until I have examined the site for myself,' he said at last.

Mina glanced at Dr Hamid. Neither could entirely restrain their amusement as the Lassiters' map indicated that the actual burial was nowhere near the gate.

'Did you discover anything new at the site?' enquired Dr Hamid. 'Were there any remains?'

Mr Hope was not best pleased at being questioned by Dr Hamid, but he made an effort to reply. 'Regretfully, there were no physical objects, only a trace of psychic energy. But I feel sure that a powerful medium could do more. I also made enquiries amongst the villagers regarding the burial and one or two did recall that Ned Copper's father had once found something unusual that had disturbed him, but they were unable to tell me any more than he had done. A few did come to me with tales of local hauntings, usually how they had encountered the shades of their ancestors in the graveyard.'

'Not far from the Goat and Hammers,' whispered Richard to Mina and she smiled.

Mr Hope ignored them and shook his head sorrowfully. 'I had thought that there would be many more such incidents, but the people here seem to have a small stock of tales. And every time I was told of one, seven others chimed in and said it was not being told rightly and it didn't happen to the speaker's aunt but the complainant's mother. Still, I may have stimulated their memories. I will return in a day or two and see what they have.'

'I have been told that Miss Scarletti is a writer of stories,' said Mr Beckler. 'She paints with words and I paint with my camera.'

'Mina writes tales for children,' said Richard. 'I haven't read them myself, but I believe they are very good.'

'They teach the difference between good and evil,' said Mina. 'Moral lessons, the true understanding of character and how to live well.'

'No ghosts?' asked Mr Beckler.

'Not one,' Mina replied.

The wind started up again and there was a busy tapping at the window like the work of a thousand tiny hammers. Mr Honeyacre rose and peered out of the window then returned to his chair dejectedly. 'I am sorry to say it is raining again and worse than before,' he said. The small hammers started to blend with each other and become larger ones and finally there was a solid deluge.

'There have been times,' said Mr Honeyacre, 'when the heavens have opened and we have been flooded with rain and when it stops one feels such a sense of relief because, of course, we think that the storm has spent itself and it is therefore impossible for there to be any more rain to fall. And that, I regret to say, is when it starts again.'

Everyone brightened a little as Mary Ann brought in the tea with some freshly baked tartlets, fragrant with warm sugared fruit. She almost dropped the tray as a great boom of thunder unfurled itself overhead.

'Don't be afraid, my dear,' said Mr Hope soothingly, 'there is no danger.'

Mary Ann moved about the room distributing cups and plates, looking unconvinced.

'Where is Mrs Jordan?' asked Mr Honeyacre. 'We should ask her to join us. She does seem to enjoy a nice pastry.'

'She has a headache and is gone to rest quietly,' said Mina. 'She has expressly asked not to be disturbed.'

'Oh, that is a great pity,' said Mr Hope. 'I did not think she was a lady who suffered from headaches.'

They sipped their tea and ate tartlets without further conversation. It was as if the rain was performing a dramatic monologue and they were all listening to it, not daring to interrupt. The cups were refreshed and Kitty fed Little Scrap half a tartlet and put a fragment of pastry in her pocket for later. Mina thought that the tiny dog ate more than his mistress.

With the eventual passing of the thunder and rain a strange quiet settled over their surroundings. No one dared comment on the weather in case the very thought provoked another downpour. Mina decided to return to the library but she had scarcely risen to her feet when the ground trembled and shook beneath her. She gasped and clutched onto the back of a chair, or she might have fallen. Dr Hamid rose to assist her, but it was Mr Beckler who seized the opportunity and was by her side in an instant, taking hold of her arm.

'What was that?' she asked. 'I know I didn't imagine it. I hope not!'

'Be calm, Miss Scarletti, I felt it too,' he said.

'We all did,' said Mr Hope. 'If I was to guess, it was an earth tremor; not the same kind as one experiences in the tropics which are volcanic in origin, but the result of an underground landslip, probably brought on by the heavy rain.'

For once, Mina was unwilling to shake off Mr Beckler's attentions as the shock through her frail body had unsettled her. For one horrible moment she had feared that it was she alone who had experienced it, a symptom perhaps of a new weakness, or a disease that would quickly claim her. She had too much to do to let go of life so soon. At least, she thought, Mr Hope had not attributed the phenomenon to a ghost.

'I had better go and look outside,' said Mr Honeyacre, and he hurried from the room. Everyone else followed him and there was an anxious gathering in the hallway as he opened the front door to look out across the terrace and down the slope to the church and the village. To their relief, all was calm and peaceful. The ground was sodden with rivulets of muddy water trickling downhill and dripping from the broken edges of the old steps, themselves harbouring in their shallows miniature rock pools that shimmered as the breeze plucked at them.

'It might have been some distance away,' said Mr Hope. 'Underground vibrations can carry for many miles.'

'Yes, we must hope so,' said Mr Honeyacre. He was about to close the door, but something, perhaps a sense of some change in the air, made him stop and look again.

The noise was quite gentle when they first heard it, a soft rumble, not as loud as thunder, more like the snores of a mythical giant. Then the ground seemed to come to life: it appeared to be breathing, its surface rising and falling, sighing and protesting. A moment or so later it gave a sudden shiver and began to move. Grassy outcrops bent and slid away. A river of mud and stones formed, widening as it went, spreading its fingers down towards the graveyard. The noise deepened and intensified. Rocks battered against rocks in a primitive percussion. The old steps leading down to the church lost their grip on the earth beneath and slithered downwards, carried by the dark tide. The gravelled carriage approach bubbled like a pot of porridge and the half constructed fountain keeled over, its walled surround breaking apart. Mina half expected the new terrace and its stairs to follow, but they held, if precariously, the lower slabs projecting into empty space and coming to rest at a tilt. At last, all was still again and they gazed out at the ruin of the land. The only sound was Little Scrap barking and barking as if his lungs would burst.

Mr Honeyacre gave little moan and staggered, looking as though he would faint. Dr Hamid took a grip on his arm, assisted him back to the drawing room, settled him before the fire and then snapped out orders that he was to be watched. Kitty went to sit with him while Dr Hamid went to fetch his medical bag. Mr Malling came running up and Mr Hope ordered him to go outside and investigate the immediately surrounding land and its safety. Mr Malling did not look pleased but he had no choice and obeyed.

The news when it eventually came was not good. Mr Malling reported that the path leading to the church no longer existed. Anyone who thought of going to church ought not to attempt it as there was the danger of starting a new landslip with consequences he hardly liked to suggest. As for the carriage drive, the part immediately outside the house was badly damaged and the portion leading to the main road was partly sunken and underwater, while the rough ground on either side looked unsafe for any mode of travel.

Mr Gillespie had a brief but serious word with Mr Malling, followed by a discussion with Dr Hamid, who was busy applying restoratives to his host.

'I will speak to Mr Honeyacre when he is recovered,' Mr Gillespie told the company. 'However, it is clear that the maids will not be able to return to their homes until the ground is safe and Mr Scarletti and Mr Stevenson will also be obliged to stay. The accommodation arrangements will have to be rethought. I am sure that this will merely be a temporary inconvenience.'

Despite these reassurances, the prevailing atmosphere in Hollow House was one of forced calm concealing incipient hysteria.

They were trapped.

Chapter Twelve

It was only a few minutes before Mr Honeyacre, who was probably thinking more of his guests than himself, insisted that he was restored. He informed Dr Hamid that he required no further attention and proceeded to consult with Mr Gillespie and the Mallings. He then called everyone together in the drawing room, although Nellie did not appear and neither did Kitty, who had gone to sit with her.

Mr Honeyacre's address was brief and to the point. 'I regret to say that, for the time being, none of us can leave the house in safety. Naturally, I wish to ensure the greatest comfort and convenience for you all, such as circumstances will allow. Inevitably, some changes will have to be made to the accommodation and this is what Mr Gillespie advises. Mary Ann and Susan will sleep in the kitchen. Mr Scarletti, it will be necessary for you to share a room with Dr Hamid. If Lord Hope is agreeable, he may share his room with Mr Beckler. That will leave a room in the west wing for Mr Stevenson. I hope no one has any objections to this?'

No one wished to add to Mr Honeyacre's woes by expressing any dissent and it was with noticeable relief that Mr Honeyacre gave orders for the new arrangements to be made before bedtime.

Mina had decided to call on Nellie and apprise her of the news when she was accosted by Mr Beckler, who pursued her up the stairs with his long strides, adopting a place several steps down so they were more on a level for conversation.

'A word, Miss Scarletti, if you would be so kind?'

Since she could not outpace him she was obliged to stop and turn to face him.

'We are destined to be in each other's company a little longer,' he observed with a flicker of his eyebrows.

'Not necessarily,' said Mina, brusquely. 'The house is a large one.'

'But I was so looking forward to your telling me all about Brighton,' he persisted. 'I have heard it is a healthful place to live and the light is particularly good for photography.'

'That is the case,' she admitted.

He leaned forward to be nearer to her face, clasping his hands together as if in supplication, his long narrow body writhing in anticipation. 'If I was to pay a visit, do I have your permission to call on you?'

'I do not accept calls from young gentlemen.'

His lips made a moue of comical distress. 'Then there must be many disappointed young gentlemen in Brighton.'

She abandoned politeness and spoke sharply. 'Mr Beckler, please desist. What you believe to be flattery I find insulting. I do not wish to be photographed and I will not receive your visits.'

'Might I not hope to know you better?' he pleaded.

'No. I am not as foolish as you seem to think. I will be blunt. I have seen through your plan.'

He paused and made a sharp intake of breath. 'You have?'

'Yes. It is too simple for words. If you want customers for your business then place an advertisement in a newspaper.'

She turned and continued on her way, but had hardly taken three steps before sounds of distress began to echo through the house. It was a wild sobbing, distant and yet uncomfortably piercing as it rose in pitch. Mina paused to try and determine its origin and then Zillah came rushing down the stairs looking unusually distracted.

'Whatever is the matter?' asked Mina.

'It's Mrs Honeyacre. Her poor Little Scrap is missing. She was playing with him only a few minutes ago, but in all the excitement he ran away and now he is nowhere to be found. He is so small that he could have slipped outside when the front door was open without anyone being the wiser and she has convinced herself that he is out there and was buried in the landslip. Miss Pet is with her now.'

Several others had now arrived in the hallway and heard Zillah's news. 'She will be inconsolable unless he is found unharmed,' said Mr Honeyacre. 'I will ask Malling to go outside and look, but I am sure that if he had seen any sign of him when he was out there earlier he would have said.' He grimaced. 'Such a little creature would not do well in the present conditions.'

'I suggest that we all search thoroughly indoors first,' said Mina. 'And as quietly as possible, so we may hear him if he moves or barks. Perhaps someone could fetch a biscuit to tempt him.'

'I have one,' said Zillah, patting the pocket of her apron.

Mr Hope joined the conference and, on learning what the matter was, instantly placed himself at the head of the expedition, allocating to all concerned the places where they should go. He, Mr Beckler, Richard, Mina and Mr Honeyacre were assigned to search the ground floor. Mr Stevenson, Dr Hamid, Mr Gillespie and Mrs Blunt, the lower floor. The Mallings were assigned to the servants' rooms, Zillah and the maids to the first floor bedrooms. Much as everyone found Mr Hope's assumption of command insensitive when in the presence of his host they all departed to their stations without argument.

The sound resulting from numerous persons all talking and walking about the house at once was, thought Mina, enough to raise an army of spectres had there been any to raise, although it was not sufficient to conceal the wails of Kitty's mounting anguish which rang through the house like the cry of a banshee. If nothing else it served to spur on their efforts.

Mina was just emerging from the library after failing to locate Little Scrap when she saw Zillah hurrying down the stairs into the hallway. 'Oh, Miss Scarletti, I think I know where the poor little puppy dog is, only I dare not go there! I think he is up on the top floor and he may have got trapped.'

'Show me,' said Mina. She ascended the staircase with Zillah offering a helping hand and at the bottom of the second flight paused and listened carefully. It was hard to be certain but she thought, in the brief moments when Kitty paused for breath, that she could detect a faint whining sound from above. 'I think you are correct.' Mary Ann and Susan were nearby, watching anxiously, neither looking willing to risk a climb to the upper floor. Mina turned to them. 'Go and fetch Dr Hamid and Mr Malling. I am sure they will know what to do.' The maids departed quickly. 'You were right not to attempt the stairs,' Mina told Zillah, as Kitty's cries rent the air once more. They both winced and covered their ears.

Mina would have preferred only her two suggested additions to the party, but when, soon afterwards, Dr Hamid appeared, Mr Hope and Mr Beckler were with him.

'I would advise caution,' said Dr Hamid, 'the floorboards are half rotten.' But Mr Hope, his appetite for peril seriously whetted, only laughed.

'Have no fear,' he said confidently, puffing out his chest, as Mr Honeyacre arrived on the scene, 'I have tackled far worse hazards than this. Leave it to me; the little dog will be saved.' Mr Hope threw back the guard rope with a flourish and began to climb.

Mr Malling arrived and stared up at the ascending figure. 'Take care, my Lord!' he exclaimed, but made no attempt to follow.

There was no stopping Mr Hope in his quest for glory. He was, mused Mina, a man to whom no challenge was too much for him to attempt, which was what made so many people think him a hero and a few to whisper that he was a fool heedless of his own danger. He was also, she thought as he disappeared around the curve of the stairs onto the upper landing, a great manipulator. Mr Hope was currently in conflict with Mr Honeyacre, who was determined to protect his wife from further distress by flatly prohibiting the holding of a second séance. The bold explorer was prepared to use every means at his disposal to ensure that his wishes were complied with. What better inducement could there possibly be than becoming the saviour of Mrs Honeyacre's prized puppy?

'Aha!' came a triumphant exclamation from above. 'I see the little fellow and he is safe and unharmed! I shall bring him down.' There was a creaking of floorboards in loud protest against the weight of the substantial Mr Hope. Mina smiled to herself. Sometimes, she thought, being small and light was an advantage. The next moment there was a sharp cry and a grinding noise then another cry. A little way down the corridor they heard another sound, a cracking, splitting noise, like a series of little explosions. All eyes were drawn to the source and, glancing upwards, they saw that the ceiling plaster in the corridor was bulging and fissures were opening.

'Oh my word!' cried Mr Honeyacre and some impulse made him run to see what was occurring, but Dr Hamid seized him by the arm and pulled him back.

Flakes of plaster began to tumble into the hallway, followed by larger fragments, until a hole opened up in the ceiling through which there descended a booted foot. The foot wriggled energetically, but only succeeded in bringing down more plaster. They could hear Mr Hope grunting as he attempted to extricate himself and a soft growl of protest from Little Scrap.

Everyone stared up at the curious spectacle of the disembodied foot.

'That is not a sight one sees every day,' Mina observed.

'Should we not try to assist Mr Hope?' enquired Mr Honeyacre. There was no note of urgency in his voice.

'He has not asked for any assistance,' said Mina.

'That is very true,' Mr Honeyacre agreed. 'I think he is the kind of man who would prefer to save himself.'

'I fear,' said Dr Hamid, 'that any further weight on the area could bring the ceiling down.'

'I agree, sir,' said Mr Malling. 'I wouldn't like to risk it.'

'I — er,' began Mr Beckler, looking from one observer to the other in some confusion, 'I think I should go and see what is happening.'

He approached the stairs, but before he could climb them there was a scuffling sound and Little Scrap, his fur coated in dust, bounded down with a prize firmly grasped between his teeth.

'Oh, my word, what is it you have there?' exclaimed Mr Honeyacre, scooping up the little dog.

Dr Hamid went to examine what Little Scrap was guarding. 'It's hard to see,' he said. 'It looks like —'

Zillah came up and offered the recalcitrant animal a fragment of biscuit and so persuaded Little Scrap to let go of his less appetising morsel.

Dr Hamid examined it. 'It is a bone,' he said. 'And, unless I am very much mistaken, it is human.'

Zillah took Little Scrap away to be washed and reunited with his mistress, while the others joined Dr Hamid in contemplating the discovery.

'A clavicle, I think,' he said. 'A collar bone.'

'Man or woman?' asked Mr Honeyacre.

'It's hard to determine. An adult, certainly.'

There was a soft cough. 'Excuse me,' said Mr Beckler, 'but I feel someone should see if we can rescue Mr Hope. I have ventured as far as the top of the stairs and can see his difficulty. He is, I believe, unhurt, but if I went any further I fear that I would find myself in a similar predicament. And there is a danger of the whole ceiling coming down.'

Mina thought it a great shame that Mr Beckler did not have his camera with him, or he might have been able to take a photograph of Mr Hope in his unusual position. She would certainly have purchased a copy.

'Oh, yes, of course,' said Mr Honeyacre. 'The whole celling — we must do something at once!' They glanced back at the foot, which made further efforts to withdraw, resulting only in a shower of plaster fragments. 'But I am not sure what is for the best.'

'I'll fetch some boards,' said Mr Malling. 'I kept the ones the builders used when they repaired the roof and they should be just the thing. If we lay them across the floor we may be able to reach Lord Hope safely and assist him.'

'That is an excellent plan!' said Mr Honeyacre. He moved cautiously a few steps down the corridor. 'Have no fear, my

Lord, help is at hand,' he called up to the protruding foot. 'Please try and keep still and we will send someone up for you.'

There was an irritated grunting from above, but the foot did stop wriggling.

'There was something else I saw while I was up there,' said Mr Beckler, 'something lying underneath the broken floorboards. That bone is not the only one. I saw it clearly. It was a skull. A human skull.'

'Are you certain?' asked Dr Hamid.

'Oh yes,' said Mr Beckler with a little smirk and an undisguised gleam in his eyes.

It was not long before the boards were brought and it was decided that the rescue party should consist of Dr Hamid, Mr Malling and Mr Beckler. Mina looked about to see if she could find Richard, but he was nowhere to be seen. She decided to say nothing. If she did not draw attention to her brother's absence half the party would be prepared to swear in a court of law that he had been there.

Since Kitty's cries had now stopped it was to be assumed that she had been reunited with her darling, a circumstance for which they were all profoundly grateful.

Mrs Malling arrived with the maids, inspected the carpet with a severe expression and ordered that once the danger was past dust sheets should be fetched from the storeroom to be laid down in case of a further snowy deluge.

At last, Richard arrived with Mr Stevenson shadowing him close behind. Mina hoped and assumed that Nellie was staying in her bedroom with her headache and unlikely to join the throng.

Once a plan had been devised the rescue party, resembling a team of Alpinists making an attempt on the Matterhorn, began very cautiously to climb the creaking stairs, carrying the boards and a lantern.

Their efforts were clearly heard from below with much annoyed exclamations from Mr Hope, during which there was a further fall of plaster dust and then large flakes. The general anxiety concerning the fate of the ceiling and the carpet was palpable. After a few minutes, and to the great interest of the watchers, the booted leg was able to ascend and it finally disappeared from sight like a celestial vision rising up into the clouds.

Soon afterwards, Mr Hope, his trousers torn and covered in dirt, appeared at the top of the stairs to muted exclamations of approval and made his way down. 'Do not fear, I am quite unharmed,' he said reassuringly. 'Please tell me that Mrs Honeyacre's charming little dog is now with his mistress and that her distress is at an end?' He looked meaningfully at Mr Honeyacre as he said so and then cast an eye over the rest of the party in case anyone needed reminding of the event that had prompted his heroism.

'I am grateful to you, of course,' said Mr Honeyacre.

Mr Malling descended the stairs. 'I am sorry to say it, sir, but there appears to be a skeleton under the floorboards. Dr Hamid says it is definitely human.'

'And now I feel sure that we have a vital clue as to the identity of the spirit that haunts this place,' said Mr Hope. 'We must recover the bones and see what Dr Hamid can make of them.'

'I'll fetch a vegetable box from the kitchen to put them in,' said Mr Malling.

Mr Honeyacre, for whom one nightmare appeared to follow the other, nodded and waved a weak hand. 'Yes, Malling, an excellent plan, see to it at once.'

Zillah returned with the news that Little Scrap was being bathed and scented and was no worse for his adventure and Mrs Honeyacre was therefore very much improved and, in a short while, would be strong enough to see her friends.

'Might I implore you all,' pleaded Mr Honeyacre, 'when you see her, make no mention of the recent discovery.'

Mr Hope nodded sagely. 'I approve the plan,' he said. 'When we next hold a séance we will therefore all be assured that any communication which is received through Mrs Honeyacre's mediumship comes direct from the spirit of this unhappy individual and is not prompted by her prior knowledge of the discovery.'

'That was not at all my meaning,' Mr Honeyacre protested.

'But it was mine,' said Mr Hope. 'You cannot prevent it now,' he added with an intense stare. 'You cannot and will not.'

'This is a conversation for another time,' said Mr Honeyacre, turning aside. Mr Hope's expression suggested that the conversation would not be long delayed.

Mr Malling arrived with a vegetable box and took it up the stairs. When the explorers returned Mr Malling was leading, lighting the way down with the lantern, while Dr Hamid and Mr Beckler followed, carrying the box between them. Both those gentlemen looked uncomfortable to be thus employed, as if the box was too small to allow as much distance between them as they might have liked.

As the box reached the corridor, Mina stepped forward eagerly to examine it.

'Miss Scarletti, perhaps you ought not to look,' suggested Mr Honeyacre, gently. 'A skeleton is a grisly thing. I would not want my dear Kitty to see one in this state.'

'Oh, I have made a special study of skeletons,' said Mina, who had read numerous medical texts on the subject of scoliosis. 'Only from drawings, of course, but I have never seen the real thing. I have to confess I am all agog.'

Mr Honeyacre sighed and accepted the inevitable.

Mina peered into the box. There was a sickly stench, but she braved it. The bones, she noticed immediately, were clean of flesh, but darkened by a coating of dust and dirt and the only clothing that seemed to attach to them were some brown strips of what appeared to be rotted linen. She recognised a skull, a hip bone, long bones of all sizes, ribs and vertebrae.

'It is complete?' she asked.

'I won't know until I have laid it out,' said Dr Hamid, 'but I feel sure that some of the smaller bones will be missing. Some may have crumbled with age, others carried off by vermin.' He turned to Mr Honeyacre. 'I would like the bones to be taken to some suitable place, the stables perhaps, where I can work on them without troubling anyone else.'

'That would be best,' said Mr Honeyacre, nodding to Mr Malling. 'There is an empty stall that would suit your purpose.'

'I'll fetch some trestles from the workshop,' said Malling, 'and then the doctor may work in comfort.'

'And I would like to see the sweepings of fallen plaster,' added Dr Hamid. 'Some small bones may be amongst them, or even a clue as to whose skeleton this is.'

'I'll bring them to you,' said Mrs Malling.

'And we must make sure the corridor is safe,' added Mr Honeyacre. 'No one must go down there before we are sure that there will be no further fall from the ceiling.'

Once Mr Malling had ensured that Dr Hamid had everything he required he proceeded to make the corridor safe. It was a relief to discover that it was not necessary to shore up the ceiling, as most of the damage was attributable to Mr Hope's foot and subsequent struggles. The larger fragments of plaster having been removed, a clean hole remained and dust sheets were laid out to catch any further powdering.

Following the landslip and the natural concerns about the safety of the terrace it was fortunate that the stable yard and stalls were still accessible by a staircase from the servants' wing. Dr Hamid put on his warm coat, took a lantern and set to work.

Mina found Nellie in their shared room with Zillah for company, looking very annoyed and extremely bored.

'I was quite prepared to feign a headache for a few hours but I feel that whole days of idleness are beyond me,' she said. 'Even the finding of an old bone in the attic is no consolation.'

'It is more than that,' said Mina. 'We have a skeleton complete with skull.'

'It would have to stand up and walk about to amuse me. Am I really doomed to remain here until the roads are mended?'

'I did do my best,' said Mina. 'In fact, I had persuaded Richard to leave and take Mr Stevenson with him, but now the landslip means we must all stay. And there is another danger. Richard has warned me that Mr Hope has expressed vile intentions towards you and is to be avoided at all costs.'

'What it is to be so desired,' said Nellie drily. 'Supposedly the wish of every woman, but it is a curse on those granted that wish. But now I really must emerge from my purdah. If you will be my ladies-in-waiting, shall we go and see Kitty?'

'How awful this all is,' said Kitty. She was sitting up in bed with a warm wrap about her shoulders. On her lap, Little Scrap, smelling of violets and with his hair knotted in a cascade of ribbons, was eating biscuits out of a silver dish. 'My poor dear child has had such a horrid time, he was so very frightened without me.'

Miss Pet was in attendance and Zillah went to sit with her, the two young girls exchanging warm assurances that each was quite safe and well after the recent commotion.

'I am so glad that your brother is here, Miss Scarletti,' said Kitty. 'He is very amusing to speak to and he should be able to divert us with his drawings, but I cannot abide Lord Hope or his friend and there is something about Mr Stevenson I do not trust. It is the way he looks about him all the time, as if he is finding fault with everything he sees.'

Mina and Nellie glanced at each other and nodded. 'Mr Stevenson is not what he seems,' said Nellie. 'He is a detective — a spy sent by my jealous husband to watch me.'

Kitty gasped. 'How cruel!'

'He does not realise that I have seen through him. Do you recall when Mr Scarletti and I took coffee with Mr Honeyacre and yourself just before you were married? Mr Stevenson was seated at the next table but he paid more attention to our party than he did his coffee. I am sure I have seen him lurking about on other occasions, too. On the day we came here he passed by in the street when we left the church and he noticed me then. Of course, he was dressed differently, but that was not disguise enough. I have a good memory for faces and knew him at once.'

'That is a nasty trade,' said Kitty. 'But now I see why he was looking about him so carefully when he arrived — it is in his nature to do so.'

'Perhaps he was looking for cobwebs,' said Mina. 'Richard says he is deadly afraid of spiders.'

'Then we should ask Mr Scarletti to make a big drawing of one and frighten him away,' said Kitty. She sighed. 'It is a pity we have none at this time of year.'

Since the day remained chill and the stable was unheated Mina ensured that Dr Hamid was brought a jug of hot cocoa to sustain him and gave in to her curiosity concerning the bones to pay him a visit, which involved negotiating the slippery cobbles of the stable yard with her tiny feet. Not for the first time she wondered if a stout staff would be a good thing to carry. She had resisted it so far, but knew that with advancing age that time would come. She had little doubt that, if she lived long enough, a Bath chair lay in her future.

Mina pushed open the stable door and found Dr Hamid in his greatcoat, engaged in laying out the bones on the wooden boards that had been so useful in the attic, which were supported at either end on trestles. The box of plaster sweepings was nearby and looked as though it had been thoroughly raked through.

'Thank you for the cocoa,' he said. 'You know me too well. How is your brother? He came to me complaining of a toothache and I gave him something to rub on his gums.'

'He is better now, but he has some serious concerns.' Mina proceeded to describe the dangers to Nellie from the prying Mr Stevenson and the egregious Mr Hope.

Dr Hamid shook his head at the sinfulness of society. 'I will do what I can to prevent distress to Mrs Jordan,' he promised.

'How is your work proceeding?' asked Mina.

'It won't be completed tonight,' he said, stretching his shoulders and rubbing his knuckles into his back, as he had been bent over the boards for some while. 'You can see that I have found the larger bones and placed them in position, but the smaller ones will take longer. And the very small ones, as I feared, are missing.'

Mina examined the layout, which resembled so closely the drawings she had studied, only now made real. 'An adult, certainly,' she said. 'Male or female?'

'Female, without a doubt. The shape of the skull and the pelvis are unmistakable. It is hard to determine her age without further examination. But I would say that she was young rather than elderly and I believe she may have borne a child.'

'The only woman associated with this house that we know has borne a child is Mrs Lassiter,' said Mina.

'We have no evidence that Mrs Lassiter is deceased,' said Dr Hamid, cautiously.

'And none that she is alive.'

'That is true. No one has been able to say where the family now resides, but we may find it out in due course.'

'Mr Hope has asked if we could all assemble in the drawing room to discuss what has taken place,' said Mina. 'Will you be able to attend? I rather think he expects it.'

'Mr Hope's discussions usually take the form of lectures,' said Dr Hamid, 'and his requests are expressed as commands.'

'There will be refreshments.'

He smiled. 'Then I will pause in my work for now and pursue it tomorrow in better light, and hopefully better weather.'

They returned indoors and on the way Dr Hamid kindly assisted Mina over the cobbles. She waited for him to suggest she ought to acquire a walking cane, but he did not.

The grouping in the drawing room consisted of Mr Honeyacre, Mr Hope, Richard, Mr Stevenson and Mr Beckler.

Kitty had chosen to stay in her room to enjoy the company of her fragrantly contented puppy dog and Nellie had remained to sit with her.

'Ah, Dr Hamid!' exclaimed Mr Hope, jumping to his feet. 'We have been awaiting your news! Can you tell us whose skeleton it is?'

'I am afraid not, and may never be able to without further information,' said Dr Hamid. 'But this I can say — the deceased was an adult female, who had given birth.'

'Then it must be Mrs Lassiter!' said Mr Hope. 'Murdered by her husband, no doubt. That would explain the restless complaining spirit that haunts this place.'

'I have seen nothing so far to tell me the cause of death,' said Dr Hamid. 'There are no injuries to any of the bones I have examined. But I have not yet completed my work.'

'Supposing she was strangled?' asked Mr Beckler, flexing his long fingers. 'That is a very common way for husbands to dispose of wives. Could you determine that?'

'Not with the bones I have, no.'

'Poisoning would leave no sign, I suppose,' said Mina. 'But that is the way wives like to murder their husbands.'

Mr Honeyacre made a sound like a whimper and pressed a handkerchief to his lips and Richard stifled a laugh.

If Mr Stevenson had any useful observations to make on the subject of spousal murder he chose to keep them to himself.

'Nevertheless,' Mr Hope went on, walking about the room, an action which always seemed to presage a long speech with which his listeners were expected to agree, 'we cannot rule out murder, neither can we say positively that the skeleton is not that of Mrs Lassiter. After all, whose else could it be?'

Mina opened her mouth to speak and then closed it again. She dared not name Abigail Falcon, the Lassiters' missing nursemaid. To do so would reveal that she had information which was not in the possession of anyone else, the pamphlet written by Reverend Tolley which she had abstracted — she would not say purloined — from the parish chest after Nellie had feloniously picked the lock. It was not something of which she was exactly proud.

'You were about to say something, Miss Scarletti?' asked Mr Hope, his expression showing that he sensed her discomfort.

All eyes turned to Mina and she was obliged to speak, choosing her words carefully. 'When Mrs Malling told me about the Lassiters she mentioned that they had employed a nursemaid to care for their child, who was ill in some way, and that both the child and the nursemaid had disappeared. She also told me that Mrs Lassiter was later found drowned in the brook, although she wasn't buried here. There is a family vault elsewhere.'

Even as she spoke, Mina recalled that according to Reverend Tolley, who had actually known the Lassiters and must be considered the better source of information, the child had not been ill and had not disappeared and he believed that the family had simply vacated the house because it was haunted. 'Of course,' she added, 'that was only a story. I am not sure where Mrs Malling heard it. Who knows how much of it is true? Perhaps none of it.'

'Was the nursemaid ever found?' asked Mr Honeyacre.

'No,' said Mina, recalling that, in both stories, Abigail Falcon's fate remained unknown.

'Do we know anything of her?' demanded Mr Hope. 'Her name? Her age? Was she a widow perhaps?'

'Mrs Malling did not say,' said Mina.

'There must have been other maidservants here over the years,' said Dr Hamid. 'Are there none who are believed to have run away, or been dismissed, or simply left the village?'

There was a thoughtful pause as Mary Ann brought in a jug of cocoa and a plate of biscuits. 'I have just recalled something,' said Mina. 'William Jesson, the boy who came up from the village to tell us about the road being under water — he said that his grandmother used to work here and it brought her trouble. He wouldn't say what that trouble was.'

'Then we must find her and interview her when the roads are clear,' said Mr Honeyacre.

Mina saw Mary Ann hesitate. 'Mary Ann, do you know William Jesson's grandmother?'

'No, Miss, I never knew her. I expect she is long passed. But Susan might know something. Susan and William are cousins. Not first cousins, further back than that. Susan did once tell me that her grandmother worked here when the other people were here, the ones before the Lassiters, but she was never happy. I don't know any more than that.'

'Were those other people the Wigmores?' asked Mina.

'I think so.'

'Then Susan's grandmother and William Jesson's grandmother might be the same person,' said Mina, who was wondering if she was also the maid referred to in Reverend Tolley's pamphlet, the one who had been ill-treated by the manservant.

'Ask Susan to come here,' said Mr Hope. 'She is not in any trouble and she may be able to help us.'

Mary Ann left and Mr Hope strode up and down again. 'Without being able to interview the villagers we must make do with what we have,' he said. 'Susan may hold the key to the mystery. And if we should find, as I am sure we shall, that there is a troubled spirit here that needs solace in order to be allowed to ascend into the heavenly realm then we must not shirk our duty.' He wheeled about and fixed his host with an intense stare. 'Mr Honeyacre, I think that you will now agree with me — it was no chance that Mrs Honeyacre's charming little dog found the bones. Animals, as I am sure you know, are extremely sensitive to spirits. Their senses are sharper, they see and hear and scent things that we do not. Little Scrap must have been led to the bones by a spirit. What a truly sagacious animal he is! If he could only speak I am sure he could tell us precisely where the most powerful psychic focus is in this house! He might even have conversed with the spirits and know all their secrets! You will now understand that we must hold another séance and that both Mrs Honeyacre and her delightful little dog must be present.'

'I believe that we must place Mrs Honeyacre's health above such considerations,' said Dr Hamid.

'But have you considered,' said Mr Hope, 'that it might be the psychic disturbances in this house that are weakening her? That these must be eliminated without further delay or her health may suffer more? Surely you must see that?'

Dr Hamid frowned. 'I can see that she finds the incidents that have taken place here very upsetting.'

'She was not so excitable when I first became acquainted with her,' sighed Mr Honeyacre.

'There you are!' said Mr Hope triumphantly. 'What do you say? Will we have our séance?'

'I will speak to my wife in the morning and ask her opinion,' said Mr Honeyacre. 'Dr Hamid and I will consult further.'

Mr Hope looked as though he was about to make a very firm reply, but at that moment there was a knock at the door.

'Enter,' said Mr Honeyacre.

The door opened and Susan stood on the threshold. She looked terrified.

'Ah, Susan my dear, come in, come in, please don't be afraid,' said Mr Hope, putting on his friendliest face.

Susan crept into the room and stood just inside the door, trembling and staring at the floor.

'Please come forward, it would be so much better if you were comfortable.' Mr Hope drew up a chair before the frightened girl. 'Sit down, do.' Susan complied as if she was afraid that the chair would suddenly rise up and eat her. 'Would you care for a biscuit?' Susan shook her head and abruptly burst into tears. 'Perhaps later.'

'Would it calm her if a lady was to speak to her?' suggested Mr Honeyacre. 'Susan, would you like Miss Scarletti to talk to you?'

Susan dabbed her eyes with her apron, sniffled loudly and nodded.

Mina went to sit by her. 'We have talked before, haven't we, Susan?'

'Yes, Miss.'

'I remember you told me all about seeing the white lady and how the rocking horse moved by itself. That must have been very frightening.'

'It was, Miss.'

'We are hoping to solve the mystery of why these things are happening in this house, so we can make them stop. The answer might lie in some of the history of Ditchling Hollow and this house. If there is anything you know that might help us we would be very grateful to hear it.'

'I don't know that I do know anything,' said Susan.

'Am I right that your grandmother used to work here?'

Susan looked understandably surprised that Mina knew this, and nodded. 'Yes, Miss.'

'That must have been a long time ago.'

'Yes, she was very young.'

'Does your grandmother still live in the village?'

'No. I never knew her. I was told she went away.'

'What was her name?'

'I think it was Susan like me.'

'Was she the parent of your father or your mother?'

'My mother.'

'Were you ever told why your grandmother went away?'

'No, only that she was unhappy. Maybe something bad happened.'

'Was she married here or elsewhere?'

'I don't know. I'm not sure she ever was.'

Mina decided not to pursue that avenue of enquiry. 'Is your grandmother also William Jesson's grandmother?'

Susan nodded. 'He told me that she was unhappy here.'

'Do you think,' interrupted Mr Hope, impatiently, 'that your grandmother ran away because the house was haunted?'

'She might have done, sir,' said Susan.

'Has your mother not told you more about her?' he demanded.

'She don't talk about her at all, sir.'

'Why do you think that is?' asked Mina.

'I don't know.'

'Then you must ask her,' insisted Mr Hope.

Susan's mouth quivered. 'You are frightening her,' said Mina. 'Allow me to continue.' She paid no attention to Mr Hope's reaction and went on. 'William told me that Ned Copper might know more. I have spoken to him but I feel he is keeping something back.'

'Ned Copper knows a lot, but he doesn't always say it. He knows about the curse on the village.'

'Ah yes, he told us about the gallows on Clayton Hill. Innocent people who were hanged there and their unquiet souls looking for justice. Were some of them from this village?'

There was a long pause and, at last, Susan slowly raised her head and gave Mina a very profound stare. There was a subtle change in both her posture and the tone of her voice, almost as if another person was speaking through her. 'There was one from this house,' she said.

There were a few moments of silence as everyone took this in. 'Susan, are you saying that someone who lived in this house was hanged on Clayton Hill?' asked Mr Honeyacre.

Susan turned the strange stare to her master. 'Yes, sir,' she said evenly.

'One of the servants, I take it?'

'No, sir.'

'By what name?'

'Redwoode.'

Mr Honeyacre pondered this. 'As we know,' he said, addressing the company, 'the sixteenth century manor house on this site was occupied by a family of that name. Sir Christopher and Lady Matilda. But neither of them is buried here and I have not heard that either was hanged. Surely had that been the case, such an extraordinary incident would not have been forgotten and they would not be honoured by a plaque in the church.'

'It wasn't either of them, sir,' said Susan. Her voice was stronger, steadier. 'Ned said it was a son. He doesn't like to talk about it much. He tells lots of old stories but this one he can't bring himself to speak of unless he has had something to get his courage up. I think that's because he knows it's where it all started. There's wicked things in it and I'm not sure I dare speak of it either.'

'Well, we can't go and fetch Ned at present,' said Mr Hope. 'Would you speak of it if I gave you a shilling?'

Susan hesitated. Mr Hope delved into his pockets but unable to locate such an item, glanced at Mr Beckler, who explored his pockets and came up with the requisite coin. Mr Hope took it, enclosed it in a napkin and rubbed it vigorously to polish it then he pressed it between his palms and muttered a prayer and finally held it up for inspection. 'There you are, Susan, it is a holy shilling now. I have blessed it and that means you will come to no harm if you tell us what you know.' He offered the coin and Susan took it and stared at it, as if trying to see if a blessed shilling was any different from the usual one. At last she put it in her pocket and began to speak. Her voice was very soft, as if all emotion had been drained away. Her expression, too, lacked feeling and her eyes stared straight ahead into a distance that went far beyond the walls of the room. All present remained silent to hear her.

'This is the story Ned Copper told me. It is the tale of the lost bones. Sir Christopher and his wife had two sons, one good and one bad. Henry was the good one and he was his father's favourite. He respected his father and always did as he was told. Edwin used to quarrel with his father. He liked to drink and gamble and do other things, too. Edwin said he loved his brother, but really he was jealous of him. When Sir Christopher's wife died he said his one comfort in the world was having a good son like Henry.

'One day, Sir Christopher told Edwin that he must mend his ways and be good like Henry and if he didn't then he would make a new will and leave all his fortune to Henry and then

Edwin would have nothing and he would be no more than his brother's servant. That made Edwin very angry.

'The very next day, Henry and Edwin went out riding together but only Edwin came back. His father asked him where his brother was and Edwin said that Henry had gone away on a journey. But Sir Christopher knew that Edwin was lying because Henry was good and he would never have gone away without saying anything. So he asked Edwin again where his brother was and this time Edwin said that Henry was unhappy and had run away. But Sir Christopher knew that Edwin was lying because if Henry had been unhappy he would have talked to his father about it and not run away.

'So again, Sir Christopher asked Edwin where Henry was. This time Edwin said that there had been an accident and that Henry's horse had fallen and crushed him. Sir Christopher was beside himself and told Edwin to take him to the spot at once, in case Henry was still alive, but Edwin said he couldn't remember where it was.

'Then Sir Christopher said he would beat Edwin until he remembered and at last Edwin confessed that he had murdered his brother and thrown the body into a well. Sir Christopher had Edwin locked away and ordered his servants to search every well there was, but nothing could be found.

'Edwin hoped that his father would show him mercy and protect him, but he did not. He never spoke to Edwin again. Edwin was tried and found guilty of the murder of his brother and sentenced to hang. The gallows were built on Clayton Hill, in the same place where the windmills are now, and Edwin was hanged there. His father ordered that the body was not to be taken down and buried, but should be left there to rot away, and it was.

'And so, the bones of both Redwoode brothers are lost. Sir Christopher wasted away and died from grief not long afterwards. Ned Copper says that when the wind blows it is the ghost of Henry calling out, begging for a Christian burial and the rain is the tears of Sir Christopher as his spirit wanders the land, still searching for his missing son and when there is a thunderstorm, it is the ghost of Edwin on Clayton Hill, cursing everyone in Ditchling Hollow for not saving him from the anger of his father. He was wicked in life and he is wicked in death, too.'

Susan stopped talking and blinked, as if coming out of a dream. She looked at the rapt faces of her listeners. 'That's all I know,' she said. 'But if you asked Ned to tell you the story he wouldn't do it for a guinea. May I go now, please?'

All eyes turned to Mr Honeyacre. 'Ah — yes, Susan, that will be all.'

Susan rose and walked out as if nothing had happened.

Mr Hope was deep in thought. 'It is far more serious than I had imagined,' he said, shaking his head. 'Old curses such as that are hard to remove. Who knows where the well is now? Shall we ever find Henry Redwoode's bones? They might have been scattered by vermin long ago. And how may we return Edwin's spirit to the infernal regions where he no doubt belongs? I shall have to give this some thought.'

'In the meantime,' said Mr Honeyacre, 'I suggest that we all try and get some rest before dinner is served. It might not be easy but we will have better appetites and think much better when we are refreshed.'

Those who departed did so with melancholy expressions that suggested it was most unlikely that they would enjoy any refreshing rest. Mina hung back in silent reflection and Dr

Hamid, seeing her still seated, understood and stayed back to talk.

'That was a very affecting story,' he said.

'I am glad you liked it,' said Mina.

'You are?'

'After all, I wrote it.'

It was a few moments before Dr Hamid understood what Mina had just said and saw the implications behind it. 'Let me be clear — you are being serious when you say this; it was not a jest?'

'Someone has stolen my story,' Mina pointed out. 'Would I jest about such a thing?'

'Er — no, I suppose not.'

'Neither am I mistaken,' she added. 'The facts are the same, the title is the same, the names of the two sons are the same. Even some of the words she used are the same, although she did not order them as well as in the original. The only difference is that the tale has been attached to this place and the Redwoode family.'

'There might just be some confusion,' suggested Dr Hamid cautiously.

'That is very generous of you,' said Mina, 'but it was clear enough to me. Of course, we don't know whose idea it was. Susan might genuinely believe the story. Even Ned Copper might believe it, too. He could have been told it by someone else.'

'I don't suppose there is a history of Ditchling Hollow in the library?'

'No, and I have looked, believe me. The books mainly deal with antiquities and spiritualism. There are histories of Sussex, of course, but that is just the county and they do not feature every village. The gazetteer makes no mention of a gallows.'

'No publications from the Scarletti Library of Romance?' he asked, not entirely seriously.

'I regret not.'

'When did you write that story?'

'About a year ago.'

'Well, someone in this region, either in the village or this house, is an avid reader and was so struck by your work that they can recall it in detail.'

'I would like to think so, but I can hardly go about searching everyone's rooms.' Richard, she mused, would have done that without a thought and charmingly talked his way out of trouble if caught. Sometimes her wayward brother had his uses, but she could hardly suggest that he indulge in such suspicious behaviour with the ever-watchful Mr Stevenson under the same roof.

Dinner was a subdued affair, the main irritant being Mr Hope persistently referring to the importance of holding another séance and Mr Honeyacre adamantly responding that nothing could be decided until he had consulted with his wife. Kitty was not at the table, having had a tray sent up to her room, but he was pleased to report that her appetite was improved. If she was able to face the next day fully rested and content then he would discuss it with her, but not under any other circumstances. Mr Hope's continued pleadings began to take on the colour of goading, even bullying, but Mr Honeyacre remained tight-lipped under pressure and made no further response.

There were other disturbing nuances in Mr Hope's behaviour. He often cast his eye at Nellie and raised his wineglass to her with a smile. The motion of his eyebrows was especially suggestive. Mina, whose experience of ardent admirers was, thus far in her life, non-existent, watched Nellie with interest in case she was ever to include such a scene in a story. Nellie, she noticed, made no response at all to Mr Hope's subtle advances and Mina assumed that, in the circumstances, this was the best thing to do. Nellie was never, of course, going to receive Mr Hope's attentions with pleasure, but further than that she refused to acknowledge that they had even occurred. Mina guessed that to such a vain man any reaction at all, even a spirited public rejection, would be seen by him as a veiled acceptance.

There were also the ever-vigilant eyes of Mr Stevenson, a man who had trained himself to look for the smallest outward signs of hidden passion. Even the most trivial behaviour on Nellie's part could endanger her reputation. Mina found herself watching Mr Stevenson, observing the direction of his stare and concluded that whether or not he suspected Nellie of any attachment to Mr Hope, he had not failed to notice that she was the object of his keen interest.

Mina did not flatter herself that Mr Beckler had any interest in her other than as a potential customer for his trade. She thought of him as an annoyance rather than a danger, like a hovering insect that buzzed without ceasing and could not be persuaded to fly out of the window. She took care not to look at him, as she suspected that if she did so she might discover him to be looking at her.

It was a source of great frustration to Mina that she had no means of pursuing her investigations, trapped as she was in the great house. If she had only been able to travel to Hurstpierpoint she might have found a library there or someone willing to talk about Ditchling Hollow and its history. After dinner, she studied the purloined pamphlet again without result and the village map, but it was so ancient and faded with markings neither she nor Nellie were able to read and she naturally did not want to show it to anyone else.

Nellie was not a great reader and Mina had never discussed with her the true nature of the stories she wrote, or revealed her *nom de plume* of Robert Neil. Now, however, she took the opportunity of unveiling her secret and that *The Lost Bones* was one of her creations. Nellie was surprised, but understood that Mina was sharing something in the strictest confidence, not to be spoken of even to her family — in fact, most especially to her family. 'If my mother was to find out it would be an unceasing topic of conversation and the subject of every letter, as she would see my degraded occupation as a personal insult.'

'I take it Richard does not know? He has never mentioned it to me.'

'Have you ever known Richard to keep a secret?'

Nellie smiled. 'He can be a little transparent. But I have seen no reading matter of that kind here. I will let you know if I do. And when we return to Brighton, I will make sure to purchase a copy of your story and read it with interest. I can quite see it played as a melodrama on the stage. Perhaps virtuous Henry could have a beautiful sweetheart who would be dreadfully affected by his loss. I can imagine her now. I suppose I shall never return to the stage, but if I could, I would like to play such a part.' She sighed. 'Are all Mr Neil's stories so bloodcurdling?'

'Many are far worse,' said Mina. 'I am only glad that Mrs Honeyacre was not in the room to hear this one. You have known her much longer than I — how do you think she does? Mr Honeyacre thinks she is improving.'

'She is, and if she was only able to spend some time away from here she would improve so much faster. She has always been such a bright cheerful thing, sparkling with life, and to see her like this is distressing to any friend who knows her well. It may be that her expectation of a family event is partly to blame, as she is so nervous and fearful. But I cannot fault Mr Honeyacre; he dotes on her and would do anything in his power to relieve her anxiety.'

'There must not be another séance,' said Mina, firmly. 'I will do everything in my power to prevent it.'

Nellie rested a gentle hand on her arm. 'Take care, my dear, you are not strong.'

Mina found sleep hard to come by that night. Too many things were troubling her and her inability to do anything to remedy them or even discover more was vexing in the extreme. She found herself revolving all the facts in her memory, pursuing avenues of action or enquiry and finding each of them leading to a wall she could not climb. She considered sitting up, lighting her candle and reading her notes again, but her tired body was demanding sleep. It took time, but eventually her troubled mind let go of thought and she drifted into an exhausted slumber. When she awoke it was still dark. Somewhere deep inside the house, a clock struck three.

For a moment, Mina wondered what could have awoken her. From the second bed a sound of even breathing with a gentle snore told her that Nellie was deeply asleep. Mina tried to settle down again and closed her eyes, but then she started and sat up, wide awake. There was noise like sighing and moaning coming from the corridor outside.

Mina slid carefully from her bed and put on her wrap and slippers. A thin yellow glow was creeping beneath her door, telling her that there was a light in the corridor, but it was not moving. She decided not to light a candle, but opened the door very carefully and peered out. A figure stood in the corridor, a dark still figure holding a lantern. Its flame illuminated the features, distorting the face until it looked like a mask, but Mina quickly realised that this was no ghost or demon, but Kitty, barefoot and clad only in her nightdress and a voluminous wrap. Soft moans were issuing from her parted lips. Mina closed the bedroom door softly behind her and approached Kitty very slowly and carefully so as not to alarm her. 'Mrs Honeyacre?' she ventured.

Kitty's eyes were open but they stared ahead unseeingly and her face bore no expression. Mina had no idea what to do, if anything. She couldn't be sure whether Kitty was asleep or awake. Even if awake, she appeared to be in a state of trance and in either event, Mina did not know if it was a good or a bad thing to wake her. She had heard of people who walked in their sleep, she had even written stories about them but until that moment she had never actually encountered one. After some hesitation, Mina decided that it was safest to do nothing at all and simply watch over her hostess to see that she came to no harm. She wondered if she should fetch Dr Hamid, but feared that if she knocked on his door loudly enough to wake him she might unintentionally wake Kitty as well.

The moaning continued and it seemed to be coming from deep inside the unconscious woman. It was a sound expressing the most profound distress.

Mina had just decided to return to her room and wake Nellie to seek her advice when there was the sound of a bedroom door opening. On hearing it, Mina hoped that Dr Hamid was awake and coming to assist, but saw to her dismay that the figure peering out into the corridor was Mr Hope. 'What is happening?' he asked. 'What is that noise?'

Mina placed a finger to her lips. 'Hush! I found Mrs Honeyacre like this and I am not sure what to do for the best. Should we fetch Mr Honeyacre? Or Dr Hamid?'

Mr Hope emerged from his room, dragging his fingers through sleep-rumpled hair. Over his nightshirt he was wearing a thick plaid dressing gown that could only have been the property of Mr Gillespie. He came up close to the motionless figure and stared at her then waved one hand in front of her face.

'They will not be familiar with this,' he said. 'It is a curious phenomenon, one that I have only read about, but have never before witnessed. Look and learn, Miss Scarletti. Even your stubborn materialism will crumble before it.'

'But what is it?'

'I believe that what we are seeing is an example of the Odic Force manifesting itself through the individual. Have you read the works of Baron Carl von Reichenbach?'

'No.'

He gave a soft chuckle. 'Ah, so you do not, as you claim, know everything.'

Mina decided not to reply to that.

'Do you see an aura surrounding her?'

'I see only the candlelight.'

'Look more carefully. What you perceive as candlelight is actually an emanation of the Force. It permeates all things, surrounds all things, but only sensitives are able to see it. You, Miss Scarletti, although you refuse to admit it, are such a sensitive.'

'But is she asleep or awake?'

'Something between the two, I believe, a condition akin to a mesmeric trance. Do not fear for her, it is harmless and in time she will awaken of her own accord. Tell me, what is the colour of her aura?'

'What colour would you like it to be?'

'You jest with me, but the aura is a great signifier of both her state of health and her power. Odic Force may be positive in some and negative in others. Von Reichenbach himself wrote that the Force has both a dark and a light side, but my feeling is that Mrs Honeyacre is specially blessed and may balance them both within her. She is a spiritual being and her current sufferings exist only because she has not yet come to a full realisation of her abilities. The spirits that roam this house are drawn to her, drawn to her power, like moths to a flame. There have always been spirits here, of course, but they have lain quiet, they have slept. She has, without realising it, awakened them. She is the key not only to the haunting here, but also to laying the ghosts of Hollow House for all time, of finally dismissing the curse of Ditchling Hollow. I see more than ever now that it is essential to hold another séance and for Mrs Honeyacre to be not only present but the main focus of the event.'

'I doubt that her husband will agree to that,' said Mina.

'Then you must persuade him!'

'I will do no such thing.'

'Why are you so obtuse? Why can you not see the truth that is in front of you?' he insisted.

'I will not be a party to anything that might endanger Mrs Honeyacre.'

'Really? Is the life of one woman more important to you than the salvation of all humankind?'

Mina was too appalled at this question to reply, but at that juncture, Kitty suddenly uttered a deep sigh and her posture slumped. Mina hurried to her, anxious that she might fall and wondering if she was strong enough to prevent it. But, to her relief, Kitty slowly straightened up, blinking and looking about her in confusion. 'Where am I?' she whispered. 'How did I come here?'

'No matter,' said Mina, taking the lantern from Kitty's hand and placing a steadying grasp on her wrist. 'You are safe now.'

'But I am not!' Kitty exclaimed. 'I am in the most terrible danger!' In the lantern's glow her face appeared white, bleached with terror, her eyes sunk in black shadows.

'There is no danger, really there is not,' said Mina soothingly. 'You were dreaming, that is all, and now you are awake.'

'It was no dream, I am sure of it. Did you not hear it, too? The tapping, the horrible tap tap tapping of the death watch!'

'No, Kitty, that was just in your dream.'

'I heard it so clearly! On and on it went. Closer and closer. Louder and louder. The death watch and it is coming for me, I know it. That was why you did not hear it. It is my death-knell and mine alone.' She began to sob.

Mina hardly knew what to say and Mr Hope was no help at all, since he only nodded sadly and knowingly. Mina wanted to guide Kitty back to her room, but realised that if she did so she would be leaving Nellie alone in her room and unprotected with Mr Hope close by, in his nightshirt, and waiting for just such an opportunity.

'Of course, I am familiar with the legend of the death-watch,' said Mr Hope. 'There are some who say that —'

'Mr Hope, I implore you!' Mina snapped. 'What Kitty needs now is rest, not more stories and legends. Go and fetch Dr Hamid at once and he will give her something to soothe her to sleep.'

Mr Hope opened his eyes very wide, since he was unused to being given orders by anybody, let alone a young female standing barely taller than a child, but he appeared to acknowledge the sense of what she said and gave a slight bow. 'But of course,' he said with a cold smile and did her bidding.

'I heard his voice in my dream,' confided Kitty when he was out of earshot. 'He said that I was the cause of all this, of the ghosts in the house, the white lady and the child. He said that we must have another séance. Do you think that is true?'

'No, of course not,' said Mina. 'Take it from me, Mr Hope talks a great deal of nonsense. It is better not to listen to him and the last thing you want is another séance. You cannot have caused the ghosts, that much is clear. Whatever is happening here, it was happening long before you came. Even Mrs Malling admits that.'

'But I woke them. They were sleeping, but now they are awake and they are coming for me. They will bleed me, they will drain me of life!'

Fortunately at that moment, Dr Hamid, resplendent in a silk dressing gown and clutching his medical bag, arrived in time to provide some much needed support. 'Come, Mrs Honeyacre, let me take you back to your room. I have something that will help you sleep and you will feel very much better in the morning, I promise you.' His voice and air of confidence were enough to begin the process of calming her and she allowed herself to be led back to her room.

Mina gazed after her, thankful that she was in good hands, but despairing of any resolution.

Mr Hope strode up to her, eyes burning with elation. 'Odic Force!' he exclaimed. 'The sceptics scoff, but they know nothing! One day, and I believe that day will not be long in coming, it will be accepted as a scientific fact! It is the key to all that we do not as yet fully understand; how ghosts manifest themselves, why some people see them and others do not, how thoughts are transferred between individuals, the power of magnets, of crystals, of electricity, of chemical action. Once I am able to return home, I intend to gather some experts in the field of animal magnetism, as I believe Mrs Honeyacre to be a valuable subject for research.'

'And I will do everything I can to prevent that from happening,' said Mina. 'Your researches are not worth the price of a woman's health and happiness. Gather your magnetisers if you must, but find another subject, a more robust individual. I came here because of an appeal for help from Mrs Honeyacre and I intend to honour that appeal.'

Mr Hope shook an angry finger at her. 'This is not over! Take care, Miss Scarletti. Progress will happen and you may find yourself crushed like a nasty little spider in its path!' He turned and stamped back to his room.

Chapter Thirteen

Daily life in the big house was obliged to go on, but the congenial atmosphere of anticipated pleasure that had marked the arrival of Nellie and her party had evaporated. All that was left was a cloud of dread at what might happen next. The two maids were busy going back and forth and although they had been the most fearful of all at the beginning, they appeared now to be the most content as they had work on hand to keep them occupied and no idleness to endure.

Kitty was once again absent from the breakfast table and Mr Honeyacre expressed a hope that she would be able to consume the piece of dry toast that she had said was all that might tempt her. As he rose from the table, having eaten very little himself, he begged Mina's presence in his study.

At this request, Mr Hope adopted a very surly expression, as if a private conference with Mina could only be an insult to him. 'I also wish to speak with you,' he said, 'and I think you will find that what I have to say is of far greater importance than anything Miss Scarletti might devise. In fact, she is mistaken on so many points that my advice is to pay no attention to her at all.'

'Thank you for your advice, Lord Hope,' said Mr Honeyacre, 'but I am a man of the world who has lived on this earth these sixty winters now and I have learned to rely on my own judgment. Miss Scarletti is a guest in my house and a lady of intelligence, and I find her deserving of my attention.'

There was an astonished silence as Mr Honeyacre conducted Mina from the room, broken only by a repressed snort of mirth from Richard.

Once in the study, Mr Honeyacre's careful façade of dignity and resolve broke into fragments of despair. 'Miss Scarletti, you must advise me,' he begged. 'I don't know what to do for the best! My poor dear wife is being frightened out of her wits. And — I apologise for any indelicacy, but it is essential that you know all the important facts. I believe that in the late summer I may become even happier in my family situation than I am now. It is more important than ever to take care of my dear Kitty. If it was not for this horrid weather, I would by now have sent her to Brighton to take the spa waters and rest. I see now that my invitation to Lord Hope was a dreadful mistake. Oh, no doubt he has the best of intentions, but the result has been that he has stirred things up abominably. Now I look back on it, we were going along quite well before, when it was just a few bumps and creaks and the maids getting nervous, which may well have been more imagination than anything else, but now it has become a nightmare. I feel as if some horrible presence in the house wants us to go — to leave Hollow House forever and let it just crumble away!' He sat down heavily at his desk.

Mina found a suitable chair and sat to face him. 'I assume that you have no intention of leaving?'

'No, no, of course not. I am very fond of this house. And Kitty was, too, before all these things started to happen. You have not seen the estate in the summer and when you do, you will see how delightful it can be.'

Mina was thoughtful. 'I can see that it might seem as if someone is trying to make you leave. Can you think of anyone who would want that?'

'Only that tormenting spirit!' said Mr Honeyacre bitterly.

'I meant someone living.'

He looked taken aback by the suggestion. 'No — why should they? How can it possibly benefit anyone?'

'Why don't we consider the idea? Let us begin with Mr Hope. Does he want to buy the estate, perhaps?'

With a theme to occupy his thoughts, Mr Honeyacre calmed a little. 'I don't believe so. He has never mentioned it. Of course, if someone has been making enquiries at the estate office in Hurstpierpoint, I won't know until I am notified by the Mallings' son, and for that I have to wait until the roads are repaired.'

'Not Mr Hope, then. Let us explore further, if only to dismiss the theory entirely. If someone wanted you to go, who would that be?'

Mr Honeyacre mused on the subject. 'The villagers are very happy to have us here. I donated substantial funds to maintain and repair the church. The graveyard was almost derelict before the Mallings restored it — choked with weeds and stones and horribly sunken in places. And I have been thanked many times for laying the new pathways. The Mallings like their place and would be terribly upset to leave. They are planning to make the garden bloom again and produce fruit and vegetables. They are quite devoted to it. Mr Gillespie has made no complaint and neither has Mrs Blunt. Both have been my loyal servants for many years. Mary Ann and Susan are well paid for their work and treated kindly. I am really at a loss.' He paused. 'I can't help thinking that Mr Stevenson knows something.'

'Mr Stevenson?'

'He claims he is a naturalist, but I don't believe a word of it. None of his conversation is about nature, in fact he seems to avoid the subject when asked. I am sure that he is really one of those land surveyors who come prowling about here from time to time. I think he has been surveying the estate for one of those dreadful factory builders.'

Mina felt unable to tell Mr Honeyacre that Mr Stevenson was not a surveyor at all but a detective employed by Nellie's husband to spy on her.

'Perhaps he is working for Mr White,' mused Mr Honeyacre.

'You have mentioned him before,' said Mina. 'Tell me more about Mr White.'

'He wrote to me last year, wanting to buy the estate. That was before I met Kitty; before I had begun the redecorating. He was going to build a brick factory of all things and a branch railway leading up to the main line to carry goods and materials. Can you imagine the dirt and the noise? Of course I said no, very firmly. I haven't heard from him again.'

'Have you ever met him?'

'No, and I don't wish to.'

Mina could not help wondering if some people might consider the dirt and the noise acceptable if they brought employment and prosperity to the area. 'Who knows about Mr White's interest in the estate?'

'Only myself.'

'Did he offer a good price?'

'Given the dilapidated state of the house at the time, it was fair, I suppose. Another man might have considered it.'

'He wanted the house as well as the land?'

'Yes, the house and everything in it, although that was little enough at the time. I don't know what he planned to do with it. Knock it down, perhaps, or maybe reduce it to a mere shell which would become the factory, I don't know. My collection was not here then, of course.'

'What was in the house when he made the offer?'

'Oh, just a few sticks of old furniture and carpets which have no appreciable value and I suppose that skeleton must have been under the floorboards then, although, whether he knew about it I have to doubt. And there were those old paintings the Lassiters didn't want and said I might have.' He gave a little gasp. 'Could that be what Mr White wanted?'

'The paintings?'

'Yes, it's possible. Supposing he knows the Lassiters and they told him about them and he has realised by some means or other that the paintings are very valuable. I haven't examined them properly because they need to be cleaned and restored. I should get them looked at.' He jumped to his feet. 'In fact, I have a mind to look at them myself, now.'

'I would very much like to come with you,' said Mina.

'Oh, by all means.'

Mr Honeyacre fetched his key from the safe and they went up to the first floor. On their way up the stairs, Mary Ann and Susan passed them by, carrying empty laundry baskets and disappearing into a bedroom.

He unlocked the door to the storeroom.

As far as Mina was aware, nothing had changed since her last visit. The cheval mirror was in its usual position in front of the window and it was still draped in a white cloth.

'And now I have a confession to make,' said Mina, with a smile. 'When I first arrived here I stood outside on the terrace and looked up at the windows. I saw that mirror with its white dust sheet and for a moment — just a moment, mind — I thought I saw a figure standing there. The figure of a woman in a white dress.'

'Oh dear,' said Mr Honeyacre, 'I do hope that didn't alarm you.'

'Since I had already been told the house was haunted, it did make me think,' Mina admitted. She decided not to mention the other mystery, how the white figure had so quickly and unaccountably vanished.

Mr Honeyacre picked up two cloth-wrapped items which were leaning against the wall. 'These are the paintings,' he said. 'Mr Lassiter, that is the nephew who managed the sale, said I might have them as they were in such poor condition that they were not worth restoring, but I am not convinced of that. My conversation with him suggested to me that he was not a great art-lover. From what he said, the Lassiters did not purchase the paintings but discovered them on the upper floor when they bought the house, so they are of some antiquity, though they may be of more interest than actual value.' He removed the wrappings, which revealed two oil paintings each about a foot square with battered frames. He laid them on top of the trunk.

Mina had no great knowledge of art, but she could see that both the pictures were very old and dirty, the surfaces so dark it was almost impossible to make out the subject. Some areas of paint had peeled from the surface and flaked away. There was no visible signature on either.

'They are painted on wood,' said Mr Honeyacre. 'Oak, I believe.'

Mina lifted up one of the pictures and gazed at it keenly, trying to make out an outline of a form. 'May I take it to the light?' she asked.

'Please do.'

Mina went to the window and let the light fall on the surface of the picture, tilting it this way and that. Mr Honeyacre stood by her side looking over her shoulder. 'A portrait, I think,' said Mina. 'A seated figure, perhaps.'

'There are so many areas of damage I am almost afraid to have it cleaned,' said Mr Honeyacre. He fetched the second painting. 'This one, I am sorry to say, is in even worse condition. Perhaps they were water damaged and not dried correctly. Even had they been by one of the great masters we could never find out and they would be worth very little. Such a pity. In my estimation these might well date from the time of the Redwoodes.' He stared closely at the second painting. 'This one may portray a family group. I think I can make out some figures.'

Mina could see what appeared to be the skirts of seated ladies and the lower limbs of a gentleman, the upper portions of the sitters having largely fallen away. Searching at the foot of the painting for a signature she saw something else. 'Can you see? There is a child here in the corner,' she said. 'Now why would they place a child there? I can almost see a little colour on its clothing and it — what is that? A toy, a whip, a rope?'

Mr Honeyacre peered at the picture then took a magnifying glass from his pocket and studied the corner of the portrait. 'Ah,' he said with a smile and handed the glass to Mina. She stared through it, adjusting the distance to obtain the best view, trying to understand what she was seeing and then she laughed. 'Oh, it isn't a child at all! It's a monkey with a curly tail and it's wearing a little red coat!'

'A family pet, I would guess. Such novelties would have been popular then. I must tell Kitty what we have found. I know she will be amused.'

'But, don't you see?' Mina exclaimed. 'This is the burial you have the fragments of. The little coffin that Ned Copper's father burned. It was not an infernal child, at all, but a pet monkey. A monkey in a red coat. No wonder it was buried outside consecrated ground.'

In the corridor outside there was the sound of the maids exiting the bedrooms, this time presumably with laden laundry baskets. The bedroom doors closed and as the maids walked down the corridor the weight of their feet and their burdens sent a little shudder through the old floorboards. As they did so, the cheval mirror tilted silently forward and the white cloth slipped to the floor. 'Oh dear,' said Mr Honeyacre, picking up the cloth and replacing it. 'I really must remember to ask Malling to repair the hinges.'

It was as they departed the storeroom that Mina was stuck with an idea. 'Mr Honeyacre, would you be kind enough to allow me to borrow that magnifying glass? I wish to be able to better examine a —' she paused — 'a book I am reading.'

'By all means,' he replied, handing her the glass.

Mina returned to her room where she was concealing her stolen treasures and unfolded the ancient map of Ditchling Hollow. When she had first examined it she had been frustrated by faded words that could not be read and portions of the drawing itself that were indistinct, but by finding the right position of the glass she was now able to see everything with fresh eyes. She could now see that the map had been drawn in 1764, the year before the first windmill was erected on Clayton Hill, perhaps during the time when the work was being planned. The hill was marked, but nothing stood upon it. She passed the glass carefully over every inch of the map and at last she saw something that made her smile.

'This is the way that stories often begin,' said Mina, when she discussed her findings with Dr Hamid. 'They start with something truthful, such as a monkey dressed as a child in a little red coat. It must have been a favourite of the Redwoodes but the kind of novelty that the farming folk of Ditching

Hollow would never have seen. So they told stories, exchanged whispers in dark places, invented the legend of an infernal child. And as time passed, the truth was forgotten and the story became more real than the truth. And then, over the years, the story was reborn and then born once more, but each time with different characters. Perhaps, later on, the child was said to belong to the Wigmores, the family who built the present house, and then later still it was rumoured to be a child of the new owners, the Lassiters, and so it goes on through each generation. And I have one other thing to mention, although, as it is not yet certain, I would rather it was not generally known until I am sure of my facts. I have discovered in my researches the location of the gallows, which I now believe was never on Clayton Hill at all, but several miles away. In 1764, the year before the first windmill was built, there was nothing on Clayton Hill. I imagine that the reputed position of the gallows must dance about depending on the story attached to it. But I will be able to check my facts more thoroughly when I return to Brighton and consult the library there.'

'I know why people tell stories,' said Dr Hamid, 'but why do they tell them as if they are true? Do they not know the difference — or are they too ready to believe?'

'Few people can resist a good story,' said Mina, 'and it is all the better if it is believed to be true. But sometimes the truth is too dull to relate so the storyteller adds drama and excitement to ensure the attention of the public. They do know the difference, but it doesn't concern them. I notice also that people prefer a story that has been played out in the place where they live. Why should we tell tales from Greece and Rome when we can invent new ones that happened in Sussex?'

'Is that how you devise your stories?' asked Dr Hamid, 'by starting with a plain truth and then embellishing it? I have read many of them, but I am still not sure how you write them.'

'It's a form of magic,' said Mina. 'I don't really understand it myself.'

After luncheon, Mina, having seen Nellie safely into the company of Kitty and Miss Pet, retired to the library. When the door opened she was surprised to see Richard, as a library was not a room he would voluntarily enter.

'I suppose you are looking for me,' she said.

'I am, and I am also trying to avoid Mr Stevenson. Though, I think I might have shaken him off at last. I haven't seen him since luncheon ended.'

'I would rather prefer to know where he was,' said Mina.

'Maybe he has given up,' said Richard. 'He hasn't found anything out, I mean there isn't anything to find, and I was getting a bit annoyed by his being a constant shadow.' He sat down and leaned forward confidentially. 'I need to tell you something about Mr Beckler. A few minutes ago, he drew me aside and asked if my pretty sister has a sweetheart.'

Mina was amazed. 'But Enid is a married woman! How does he know her?'

Richard rolled his eyes. 'Mina dear, he has never met Enid. He meant you.'

'I don't understand.'

'He obviously admires you.'

'Oh, no, that is quite wrong,' said Mina with a laugh. 'He is a photographer, remember? All he wants is new customers. That is the reason for his flattering remarks. Nothing more.'

Richard shook his head emphatically. 'It is far more than that. He made it very plain to me that he has a tender regard for you. He asked me to put in a word for him. That's what chaps do for each other when there is a lady they are sweet on.'

Mina was mystified. 'What sort of a word?'

'Oh, the usual kind of thing, you know.'

'I don't know.'

'Just to tell you that I thought he was a fine fellow and so on.'

Mina threw down her pencil in exasperation. 'He isn't, Richard. He really isn't. This is all some ridiculous scheme to drum up business and he goes much too far.'

'He knows you think that and he said that you have mistaken his intentions. My dear sister, he means to court you.'

'Now that is ridiculous. What would Mr Hope think of it? Mr Hope is undoubtedly encouraging and supporting Mr Beckler in his attempts to photograph spirits, whereas if he had his way, I would be locked up as mad woman. Mr Beckler cannot be unaware of that. I would be the very last woman he would pay court to.'

'But Mina, dear —'

Mina waved him away impatiently. 'No, just leave me to my books. If you want to do something useful, try and find out where Mr Stevenson is and what he is doing.'

'Very well,' said Richard, 'but you will see that I am right.'

Mina was left once more alone, but she found it hard to concentrate on the pages in front of her. She was reading a fanciful ghost tale about a maidservant who had been frightened out of her wits at macabre happenings, only to find that her master had murdered three wives, all of whom he had married for their fortunes and then buried their corpses under the kitchen flagstones.

It was at that moment, when contemplating the general villainy of husbands and how pleased she was not to have one, that Mina realised how obtuse she had been. She had assumed from the start that the purpose of Mr Beckler's flattery was to obtain a customer for his business. But why should that be, she now reasoned, when he lived in Twickenham and there were many good photographers in Brighton? No, it was more than that, and it was far far worse.

Mr Beckler was Mr Hope's creature and acted on his master's instructions. She had seen evidence of this time and time again. Therefore, if he was trying to court Mina, he was doing so because Mr Hope had told him to. Neither man could know that Mina had been warned by a doctor many years ago that she should never marry or bear children and that she had put all such ambitions firmly from her mind. They might well imagine that she yearned to be a wife and mother as other women did, but was wretched in the belief that no man would ever make her an offer.

Did Mr Hope really imagine that being occupied with marriage and children would silence her? Or was he hoping that the ordeal of childbirth would prove fatal? It was then that the full force of the dreadful truth finally struck Mina. Mr Beckler's courtship, if that was what it was, was not intended to lead to marriage. Mr Hope, as he had made abundantly clear, wished to destroy Mina; not necessarily by taking her life but by erasing any respect and credibility she might have earned. Mr Hope, horrible as it might seem, had instructed his acolyte to romance Mina and then shame her in order to blight her reputation. She felt suddenly nauseous. It was an insight so shocking, so disgusting, that she felt unable to confide it to anyone.

Mina did not feel safe where she was, since anyone might enter and find her there alone and in a state of distress. She retired to her room, which she felt did offer a measure of privacy. There was water in the jug and she poured some into the basin and washed and dried her face. Gradually, she felt calmer. The sooner she could leave the house and return home the better.

She managed to find some solace in a book and was quietly reading when Nellie entered.

Mina saw at once from Nellie's expression that something was dreadfully wrong. 'What is the matter?' she asked.

Nellie said nothing but sat on the bed. She was clutching a slip of paper in her hand.

'Is it that horrid Mr Hope?' asked Mina. 'If so, something must be done!'

'Oh, he is the least of my troubles,' said Nellie.

Mina left her chair and went to sit beside her friend. 'Shall I fetch Dr Hamid?'

Nellie shook her head. Mina reached out and teased the paper from her hand. She did not resist. The note read:

You enchantress, you have bewitched me with your beauty. I am your humble slave. Meet me in the drawing room at midnight. AWH

Mina wrinkled her nose in disgust. 'Did Mr Hope hand this to you himself?'

'No, it was his minion, Mr Beckler.'

'Unspeakable!'

'But that is not the worst. I was in the parlour a little earlier with Kitty and Miss Pet and they went to take Little Scrap to play in the hall when your brother came in. He asked me if I had seen Mr Stevenson and I said I had not. I told him to go and I thought he would, but he stayed. We — had a conversation and he made a very tender declaration to me. He alluded to what we had once been to each other. He also alluded to meetings we had had since I was married. He was quite emotional. You know how Richard is when he is — the way he is.'

'But the two of you were alone in the room? No one saw or heard you?'

'So we thought. I said I would go to join Kitty and as I rose I saw a movement behind the curtains and then I saw the tips of some shoes. There was no mistaking Mr Stevenson's coarse boots.'

'What did you do?'

'What could I do? I left the room. I could not tell him he had been discovered, or threaten or bribe him. Especially with Richard there. Who knows what he would have done? Your brother is a dear fellow, but he does need to be protected from his own folly. So there it is, my marriage is over. I will be poor again and return to the stage and look for a gentleman of means who will protect me. That is my future.' Nellie sounded regretful rather than distressed.

Mina gave Nellie a sisterly hug and Nellie returned it warmly.

'It is hard to know what to do about Mr Stevenson,' said Mina. 'The man knows too many tricks, and any scheme we might devise could only make things worse. But I promise to give it some thought, and perhaps I will find an answer — or we may be fortunate, and on the way back to Brighton he will sink into the mud and slime where he belongs. I only wish we could do something about Mr Hope. Will you send him a sharp reply?'

'I feel it is best to have no communication with him at all. And I decline to tell Mr Honeyacre what that vile beast of a man is up to. He has quite enough upset to deal with.'

'Especially as he is unable to order Mr Hope to quit the house,' said Mina. She thought for a while. 'Might I suggest a plan? Mr Hope is vain enough to take your lack of response as assent, but that is to our advantage. He is bound to go to the drawing room at the appointed time and when he does, there should be someone waiting for him. In fact, it would be better for safety if there were two people; Dr Hamid for his authority and good sense, and Richard as he would wish to protect you and would be most offended if he was not allowed to do so. We will show them this note, and I am sure they will know what to say. But we ought to be on our guard in case Mr Hope should attempt to gain entry to our room. Naturally the door will be locked, but we must remain alert until we are told by our gallant protectors that we are safe.'

All the plans had been made, and the arrangements completed to Mina's satisfaction. As she and Nellie prepared to rest, both fully dressed but taking it in turns to refresh themselves with naps, Mina could not help but wonder how her scheme would be resolved and consider what a wonderful story her adventures in Hollow House might make if her *alter ego* Mr Robert Neil were ever to write it as a work of sensational fiction.

Rest did not come easy, however. Mina was just on the cusp of sleep when she became aware of footsteps outside her room. It was hard to tell but she thought that two or maybe even three people were creeping towards the servants' stairs at the eastern end of the corridor. No sooner had they passed by then she heard the squeak of a hinge. A door had opened at the western end. Mina listened carefully but detected no further sound. 'I am not sure,' she whispered to Nellie, 'but that might have been Mr Hope leaving for his assignation in the drawing room.'

'How I wish I could see him discovering that his vile scheme had been anticipated,' said Nellie, with a grim smile.

'Once the gentlemen have spoken to him, he would do well to return to his room and never trouble you again,' said Mina.

They waited together, but hardly more than a moment or two passed before there were further noises, footsteps at the eastern end of the corridor and a creaking and scraping impossible to identify. There followed at the western end the soft pattering sound of cautious footfall, probably from more than one individual, then several doors opened and closed in quick succession.

'What can be happening?' said Mina in astonishment. 'Is the entire household awake?'

Then came a knock at their door. Neither of them spoke, but the knock came again.

'Miss Scarletti?' The urgent whisper was immediately outside.

Mina drew Nellie aside. 'It's Mr Beckler,' she said quietly. 'The despicable creature. He believes his master is downstairs with you, and I am alone.' Mina's annoyance got the better of her and she approached the door. 'Mr Beckler, kindly return to your room and do not bother me again.'

To her surprise she heard a little squeal followed by a nervous laugh. 'I felt something brush past me, but there was nothing there. Miss Scarletti, there are curious things happening which you must see and hear for yourself.'

The next sound was almost melodious, the rattle of twigs and dry logs beating rhythmically together. Mr Beckler gave a little gasp. 'There is a skeleton in the corridor,' he said, and there was no mistaking the tremor in his voice, half excitement, half fright, 'It's waving its arms at me. Oh, please come out and see!'

Mina returned to where Nellie stood and spoke softly. 'This annoyance must end. I mean to confront him. But I won't leave you alone until you are safe from Mr Hope. If you are equal to it, we will go together and protect each other.'

Nellie nodded eagerly.

Mina went to the mantlepiece and removed the candlesticks. She handed one of them to Nellie. 'If it is necessary to strike him, I trust you will do so,' she said.

'With pleasure,' said Nellie.

Mina unlocked the door and threw it open. Mr Beckler was leaning against the far wall, staring along the corridor, then he turned to see Mina and Nellie. His profound astonishment was gratifying to both ladies.

'As you see,' said Mina, 'Mr Hope's little ruse has failed. Some gentlemen were waiting for him in the drawing room and are even now explaining to him the folly of his actions.' She glanced down the corridor, which was empty. 'And there appears to be no skeleton.'

He turned back to look. 'It was there a moment ago! I promise you! It was dancing about!'

'Then we shall go and look for it. All three of us. If you have the courage to face it, that is. And if I find you have been telling me untruths it will be the worse for you.'

From Mr Beckler's expression he would have found an animated skeleton preferable to an angry Mina.

The unclouded moon was throwing sufficient light down the corridor, and they crept towards the window, looking about them but seeing nothing of note. Faced with the servants' stairs, they detected noises coming from the attic; a shuffling that resembled the movement of rats. Mina glanced at the others, pressed a finger to her lips then pointed upwards and they ascended the stairs as quietly as possible. At the head of the stairs was a small landing with single dark door and a yellow light flickering from below.

Mina was leading the way and driven by excitement she abandoned caution and pushed the door open. Nellie and Mr Beckler rushed in after her. There in a small dingy and unfurnished room illuminated by a single candle they confronted Mrs Malling, wearing an unflattering costume of billowing white muslin over her day dress, and a glowing skeletal shape with the head of Mr Malling. Too late, and with a look of alarm, he pulled on a black hood, which was painted with a phosphorescent skull.

'Oh, do take that off, Mr Malling!' snapped Mina. 'Really, I am disgusted with the pair of you!'

He removed the hood with a sigh and a slump of his shoulders. Both looked suitably crestfallen.

'We didn't mean any harm,' said Mrs Malling, sulkily.

'It was just a game,' said Mr Malling.

Mrs Malling nodded and took up the theme. 'That's right. We knew that Mr Honeyacre hoped to see a ghost — all those books he has on hauntings and spirits — so we thought we'd give him what he wanted.'

If Mrs Malling thought Mina would swallow that explanation she was to be disappointed. 'If you knew anything of the matter and I know you do,' said Mina, sternly, 'you would be well aware that your employer is not happy to be living in a haunted house, his poor wife is being made ill with terror, and the maids are frightened out of their wits!'

At this the Mallings glanced at each other and Mina sensed that there was more to discover. 'Whatever you are doing, this is no game, no joke,' she said. 'You are still lying to me even now.'

They were silent.

'Now take off those ridiculous costumes and go back to your own rooms. I will talk to both of you in the morning.'

'Will you tell Mr Honeyacre?' asked Mrs Malling.

'I certainly have no intention of concealing it from him. Now go. It's too late an hour for me to make any decisions. But make sure that tomorrow you tell me all the truth.'

Once Mrs Malling had divested herself of the white draperies and Mr Malling had doffed the black cloak with its skeletal painting it was a shamefaced pair who descended the stairs.

Nellie picked up the cloak and hood. 'Such an old illusionists' trick,' she said, 'black fabric with paint on the front and none on the back. If you turn around you can vanish in an instant. I wonder, did they think it up for themselves or did someone teach it to them?' She raised the garments cautiously to her nose. 'Phosphorus; probably obtained from soaking match heads.'

Mr Beckler edged forward and hovered over Mina. 'You are very pretty when you are angry, Miss Scarletti,' he said. She brandished the candlestick at him and he flinched.

At that moment screams of terror rang out from the corridor below. Mina and her party descended the attic stairs to be greeted by the sight of the Mallings cringing in revulsion from what appeared to be an enormous spider-like creature with a shiny black body. It was rearing over the unfortunate Mr Stevenson, who was lying on the floor, curled into a ball and sobbing. Dr Hamid and Richard had just emerged from Mr Hope's room and were trying to understand what it was they were seeing.

Before anyone had an opportunity to react the spider abruptly unfolded itself and rose up with a tinkling laugh, proving to be none other than Kitty Honeyacre, formerly Princess Kirabampu the oriental contortionist, in a black silk fringed robe and face paint. 'I hope I didn't frighten you all,' said Kitty, 'but it was far too good an opportunity to miss.'

At that moment, Mr Honeyacre emerged from the storeroom bringing with him Susan, who was wearing a red coat and the shreds of a painted mask. The girl had a surly look and was struggling to escape but was being clasped firmly by the arm. 'What is happening here?' he demanded and then he saw Kitty. 'My dear! You should be resting in your room!'

Kitty took his hand. 'Oh, have no fear, Benjamin, I am well. As for Mr Stevenson, he has taken fright at a shadow. But what has Susan done?'

'This miscreant,' said Mr Honeyacre, giving the girl an angry shake, 'has been carrying out the most foolish escapade. I was taking a walk, hoping the white lady might appear to me, when I heard the sound of the rocking horse in the storeroom. When I went to confront the spirit I found the girl riding the horse and pretending to be a ghost. What can she have been thinking of? I hardly know what to do with her!'

'I suggest,' said Kitty, gently, 'that a decision can be made in the morning.'

'Whatever you think best,' said Mr Honeyacre, gazing into the eyes of his smiling wife. 'Mrs Malling, take the girl away and guard her well.'

Mr Stevenson, who had shamed himself beyond redemption in front of several reliable witnesses, would also have to be dealt with later. He was in a disgusting condition, babbling and gibbering incoherently and in urgent need of clean underlinen, and it was felt to be unwise to leave him alone. Dr Hamid took charge, ordering Mr Malling to remove Mr Stevenson to his room and do what was necessary to restore his dignity. Mr Malling was detailed to sit with the patient and alert Dr Hamid at once in case he should show signs of feverishness and incipient frenzy.

Mina could hardly object to these decisions although she was not sure what stories the Mallings would devise to try and exculpate themselves. She gave them both a warning look before they departed.

Mr and Mrs Honeyacre decided to return to their room, walking arm in arm in the most affectionate manner.

Mr Beckler was preparing to creep back to his room unnoticed, but Dr Hamid interrupted him. 'I think you should know that Mr Hope is unwell,' he said. 'Mr Scarletti and I were having a conversation with him in the drawing room and he appears to have imbibed too much brandy. We have brought him back to the room and laid him on the bed and I managed to get him to swallow a glass of water. I should warn you; he will have a sore head in the morning.'

Mr Beckler looked puzzled. 'Mr Hope can tolerate a great deal of brandy, far more than most men. How much did he drink?'

'I am not sure,' said Dr Hamid. 'Now I come to think about it, I didn't see him have more than two glasses. Of course, capacities vary but a man of his size ought to have more tolerance for it.'

Mr Beckler went to see for himself and Mina peered into the room to see Mr Hope lying on the bed, fully dressed, semi-conscious and mumbling.

Richard crept over to Dr Hamid. 'I — er — I may know something about that,' he said with an awkward little laugh.

Mina, with an all too familiar sense of dread, turned to her brother. 'Richard, what have you done?'

He shrugged. 'I wanted to make sure he was in no position to trouble Mrs Jordan so when I poured out his second glass of brandy for him, I might have added something to it.'

Dr Hamid stared at him. 'Might have? What do you mean?'

'Well — I did.'

'What?' Dr Hamid gave a groan. 'Oh no, don't tell me you gave him one of those drops I gave you for toothache. It was just the one, wasn't it? I said one drop rubbed on the gums or in a teaspoon of brandy.'

'Ah, well, it was more than that, I think.'

'You think?' exploded Dr Hamid.

'Yes, well, he had a whole glass of brandy to drink and that was quite a lot of teaspoons so I thought I would have needed more drops. I wasn't expecting it to work that fast, I must admit. But I'm glad it did.'

Dr Hamid stared at Richard and he did not look friendly. 'How many drops did you put in, man?'

Richard backed away defensively. 'I don't know. I didn't count them. About half the bottle. But it will be alright, won't it? When he wakes up he'll just think he fell asleep from the drink.'

'When and if he wakes up,' said Dr Hamid. 'Mr Scarletti, you are a great fool, but I hope you are not a murderer. Now listen to me carefully. I want you to — ' he paused, 'no, I need someone sensible.' He looked around and, as luck would have it, Zillah and Miss Pet arrived at that moment. 'Ah, good, Zillah, Miss Pet, I want you to go as fast as you can and fetch me fresh towels, a large basin, plenty of warm water, salt and a funnel.'

The two young women nodded and departed at a run.

'And now I need to keep him awake long enough to be able to swallow. Where are you going, Mr Scarletti?' he called out, as Richard was trying to slip away.

'I — er — didn't think I was needed,' said Richard.

'Oh, you most definitely are! You are going to assist me, and I am warning you now, you will not enjoy it.'

Something in Dr Hamid's expression and manner alerted Richard to the fact that things were very serious indeed. 'Oh! Right! I'm your man! Yes!' he exclaimed.

Dr Hamid rolled up his sleeves and went to attend to the patient. To his surprise, Nellie followed him into the room. 'Oh, Mrs Jordan, it really won't be necessary for you to assist.'

She smiled. 'I used to be on the stage, Dr Hamid. Drink and soporifics taken to excess were not an uncommon thing to deal with. I have seen far worse than this.'

There was nothing more for Mina to do, especially as both the gentlemen who might have caused Nellie harm were currently incapacitated, but she decided to wait a little to see what transpired. Zillah and Miss Pet returned quickly with the articles required and took them to Dr Hamid, who assured them that he needed no further help and closed the bedroom door firmly. The noises that emerged were resoundingly unpleasant. Mina was considering a return to her room when Zillah and Miss Pet came to address her.

'Miss Scarletti,' said Zillah, 'I think you ought to know that we made a discovery in the apartments of Mr and Mrs Malling and we feel that you ought to see what we found.' Zillah took a ribbon-wrapped packet of letters from her apron pocket.

'Are these personal and private papers?' asked Mina.

Miss Pet lowered her gaze. 'Yes, they are. We went out ghost-hunting and saw the Mallings creeping about. They were behaving very strangely.'

'So you took the opportunity of searching their rooms?' said Mina. 'I won't ask how you got in.'

'I am the one to blame,' said Zillah. 'If it was wrong to abstract papers of that nature, even in the cause of truth, I will return them at once.' Miss Pet said nothing but gave Zillah's hand a gentle squeeze.

'That won't be necessary,' said Mina, taking the packet and glancing through the collection of letters, 'sometimes, needs must.'

Chapter Fourteen

Mina awoke the following morning to a quiet house. Nellie was soundly asleep and Zillah was pulling back the curtains to reveal a cloudless sky and the first blushes of sunrise.

'It might be best to leave Mrs Jordan to sleep a little longer,' said Mina. 'She did not retire until very late.'

'I think the only people who had a good night's sleep last night were Mrs Blunt and Mr Gillespie,' said Zillah as she helped Mina out of bed. 'They are both about but hardly anyone else is apart from myself and Dr Hamid. He has just had two cups of strong coffee and gone to see his patients.'

'What about Mary Ann? I saw nothing of her last night.'

'I think Susan plied her with sherry so she could creep away to perform her mischief. At least, she looks a little the worse for something this morning and Mrs Blunt has been complaining that there is nothing left for the tipsy cake and has ordered her to light all the fires as punishment. Oh, and I returned those letters to Mr and Mrs Malling's room as you asked. They won't suspect anything.'

Mina took her time to dress and went down to breakfast which she began alone, but eventually Dr Hamid, looking strained and tired, joined her at the table, after piling a plate with hot food and pouring more coffee.

'You have been rather busier than you expected when you came here,' Mina observed. 'I am sorry that this was not the amusing visit that was promised. How is everyone faring?'

Dr Hamid rubbed his eyes. 'I am relieved to say that Mr Hope is out of danger and fortunately has little memory of what occurred, otherwise your brother would now be facing a charge of attempted murder. Hope thinks that he simply took too much brandy, or it was a bad bottle. I have not enlightened him and have advised bed rest. I can also report that after assisting me, your brother, if he ever had any ambitions to enter the medical profession no longer considers that a possibility. There were moments last night when he was in a worse state than Mr Hope.'

'And Mrs Honeyacre? I must say she appeared extremely well after her little joke at Mr Stevenson's expense. In fact, she was quite back to her old self — if that is,' Mina added with a smile, 'she ever left it.'

His expression showed that he understood her meaning. 'Yes, I wish more people were as well as Mrs Honeyacre. I saw her this morning and found her in perfect health and good spirits. She has explained some facts to me concerning her behaviour during the last few days and will want to speak to you in due course. As to Mr Stevenson, I was obliged to give him a sedative or he might have injured himself. Zillah is sitting with him now and will alert me if I am needed.' He paused. 'But I have yet to enquire about my most important patient. I hope you have not overtired yourself. You really should take more care.'

'I promise I will rest when I am home, but today it is my intention to finally expose all the secrets of what has been happening at Hollow House. Some of them I already know, some I can guess and there are others that will be revealed when I ask the right questions. For once I am quite pleased that the house is cut off from the outside world or certain of its inhabitants might have been tempted to abscond.'

Dr Hamid was about to comment on this when there was a loud knocking at the front door.

Mina and Dr Hamid exchanged looks of astonishment and went to the hallway where Miss Pet was admitting the visitor, a young clerical gentleman, looking a little damp and wearing a long cloak and riding boots. A horse, muddied well above its hooves, stood patiently at the head of the carriage drive.

'Reverend Ashbrook,' said Miss Pet.

'Please excuse this unannounced visit,' said the young gentleman, disarmingly, 'but I was most distressed at being unable to take the service at St Mond on Sunday. In view of the dreadful weather I thought I would call and see if everyone was well or in need of anything.'

While Miss Pet took charge of the Reverend's cloak and boots and provided him with dry shoes, Mina greeted him and introduced Dr Hamid, explaining that Mr and Mrs Honeyacre were resting. 'I can assure you we are extremely grateful for your call. If you would come into the parlour I will have refreshments sent and we can talk there. Miss Pet, would you go and ask Mrs Blunt to prepare a tray and also see if Mr Malling is about, so he can take care of the Reverend's horse.'

'I will advise Mr and Mrs Honeyacre that you are here,' said Dr Hamid.

Mina and the young clergyman were soon settled in the parlour before the fire. 'I am curious to know how you were able to reach us,' asked Mina, 'We have had the most dreadful weather, which, as you must have seen, resulted in a landslip and we have not been able to stir from the house for some days.'

'The road from Clayton has been nothing but mud for some time, but it has improved a little and today I risked hiring a horse to see if I was needed here. I am glad to say he was able to keep his feet and we met with no accident.'

'Did you come up the carriage drive? I had understood that it was sunken and below water.'

The Reverend looked surprised. 'It was not so this morning. But as we know, even the worst floods will eventually recede.'

Mary Ann, looking pale and headachy, brought in a tray with tea, toast, butter and preserves. 'Is Mrs Malling about?' asked the Reverend. 'Her son has been most anxious to reach her and insisted that I deliver this letter.'

'Mary Ann, bring Mrs Malling here,' said Mina.

Mary Ann gave her a gritty-eyed stare and departed.

'In recent weeks I have heard rumours of curious things happening here,' said Reverend Ashbrook, 'and I am not referring to the weather.'

'Oh, we have had a fine little masquerade,' said Mina, pouring the tea. 'But before I tell you of that I was hoping that you would be able to enlighten me on a number of things. I have heard something of the village and its history and legends and would appreciate it if you could tell me more.'

'Of course.' Reverend Ashbrook looked grateful for the hot tea and the offer of toast, which he buttered well, adding large spoonfuls of jam. 'What would you like to know?'

'Do you remember the Lassiter family? They may have been before your time.'

'I do remember them, yes. I was very young when they lived here, but my predecessor, Reverend Tolley, once preached at St Mond's and he knew them well. He was my great-uncle. Sadly, he passed away last year.'

'So he would have known all about the haunting that took place when they lived here?' Mina prompted. 'It is the talk of the village, you know.'

To her surprise Reverend Ashbrook laughed until he coughed and was obliged to gulp some tea to wash away toast crumbs. He put his plate down. 'Oh, yes, that was a great to-do. Very amusing in its way. What have you been told?'

'I have been told several different stories, all conflicting.'

'Yes, well the truth is almost certainly more mundane. The Lassiters purchased the estate in order to establish a racing stables here but found it unsuitable for their purpose and removed to Kent, I believe. Later, for reasons of Mrs Lassiter's health they went to live in Italy, where they still reside, although the son, George, was sent back to England when he was of university age.'

'There were rumours that he had died in childhood.'

'He was very much alive when he paid a visit to my great-uncle two years ago.'

'I see. But what can you tell me about the haunting?'

'At the time there was a considerable upset and my poor uncle, to his eternal regret, did become entangled in it. He even wrote a pamphlet on the subject. Later, he could hardly bear to speak of it, but towards the end of his life when he knew I was to come here to preach he told me the entire story. But I was not to tell it to a soul while he lived.'

'Then am I to be the first to hear it?' said Mina eagerly.

He smiled. 'You are the first to enquire, so yes. Young George was terribly spoilt as a child, though he seemed sensible enough when my uncle last saw him. The Lassiters employed a nursemaid called Abigail Falcon and she found the boy difficult to deal with, while the parents, of course, would never believe ill of their precious son. Apparently, one day George threw a tantrum and broke some crockery. The maid, knowing that she would be blamed, claimed that the crockery had broken by falling off a shelf by itself while she was not in the room. Realising that this explanation might not be convincing she was obliged to fabricate a ghost. After that there was a series of incidents and the parents and visitors all saw things occur for which they were certain the maid could not have been responsible. And I rather think she came to enjoy the excitement and attention.'

'Was Abigail Falcon from Ditching Hollow?' asked Mina. 'I visited the church and found no —' she paused, as she had been about to say parish records, 'gravestones with that surname.'

'I believe she came from Burgess Hill,' said Reverend Ashbrook. 'At any rate, her deception took in everyone, including, I am sorry to say, my uncle. They asked for his advice and he paid them a visit and saw a great deal of things that convinced him that the house was haunted. He was above seventy by then and his eyesight was failing, so I really don't think he had anything with which to reproach himself. When she eventually confessed everything to my uncle he was quite astonished at how he had been taken in. I think he destroyed all the copies of the pamphlet — at least I have never seen one.'

'Do you know what happened to the nursemaid? I have been told she didn't go away with the Lassiters.'

'Well, you should ask her daughter, Susan.' He sipped his tea and made a fresh assault on his toast.

'Susan?'

'Yes.'

'You mean Susan Parker, one of the maids here?'

'Yes. Are you surprised?'

Mina thought about this. 'Now that you mention it, no. Then Abigail must live in the village.'

'Yes, I think she went away after the Lassiters left, married and came back a few years later as Abigail Parker. Since she had only ever lived and worked at the house, I doubt anyone in the village realised who she was.'

'Did Abigail ever reveal to your uncle how she had made people believe the house was haunted?'

'Yes, it was really rather simple. She used black thread and horsehairs to make things fall from shelves when she was not near them. Sometimes she would simply place things in a precarious position so that the footsteps of someone passing nearby would dislodge them. Once she even made stones fall from the ceiling.'

'Stones from the ceiling? Dear me, how did she achieve that?'

'By sprinkling them through a crack in the plaster, apparently. I do hope her daughter has not been up to similar tricks.'

Mina was not sure what to say, but at that moment Mrs Malling arrived. The housekeeper approached the visitor cautiously, smoothing her apron and looking at Mina with some trepidation.

'Ah, Mrs Malling,' said the Reverend brightly, 'I am pleased to say that your son is very well indeed and hopes to pay you a visit soon. He begged me to give you this letter, which he says is highly important. I do so hope it is good news.'

Mrs Malling thanked him in a whisper, took the letter and slipped it into her pocket. 'May I be excused to read this in private?' she asked.

'You may, but I wish to speak to you when you are done,' said Mina. 'Both you and Mr Malling, together, in the library. I will send for you when needed.'

'Yes Miss,' said the housekeeper and hurried out.

Reverend Ashbrook was about to make a comment but was forestalled by the arrival of Mr Honeyacre and Kitty both looking very much better than they had the evening before. They greeted the clergyman warmly and Mina left them to their conversation. Her discussion with the Mallings would not be as friendly and she realised that, without knowing how they might react, it was better for her not to tackle them alone.

Later that morning, Richard, looking red-eyed and haggard, emerged from his bedroom and wandered into the dining room. After surveying the hot dishes he took only coffee for breakfast.

Mina joined him. 'I hope you are feeling better after your ordeal,' she said.

'Oh, I suppose I shall recover from that eventually and trust I will never dream about it,' he said unhappily. 'But there is far worse. Did Nellie tell you what happened with Mr Stevenson in the parlour?'

'She did.'

'I didn't know the horrid sneak was hiding behind the curtain! That wasn't fair! What sort of gentleman does that?' He sipped his coffee and pulled a face. 'Do you think if I told him there was nothing in it he might believe me? It was only one little kiss.'

'You kissed her?'

'Well, what is a fellow to do?'

'You might have been sensible, but that is obviously far too much to expect. Please, Richard, don't try and speak to Mr Stevenson again. In fact, you should have nothing to do with him at all. You'll only make things worse.'

'I don't suppose all that business with the fright he got might have made him forget it,' said Richard, hopefully.

Mina was thoughtful. 'Leave it with me, I'll see what I can do. In the meantime, I have a task for you. When you have finished your coffee, go and fetch Mr and Mrs Malling and tell them I want to speak to them both in the library. Bring them to me and then stay there to act as a witness, but you must remain silent.'

When Mina faced the Mallings across the library table Mrs Malling was redder in the face than she had been only shortly before. She held the open letter before her and gazed at it as if it had been poisoned.

'I need the truth, now,' said Mina. 'I know what you have been doing and I even know how some of it was done, but what I need you to tell me is why?'

'You haven't told Mr Honeyacre about us, have you?' pleaded Mrs Malling. She glanced at Richard who was sitting in one corner of the library, awake, but too weary to fidget.

'What I have already told him or choose to tell him in the future is my business,' said Mina. 'It will depend entirely on what you tell me today. You must be honest and hide nothing.'

Mrs Malling took a handkerchief from her pocket and wiped her face with it. 'I hadn't meant it to end up like it did,' she said. 'I didn't know Lord Hope and his friend would come here, and that spying man, and I still don't understand about Mrs Honeyacre and that horrid black creature with all its legs a crawling about.'

Mina waited and at length Mrs Malling breathed out with a puff of her cheeks and put the handkerchief away. 'You might know that our son Albert is a clerk at an estate office in Hurstpierpoint. And he wants to get married, only that's never easy on a clerk's wages and he thinks he might have to wait a long time. Well, there is this man, very rich he is, Mr White, he owns a lot of properties and builds houses and other things. He wrote to Mr Honeyacre last year, that's before master came here to live, saying that he wanted to buy up the estate and make it into a brickworks, but Mr Honeyacre said no. In fact, he was very indignant and said he wouldn't have the countryside made into a nasty dirty factory.

'Last month, Mr White paid a call at the office and told Albert that he was still interested in buying the estate if he could get it for a good price. When Albert told Mr White that we worked here he promised him a commission if we could find some way of persuading Mr Honeyacre to sell up. It was a very good commission, too, enough for him to get married on. And Mr White also promised that when he bought up the estate he would live here, in Hollow House, and we would still have our places and a good salary. It wasn't just promises, he signed a paper and everything.

'I didn't see how it could be done, making Mr Honeyacre change his mind, but then I remembered all those ghost books in the library and that was when I thought we might be able to convince him that the house was haunted. And I didn't think that Mrs Honeyacre would want to live in a haunted house, because I know theatrical people are great believers in ghosts, so she would tell her husband that she wanted to leave, and he dotes on her and would do anything for her.'

'It's just stories, that's all,' said Mr Malling, gruffly. 'We didn't think she'd get as upset as she did. We didn't think any of it would go as far as it did.'

'So you decided to report that things were happening and hoped imagination would do the rest?' asked Mina.

They nodded.

'All the time saying that you didn't believe in hauntings to remove suspicion from yourselves? How did Susan become involved?'

'I asked her if she knew some ghost stories and suchlike,' said Mrs Malling, 'and she told me that her mother knew how to conjure up ghosts. Or at least make it look as if she had.'

Mina had one very important question to ask. 'Susan told us all a story about Sir Christopher Redwoode's sons. *The Lost Bones*, she called it. That was all made up, I am sure. Do you know how she learned the story? I don't think she made it up herself.'

'Oh, it was in one of those cheap story books,' said Mrs Malling. 'I wouldn't encourage the maids to read things like that, but one of the shops in Hurstpierpoint was using old copies as wrapping paper.'

Mina bit the inside of her lip and did her best to avoid revealing her emotions.

'The noises in the corridor, the first night I was here?'

'That was me,' said Mr Malling, 'I walked along pulling a coil of rope. But all what Mrs Honeyacre did, we never put her up to that.'

'Would you mind telling me how you achieved the things that happened at the séance?'

'That was all Susan's idea,' said Mr Malling. 'It was done with black sewing thread. Not tied on to things, just passed around them so it could be pulled away afterwards. Quickly done and nothing left to see.'

'The Chinese vase? That didn't fall. Was it meant to?'

Unusually, Mr Malling's expression softened for a moment. 'That was one of Mr Honeyacre's favourites. I didn't want to break it, so I put some clay on the bottom.'

'And the stones? How was that done?'

'Susan dropped them through. When I took the maidservants back to the village that night Susan came back with me and hid upstairs. She had a plan and told me what to do. I think her mother had done something very like it before. I had overseen the workmen who fitted the lights in the dining room, so I knew how to loosen the screws so there was a gap to put the stones down. She was able to make the lights move as well. Then after the séance when everyone was still downstairs making things tidy I went up and put things back the way they had been. And Susan went home.'

Mina recalled Miss Pet saying she had heard a noise like a chirping bird before the séance and realised that this must have been the squeaking caused by loosening the metal screws supporting the chandelier. Afterwards, in the commotion following the séance, the noise of tightening the screws had not been noticed.

'The thing is, it turns out that it's all been for nothing,' said Mrs Malling. 'This letter I just had from my son; he's learned that Mr White has gone back on his word. He went and bought another estate and doesn't even want this one now. And he promised that he would employ the servants of the place he has just bought, but then he didn't, he turned them all out at a moment's notice. He does that all the time, it seems, makes promises that he doesn't mean to keep if it doesn't suit him. And he's too rich to sue. So Albert wanted to warn us to have nothing to do with him.'

'Can you explain the skeleton found in the attic?' The Mallings glanced at each other. 'I was told you keep the churchyard tidy; that it had been much neglected when you first came here. I hope you didn't dig something up.'

'No, we'd never do that! It was an old burial, come up to the surface and the coffin all rotted away,' said Mr Malling. 'We took up the bones and we were going to hand them over to Reverend Ashbrook but then we thought —'

'They were going to be buried again proper in any case,' said Mrs Malling defensively.

'How did you know that we would find them?'

'We didn't know. There are men are coming next week to replace the floorboards so we thought they would find them.'

'Are you going to tell Mr Honeyacre?' asked Mr Malling.

'I have one more question,' said Mina. 'After the landslip, was the carriage drive really sunken and under water and impassable as you said? We all took you to be telling the truth, but now I must doubt it.' There was an embarrassed silence. 'I see. That was a fine scheme to keep us all trapped here and afraid. I must say I am surprised that you didn't both run away after our conversation last night.'

'We've nowhere to go,' said Mrs Malling, miserably. 'We're hoping Mr Honeyacre will be merciful. We want to stay here. We'll pay for all the broken crockery. We'll work for nothing if he wants.'

'If you were my employees you would now be packing your boxes and leaving without a character,' said Mina, severely. 'But I can't make that decision. That is for Mr Honeyacre. What I would like you to do now, Mr Malling, is go down to the village — I assume that it can still be reached via the carriage drive — and discover if the roads to Hassocks Gate are passable. If they are, we can start making plans to go home.' She rose to her feet. 'By the end of today you will both have made a full confession to your employer. Who knows what he will do? He is a good man.'

Mr and Mrs Honeyacre made a late and leisurely breakfast — Kitty working her way through a plateful of bacon and kidneys — and reported that Reverend Ashbrook had departed after promising to come on Sunday to take service. Kitty, Mina noticed, had a sparkle in her eye and a freshness of colour that had been lacking before and she wondered if the previous pallor was due more to the art of the theatre rather than any fault in health. She was not surprised when Kitty asked to speak to her in the parlour after breakfast.

Mina still felt guilty over her raid on the parish chest. Fortunately, she had learned from the Reverend's comments that he had never seen the pamphlet and therefore, even if he was to examine the contents of the chest, was unlikely to realise that it had been burgled. It was with a conspiratorial air that she handed the packet of papers to Miss Pet, asking her if, on the following Sunday, she could ask Reverend Ashbrook if she might examine the parish records and in so doing surreptitiously return the documents to their proper place.

In the light of the parlour fire Mina studied her hostess's glowing complexion and merry eyes. 'I feel there has been some duplicity here,' she said, although she spoke lightly and not in an accusing tone. 'Mrs Jordan did comment that she had never seen you so fearful before and now I feel sure that it was all pretence.'

Kitty gave one of her little careless laughs. 'Did you not notice that it was all I could do to keep my face still when Mr Hope talked about his precious Odic Force? Of course, I have seen Nellie mesmerised on stage a hundred times when she did the mind-reading trick, so I knew what to do. I am sorry to have deceived my friends, but I know you will forgive me. And all is well, now, since I have had a very comforting conversation with my dear Benjamin and he has agreed to accede to my wishes. You see, I knew when we came here that he loved this house and it was his dream to make it a charming residence. Naturally I wanted him to be happy and would never have insisted he abandon it, although I was sure I could never be content here. When I heard the reports of hauntings — and I swear I had nothing to do with those — I simply made use of the situation. And the fact that a happy family event is probable meant that there were some things that were quite unfeigned.' She patted her abdomen. 'I must say Dr Hamid's recipe for ginger tea has been a boon. But the future is now settled. My dear husband and I have decided to spend a month here and a month in Brighton, turn and turn about. That will satisfy us both.'

'Your appearance as a monster spider was very impressive,' said Mina.

'It is surprising what one can do with only a black silk wrap,' said Kitty. 'My main purpose was to force that odious man to reveal his true purpose here, which he did. He will think again before he spies upon poor Nellie.'

Later in the day the Mallings reported that the floods were receding and the way to Hassocks Gate would be clear by next morning assuming, of course, that no further rain was to descend. Zillah was kept busy packing for the guests' departure. She was a little despondent at leaving her new friend, but Mina reassured her that Miss Pet would be in Brighton for half the year whenever the Honeyacres were in residence and she was cheered by that prospect.

Mina had one more serious conversation planned before she departed. Mr Stevenson had come to himself but was still huddled in his room wrapped in blankets and looking grey and jaded. He was understandably unsure as to how many people had actually witnessed his hysterical collapse and confession. Mina was pleased to advise him that it was everyone who mattered.

'Poor Mr Stevenson,' she said. 'Your terror of spiders must cause you severe difficulty in your profession as spy and detective. How do you manage when lurking on street corners, or hiding in cupboards or under beds? Are there no cobwebs to become entangled in, none of the horrible beasts to crawl inside your collar?'

He shuddered. 'How cruel you can be! I did not choose this thing. I have been that way from a child.'

'Do your clients know of it?'

'I prefer them not to, of course. But you must have guessed that.'

'I have. The events that have taken place in this house, would, if they became generally known, adversely affect your professional reputation.'

Mr Stevenson nodded, unhappily.

'However, I have no intention of destroying your business. Many people despise what you do, but some of them might be the very people who will one day be glad of your services. So, I am giving you my solemn promise that I will not broadcast the details of what I have seen and I will also persuade the others to do the same.'

Mr Stevenson, who had been prepared for something a lot less friendly and amenable, looked firstly surprised, then relieved, then grateful.

'Miss Scarletti, I — I hardly know what to say; that is most kind and generous of you. I am in your debt.'

'Indeed, you are. In fact, my observation is that it would be all to the good if everything that took place here since your arrival was quietly forgotten. Don't you agree?'

'Ah,' said Mr Stevenson. 'Yes. I understand you.'

'But before you do so,' said Mina, taking out her little notebook, 'I would like you to tell me everything that happened to you last night.'

'That was a narrow escape,' said Mina to Richard later.

'But I can't believe how underhand the fellow was,' Richard protested. 'He pretended to be my friend, he shared his whisky flask with me and now I see it was all a plan to win me over and make me say something I ought not to.'

'No one could have predicted that,' said Mina, comfortingly. 'Even from someone you knew was a private detective hired by a jealous husband to spy on you.'

'Exactly! And now I think that I might not be a detective after all if that is what it means. Not to mention all that standing about in the cold and wet. But it was rather fun the other day when I went up in the pulpit. Imagine standing there and saying things to people and they all have to listen to you. It can't be that hard. You could write my sermons for me. And I'd only have to do it once a week.'

With only a few hours remaining to explore Mr Honeyacre's library Mina was making the most of her time when her host came to see her. He had a solemn look that told her at once that he had spoken to the Mallings. She put her books aside.

'Miss Scarletti,' he said with a deep sigh, 'I have had a conversation with Mr and Mrs Malling of a most painful nature. They tell me that you know everything and urged them to come to me and confess all. You did the right thing and I am most grateful. Unpleasant as it is, I should not be left in the dark as to the behaviour of my servants. Susan has been dismissed, of course, since her motives were pure mischief. I am sure that Mary Ann had nothing to do with the circumstances, being highly impressionable. As to the Mallings, I have yet to make a decision. They have served me diligently for several years, they are exemplary servants, but they have done things I can scarcely forgive. If Kitty had been harmed I would not now even be hesitating.'

'Perhaps you should seek Mrs Honeyacre's opinion,' Mina suggested.

He nodded. 'Yes, I think I will. Thank you, Miss Scarletti. Once again, you have my eternal gratitude.' He rose to depart and Mina returned to her reading. She did not, therefore, notice that as Mr Honeyacre left, another person had entered the room.

There was a gentle cough and she looked up to see Mr Beckler standing just inside the door.

'I — um,' he began.

'Please go,' she said.

'I have something to say to you.'

'I don't wish to hear it.'

'It's an apology.'

She made no reply and he advanced into the room. 'Will you allow me to speak?'

'I can't very well stop you speaking, but I can choose not to listen.' She closed her book and stood up.

'I'm sorry,' he said. 'I'm sorry if my behaviour has upset you.'

'You have done more than just upset me,' she said, harshly. 'To begin with I imagined that you were flattering me as a potential customer for your business. That was merely annoying. And then my eyes were opened and I understood your real motive. You are Mr Hope's creature and the instrument, as he intended, of my destruction. Admit it.'

He cringed at her words. 'Yes, I am. I was. But no more, I promise.'

'You revolt me,' said Mina. 'Never address me or even come near me again.' She left the room and closed the door.

The next morning, Mr Hope's servant arrived from the newly reopened Clayton Road in the repaired carriage with rested horses. Mr Beckler had hoped to take photographs in Hollow House but found that there had been some damage to the camera in the accident and the plan had to be abandoned. Mr Hope and Mr Beckler departed for Middlesex. No one was sorry to see them go.

Mina, Nellie and Dr Hamid, their boxes packed, prepared to leave Hollow House. Mr Honeyacre had allowed the Mallings to remain a month longer while he decided their fate and it was Mr Malling who was to drive them to Hassocks Gate to take the Brighton train. Richard begged to accompany them so he could return to London, as he did not wish to spend any more time in the company of Mr Stevenson, who, it was agreed, would be conveyed to the station later.

Before she stepped into the carriage Mina looked up at the window of the storeroom. Now that she was not seeing it through a curtain of misty rain it was quite clear that she was only seeing a mirror draped in a white sheet. She pointed it out to Mr Honeyacre and told him how she had been deceived on the day of her arrival by the falling dustsheet.

'I still think there may be the ghost of a white lady here,' he mused. 'I wonder if I will ever see her?'

'You may do,' said Mina, 'but only when the sky is very clear and the full moon shines through the east window.'

Chapter Fifteen

The next two weeks were a storm of activity as the whole of fashionable Brighton was busy with preparations for the Fancy Dress Ball to be held at the Pavilion on the evening of the seventh of February. Artists in hair were devising elaborate new styles that defied both nature and architecture. Milliners, dressmakers and costumiers were in deadly rivalry, jealously guarding their new designs and small wars were being fought over fabric. Mr Jordan's new venture, informed by Nellie's sense of costume and glamour, was thriving. Mina was pleased to note that there had been no painful rift in Nellie's marriage, which suggested that her carefully chosen words to Mr Stevenson had had their effect.

Nellie, true to her promise, had arranged a ticket for Mina and had her measured for a costume as a Spanish lady so she could protect herself from bad vapours with a fan and a cunningly concealed sachet of herbs. Mina could therefore devote her time to her most important task, committing her new story to paper. It was obvious that if she was to write the events of that remarkable night as a piece of fiction — or at least a piece of fiction that would satisfy the tastes of her readers — she would have to introduce dramatic scenes of mystery, magic, violence and horrible death that had not in fact occurred, or were at the very least somewhat exaggerated. Nevertheless, when she reflected on what had actually happened, there were genuine circumstances enough, the memory of which she would savour forever.

She thought at first that the task would take weeks, even months, but when she sat at her desk and made a start her pen began to fly over the paper as if possessed. In a matter of days — days during which Rose had had to remind her to eat and rest — she had material enough to send to Scarletti Publishing.

Before long, Mina received a small package from the publishing house in response to the first three parts she had written and opened it eagerly.

Dear Miss Scarletti

I enclose for your attention the proof copies of the first three parts of A Night in a Haunted House, *which we propose to publish monthly starting on 1 March under the nom de plume Robert Neil. I look forward very much to receiving the final part in due course.*

Might I add that it is an extraordinary work of the imagination, possibly one of your finest, and once again you leave me wondering where in the world you get your ideas from!

With very best wishes

D Greville

Fiction editor, Scarletti Publishing

Smiling, Mina took out the proofs and began reading them before starting work on the fourth and final part of the story.

A NIGHT IN A HAUNTED HOUSE

BY
ROBERT NEIL

(Author of *The Haunted Nun* and *Bessie the Pirate Queen*, available in bound volumes price 1s, from all good booksellers)

Published in four parts by the Scarletti Library of Romance

PART THE FIRST

It was with some trepidation, but also a feeling of excited anticipation that diminutive Miss Claretti agreed to spend the night at the manor house of her good friend, the venerable Mr Sweetacre and his charming young wife, Kate. Their home was situated on the edge of Ditterling Hollow, Southshire, a gloomy little village, whose inhabitants eked out a miserable living by tilling the thin soil that barely allowed the growth of a few bitter-tasting vegetables. The dreary streets were dominated by a grim hillside atop which there stood the largest and blackest windmill in the county. The windmill, so Miss Claretti had been told, had not been used for the grinding of corn for over a hundred years. The hill had a dreadful reputation as it had once been used to bury the ashes of witches who had been burned at the stake and few dared to venture there. The windmill was now occupied by a hideous-looking wise woman, who spent her time collecting such fragments of charred bone as she could discover and using them to cast spells. She had one familiar, a large dog that roamed the fields at night and was reputed to glow in the dark.

There had been a small church in the village, but following a collapse of the roof, which had crushed the incumbent minister to death, it lay derelict, leaving the villagers comfortless in times of distress.

Miss Claretti had received a letter from Mrs Sweetacre begging her to come and stay at Ditterling Manor, as she and her whole household were in a constant state of terror over the appearance of a number of ghosts, which prowled the corridors at night, making a great din, moaning and rattling chains, as if overcome with a terrible and inexpressible grief. A room which had once been a nursery was haunted by the ghost of a child in a red velvet coat who rode the rocking horse at night uttering piercing shrieks of evil laughter. Now, my readers might feel that unlike the heroine of my story, they would not have set foot in such a house, or even approached it, but little Miss Claretti was stronger than she looked, and quite unafraid of ghosts, and she agreed to spend the night there.

She did not travel alone, but was accompanied by her good friend, Mrs Eleanor Johnson, once a renowned actress who had given up the stage to make a dazzling society marriage, and Mrs Johnson's pretty and accomplished maid, Zena. Also of the party was wise and kindly Dr Haroon, since it was considered that in a household where many of the occupants were afflicted by hysteria, the skills of a medical man might well be required.

The journey to Ditterling Hollow was fraught with the most dreadful dangers due to the state of the roads that resembled rivers of dark mud more than they did passable thoroughfares. Several times their coach was almost upset and it seemed that the travellers would either drown in evil-smelling mire or be thrown bodily from the fallen vehicle. It was with some relief that they finally reached their destination without accident.

Ditterling Manor had once been a large handsome house, but in recent years it had been neglected and looked ready to crumble into a ruin. Its stones were as black as thunderclouds and heavy draperies were required within to prevent cold draughts from sweeping through every room. The floorboards were half rotten and creaked horribly underfoot, grotesque faces stared from ancient oil paintings and burrowing beetles tapped and clicked from its wooden rafters.

Mr and Mrs Sweetacre were, however, most welcoming and Zena at once became good friends with Mrs Sweetacre's maid Petronella. The visitors were afforded every comfort available. The cook, Mrs Bunn, was highly skilled. Mr Gillery, the master's manservant, was a model of good deportment. The housekeeper, Mrs Miller, and her husband who looked after the property for Mr Sweetacre were industrious people who seemed unafraid of the hauntings; indeed, they often declared that they did not believe in ghosts at all. Nevertheless, Mrs Miller liked to tell strange tales from which Miss Claretti gathered that no less than three young women had gone missing from the house and were reputed to be either murdered or suicides. A young boy had once occupied the nursery where he used to spend many hours riding a rocking horse. The ignorant villagers had believed the child to be a changeling and everyone who encountered him was afraid, since he had a look of great malevolence and it was thought that anyone who crossed his will would suffer a terrible fate. The boy's nursemaid was said to have sacrificed herself by jumping into the nearby brook holding the struggling child, thus putting an end to the evil. Neither body had been found but their ghosts were rumoured to appear in the house very frequently. One curious aspect of the house was that all the mirrors were covered during the hours of darkness, since it was said that anyone who looked in them at that time would be sure to see a spectre standing at his or her shoulder. It was also believed that somewhere in the house the corpse of a murdered wife would be found walled up, but so far no one had been able to locate it.

An elderly villager called Noddy Cooper had claimed that the witches who had been burned on the hilltop had placed the whole village under a terrible curse and no one who lived in

Ditterling Manor would ever know contentment. Most frightened of all were the two maidservants, who refused to stay in the house after dark. Maria was old Cooper's granddaughter and a fervent believer in the legends of the village and Sally was a nervous girl who said that she had fainted clean away when she had first seen the ghost of the child. Both had seen the spectre of a white lady that was able to walk through walls.

Mr Sweetacre, determined to protect the health of his young bride, informed Miss Claretti that he had decided to patrol the house that night with a dark lantern and accost any ghost he might see. Mrs Sweetacre was told to stay in her room, comforted by her puppy dog, Spot, to lock her door and only open it to admit her husband who would knock in a secret way.

While these plans were being laid, Miss Claretti received the most terrible shock. Who should unexpectedly arrive at the house but the notorious Viscount Hogg, an adventurer and an incorrigible roué who liked to investigate hauntings. Hogg thought so well of himself that he was convinced that all ladies could not help but fall in love with him. He at once began to make great eyes at Miss Claretti's friend Mrs Johnson in the most revolting manner and she naturally regarded his attentions with disgust. Mr Hogg was accompanied by a Mr Bickley, a man of repellent aspect, as thin as a skeleton with a pale cadaverous face. He purported to be a master of the art of photography although he had brought no camera with him to support his claim. Mr Bickley attempted to use his supposed profession to worm his way into the good graces of everyone present by the most obsequious and nauseating flattery. Mr Bickley, it transpired, was cut from the same cloth as his master, since he addressed Miss Claretti in a thoroughly indecent manner. Mrs Johnson and Miss Claretti decided to preserve their safety and protect each other by sharing a bedroom.

There were two more unexpected arrivals at the house, both of whom Viscount Hogg had taken it upon himself to invite without troubling to consult his host. One was Miss Claretti's brother Rickard, a handsome good-natured youth, but unencumbered either by fortune or intellect and inclined to the most dreadful recklessness. The other was a recent visitor to the village, a man calling himself Smith, although no one believed that that was his real name and he was largely suspected of being a spy for an unscrupulous property dealer called Mr Blank, who was hoping to acquire the estate at a low price. Mr Smith, who resembled a rat and wore coarse ugly boots, liked to prowl about the house poking his long nose into everyone's business.

After dinner, Viscount Hogg had the audacity to convey a note to Mrs Johnson inviting her to a secret rendezvous with him in the drawing room at midnight. This information she at once revealed to Miss Claretti, Rickard and Dr Haroon who were shocked at the insulting implications of this despicable communication.

'The man is worse than I thought!' exclaimed Dr Haroon. 'He is sure to come to grief one day, shot dead by an outraged husband.'

'If had a gun I would shoot him at once,' said Rickard, boldly.

'Then it is as well that you do not have one,' said his sensible sister.

'Pray do not attempt violence on Viscount Hogg,' said Mrs Johnson. 'He is a vile creature but in any such encounter his lofty rank in society ensures that he is bound to be believed the innocent party. I wish neither of you to suffer in my defence.'

'But we cannot allow him to continue his dreadful behaviour,' said Rickard.

'I suggest,' said Miss Claretti, 'that tonight, you and Dr Haroon wait for Viscount Hogg in the drawing room and, should he appear, make it very plain to him that you have learned of his loathsome plans and he ought to desist at once. You know enough of his dubious past to prove that you understand his nature. If he professes to be a gentleman he ought to behave as one.'

With this scheme in place, Miss Claretti and Mrs Johnson retired to their room and secured the door. All at once they heard a foul wind spring up, so fierce that it made their window panes vibrate with a sound like drumming. Miss Claretti peered out and saw that snow had begun to fall, cascading in large whirling flakes like leaves of paper, turning the sky a blinding white and carpeting the ground thickly. 'I hope we are not obliged to remain here any longer than we had planned,' said Miss Claretti, as the snow cover seemed to deepen with every passing moment.

Mrs Johnson shivered and it was not only from the chill in the air. 'Let us sleep turn and turn about and remain in our day clothes,' she said. 'Then if there is any danger one of us will always be on the alert and we can protect each other.'

Miss Claretti agreed. Little could either know what horrors the night would bring.

It wanted but fifteen minutes to midnight when, in the servants' quarters, a door opened and the two ladies' maids, Zena and Petronella, peered out of the room they shared. Both were clad in dark gowns and carried lanterns draped in black cloth. They waited awhile to enable their eyes to become accustomed to the gloom before they moved off.

'This is such an adventure!' said Zena, her eyes shining.

'I knew you would be brave enough for it, my dear,' said Petronella, squeezing her friend's hand in encouragement.

'Whatever is strange in this house we will discover it and end all the unhappiness and fear.'

'We must go quietly. I am wearing my very softest shoes and will not be heard.'

'And I my new slippers that you so beautifully stitched for me.'

They smiled and began to creep slowly along the corridor past the doors of the servants' rooms.

'Hush!' said Petronella suddenly, laying her hand upon Zena's arm. They stopped and listened. Behind them and coming closer they could hear footsteps. They exchanged glances. Up ahead was a laundry cupboard and Zena managed to open it soundlessly. They squeezed inside, huddling closely together, their arms about each other's waists. Fortunately, they were slender enough that there was just enough room for them both. Petronella drew the door almost closed leaving a small gap for her to peer through.

The footsteps came nearer and both maids held their breath, anxious not to be discovered. Whatever or whoever was passing along the corridor was tangible enough to make a noise and visible enough to be perceived as two distinct silhouettes. One figure carried a small candle in a lantern with a hand over the slits so as to conceal much of the light. The other carried something wrapped in a parcel. Petronella stifled a gasp and moved back from the door. Zena craned her neck, not daring to speak. At length the figures had passed beyond their hiding place and were far enough away not to overhear their conversation.

'What did you see?' asked Zena.

'There were two people,' said Petronella. 'I could not see who they were, but from their proportions I suspect that they were Mr and Mrs Miller.'

'I wonder what they are about?'

'The same as us, perhaps, hunting for ghosts?'

'There will be more ghost-hunters in the house than ghosts,' said Zena with a smile.

'They were carrying something besides the lantern. I couldn't see what it was.'

Zena thought carefully. 'Did you not tell me that the Millers have always said that they didn't believe the house was haunted?'

'They have claimed so, yes,' agreed Petronella.

'They why are they looking for ghosts? And in the middle of the night? If there was some natural explanation for the haunting such as the settling of an old building it would be more easily detectable during the day than at night.'

'Unless,' said Petronella, 'they have laid traps and are going to inspect them. That is a very good scheme.'

'We need to find out what they are doing,' said Zena.

'We do.'

'But we must use our resources with care. You, my dear, must follow Mr and Mrs Miller, but do not confront them. If they should see you, pretend to be sleepwalking. That is very easy to feign. All you need to do is stare straight ahead. I will see if they have any clues in their room.'

'That is a good idea, but their room may be locked.'

Zena removed a hairpin from her pretty tresses. 'That will not present any difficulty.'

They emerged from the cupboard and, after an encouraging embrace, went their separate ways.

Mrs Bunn had retired to her room where, as she was often proud to claim, she enjoyed a sleep that could not be disturbed by the loudest thunder and would not wake till wakefulness was required. She attributed the soundness of her slumber to a clear conscience on all subjects, although there were suspicions that a nightly noggin of brandy assisted the matter. Long before the midnight hour had come she was snoring robustly, her trusty meat-axe, an implement that her brawny arm had used to butcher many a carcass, laid by the side of the bed in case of burglars. So sound asleep was she that she did not hear or see the hand that purloined that gruesome weapon.

In the next room, Mr Gillery, Mr Sweetacre's loyal manservant, also enjoyed a dreamless and untroubled sleep.

Below stairs, all was quiet in the kitchen. The housemaids, Maria and Sally who usually refused to sleep at Ditterling Manor because of the nightly hauntings had been obliged to stay in the house because the turn in the weather had prevented them from walking to their homes in the village. They were wrapped in blankets and lying on the kitchen floor. The gentle warmth exuded by the range was most conducive to sleep, but, despite this, both were restless. Maria readily agreed to Sally's suggestion that they should encourage restfulness by sampling the bottle of sherry that Mrs Bunn had been saving to make a tipsy cake. Neither were used to strong drink and before long they confessed to each other that they were a little drowsy and settled down comfortably before slipping into a peaceful slumber.

Alone in her room, Mrs Sweetacre carefully locked her door as she had been advised, but when she looked for her puppy dog Spot, she was unable to find him. Knowing that it would be impossible for her to sleep without the company of her darling, she decided, despite all her husband's careful warnings, to take a lantern and venture out into the darkened corridors of Ditterling Manor.

Mr Smith's unexpected arrival had resulted in him being allocated a tiny room in the servants' wing, but he found that this arrangement suited his purpose, since he could come and go as he pleased. He had told his host that he was an expert on the flora and fauna of Southshire, on which subject he was writing a book. This was a double lie, since Mr Smith knew nothing of nature and had no literary ability whatsoever. Mr Smith was a secret agent, a collector of scandal that he would use to pursue his real profession, blackmail. Poor Mr Sweetacre, little realising what a treacherous reptile he had admitted to his home and hospitality!

Mr Smith, being an expert on foul deeds, well knew that these were generally done at night under cover of darkness. He had no fear of ghosts and often boasted that if he ever saw one it would fear him far more than he would fear it. Mr Smith was afraid of nothing, or so he claimed; however, this was not entirely true. The one thing he could not abide was a spider. It was not likely that he would encounter such a beast in the month of January, but even the tiny corpse of a deceased one, all dried up, its horrid black legs shrivelled and clenched into a little ball of evil was enough to produce revulsion and terror. In fact, it had been a source of great relief to Mr Smith to observe when he arrived at Ditterling Manor that it was kept very well swept and there was no sign anywhere of cobwebs.

He was wholly unafraid, therefore, as he prepared to creep from his room carrying a tiny stub of candle in a lantern; his object, to prowl about the house in the hopes of uncovering some impropriety from which he could make a profit.

There was a slight noise outside his door and he carefully opened it a little, a skill he had practised well in his nefarious career of spying and snooping. He was thus able to see the shapes of two persons gliding past, carrying a lantern and a parcel of some sort, and soon afterwards, two more shapes, clad in black, both female, emerging from a laundry cupboard. All of these circumstances were highly suspicious and excited his interest. After a whispered conversation one of the females walked back past his door and quickly effected entry to another room, while the other went in the opposite direction.

Whatever was happening, Mr Smith sensed that dark deeds were afoot. He liked dark deeds and, smiling to himself, slipped out of his room and followed the retreating figure. He might have interrupted the woman in the room to discover what it was she was about, as the slight hesitation in opening the door suggested that it was not her own room she was entering, but on reflection he decided that it was better to allow her to go about her business. The dimensions of the figure indicated that she was one of the servants and therefore susceptible to either threats or bribery, in both of which he had some expertise. He had no doubt that he would be able later on to discover her identity and extract from her both her purpose and what she had discovered.

Midnight was fast approaching and the ghosts of Ditterling Manor were preparing to walk.

PART THE SECOND

In the gloom of haunted Ditterling Manor, Mr and Mrs Miller pursued their silent course along the corridor, on a mission that they had kept a careful secret from all the occupants of the house. Mrs Miller held a lantern, while her husband clutched a parcel that exuded strange pungent odours. They said nothing to each other, but from time to time, Mr Miller pressed the back of his hand to his forehead to wipe away the bloom of perspiration that could only come from fear and anxiety. They passed like drifting spectres from the servants' wing to the main portion of the house, where the full moon was casting its beams down the corridor. There they were met by a third shadowy individual and it was a meeting that was clearly anticipated. The third figure had brought a sack that contained something that wriggled. A few whispered words were exchanged and they nodded and walked on. They all knew what needed to be done.

It now wanted but five minutes of midnight and as the night plunged on towards the witching hour, the time when ghosts and demons venture forth, corpses rise from their graves to torment the living, and the forces of darkness are at their most powerful, the villainous Viscount Hogg slipped quietly from his room. He wore only a nightshirt and a dressing gown, the shameless *dishabille* he preferred for his amorous adventures, of which there had been too many to count. The enchanting Mrs Johnson had not replied to his note, but he did not see that as a refusal. Perhaps, he thought, she dared not put her acceptance in writing in case it fell into the wrong hands, her husband's for example, or a blackmailer's. Or maybe it was simply a female whim. Women in his experience were fickle creatures, demure one moment and enticing the next. All women, he assured himself, would fall under his spell if he so pleased, but there was a type he especially admired. Not that childish whining Mrs Sweetacre forever cuddling her unpleasant little dog, nor the acerbic Miss Claretti who thought herself so very clever. Mrs Johnson was a woman of splendid proportions and bold spirit and she could not help but excite his attention. Virtuous she might claim to be, but he had no doubt that before the night was over she would be in his thrall.

He descended the stairs and, as he did so, heard movements on the floor he had just left. Were the ghosts of Ditterling Manor walking? For once, they would have to wait. He had other more pressing business to attend to.

Mr Smith was confused. Unused to the layout of the large house he had turned the wrong way, found himself unexpectedly faced with a flight of stairs that ought not to have been there and been obliged to retrace his steps. By the time he reached the main corridor all the persons he had been following had vanished, leaving no clue as to where they had gone. Clearly, he could not go into the bedrooms without a good excuse. He tried peeping through keyholes but learned nothing. All the rooms were silent and dark. He wondered if it was better to hide in the shadows at the top of the staircase to see if anyone should leave a room and then follow, or continue his tour of the house.

There was the sound of a door opening and he quickly ducked into the nearest room, one that he knew to be the water closet, and fastened the bolt on the door. As he waited there was a pull at the door handle then the sound of someone entering the room next door, the one with an ancient cast iron bathtub. The steps in the corridor moved past and there was a soft creak on the top step of the staircase. He opened the door and peered out. No one was waiting outside, but someone, a man, was creeping down the stairs very slowly. This looked promising, so he left the water closet and silently followed the man, whom he felt sure could be up to no good. The size of the individual suggested that he was none other than Viscount Hogg, whose reputation virtually ensured that he was about some act of a nefarious nature, moreover, Mr Smith was well aware that the nobleman possessed more than enough wealth to be able to pay a handsome sum in blackmail.

Smith was halfway down the stairs when he thought he heard another door open in the corridor, but by now he had cast his die and continued on his way down.

Miss Claretti was unable to rest, since she was impatient to know what was happening downstairs. She disliked inaction, yet she knew that it would be dangerous to leave Mrs Johnson alone and unprotected. The hour of midnight approached and both ladies listened carefully and heard the sound of a door opening and footsteps moving towards the stairs. Undoubtedly it was Viscount Hogg, on his way, as he thought, to a secret tryst with Mrs Johnson in the drawing room.

'Once he is disappointed he will guess that you have remained here, but I hope that by then he will have received a sound warning from the gentlemen. He would not dare try to enter this room,' said Miss Claretti.

The old house was moving about them, its venerable boards bending and shifting, groaning and protesting, and they might almost have imagined a fluttering like the sound of many slippered feet passing back and forth. Outside the wild wind howled and snowflakes battered the windowpane like desperate moths throwing themselves against a lamp.

There was a gentle knock at the door.

Mrs Johnson started and gave a little gasp. 'Surely not?' she whispered.

'But he has hardly been gone two minutes,' said Miss Claretti.

The knock sounded again.

They stayed quiet.

'Miss Claretti?' came a voice they recognised at once.

'It's Mrs Sweetacre,' said Miss Claretti. 'She should not be about.'

She opened the door. Miss Sweetacre stood there, still in her day gown, her hair dishevelled under her cap, a loose black silk wrap about her shoulders, its deep fringes sweeping the floor, the light of her lantern reflected in her eyes in a strange mad gleam. 'Oh Miss Claretti, have you seen little Spot? I can't find him anywhere!'

'He is not here,' said Miss Claretti. 'But I promise if I do see him, I will bring him straight to you.'

'Oh, what can I do!' exclaimed Mrs Sweetacre. 'He may be in the most terrible danger!'

'Please don't upset yourself,' said Miss Claretti. 'Your husband asked you to stay safe in your room. Do go back, or he will not know where you are.'

'I can't!' wailed the distracted woman. 'I must have my darling or I can get no rest! I will look everywhere until he is found!' Before Miss Claretti could reason with her further, Mrs Sweetacre turned and hurried away.

'What can we do?' asked Mrs Johnson.

'Nothing, I fear. But Mr Sweetacre is about and he should be able to calm her.'

They had hardly settled again, Mrs Johnson reclining on her bed and Miss Claretti in an armchair, listening to snowflakes making a constant damp patter against the window, when there was another knock on the door.

'Really,' said Miss Claretti, 'this house is busier by night than it is by day.' She rose and crept forward with some caution in case the presence outside was Viscount Hogg.

'Miss Claretti?' came a voice, 'it is I, Bickley. Please let me in. I would like to talk with you.'

'The audacity!' hissed Miss Claretti to Mrs Johnson under her breath. 'Of course, he must imagine that Viscount Hogg is in the drawing room with you and that I am therefore alone and vulnerable. I have half a mind to admit him and dash his brains out with a candlestick. No jury in the land would convict me.'

The knocking sounded again. Miss Claretti, now thoroughly exasperated, strode up to the door. 'What do you want, Mr Bickley?' she said sharply. 'Do you mean to wake the dead at this unholy hour? Go back to your room!'

'I wanted to explain myself.'

'Explain yourself tomorrow morning. Now go away!'

'Are you alone?'

'Whether I am or not is none of your concern.'

There was a sudden yelp from the other side of the door then an embarrassed laugh. 'I thought I felt something brush past me just now, but there was nothing there.'

'Go back to your room, Mr Bickley, and don't bother me again.'

Miss Claretti listened carefully, hoping to hear his retreating footsteps, but instead she heard a sound that appeared to be coming from further down the corridor. It was like hollow dry sticks or wooden pipes clattering together. Mrs Johnson came up and pressed her ear to the door then gazed at Miss Claretti in amazement. Whether the sound was human, animal or the product of some infernal instrument of percussion was unclear. Then there began the sound of a keening flute, now high, now low, the tone however always indicative of unrelenting misery.

'Mr Bickley, are you responsible for that noise?' asked Miss Claretti.

He made a gasping sound and his voice sounded peculiar, as if his throat was closing up with terror. 'No, but I can see what is.'

Miss Claretti finally succumbed to her curiosity, unlocked the door and peered out into the corridor. Mr Bickley was cowering against the far wall, trembling with fright. The soft light of the closed moon showed that his face was contorted, his eyes wide with fear. Miss Claretti and Mrs Johnson, clasping hands for assurance, walked out. There was nothing to be seen. The unearthly noise abruptly ceased.

He stared at them, astonished to see the two women. 'Your ruse did not work,' said Miss Claretti scornfully. 'You and your master should be ashamed of yourselves. Now, what did you see? A ghost? A demon? A monster?'

'It was a skeleton,' he said. 'I couldn't conjure that up or mistake anything else for it. And I am wide awake, not dreaming.'

'Where was it?'

His hand shook as he pointed to the far end of the corridor.

'It is not there now. Where did it go?'

'It vanished. In the blink of an eye.'

'Then we will go and hunt it. All three of us.'

Miss Claretti took a candlestick from the mantelpiece in case defence should prove necessary and secured her bedroom door. 'Come now, Mr Bickley,' she said, 'you have two ladies to protect you. Have no fear.'

The three unwilling adventurers began to creep down the corridor.

Meanwhile, downstairs, the drawing room was in darkness, apart from a faint glow from the last embers of the fire. Dr Haroon and Rickard sat silently waiting for their quarry. Since their characters were so very different they rarely had a great deal to say to each other. Rickard knew Dr Haroon to be a man of learning who commanded the respect and admiration of all who knew him. Dr Haroon regarded Rickard as a wastrel who lived a life of idleness and tolerated him only because he was also without guile. The absence of conversation was not therefore a great trial to either of them.

Outside, the wind made its strange music, as the snow fell relentlessly. Inside, there was only the occasional whisper of ashes settling in the fireplace and the kind of noises that old houses always make at night. The clock began to strike midnight.

Footsteps approached and Dr Haroon rose and secreted himself behind the door, while Rickard hid behind a curtain. Viscount Hogg entered and looked about him, but seeing no one, helped himself to some brandy from a decanter, seated himself comfortably before the fireplace and waited. It was only moments before he was confronted by the two other men, something that caused him no discomfiture at all.

'Dear me!' exclaimed the Viscount with a broad smile, 'So we are three! Mrs Johnson is a very busy lady, but I am sure she is woman enough for all of us. I had always suspected her to be an unmitigated strumpet.'

'That is a grave insult to a virtuous lady!' exclaimed Rickard, angrily. To his astonishment and that of Dr Haroon, Viscount

Hogg simply threw back his head and laughed. It was an action he was doomed to regret.

Mr Smith reached the bottom of the stairs. He had spent too long wandering about the house and found to his dismay that his candle was guttering. He was not sure where the figure he had been following had gone and walked about the hall listening at doors until he heard what he thought were voices in the drawing room. He had been hoping to hear the tones of both a man and a woman but only heard what he thought were male voices. Perhaps he had interrupted no more than some gentlemen guests helping themselves to Mr Sweetacre's brandy, very small grist to his disreputable mill. He decided to wait outside to observe who emerged and as he stood by the doorway his candle went out and he was plunged into almost total darkness. The only light in the hallway was now the faint moonlight that breathed softly through the worn and threadbare curtains.

There came from the drawing room a burst of laughter like the infernal cackling of a demon. The next moment the laughter abruptly stopped and devolved into a gurgle. Then there were louder voices, exclamations, the thud of a heavy object falling to the floor and a groan. A brief silence was followed by some urgent whispering.

Mr Smith held his breath. After what appeared to be an age the door of the drawing room opened softly and a head peered out. Mr Smith, thinking he recognised the silhouette of Dr Haroon by the shape of his beard, tried to press himself flat again the wall, hoping he would not be observed. There were some more whispers and then two figures emerged carrying a third one between them. The third figure was limp and unmoving.

Mr Smith suppressed a gasp of horror. Had murder been done? He was not about to challenge two desperate men and become their next victim. He felt the hairs on his head rise up in terror knowing what his fate would be if he were discovered. He was standing next to a hall chair and carefully, silently, lowered himself to crouch down beside it, hoping that his form would melt into a pool of darkness.

The two murderers, or so he supposed them to be, proceeded slowly up the stairs with the corpse of their victim and faded into the shadows. Smith stood up slowly. He dared not follow them and now was unsure of his way. Footsteps pattered swiftly down the stairs, accompanied by a tiny light, which showed the wild hair and staring eyes of a frantic Mrs Sweetacre. He backed against the wall once more as she ran about in a circle, then, sobbing, ran up the stairs again.

He became aware of a new sound, like the scraping of twigs, bare wintry branches caught in the wind and the low howl of a reed pipe. He determined to follow it and started groping his way about the hall. As he did so he sensed that the noise was behind him and realised that he was not alone. He turned and saw in the darkness the stark white glimmer of a skeletal figure.

He gasped but rallied his courage. 'You — who are you? What is your name?' he demanded.

The figure was silent. Did a skeleton even have the ability to speak? he wondered. It waved its thin pale arms at him, the skull moving from side to side. He braced himself and strode towards it, and then unexpectedly it vanished. He stopped, disoriented once again. 'Where are you? Come back!' But there was no sound.

'Who is there?' came a voice and Mr Smith recognised the tremulous tones of Mr Sweetacre. A slight adjustment to his host's dark lantern cast a soft light in the hallway.

'It is I, Smith. I heard a noise and came to see what the matter was.'

'There was a curious sound just now. Was that you?'

'No, but I heard it too. I thought it came from down here. It stopped and then I saw something, a skeleton.' Mr Smith decided it might be unwise to tell his host that he had witnessed the aftermath of a murder. Ghosts, skeletons and adulterers he might pursue in the dark but not killers.

'Where?'

'It was here in the hallway. Not a dried-up dead thing, but it moved, it walked and then quite suddenly it vanished. I challenged it to speak but either it could or would not. And — I also saw Mrs Sweetacre.'

'Surely not! I have told her to keep to her room!'

'She seemed most distracted, but I don't know what the matter was.'

Mr Sweetacre stared about him and uttered a cry. 'Do you see that! There! On the stairs!'

Mr Smith turned and saw most clearly a female figure clad all in white at the top of the staircase. It was poised and motionless and the head was heavily veiled so that its features could not be seen, and it appeared to be hovering with its feet not touching the floor. There were chains about its wrists and a line of heavy links trailed back into the darkness so that it was impossible to see where they ended.

Mr Sweetacre lifted his lantern and went to the foot of the stairs. 'I see you, spirit! Speak to me! What is your name?'

The figure only shook its head sorrowfully.

'Perhaps it can't speak,' said Mr Smith.

'Oh, spirit, I would learn of your sorrow!' called Mr Sweetacre.

The chains clanked as the figure crossed its arms across its breast and hung its head as if to say that its sorrows were deep and inexpressible.

'Should we approach it?' suggested Mr Smith.

'I dare not be too bold or I might chase it away,' said Mr Sweetacre. 'I always knew that I would not fear a ghost if I saw one. Why, this one cannot mean us any harm. It is a sad creature and I would give it comfort.'

Mr Smith began to climb the stairs, but he had not progressed far before the ghost suddenly threw out its arms in an attitude clearly banning him from coming closer. The chains slid across the stairs like scaly serpents, making a low slithering rattle and the spectre uttered a noise like a hiss. Mr Smith hesitated. Then the spirit began to laugh, a deep guttural mirthless laugh. Suddenly it threw back the veil and they saw its face, deep empty sockets where there had once been eyes, sunken cheeks, bleached white flesh and teeth that came to sharp points. Mr Smith, less confident than Mr Sweetacre of the harmlessness of the apparition stopped in his tracks and after a moment or two, slowly backed down the stairs.

'That is a Hellish sight,' he said.

Mr Sweetacre said nothing but made rapid gasping breaths.

The apparition turned and began to glide away.

'I will follow it!' said Mr Sweetacre.

'Surely not!'

'A disembodied spirit cannot hurt me, and even if it could, I will gladly risk all to save my dear wife from this constant fear!' Mr Sweetacre was not usually a bold man but strengthened by resolve he began to mount the stairs.

Zena, having entered the Millers' apartment by the dexterous application of her hairpin to the lock, held up her lantern to cast a gentle light on her surroundings. She was in a small parlour and all was very tidily arranged as she might have expected. A noise outside alerted her and she pulled the curtains aside and peered out of the window. The room overlooked the stable yard and she could hear the sound of restless horses protesting against the howling of the wind. Moonlight was reflected from the falling snow, which was thickly coating the stable roof and obscuring the cobbles. In the far distance she thought she saw the silhouettes of a line of figures, dark against the snow, moving towards the house, some of them bearing lighted torches; then they were hidden from her view by a dip in the land.

The chief item of interest in the room was a writing desk and on it stood a photographic portrait of a youth who was sufficiently similar in appearance to the Millers to suggest that he was their son. The photograph was draped in black crape. Zena began to examine the contents of the desk with meticulous care. There was a row of neatly arranged and labelled folders of household papers which contained nothing unusual, but she noticed that they projected a little further than she might have expected, which suggested that there was something hidden behind them. She removed the folders and, sliding her hand into the recess they had occupied, discovered what appeared to be the door of a small compartment. Feeling her way with her fingertips she encountered a small spring and on pressing it there was a click and the compartment opened. Zena drew out a small package of letters. Why had they been so carefully concealed? she wondered. There was only one way to find out.

Meanwhile, Petronella had pursued her quarry to the main corridor of principal bedrooms, leaving sufficient space between herself and the others so as to avoid being seen. The house was a veritable hive of movement that night. On seeing a new shadowy figure up ahead and coming towards her she was obliged to try and slip into the water closet only to discover it occupied and quickly entered the bathroom. The footsteps moved past then the door of the water closet opened and whoever had been in there departed. After a brief wait, she was just about to emerge then she heard someone knocking on a door and the voice of Mrs Sweetacre saying that she had lost little Spot and was searching for him. Her mistress conversed with someone and then abruptly ran past her door. Petronella knew that it would be impossible to console her mistress until Spot was found and determined to make that her most important task. The little puppy was of an inquisitive nature and could be almost anywhere, although he did prefer places that were warm and where there was something to eat. She decided to look in the kitchen. On peering out of the bathroom she found that the individuals she had been following had vanished. The shadowy figure of a tall man was standing outside one of the other bedrooms knocking on the door and imploring Miss Claretti to admit him. It was that scoundrel Mr Bickley and she decided to give him a fright. She occluded the light on her lantern and brushed past him as she proceeded down the corridor, which made him squeak in alarm.

At the end of the corridor was a door leading to the servants' staircase. It was usually closed, but when Petronella pushed it, she found it slightly ajar. She opened the door and crept down the stairs.

Mr Smith, left alone in the dark hallway and hardly knowing which way to go was pondering this dilemma when he heard a soft feminine voice calling him. 'Oh Mr Smith…' He looked about him and saw, floating in the darkness of the hall, a face. It was not the demonic face of the white lady but a shapely pale countenance, half hidden in a cloudy mist.

'Who are you?' he gasped.

'I am the ghost of Ditterling Manor,' it breathed.

'You are not the white lady?'

There was a laugh like the tinkling of a little bell. 'No, she is not from the heavenly regions. She is a harbinger of doom and death. Do you not hear her knocking? If you do, she is your doom.'

'But Mr Sweetacre has followed her. What should I do?'

'Oh, poor Mr Sweetacre, it is far too late to help him now. You must come away. Follow me.' The voice was gentle and melodious. Mr Smith was inclined to follow it and he did.

PART THE THIRD

Miss Claretti, Mrs Johnson and Mr Bickley, the two ladies clasping hands for mutual support and to show their shared antagonism towards their unpopular companion, slowly advanced down the corridor to the place where, so Mr Bickley claimed, the skeleton had appeared to him. There was a window overlooking the side terrace and they peered out. Mr Bickley, his height giving him some advantage, uttered a groan. 'This is a strange place.'

Dark shapes were moving across the snow. A few carried lighted torches. Some of the travellers were human in form but others were not. Some left footprints, but others left none. All trudged in the same direction towards the desolate plain that lay in front of the house. Somewhere a dog howled.

'It is as if they are coming to a great assembly of spirits,' whispered Mr Bickley. 'Are you afraid?'

'Of things made of shadows and air? No.' Miss Claretti turned to Mrs Johnson. 'I mean to pursue the household ghosts. Will you come with me?'

'I will!' said Mrs Johnson boldly and Mr Bickley, who appeared a little nervous of being left alone, had no alternative but to accompany them. The door at the end of the corridor was unlocked and they pushed it open. There was a staircase leading down to the kitchen and another going up. As they hesitated they heard a shuffling noise from above.

'Vermin?' ventured Mr Bickley, but then they heard what sounded like whispers and the movement of feet.

'Ghosts,' said Mrs Johnson.

'People up to no good,' said Miss Claretti. She grasped the candlestick firmly in her little fist.

'We should alert someone,' said Mr Bickley. 'Wait there and I will ring for the servants.' It took hardly a minute for him to do so and return, but his expression was grave. 'I went to wake Dr Haroon, but his room was empty.' They listened, but nothing stirred.

'Walk ahead,' said Miss Claretti. 'Go up the stairs and tell me what you see.'

Bickley hesitated, but at last he began to creep up the stairs and the two ladies followed. Quite what they were expecting to see none of them could say. Nothing perhaps, simply an empty room, from which any malefactors had escaped, some birds finding shelter from the cold, or maybe an assembly of ghosts. What they did find was very much worse than they could possibly have imagined.

The letters in the Millers' desk, the ones Zena had drawn from the secret compartment, made terrible reading. Only six months before, the couple's only son, disappointed in love and in a fit of melancholy, had taken his own life by throwing himself out of a moving train. There were notes he had left for his friends and relatives, letters of condolence and a newspaper cutting describing the inquest. The other documents were quite different — a collection of filthy scraps of paper, smeared with dark red stains. As Zena managed to make out the words scrawled on those papers she realised that out of grief and desperation, the Millers had taken a terrible step. They had gone up to the black windmill that overlooked the village and consulted the dreadful hag that lived there. In return for a payment of gold, they had received instructions for bringing the dead back to life. It wanted only a full moon and a blood sacrifice to achieve their aims.

Petronella had made her way down the stairs. She knew the servants' passage well, a narrow place lined with shelves and cupboards. Her lantern was dim but it was enough. She had no wish to awaken the sleeping maids in the kitchen and walked carefully past the bundled forms, looking about her in case Spot was there. There was no sign of the little dog, but she noticed something strange. Lifting her lantern carefully and allowing light to fall on the sleeping forms, she saw that one of the maids was very pale and in a deep snoring slumber, which suggested that it might be hard to rouse her. A sherry bottle out of its usual place told the tale. The other maid, however, had vanished. In her place was merely a rolled up blanket.

There was now, in addition to the dog, a missing girl to find. Petronella walked determinedly on. After a careful inspection of the washroom and scullery she mounted the steps to the main hallway, which was in complete darkness. A light was descending the stairs and she recognised the figures of Dr Haroon and young Mr Rickard Claretti, creeping very slowly as if they preferred not to be seen.

'Dr Haroon,' she said, appearing out of the shadows, and they both jumped and looked undeniably guilty. 'It is I, Petronella. I would be obliged if you were to go to the kitchen where one of the maids may need your attention. She is either ill, or drunk. The other one is missing and I fear the worst.'

'I will go at once,' said Dr Haroon. He glanced at young Rickard.

'Oh — yes, I will — er — attend to the other matter,' said Rickard. He was carrying what looked like a bundle of towels that he was attempting to hide behind his back.

'Is anything wrong?' asked Petronella.

'Oh, nothing. Nothing at all. I think I might have spilled some brandy in the drawing room when I was there after dinner and I'm going back to attend to it before it ruins Mr Sweetacre's best carpet.' He began backing away.

'And if you should find Mrs Sweetacre,' said Petronella, 'she is running about very distractedly as she has lost her little puppy dog. I am hoping to find them both.'

Rickard nodded and dashed away before any further conversation was possible.

At that moment Zena arrived in the hallway and hurried up to Petronella. 'Oh, my dear, I am so relieved you are safe! I have found out some terrible things about Mr and Mrs Miller. I know their secrets and they are too dreadful for words. Do you know where they have gone?'

'No, but they are not in the kitchens. Let us look upstairs.' As Dr Haroon went to attend to the unconscious maid, Zena and Petronella ascended the stairs to the main corridor. Hardly had they reached the landing when they heard a strangled gurgling sound that appeared to be coming from one of the bedrooms. They decided to investigate.

Mr Smith followed the dark shape with its pale but beautiful head. Its voice had mesmerised him. It exuded a power of attraction, like a magnetic force, drawing him on. His head seemed to spin and he had no idea where he might be. There was the sound of a door opening and the face turned to him. 'Come,' it said and a white hand extended from the darkness and beckoned him. He was powerless to do anything other than obey.

He followed the shape into a room but saw no detail of his surroundings. He began to stumble around in the dark but the figure told him to hush. There was a strange rustling noise, the sound a nest of insects might have made, all running about with their horrid scaly legs, but that was impossible, he knew.

At that time of year, there could be no insects. 'Close your eyes and you will understand why you are here,' said the voice.

He closed his eyes. All was now silent apart from the sound of his own ragged breathing. Somewhere in the room, he knew there was another creature, but what it was and why it had brought him here he dared not think. After what seemed like an age, he decided to risk opening his eyes. There was a faint glow in the room from a single candle, casting a pale flush over the walls, and he now knew that he was in the bathroom. The large shape of the old iron bath, its legs cast in the form of lions, dominated the room. Of the mysterious figure, however, there was no sign. Then there came a new sound, almost like a laugh, a low chuckle of anticipation. It came from within the bath and it was followed by a dry rustling like paper or silk or twigs and then a clicking scraping skittering as if something, a trapped bird perhaps, something with sharp talons was inside the bath and trying to gain a purchase on its curved inner surface in an effort to climb out.

He crept closer to look but was still about two strides away when he saw a large black claw rise up and clutch at the side of the bath. Then there rose up a head, a pearl grey head with fierce red eyes, followed by an ugly black body borne along by multiple legs. Mr Smith did not stop to think whether it was even possible for a spider to be that size, all he knew was that there was one in the room with him. His throat constricted in terror and he jumped back and then began groping madly about the room trying to find the door. It eluded him in the semi darkness. When he did find what felt like a handle he pulled and shook and twisted it for all he was worth, but somehow could not get it to open. He turned and faced the creature, which was now halfway out of the bath and staring at him with slowly blinking eyes and a smile on its face then he sank to the floor, crying and gibbering in terror.

Then the spider spoke to him.

Zena and Petronella found themselves in the room occupied by Viscount Hogg. The nobleman lay on his bed, clad only in his nightclothes and the lantern light revealed a ghastly sight. His throat had been cut from ear to ear and from the great gash there trickled a flow of dark blood, cascading down his chest. He was still just alive, as from his open mouth there came a horrid bubbling sound, the sound of a man drowning in his own gore.

'There is nothing we can do for him,' said Zena.

As they stood considering whom they might fetch to assist them there was a new disturbance from outside and they peered out of the window. In front of the house a bonfire had been lit and around it a coven of unearthly shapes had assembled. A figure, that of an ancient female clad in the most hideous rags was brandishing a staff topped by a skull and declaiming words in a language neither girl could understand.

'Who can help us?' exclaimed Zena.

'There is one person here with the understanding, the courage and the resolve,' said Petronella. 'One person whose advice we can truly trust. Miss Claretti will know what to do. Let us look for her.'

They emerged into the corridor when they heard, coming from the bathroom, sounds that could only have been made by a human being in dire extremity. They decided to go in.

'Are you afraid, Mr Smith?' purred the spider in the bathroom. 'You are a despicable creature. You present yourself to the world as a respectable person, you say you are a lover of nature, but you are neither. You claim to be a writer, an honest and noble profession whose members toil long hours for inadequate reward, yet you are not. You are a liar, and a spy. You serve men who make themselves rich by cheating others. You are the tool of those who harbour hatred and jealousy and greed. You are a destroyer of happiness, a breaker of reputations. Admit it, Mr Smith, admit it!'

'Yes, yes, I admit it!' he blubbered. 'I am a private detective working for Mr Blank the property dealer. He sent me here to learn all I can about the estate and its owners to enable him to buy it up cheaply.'

'Is that all? What has he authorised you to do?'

'Anything! Blackmail, bribery, sabotage. I do all of those things for the right price.'

The spider made a clicking noise expressing disapproval. 'And what should be the fate of vermin like you?'

'I — I'll go away! I promise! Spare me and I'll never work for Mr Blank again!'

The spider uttered a cackling laugh. 'Oh, I can promise that you will not work for him again. Him, or anyone else.' It heaved its huge shape from the bath. Mr Smith sobbed. The horrible thing must have been three feet wide, black and shining. He had no doubt that it intended to eat him. He gazed around him for a weapon, but there was nothing. He curled into a ball of terror and whined.

The bathroom door opened.

Mr Sweetacre, creeping along the corridor with his dark lantern, heard a noise he had been dreading, yet it filled him with a strange excitement. Here at last, he thought, lay the secret of why Ditterling Manor was so cursed. Inside the haunted nursery he heard the creaking of the rocking horse, the toy that had been so beloved of the infernal child. He pushed at the door expecting it not to open, but to his surprise, it did, and he gathered all his courage and entered. There at the far end of the room he saw the rocking horse move, as if under its own volition. He crept forward.

'If you are the ghost of the child that once lived here then appear before me,' he cried.

There was a burst of evil laughter. The curtains flapped in the wind of a storm that seemed to have sprung up from nowhere and as they billowed filling the room with whirling flakes of snow, so a figure appeared, very small at first then steadily growing and forming itself into the unmistakable proportions of the white lady of Ditterling Manor. Beside her the rocking horse moved and there appeared upon its back a form the size and shape of a child, but scarcely human, clad all in blood red, its face covered in dark fur with sharp teeth and yellow eyes.

The white lady pointed to Mr Sweetacre who stood his ground. 'You are cursed!' She screamed. 'You and everyone in this house are cursed!'

'What must I do to break the curse?' asked Mr Sweetacre.

'You must die!' She clenched her fist.

Mr Sweetacre felt a pressure on his chest as if the ghostly hand had taken hold of his heart and was squeezing it. He gasped and sank to his knees. All went dark before his eyes.

Mrs Sweetacre ran into the room, hardly knowing where she was. Before her, her beloved husband lay dying and the ghosts eyed him in malevolent fashion. She screamed and hurled her lantern at the spectres. The candle fell and ignited the old desiccated and threadbare curtains, which were almost instantly aflame.

When Miss Claretti and her companions reached the top of the stairs they saw that the walls of the attic room were smeared with indescribable filth and painted with magic symbols. An altar had been constructed from boards laid across wooden trestles on which human bones were displayed. Dishes of herbs were burning, filling the room with a ghastly stench. Mr and Mrs Miller in gross costume, stood at the altar and there, tied to the boards, its tiny muzzle bound with rope, was little Spot the puppy. The expression of terror in the little dog's eyes was painful to behold. One of the maidservants, clad only in her nightshift was dancing about the room in a frenzy. Mrs Miller wielded the meat axe, raising the horrid weapon over the form of the whimpering dog and was about to bring it down and sever its tiny body in half when Miss Claretti prevented her by hurling the candlestick across the room. It struck Mrs Miller smartly on the hand and the axe clattered to the floor.

Before anyone could move, Miss Claretti darted forward and took up the axe, brandishing it angrily at Mr and Mrs Miller. On seeing this, any courage they might have had drained away and they cowered back in fright. Mrs Johnson took the opportunity to release little Spot from the ropes and gathered him into her arms where he mewled most piteously.

The maidservant, who seemed to be half demented, perhaps from the noxious vapours she had inhaled, shrieked loudly and then, baring her teeth like a wild animal, advanced on Mr Bickley. Terrified by this demonic creature, he backed away and as he did so the old floorboards crumbled to dust beneath his feet and he plunged through them with a scream.

Zena and Petronella had managed to drag Mr Smith out of the bathroom, but he had lost his mind. Unable to stand up, he was lying pressed against the wall, gibbering with fright. The spider ran out into the corridor and was about to attack the two ladies when Mr Bickley fell through the ceiling and crashed heavily onto the hideous creature. This did no more than anger it and it shook itself, turned on him and tore him limb from limb. At that very moment, a loud noise began to reverberate throughout the house, a steady repeated and determined thumping at the front door. Who could the mysterious visitor be?

Mina, satisfied with her creation, selected a newly sharpened pen and began the next section.

PART THE FOURTH

The hammering at the door of Ditterling Manor was like a death-knell, a harbinger of doom announcing the imminent demise of everyone in the cursed house. As the flames took hold, the old wood and dusty curtains spat their sparks and ignited everything about them. Miss Claretti looked about her and saw no avenue of escape. Within, there was consuming fire. Outside, there were howling demons bent on her destruction.

Knock! Knock!

Who or what could be at the front door demanding admission? Was it too much to hope it was a saviour or was it as she feared, an infernal creature risen from the abyss and bent on their destruction?

There was only one way of being sure. Miss Claretti called to her friends and roused them to a resolve of going to the door and, if necessary, defending themselves against what lay without and making an escape. All agreed and seized whatever weapons were at hand then they rushed down the stairs. Whatever was outside was undoubtedly large and powerful. At each booming strike the door, large and solid as it was, seemed to cave inwards and threatened to come off its hinges.

It was only a matter of time. As they waited and prayed, Mr Gillery, awoken by the noise, joined them carrying an ancient blunderbuss. The gentlemen sought to send the ladies away, but Miss Claretti told them that there was nowhere in the house that could be deemed safe. Neither she nor Mrs Johnson consented to leave.

With a loud crash the door finally gave way, but before anyone could move, Mrs Bunn arrived, brandishing an iron roasting spit and with a roar of defiance charged at what lay outside.

Mina, disturbed in her composition by actual knocking, looked up from her desk as Rose entered. 'Excuse me, Miss, but Mrs Jordan and Miss Zillah are here to dress you for the costume ball.'

Mina laid her pen aside with a touch of regret, as she had thought of a clever device to enable Miss Claretti and her friends to escape unscathed from the fire-blackened ruins of Ditterling Manor and was looking forward to writing it.

The Pavilion was crowded with a glittering company of some thousand persons and Mina was astonished at the beauty, richness and good taste of the costumes. There were ladies and gentlemen who might have descended from oil paintings, sprung from the pages of storybooks or even magically arrived from past times. Here were Marie Antoinette, Little Bo Peep, Lady Teazle, and Good Queen Bess; Sir Walter Raleigh, Dick Turpin, Mephistopheles, and Rob Roy and a great host of others, all mingling with elegance, charm and good humour.

Mina's dress, the finest she had ever worn, was a cerise skirt overlaid with black lace, a black silk bodice trimmed with cerise ruffles and a mantilla draped over a high comb in her hair. Nellie was in blue and white silk with a pink rose corsage and a towering coiffure of powdered hair. Mr Jordan was there, too, and in common with some of the less adventurous gentlemen, was in evening clothes, which made him resemble a waiter rather than a guest. Richard was clad as a matador, dashingly handsome in red satin trimmed with gold, although Mina secretly thought that he was better suited to the costume of a court jester.

The music room, the banqueting room and the saloon had all been designated for dancing, each having its own band, and while no special decorations had been supplied apart from some exquisite floral arrangements, no more seemed to be necessary since nothing could outshine the beauty of the costumes.

Mina did not feel that dancing would be her great forte but was happy to watch as couples whirled their way around the rooms in waltzes or enjoyed a quadrille or a polka. For those less inclined to dance there were comfortable divans in the south drawing room, where quiet *tête-à-têtes* could be enjoyed and no doubt something in the nature of flirting and scheming and a great deal of nonsense was taking place.

Along the length of the banqueting room tables had been laid out with a bewildering variety of refreshments and as soon as one platter was emptied a member of the attentive staff would replace it with a laden one.

A waiter was moving about the company with a silver tray offering small printed cards to those in attendance and Mina took one. It advised her that a new establishment was to open in Brighton in the spring, one that enjoyed the patronage of the aristocracy. Each card was a special introductory voucher for the business of photographic artist, Mr A Beckler…

HISTORICAL NOTES

The Weather
It is a standing joke in my family that whenever I visit Sussex we get torrential rain. The records for January 1872, when Mina visited, do suggest that it was very wet with occasional flash floods.

Sussex Villages
Ditchling Hollow is a fictional Sussex village. However, the other named villages nearby, Clayton, Hassocks (the railway station of Hassocks Gate is nowadays just called Hassocks), Burgess Hill and Hurstpierpoint and the town of Horsham, are all very real.

The Clayton Hill Windmills
They can still be seen today and are known affectionately as Jack and Jill.

Clayton Railway Tunnel
The Clayton railway tunnel on the Brighton line was opened in 1841. Its ornamental north portal, which resembles a castle in miniature, is a Grade II listed building. On the morning of 25 August 1861 three trains left Brighton station within a few minutes of each other. The first train passed through the tunnel but due to signalling errors the second train stopped in the tunnel and the third one ploughed into it. Twenty-three people were killed and 176 injured. It was, at that date, the worst ever British railway disaster.

On Saturday 27 October 1871, 24-year-old Charles Tune, who had been ill for some months, took the train from

Brighton to London Bridge Station. Halfway through Clayton Tunnel, he threw himself from his carriage. He was seriously injured and died a few hours after reaching hospital. (*The Times*, 2 November 1871, p. 10)

Mr Hope's Search for Dr Livingstone

Dr Livingstone was located by Henry Morton Stanley in November 1871, however news of the discovery did not reach England until May 1872, so in January 1872, Mr Hope still believed Dr Livingstone to be missing.

Odic Force and Baron Carl von Reichenbach.

I did not make this up. I wouldn't have dared. Baron Carl von Reichenbach (1788-1869) was a respected man of science who suggested that there was a force of energy within and connecting all living things. He studied, amongst other things, hysteria, somnambulism and mesmerism, and believed that there were some individuals whose nervous systems were unusually sensitive. These 'sensitives' were especially responsive to the Odic Force. He first published his studies in the 1850s, and they were later available in English translation.

The Brighton Fancy Dress Ball, 1872

A highlight of the fashionable season, it was held at the Royal Pavilion on 7 February and was reported in the *Brighton Gazette* on the following day.

Table-Tipping

Mina's comment on 'an eminent professor' must have been referring to noted physicist Michael Faraday, who, like many scientists, became interested in the 1850s fashion for table-tipping séances. He conducted a number of experiments which revealed that the movement of the tables was caused by the involuntary muscular action of the sitters. See his letter to the editor of *The Times*, 30 June 1853, p.8.

Spirit Photography

Mr Beckler's visit to Hollow House for the purpose of trying to photograph spirits was more possible in 1872 than formerly. He would have started his career using the wet-plate collodion process, which required preparation of the plate, exposure and development to be completed in the space of about fifteen minutes. Outside his own studio, he would therefore have needed to bring a portable darkroom in addition to the camera and chemicals.

1871, however, saw the invention of dry plate collodion. The glass plates could be prepared in advance, allowed to dry and taken to the site. It was no longer necessary to complete the processing in a short time and no portable dark room was required.

In 1869, photographer William Mumler was tried for fraud in New York after selling spirit photographs he had taken in his studio using the wet plate collodion method. It was impossible to prove how he had achieved his results, although the best theory is that the spirit was a double image produced when the plate was not properly cleaned after a previous picture had been taken. He was acquitted.

Unusual tricks of the light have often been responsible for reported sightings of ghosts. Mary Ann might well have seen an effect of the full moon in the upper corridor of Hollow House on 26 December 1871.

The Yellow Wallpaper

One hopes that Mina's ennui described in Chapter 1 will not

result in the same symptoms as the main character of Charlotte Perkins Gillman's short story.

The Stockwell Poltergeist Hoax

Details of this incident can be found at
https://en.wikipedia.org/wiki/Stockwell_ghost

Sapere Books is an exciting new publisher of brilliant fiction and popular history.

To find out more about our latest releases and our monthly bargain books visit our website: **saperebooks.com**

Printed in Great Britain
by Amazon